W9-DAG-563

THE FAMILIARS

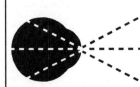

This Large Print Book carries the
Seal of Approval of N.A.V.H.

THE FAMILIARS

STACEY HALLS

WHEELER PUBLISHING
A part of Gale, a Cengage Company

Farmington Hills, Mich • San Francisco • New York • Waterville, Maine
Meriden, Conn • Mason, Ohio • Chicago

**LIBRARY OF CONGRESS CIP DATA ON FILE.
CATALOGUING IN PUBLICATION FOR THIS BOOK
IS AVAILABLE FROM THE LIBRARY OF CONGRESS**

ISBN-13: 978-1-4328-6492-7 (hardcover alk. paper)

Published in 2019 by arrangement with Harlequin Books S.A.

Printed in Mexico
1 2 3 4 5 6 7 23 22 21 20 19

To my husband

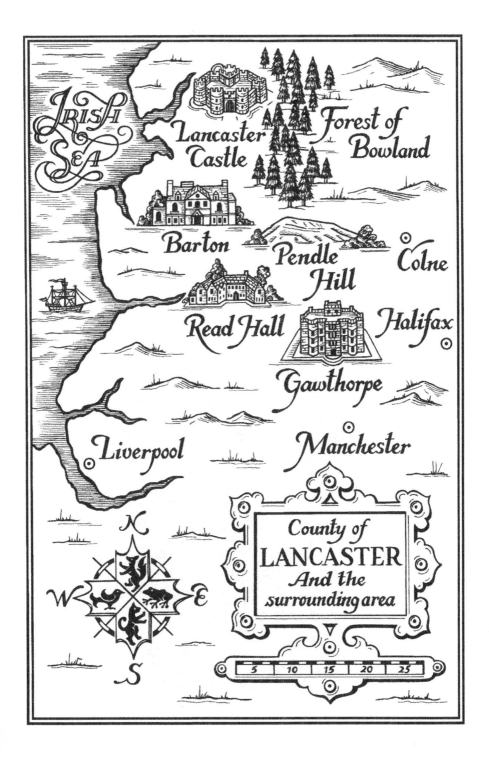

PART ONE

LANCASHIRE,
EARLY APRIL, 1612

"Be ever well in blood, for otherwise she will not long be at your commandment but make you follow her."
THE BOOK OF FALCONRY OR HAWKING,
GEORGE TURBERVILLE, 1543–1597

"PRUDENCE & JUSTICE."
SHUTTLEWORTH FAMILY MOTTO

CHAPTER ONE

I left the house with the letter because I did not know what else to do. The lawn was wet with late-morning dew that soaked my favorite silk rose slippers, for in my haste I hadn't thought to put on pattens. But I did not stop until I reached the trees overlooking the lawns in front of the house. The letter I had clutched in my fist, and I opened it once more to check I hadn't imagined it, that I hadn't drifted off in my chair and dreamed it up.

It was a chill morning, misty and cool with the wind racing down from Pendle Hill, and though my mind was in turmoil I'd remembered to take my cloak from its place at the end of the wardrobe. I'd given Puck a perfunctory stroke and was pleased to see my hands weren't shaking. I did not cry, or faint, or do anything at all except fold what I had read back into its old shape and go quietly down the stairs. Nobody noticed me,

11

and the only servant I saw was a brief glimpse of James sitting at his desk as I passed by his study. The idea that he might have read the letter himself crossed my mind, as a steward often opens his master's private correspondence, but I dismissed the thought quickly and left through the front door.

The clouds were the color of pewter jugs that threatened to spill over, so I hurried across the grass toward the woods because they were a good hiding place, and I needed to think. I knew in my black cloak I'd be conspicuous among the green from servants' prying eyes at the windows. In this part of Lancaster, the land is green and damp, and the sky wide and gray. Occasionally you see the flash of a deer's red coat, or a pheasant's blue neck, and your eye is drawn swifter than they can disappear.

Before I reached the shelter of the trees, I knew the sickness was coming again. I pulled the hem of my skirt away from where it splattered the grass, then used my kerchief to wipe my mouth. Richard had the laundrywomen sprinkle them with rose water. I closed my eyes and took several deep breaths, and when I opened them I felt very slightly better. The trees shivered and birds sang merrily as I went deeper, and in less

than a minute I had lost Gawthorpe altogether. The house was as conspicuous as I
was in these parts, made of warm golden
stone set in a clearing. But while the house
couldn't keep you from the woods, which
seemed to draw ever closer and were visible
from every window, the woods could keep
Gawthorpe from you. Sometimes it felt as
though they were playing a game.

I needed to think. I took out the letter and
opened it again, smoothing out the creases
that had formed in my tight little fist, and
finding the paragraph that had left me reel-
ing:

You can divine without difficulty the true
nature of the danger that your wife has
been in, and it is with solemn regret that I
impart on you my professional opinion as
a physick and expert in matters of childbed: that upon visiting her last Friday sennight, I drew the deeply unfortunate con-
clusion that she cannot and should not
bear children. It is with excessive impor-
tance that you understand if she finds
herself once more in childbed, she will not
survive it, and her earthly life will come to
an end.

Now I was out of sight of the house and

could react with some privacy, my heart was beating furiously, and my cheeks were hot. Another surge of sickness overcame me, and I almost choked on it as it burned against my tongue.

The sickness came morning, noon and night, wringing me inside out. At the most, it was forty times a day; if it was twice, I felt lucky. Veins burst in my face, leaving delicate crimson stems around my eyes, the whites of which turned a demonic red. The awful taste in my throat would last for hours, sharp and choking as the blade of a knife. I couldn't keep food down. I had no appetite for it anyway, much to the cook's disappointment. Even my beloved marchpane lay in broad, unsliced tablets in the larder, and my boxes of sugar candy sent from London gathered dust.

The other three times I hadn't been this ill. This time it felt like the child growing inside me was trying to escape through my throat instead of between my legs, like the others who announced their untimely arrivals in red rivers down my thighs. Their limp little forms were grotesque, and I watched them be wrapped like fresh loaves in linen.

"Not long for this world, the poor mite," the last midwife said, wiping my blood off her butcher's arms.

Four years married, three times in childbed and still no heir to put in the oak cradle my mother gave me when Richard and I married. I saw the way she looked at me, like I was letting them all down.

Still, I could not fathom that Richard knew what the doctor had said, and had watched me fatten like a turkey at Christmastide. The letter was bundled in among several papers from my three childbeds, so it was possible he could have missed it. Would he have done right by me withholding it? Suddenly, the words seemed to fling themselves from the page and wrap around my neck. And written, too, by a man whose name I did not recognize, so wreathed in pain was I when he visited that I could not recall a single detail about him: his touch, his voice, or whether he was kind.

I'd not stopped to catch my breath, and my slippers were truly ruined now, soaked with greenish mud, for it had been raining. When one of them got stuck and came off, sending my stockinged foot into the wet ground, that was more than I was prepared to take. With both hands I made the letter into a ball and threw it as hard as I could, taking a brief moment's satisfaction when it bounced off a tree several yards away.

If I had not done that, I might not have

seen the rabbit's foot a few inches from where it landed, nor the rabbit it belonged to — or at least what was left of it: a mangled mess of fur and blood, then another, and another. I hunted rabbits; these had not been slain by a hawk or a falcon making a neat little kill before circling back to its master. Then I noticed something else: the hem of a brown skirt brushing the ground, and knees bent, and above them a body, a face, a white cap. A young woman was kneeling not ten feet away, staring at me. Every line of her was alert with an animal tension. She was shabbily dressed in a homespun wool smock with no apron, which was why I did not see her straightaway among all the green and brown. Flax-colored hair spiraled down from her cap. Her face was long and narrow, her eyes large, their color unusual even from a distance: a warm gold, like new coins. There was something fiercely intelligent, almost masculine, in her gaze, and though she was crouched down and I standing, for a moment I felt afraid, as though I was the one who had been discovered.

Another beast dangled from her hands, one eye resting on me without blinking. Its fur was stained with red. On the ground next to the woman's skirts a roughly hewn sack lay open. She got to her feet. A breeze rustled the leaves and grasses around us, but she remained perfectly still, her expression unreadable. Only the dead rabbit moved, swinging slightly.

"Who are you?" I asked. "What are you doing here?"

She began bundling the rabbits into her sack, bent over like a cripple. My crumpled letter lay pale and bright among the massacre, and she paused when she saw it, her long fingers hovering, stained red with blood.

"Give it to me," I snapped. She held it out from where she stood, and in a few quick strides I'd snatched it from her. Those golden eyes did not leave my face, and I thought a stranger had never looked at me so hard. Briefly I wondered how I must appear, with no outdoor shoes and my slipper lying in the mud. No doubt my face was flushed from vomiting, and the whites of my eyes would be red. The acid in my mouth made my tongue sharp.

"What's your name?"

She did not speak.

"Are you a beggar?"

She shook her head.

"This is my land. You have been poaching rabbits from my land?"

17

"*Your* land?" Her tone was accusatory, or surprised. Her voice was soft, her accent local like my servants'. It broke the strangeness of the situation like a pebble tossed in a pool. She was just an ordinary village girl.

"I am Fleetwood Shuttleworth, the mistress at Gawthorpe Hall. This is my husband's land you are on. If you are from Padiham you would know that."

"I am not," was all she said.

"You know the penalty for hunting on another man's land?"

She lowered her eyes, taking in my thick black cloak, my gown of copper taffeta peeking through the bottom. I knew my skin was dull, my black hair made it sallow, and I did not wish to be reminded of this by a stranger. I suspected I was younger than her, but I could not guess her age. Her dirty dress appeared not to have been brushed or aired in months, and her cap was the color of mutton's wool. Then my eyes fell on hers, and her gaze met mine, level and proud. I frowned and raised my chin. At four feet eleven inches, everyone I met was taller than me, though I did not intimidate easily.

"My husband would bind your hands to his horse and drag you to the magistrate," I said, more boldly that I felt. When she did not speak, and the only sound was the trees

18

hissing and shuddering, I asked again, "Are you a beggar?"

"I am no one." She held out the sack. "Take them. I did not know I was on your land."

It was a strange answer, and I wondered what I would tell Richard, then I remembered the letter in my fist. I squeezed it hard.

"With what did you kill them?"

She sniffed. "I did not kill them. They were killed."

"What an odd way of speaking you have. What is your name?"

I had barely finished when in a flash of gold and brown she turned and ran away through the trees. Her white cap flitted between the trunks, the sack bouncing against her skirts. Her feet thudded onto the earth, quick and deft as an animal, before the woods swallowed her whole.

CHAPTER TWO

The sound of Richard's waist belt preceded him everywhere. I think it made him feel powerful — you heard his money before you saw it. If, say, you were a thief, and you had the idea of relieving him of his coins, you would swiftly change your mind when you saw the dagger, followed by the look in his eye that not so much asked for a fight, but welcomed it as a friend. When I heard the familiar jangle and the tread of his kid leather boots on the stairs, I took a deep breath and brushed some imagined dust off my jacket. I stood as he entered the room, bright and invigorated from a business trip to Manchester. His gold earring caught the light; his gray eyes gleamed.

"Fleetwood," he greeted me, putting my head between his hands.

I bit my lip where he kissed it. Could I trust my voice to speak? We were in the wardrobe, where he knew he would find me.

Even though nobody had lived at Gawthorpe before us, it was the only room that truly felt mine. I had thought it extremely modern that Richard's uncle, who designed the house, had thought to include a room just for dressing when he had no wife. Of course if women designed houses they would be as much a part of the plans as a kitchen. Having come from my own house of gray stone under gray skies to Gawthorpe, with its rich, warm color, as though the sun was always rising on it, and three floors of gleaming windows, bright as the crown jewels, and the tower in the middle, I had felt more like a princess than a mistress. Everything was new, including us, though part of me felt old as time. Richard had led me through the maze of rooms and all the fresh plaster and shining panels and little passageways teeming with decorators and servants and carpenters like ants in a nest made me feel dizzy. I tended to keep at the top of the house, out of the way of everyone. If I had a baby in my arms or a child to take down to breakfast I might feel differently, but while I didn't, I kept to my rooms and my wardrobe, with its pleasant view of the rushing River Calder and Pendle Hill.

21

"Conversing with your clothes again?" he said.

"They are my constant companions."

Puck, my great French mastiff, roused himself from the Turkey carpet, stretching and yawning and revealing a jaw so wide it could fit my head inside.

"You fearsome beast," said Richard, going to kneel by the dog. "Not for long will you be the singular object of our affections. You will have to share them." He sighed and got to his feet, weary from a long ride. "You are well? And rested?"

I nodded, tucking a loose strand of hair under my cap. Lately it had been falling out in great black clumps when I combed it.

"You are troubled. You have not . . . You are not . . ."

"I am fine."

The letter. Ask him about the letter. The words hung thick, an arrow poised on a pulled bow, but there was nothing but relief in his lovely face. I held his stare for a moment too long, my dark eyes on his light ones, knowing my opportunity to ask him was passing, slipping through my hands like sand.

"Well, Manchester was a success. James always thinks he should go with me on these trips but I fare just as well alone. Perhaps he is only exasperated because I forget to write down receipts. I've told him I keep them as well in my head as in my jacket." He paused, ignoring Puck sniffing at him. "You are in a quiet mood."

"Richard, I read the midwife's correspondence today. And the doctor's, who delivered the last."

"That reminds me." He reached deep into the emerald velvet of his doublet, his face lit with a childlike excitement. I waited, and when he withdrew his hand he dropped into mine a strange object. It was a small silver sword, long as a letter opener, with a shining gold hilt. But the end was blunt — it would not cut a cake — and all over were little spheres dangling from miniature hooks. I turned it over in my palm and it made a pleasant tinkling sound, like horses coming to a halt.

"It's a rattle." He beamed, shaking it so it jangled. "They are bells, look. It's for our son."

He did not even try to disguise the longing in his voice. I thought of the drawer that I kept locked in one of the bedrooms. Inside were half a dozen things he'd bought the other times — a silk purse with our initials, an ivory horse that could fit in a palm. In the long gallery was a suit of armor he

23

bought to celebrate the first time my stomach grew. His faith that we would have a child was clear and strong as a stream, even when he was trading wool in Preston and passed a trader selling miniature animals; when he was with our tailor and saw a bolt of silk the exact color of an oyster's pearl. With the last one, only he knew if it was a son or daughter, and I did not ask, because I was still not a mother. Every gift he gave me was a token of my failure, and I wished I could burn them all and watch the smoke rise from the chimney and be swallowed by the sky. I imagined where I would be without my husband, and my heart was full of grief, because he had given me happiness, and all I'd given him were three absences, their souls extinguished in the gentlest breeze.

I tried one more time. "Richard, is there anything you wish to tell me?"

Puck yawned and settled on the carpet. Richard's earring glinted. A deep voice called his name from a distant floor below.

"Roger is downstairs," Richard said. "I should go to him."

I put the rattle on the chair, eager to be rid of it, leaving Puck to sniff curiously at it. "Then I will come down."

"I came upstairs only to dress. We are going to hunt."

"But you have been riding all morning."

He smiled. "Hunting is not *riding,* it is hunting."

"Then I will go with you."

"You feel fit for it?"

I smiled, and turned back to my clothes.

"Fleetwood Shuttleworth! My eyes, look how pale you are," Roger's voice boomed across the stable yard. "You are whiter than a snowdrop but twice as beautiful. Richard, have you not been feeding your wife?"

"Roger Nowell, you do know how to make a woman feel special." I smiled, drawing up on my horse.

"You are dressed to hunt. Have you accomplished all your ladylike pursuits of a morning?" His voice carried to every beam and corner of the stable yard as he sat astride his horse, tall and broad with a gray eyebrow raised in question.

"I am come to spend time with my favorite magistrate."

I pushed my horse between the two men's. Roger Nowell was easy company, and I admit now that I suppose I was a little in awe of him, having no father to compare him to. He had enough years to be my or Richard's father — grandfather, even — and as ours were both long dead, he became a friend to us when Richard inherited Gawthorpe. He'd arrived on his horse with three pheasants the day after we'd arrived and stayed all afternoon, explaining the lay of the land and everyone in it. We were new to Pendle and this part of Lancaster, with its rolling hills and shadowy forests and strange people, and he was a wealth of knowledge. An acquaintance of Richard's long-dead uncle Richard who had been the chief justice of Chester — who provided the closest link the family ever had to the crown — Roger had known the Shuttleworths for years, and settled himself in our household like an inherited piece of furniture. But I liked him from the moment I met him. Like a candle, he burned brightly, and his mood would flicker easily from one to the next. But as wax runs down the sides, he had his way of drawing you in smoothly until you were stuck.

"News from the palace — the king may finally have found a suitor for his daughter," Roger announced.

The hounds in their kennels were driven wild by the sound of us and were brought out, teeming and panting around the horses' legs.

"Who is it?"

"Freidrich V, Count Palatine of the Rhine. He will come to England later in the year and hopefully put an end to the parade of jesters trying for the princess's hand."

"Will you go to the wedding?" I asked.

"I hope to. It will be the grandest the kingdom has seen in many years."

"I wonder what sort of gown she will wear," I thought aloud, but Roger didn't hear me over the whines and barks of the hounds, and he and Richard moved out of the yard to begin the hunt. With the hounds on leashes I realized the quarry would be hart, and I wish I had asked before. A hart at bay was not a friendly sight, with its antlers slashing and eyes rolling; I would have preferred almost anything else. I thought about turning round, but we were already in the forest so I followed Richard's slim, dark green back and Roger's wide brown one. Edmund the apprentice acted as whip, riding alongside the dogs. As we went through the trees I heard glimpses of their furtive conversation and rode silently behind them, half listening. An image from the day before came to me: spilled blood, glassy eyes and the strange golden-haired woman, and I shivered.

"Richard," I interrupted. "There was a trespasser on our land yesterday."

"What? Where?"

"Somewhere south of the house, in the woods."

"Why did James not tell me?"

"Because I did not tell him."

"*You* saw him? What were you doing?"

"I . . . went out walking."

"I told you not to go out alone, you might have got lost or tripped and . . . hurt yourself."

Roger was listening.

"I am *fine*, Richard. And it was not a man but a woman."

"What was she doing? Was she lost?"

That's when I realized I could not tell him about the rabbits because I had no words for what I'd seen. Out of the corner of my eye I thought I saw a flash of white, like a cap through the trees, but when I looked there was only green. "Yes," I said eventually.

Roger was amused. "You do have a wild imagination, Fleetwood. You had us thinking you were attacked by a savage in the woods when really a woman had got lost?"

"Yes," I replied faintly.

"Although now even that isn't without harm — you may have heard of what happened to John Law the peddler at Colne?"

"I have not."

"Roger, you don't need to frighten her with tales of witchcraft — she already has nightmares."

My mouth fell open and my face grew scarlet. That was the first time Richard had told anyone about The Nightmare, and I would never have believed it of him. But he continued to move ahead of me, the feather in his hat trembling.

"Tell me, Roger."

"A woman traveling alone is not always as innocent as it seems, as John Law found out and will never forget as long as he lives — and that might not be long, Lord have mercy." He settled back in his saddle. "Two days ago a man came to Read, name of Abraham Law."

"I do not know him."

"Well, you wouldn't because he is a cloth dyer from Halifax. The lad has done well for himself, considering."

"And he found a witch?"

"No, *listen.*"

I sighed and wished I hadn't come; wished I was sitting in the parlor with my dog.

"John was traveling on the woolpack trail at Colnefield when he came across a young girl. A beggar, he thought. She asked him to give her some pins, and when he said he would not . . ." He paused for effect. "She cursed him. He turned his back and next thing, heard her speaking softly behind him, as though she was talking to someone. It sent a shiver up his spine. He thought at first it was the wind, but he turned back, and her dark eyes were fixed on him, and her lips moving. He hurried away, and not thirty yards on, he heard running feet, and then a great thing like a black dog began attacking him, biting him all over, and he fell to the ground."

"A thing *like* a black dog?" Richard asked. "You said earlier it *was* a black dog."

Roger ignored him. "He held his hands to his face and begged for mercy, and when he opened his eyes the dog had disappeared. Gone." He held his large hands up. "And the strange girl with it. Someone found him on the path and helped him to a nearby inn, but he could barely move a limb. Nor could he speak, and one of his eyes stayed shut to the world, and his face was all fallen down on one side. He stayed at the inn, but the next morning the young girl appeared again, bold as brass, and begged his forgiveness. She claims she wasn't in control of her craft, but that she did curse him."

"She admitted to it?" I remembered the girl from yesterday and goose bumps covered my skin. "What did she look like?"

"She certainly looks like a witch. She is very thin and rough-looking, with black hair and a sullen face. My mother says never trust someone with black hair because they usually have a black soul to match."

"*I* have black hair."

"Do you want to hear my story?"

My mother always said I was a pain for interrupting, and threatened to sew my mouth as a child. She and Roger's mother would have plenty to discuss.

"I am sorry," I said. "Is the man well now?"

"No, and he may never be again," Roger said gravely. "That is worrying in itself, but there is something that troubles me more — the dog. While it is free to roam Pendle, no one is safe."

Richard was far ahead by now, keeping up with the hunt. The thought of the animal did not frighten me — after all, I had a mastiff the size of a mule. But before I could point that out, Roger began again. "At the inn, a few nights after it happened, John Law woke to the sound of something next to him, breathing over him. The great beast stood over his bed, the size of a wolf, with bared teeth and fiery eyes. He knew it to be a spirit — it was not of this earth. You can understand his terror — a man who is unable to move or speak save for groaning out. Then who should be standing over his bed in its place, not a moment later, but the witch herself."

I felt as though my skin had been brushed with feathers. "So it turned into the woman?"

"No. Fleetwood, have you knowledge of a familiar spirit?" I shook my head. "Then I will direct you to the gospel according to Leviticus. In short, it's the Devil in disguise. An instrument, if you will, to enlarge his kingdom. This witch is a dog, but they can appear as anything — an animal, a child. It appears to her when she needs it to do her bidding, and she told it last week to lame John Law. A familiar is the surest sign of a witch."

"And you have seen it?"

"Of course not. A creature of the Devil is hardly likely to appear to a God-fearing man. Only those of questionable belief might sense its presence. Low morals are its breeding ground."

"But John Law saw it. You said he was a good man."

Roger waved me off, impatient. "We have lost Richard. He will not be happy with me for lagging behind indulging you. This is what happens when women come on hunts."

I did not point out that it was me indulging him — if Roger had a story, he wanted it heard. We set off at a canter, and slowed down again when the hunt came back into view. We were a long way from Gawthorpe now, and I was not in favor of the thought of a full afternoon riding.

"Where is the girl now?" I asked as we fell behind again.

Roger adjusted his grip on the reins. "Her name is Alizon Device. She is in my custody at Read Hall."

"In your *house*? Why did you not put her in the gaol at Lancaster?"

"She is not dangerous where she is. There is nothing she can do — she would not dare. Besides, she is helping me with some other inquiries."

"What kind of inquiries?"

"My, my, you are full of questions, Mistress Shuttleworth. Must we *talk* the quarry to death? Alizon Device is from a family of witches — she told me so herself. Her mother, her grandmother — even her brother — all practice magick and sorcery, no more than a few miles from here. They are also accusing their neighbors of murder by witchcraft, one of whom *lives on Shuttle-*

33

worth land. Which is why I thought Master Shuttleworth over there ought to know about it."

He indicated his head at the expanse of greenery before us. The hounds, Edmund and Richard were again nowhere to be seen.

"But how do you know she is telling the truth? Why would she betray her family? She must know what it means to be a witch — it's certain death."

"Your guess why is as good as mine," Roger said simply, although I detected something below. He could be forceful and bullying when he wanted; I had seen it with his wife, Katherine, who was a tolerant sort of woman. "And the murders she claimed her family are responsible for all happened."

"They have *murdered*?"

"Several times. You would not want to cross a Device, as all the people who died did. Do not fear, child. Alizon Device is safe in custody, and I am to question her family tomorrow or the next day. I shall have to notify the king, of course," he sighed, as though it was an impediment. "He will be pleased to know it, I'm sure."

"What if they escape — how will you find them?"

"They'll not escape. I have eyes all over Pendle — you know that. Not much gets past a high sheriff."

"Former high sheriff," I teased. "How many years has she? The girl with the dog?"

"She does not know, but I would say she is seventeen or so."

"The same as me." After a moment of thoughtful silence, I spoke again. "Roger, do you trust Richard?"

He raised a bushy eyebrow. "With my life. Or what's left of it — I am an old man now, with my family grown and the best days of my work behind me, most regrettably. Why do you ask?"

The doctor's letter I'd tucked into my pocket, deep beneath my riding clothes, beat against my ribs like another heart. "No reason."

CHAPTER THREE

Lent was not yet over and though my appetite was poor, I longed for a cut of stewed beef or a strip of soft, salted chicken. Roger stayed for dinner and rubbed his hands together as the servants brought out silver platters of pike and sturgeon. I knew I wouldn't touch any of it, even though I was hungry after the hunt, from which we had come back empty-handed as a chill mist descended. It pressed in now at the windows, and the dining chamber was cold. I broke my bread into pieces and sipped my wine, wondering when the time would come when I would be able to eat everything on my plate again. I hadn't told any of the servants, including Sarah who helped me to dress, but a cook is always the first to know of her mistress's condition. The other servants would have seen me hold my fingers out to Puck, offering him bits of things on my plate, but I had done that since he was young. My dog was growing fatter as I seemed to shrink. Richard once remarked Puck ate better than most of Lancaster.

When I could take the sight of the fish heads no longer, I went to my chamber to lie down. At the top of the house it was quiet, away from the clatter of sauce dishes and knives, and the fire had been lit. Usually I would have drawn the drapes to help my headache but I felt too sick and tired, so I kicked off my slippers and lay down, staring out the window with my hands on my stomach. There had been too much to think about this morning, but the doctor's letter came back to me, pressing in like the mist. I suppose in the end it came down to who would survive in the end: would it be me, or the child, or both, or neither? If the doctor was to be believed — and no doubt he was — the child was fattening like a conker in a spiked green shell, and eventually would split me open. A child was what Richard wanted more than anything, and where I had failed before perhaps I would not this time . . . but at the cost of my life? Women carried life and death in their stomachs when they conceived; it was a fact of life. To hope and pray I might not join the departed was as useful as wishing the grass blue.

"Will you stay there and kill me?" I asked the empty room. "Or will you let me live? Shall we try to live together?"

I must have fallen asleep because when I woke there was a jug of milk next to the bed. I reached over to dip in my littlest finger and lick it. My mother used to say the most beautiful girls had skin like fresh milk, plump and creamy. Next to it, mine looked like old parchment. The fuss she made when Richard came to Barton for the first time with his uncle Lawrence; she wouldn't settle, fluttering around me like a moth. "Show him your hands," she said. "Keep them folded." She didn't need to say my face wasn't my best feature — I knew that already. Still, none of it mattered, because we both knew my best feature was my name and the money it brought. Mother said Father was closefisted, but when I asked why we lived in a drafty house and had to share a bedroom, she drew her lips into a thin line and said an old house was better than a new one.

The night of Richard's coming, as Mother and I got into our beds, she asked me if I liked Richard.

"Does it matter?" was my petulant reply.

"It matters greatly to your happiness. You

will spend every day of your life with him."

He will save me from this miserable life, I thought. *I could not like him more if I tried.*

I thought of his pleasant, unlined face and light gray eyes. The beautiful jewelry he wore in his ears and on his hands, a piece of which I would take so he could lead me to my new life, away from the path that had been trimmed and swept for me by my mother, with a monster lurking at the end of it.

"Do you like the playhouse?" he asked me in my mother's parlor.

His uncle and my mother stood at the window, talking and glancing over at us. I knew my mother had tilled the ground for this marriage, but if Richard refused, nothing could be done.

"Yes," I lied, for I had never been.

"Excellent. We shall go every year to London. That's where the best ones are. Twice, if you wish."

How could I not be charmed and delighted by this young man, who did not treat me like an infant as everybody else did? I thought of his face every waking hour and every dreaming one, too. The wedding date was set in the parish church, and I could not wait for every morning to arrive and the nightfall after it, because each one drew me closer. I thought about what sort of mistress I would be: kind, and wise, for I wasn't beautiful. A mother, one day, adored by her children and her husband. Whatever Richard wanted I would give him. His comfort would be my occupation; his happiness my life's work. For he had bestowed the greatest gift on me: accepting me as his wife, and I would live out the rest of my days with gratitude.

I heard my mother shifting in her bed. "Fleetwood," she said. "Are you listening? I asked if you liked Richard."

"I suppose he will do," I had replied, and blew out my candle with a smile.

I rose awkwardly, my limbs stiff, and went into the long gallery at the front of the house to walk back and forth. To my surprise, Roger was there, examining the royal coat of arms above the fireplace with his hands clasped behind his back.

"Fear God, honor thy king, eschew evil and do good. Seek peace and ensue it," I recited the motif on the mantel from memory.

"Very good, Fleetwood. Consider it a promise from your justice of the peace."

"Richard's uncle Lawrence had that put in. I think he hoped King James would hear about it and not feel the need to visit."

"The Shuttleworths are loyal to the crown, of course." There was an edge of warning in Roger's tone.

"Faithful as dogs."

Roger was thoughtful. "More demonstrations of loyalty need to be made in these parts. But how to make them?"

"I think it is not so much lack of loyalty but confidence. Besides, he would surely avoid these areas, with their old ways of faith."

"This corner of the kingdom with its Catholic heritage causes His Majesty a great deal of anxiety. A lot more could be done to honor thy king and eschew evil, as you Shuttleworths say." He learned forward and frowned. "I had not noticed the words around the king's arms. What does it say?"

"*Honi soit qui mal y pense.* 'Shame on him who thinks evil of it.' "

He made a face, as though he was considering it. "Indeed. But thinks evil of what, Lawrence will never be able to tell us. Maybe I will ask the king himself."

"You're at court soon?"

Roger nodded. "His Majesty requires all of Lancaster's justices of the peace to make a record of every person who does not take communion at church."

"For what purpose?"

"Oh, Fleetwood, you need not concern yourself with matters of the court, they hardly affect the life of a young gentlewoman. You do your duty and give your husband lots of little Shuttleworths, and I will do my duty in keeping Pendle safe." I must have looked displeased, because he became genial and looked more kindly on me. "Well, if you must know, His Majesty is still very . . . uneasy after the events at Parliament seven years ago. And you may have heard the whisperings about some of the treasonists escaping to Lancaster. Something must be done to demonstrate the county's loyalty to the crown, because currently the king is very mistrustful of our little part of the north, and the lawless people within it. He thinks us a pack of wild dogs, compared to the genteel lords and ladies of the south. We are very far from society here, and I think he is afraid. But do you know what else he is mistrustful of?"

I shook my head.

"Witches." There was a gleam of triumph in his eye, and it took a moment for me to understand.

"You mean Alizon Device?"

Roger nodded. "If I can convince the king that the people of Lancaster are under threat from the thing he hates most, his

42

sympathies might extend to us, and he might grow less suspicious. If I am seen excavating the *bad seeds,* if you will, the county may grow and prosper, and we may rejoin the kingdom with a new reputation."

"But Catholics and witches are not the same thing. There are plenty of the first here, but not the latter."

"More than you think," was Roger's easy answer. "And the king sees them as the same thing, besides."

"Well, I doubt very much that the king should worry about us storing gunpowder around here. It's far too wet," I said, and Roger laughed. I wondered if I should tell him about my letter, folded deep in my pocket. Might he know already? "Where is Richard?" I asked instead.

"He has some business with his steward and then he is showing me his new falcon before accompanying me back to Read. Will you join us?"

"He spends more time with that creature than me. No, thank you. But you could tell him to ask Henry Hopwood the tailor, to call. I need some new clothes."

Roger laughed as we passed the entrance to my chambers and reached the top of the stairs. "You and my Katherine are two equal forces. But still, neither of you are a match for Richard. He has the largest collection outside of the king's wardrobe." He paused at the top of the staircase. "You will come and see Katherine soon? She often asks after you and your latest fashions. She is fascinated to see what the young people are wearing."

I smiled and bowed as he descended the staircase that curled around the tower, but before he disappeared I called his name again, because I felt a sudden ache, and wanted desperately for him to embrace me as a father might. Roger certainly smelled as a father might — or so I imagined — of woodsmoke, and horsehair, and tobacco. He stood waiting below the portrait of my mother and me as a child — the one I would not hang in the long gallery or anywhere else. The reason was nobody paused for long on the stairs, meaning guests walked past it and often forgot to mention it by the time they reached the next floor. In the picture, which was about the same height as me, my mother dominated the frame in her wide collar and gown of scarletwork. I occupied the bottom left corner, my mother's arm bent toward me as though about to hurry me out of the frame. A little blackbird sat on my hand, the pet I kept in a cage in my room made immortal.

I could still recall the unpleasant silence while sitting for it in the great hall at Barton, and the pointy-faced artist with the colored oils on his lips; the blackened tip of his tongue that flicked out of his mouth like a serpent.

"Roger . . ." My voice died in my throat. "Do you think John Law will live?"

"Do not fret," Roger said. "His son is caring for him."

I went back to my chamber and wondered how Roger Nowell slept with a witch in the house, and decided soundly.

I'd hidden the pan under the bed for when I needed it and covered it with a cloth, but Richard still recoiled when he walked into the bedroom. I was lying in my nightdress, weak and empty, what little pike I'd had at dinner clinging to the bottom of the bowl. Richard sighed and came to kneel by me.

"Are you no better? You've barely eaten. I so want you to be well."

I pulled at my nightdress so the tiny mound of my stomach showed through. Richard gazed at it, resting a gentle hand on the bump. I twirled his gold ring, the one his father gave him that he never took off. I could not decide what was worse: how sick I felt or not knowing if my husband was keeping this great truth from me, for at some point that evening it had dawned on me as I sat in my chamber with only the candles' cheerful sputter for company: of course Richard valued his child's life more than mine. Would any man not who had a great deal to leave behind?

"Richard?" I asked. "What will happen if I cannot give you an heir?" I thought of the old kings' wives' necks on the chopping blocks. What would be better: to go messily and painfully, thrashing about in a blood-soaked bed; or clean and resigned, wearing your best dress? Divorce was decades old, but the word struck as much fear as death.

"Don't speak such things. It will not happen this time — the Lord will be kind to us. We will employ the best midwife."

"We had a midwife last time. She did not stop it from coming out dead."

He stood to undress, the candlelight casting off his buttons, then settling on his bare skin. I watched him change into his nightshirt, then he came to my bedside and took my cold hand and held it, pink against gray. Although his voice was calm, his face was worried. "Until you are well again, I will sleep in the dressing room."

My stomach lurched. "No! Richard, please, I won't hear of it. I'll not be sick again. I'll have a maid remove the pan." I tried to climb out of bed but Richard stopped me.

"I will only be in the next room until you are better, which will be very soon."

"Richard, don't. Please. I don't like sleeping alone, you know I don't — The Nightmare."

When I woke soaked with sweat and blind with terror, he would hold me until I stopped trembling. It only happened a few times a year, but he *knew* I would be terrified if he was not there.

"Please don't sleep in the dressing room. Please stay with me, I'm afraid."

But he kissed my forehead, and with a pained face left with my undigested dinner at arm's length. I slid down in our bed, feeling tears press at my eyes as I thought about how he would never have done this when we were first married. After the wedding, in the house on the Strand, I could not sleep with the chaos outside the window. London was new to me, and everything in it — carriage wheels rolling, and the sounds of boatmen coming ashore, and the cries and bells and crowds of people. Richard would sit up with me at night, reading or drawing or just lying quietly stroking my hair. When it got colder and we moved farther out to the fields and wide skies of Islington, I told him I'd grown used to the sounds of the Strand, and now wouldn't be able to sleep because it was too quiet. He laughed and said I was far too spoiled and the only thing for it was for him to make the noises for me. Night after night, just as I was about to fall asleep, he neighed into the darkness, or gave the cry of a knife sharpener, or juggled like a coal seller pretending to scald his hands. I'd never laughed so much in all my life.

Once, when it was snowing outside and the fire was low in the grate, I asked to see what he was drawing. He told me to wait until he was finished. I watched him work, his face taut with concentration, his hands making quick little movements and soft noises on the page. When he turned the paper around, I saw myself. I was wearing a beautiful trimmed hat, a fine ruff and collar and elegant Spanish slippers. Around my shoulders was a cloak that flowed off the page, pressed with Paris buttons. I could almost feel its thickness.

"What color is it?" I whispered, running my fingertips along the lines.

"The cloak is of branched satin and orange wool," he said proudly. "I'll have it made tomorrow and this is what you will wear to ride home in. To Gawthorpe."

Nobody had ever done such a thing for me before. When the winter ended, we arrived at the brand-new house that no one had ever lived in, just as he said. The journey took nine days, and all I could think about the whole way was arriving in Lancaster as Mistress Shuttleworth, wearing an outfit the likes of which not a soul in these parts had ever seen. Richard looked equally fine in an outfit he designed himself, a dagger and sword at his hip. Villagers lined the streets as we drew closer to our new home, smiling and waving. But with time the picture had changed in my mind, and all I could see was two children dressed for a play.

I blew out the candle and listened for noise from the other room. That was the first time in our marriage we were both in the house and I was sleeping alone.

He did not come to me the next morning, going down to break his fast without waking me. He read his correspondence while I sat opposite, trying to force bread and honey into my mouth and keep it down. I watched his face, creasing or brightening as he read; I did not ask who wrote. As the servants passed in and out of the dining chamber I wondered who knew a truckle bed and fresh linen had been placed in the dressing room next to our bedroom. As though in answer, one of the kitchen girls caught my eye and looked hurriedly away, the tops of her ears turning red. I felt cold, and could not eat or say what I wanted to, so like a coward I went to walk up and down the long gallery and pray, hoping for a sign from God. I watched the trees and the sky, and felt that burning itch to be outside without my thoughts instead of inside with them.

Richard was in the great hall, seated with James the steward, the household ledger open between them. The Gawthorpe ledger was as important in our house as the King's Bible: everything we bought, every bill we paid and everything that came in or out of Gawthorpe — whether on wheels, horseback or rolled in a barrel — was inked on its thick pages in James's immaculate hand. Suits of armor, tapestries and other frivolities that Richard liked to spend his money on were committed in ink, as well as everyday things: stockings for the servants, cork for the wine. But like me, Richard took little interest in it, preferring to leave it to our men, so when I found him I knew he would be impatient: talk of quit-rents and profits bored him. As if reminding him to take the estate's business seriously, the grave portrait of his uncle the reverend Lawrence sat overlooking them, the words *death is the way unto life* painted at his shoulder.

I swallowed. "Richard?"

He looked up quickly, welcoming the distraction. Then two things happened at once: James turned a new leaf so the pages were blank, even though they had only been halfway down the last, and I noticed Richard was dressed to travel.

"You are going away?"

"Lancaster. I leave tonight."

"Oh. Did someone write to you this morning?"

"Only my sisters with news from London. They always write me a letter each but it might as well be one — they only talk of the same people and plays and the latest victim of scandal. At least there is more to entertain them there than at Forcett with my mother. I expect they'll never want to move back to York. Did you need me?"

Yes, I need you. The room rang with silence. James's feather quivered, its inky point eager to scratch. I wanted to say "Don't go," but instead replied, "How are the Mistresses Shuttleworth?"

"Eleanor hints at something that has quite excited her, but Anne refers to it not at all."

"Perhaps she is engaged."

"It is not like Eleanor to be subtle."

"Perhaps she hopes to be engaged, then." I continued, though James cleared his throat pointedly. "I am going into Padiham this morning for some linen from Mrs. Kendall's. Is there anything you need?"

"Why don't you have one of the servants go?"

"They will get the wrong thing."

"You are well enough?"

Lawrence's gray eyes stared at me from the frame. *Death is the way unto life.* "Yes." I did not want him to go; he was always going, and I was always staying. "When will you be back?"

"In a few days. Shall I check on Barton on my travels?"

"Why? My mother no longer lives there, there will be nothing but empty rooms and mice."

"I should look in every now and again to check all is in order."

James sniffed and shifted in his seat. I was taking up valuable time with his master. Perhaps then Richard looked at me properly, for he came to me, tilting my chin to his face with his finger.

"And how about we fit in a trip to London soon? Eleanor and Anne have made me miss it. We can get you one of the best midwives, and the Lord knows we are starved of entertainment in these parts. This dreary hall could use some joy. James, find out if there are any players traveling in the area that could come and perform. Or send for some." He wrapped an arm around my waist and held my hand as though we were about to dance. Puck shuffled up to us, grunting curiously. "Otherwise I shall have to train Puck to be a dancing bear. Behold!"

He discarded me and pulled the dog up to his height so Puck's great paws rested on his shoulders and his monstrous head was level with Richard's. I could not help but smile as they sauntered in an awkward dance, Puck's tongue lolling as his feet staggered on the stone flags before he crashed ungracefully to the ground. He came immediately to me for a rewarding pat.

"Useless creature. We will have to work on our routine," said Richard.

He left me with James, and James with their unfinished business. I knew I was not the only person in the household left disarmed at times by my husband's shifting moods that were like clouds scudding across the sun. I watched him go, feeling his kiss feathery light on my cheek, and the weight of everything else heavy as a wet cloak around my shoulders.

CHAPTER FOUR

I'd heard of wise women, who could give you a cup of something and make you bleed so your stomach went flat again. Just as there were herbs and potions to make it come out, were there not different ones to make it stay in, make it live? The little I'd heard was in snatches of conversation I was on the edge of, when the servants hadn't known I was sitting quietly in the next room, or from pursed lips at a dinner table in some hall or other, before the topic swiftly moved on to one more tasteful. If only I had a friend I could ask; I could hardly speak to the apothecary myself.

The ride from Gawthorpe to Padiham was a pleasant one through wide-spaced trees until the land opened out onto the road. It was cold and bright, and I was glad my thick wool cloak covered me. I tied the horse outside the clothiers, stroking her coal-black mane once, twice, before leaving her.

"Good morning, Mistress," said face after plain face.

I returned their greetings, noticing them greedily examining every inch of me, from my hat to my gloves. It was impossible to be inconspicuous.

I paused at the apothecary's door, my hand half raised to push it open. In the dark, narrow little shop, with all its scents that pressed in and made my head spin, were dozens of miniature bottles and tapestries of herbs hanging from the walls. It was very possible some might stop the sickness coming, stop the child leaving. Stop me from dying, even. But it was a different language, and one I could not speak.

I ordered my linen from Mrs. Kendall the clothier and thought I saw her bright little eyes flick down my front. It was hard to tell with village people, if they suspected you were in childbed or were admiring your Paris buttons.

"Mrs. Kendall," I imagined whispering. She would no doubt grow confidential and press her round stomach against the counter, leaning forward. "Do you know a wise woman?"

"What for, Mistress?" she'd ask in astonishment.

"To help me grow a baby."

"All you need is a husband for that!" And she'd slap her red hands on her apron as tears streamed down her round face while she laughed and laughed. Then the whole town would know, and it might get back to my servants, who would tell in turn how the master had quitted my chamber, and us not five years married. No, it would not do.

I rode my horse out of the town and took a shortcut through the woods. It was easier to think there than in the house, which was too quiet when Richard was away. I'd found the scale of Gawthorpe and the silence of it frightening at first. Wherever Richard went I would follow, and he called me the little ghost. If there were any ghosts, he said, which there weren't because the house was so new it shone like a minted coin, they would think I was one of them, so would leave me alone.

I suppose if only I had been more assertive, Miss Fawnbrake would never have arrived. When Richard called me into the hall, I saw her wide back turn from where she was standing at the fireplace so she could regard me with her glassy, vacant eyes that were too far apart, like those of a fish. Ten or more years older than me, she looked all wrong — her ruff was floppy and needed starching; her dress was too tight. Even her name was wrong: Miss Fawnbrake belonged to a coltish, beautiful young woman, and she was none of those. But what unnerved me the most was how she stood at Richard's shoulder as though she had lived at Gawthorpe all her life. Richard was telling me he had found me a lady's maid, to keep me company in the house. Dread poured into me, filling me from bottom to top as he told me how I'd be like a lady at court, who had women to sit and read with them or play games and music. In my meekness I could only stare at her hands, which were pink and dry like smoked ham, folded patiently with too much wrist showing because her sleeves were short. Richard knew I didn't play music or practice my Latin vocabulary; he knew I liked to hunt and be outside with my dog, and the house was the problem, and him being away. Did he not?

By this point I'd lost the first baby, but this was worse. I'd gone tearfully into the dining chamber, where Richard came to me, leaving Miss Fawnbrake curling her swollen knuckles.

"I don't want a nurse, Richard," I had told him, my voice cracking.

"You prefer to be alone? Fleetwood, you say the suits of armor frighten you."

"They do not anymore." Hot, salty tears were falling down my cheeks, and I began to cry like the infant I was. My husband did not see me as mistress of the house. "I am not a child, Richard," I'd sobbed.

If only I could go now to that frightened girl, I would kneel on the Turkey carpet and take her cold little hands in mine; if only I could have done it years before that and said things will get worse before they get better, but better they will. Would I believe myself?

Recalling her rough pink hands and her bloated, pockmarked face still makes me queasy. She was with us for eight months and I lost two babies in that time, one after the other. When I began bleeding and begged her not to tell Richard, she marched from the room to inform her master. Richard raced upstairs to find me hunched over the bed as pain folded me in half again and again. I wish he had not seen how incapable I was, how keenly the child did not want me as its mother. The first time I'd miscarried, before Miss Fawnbrake arrived, we'd been walking in the long gallery, talking about commissioning our portraits, when I felt a strange plucking below, and thought my bowel had opened. I did not know what was happening, did not know there had even been a baby, and Richard had tucked me in bed and washed me with a warm cloth and fed me broth and marchpane. He was sad, but also delighted that we had conceived.

"We will have a baby by Christmastide!" he had said, smiling, and I had smiled weakly back, believing him.

There had been no pain, just sorrow, and love. But then Miss Fawnbrake arrived, and there had been a great deal of pain, and even more sorrow, and guilt, and everything else.

The third time was worst of all. Richard was away, and I'd been playing with Puck on the lawn outside the house, tugging him around by a stick he had clamped in his mouth. My stomach was big by that time, as though I'd swallowed a globe. A line had appeared down my front, and in my inexperience I thought that's where the skin would come apart and my baby be lifted out when it was ready. That afternoon I'd fallen over more than once, and got muddy and wet, my playful Puck jumping all over me when I was down, licking my face and making me laugh. I remember the laughter dying in my throat when I saw Miss Fawnbrake watching me from the dining room window, and then for a long time it never came back, because that evening while I dressed for bed, the pains started again and didn't stop for three days. A doctor was called, Richard arrived from York, and in a blur of pain and darkness I remember the feeling of something leaving me, and a midwife holding what looked like a white rabbit by its feet. For two weeks I did not leave my bed. Miss Fawnbrake was a malignant shadow in the corner, and one day she disappeared, and came back with Richard, who for the first time in our marriage raised his voice at me.

"What is this about you rolling around on the lawn like an animal? Letting the dog trample all over you? Fleetwood, it's like you have no interest in becoming a mother and insist on behaving like a child."

He may as well have called me a murderer. If there had been a knife with my untouched bread, or a red-hot poker in the fireplace, I would have rammed it into Miss Fawnbrake's pallid chest, and proved him right. Once Richard could see how much passion she inspired in me, and how I ground my teeth when she walked into a room, he finally deigned to make rid of her with the idea that her presence was causing me to miscarry. While I did not think him right, I did not think him all wrong either. How I dreaded her face appearing at the door each morning to dress me, and how I hated the low, confidential conversations she conducted with my husband, with the servants. Before I could tell Richard about my day she had done it; before I could greet him at the door she'd taken his cloak. If she could have carried his child for him, no doubt she would have done. When Richard dismissed her, that night I found one of Puck's turds beneath my pillow, dug from the grounds and carried up four flights of stairs in her chapped, swollen hands. Never again would I have a companion — it was like having a sister who hated you.

Halfway home, my horse's steady rhythm jolted to a shuddering halt and, before I realized what was happening, she began backing up and rearing, her eyes rolling and nostrils flaring. Surrounded by tree trunks and a chorus of rustling leaves, at first I did not know what had startled her. I knew she disliked harts and even deer, as she was not a hunting horse. Then a movement ahead drew my eyes, which fixed suddenly on the source of her alarm. A red fox was tensed ten yards ahead, large as a young doe and just as sleek. I had only a second to take in its pointed face and flattened back, its bristling tail frozen in a perfect line behind it. What I remember thinking before I fell was how unmoved by us it was, as though we had disturbed it in some private reflection.

The last thing I saw before my horse flailed again with the effort of communicating her terror was the animal's reproachful golden eyes. I hit the ground with a crack, landing on my left wrist and feeling several things at once: the pain in my arm, the wet ground underneath and the mounting knowledge that the horse was going to crush me underfoot. For she was panicking, rearing and bucking around the ten-yard-wide clearing that I was lying in. I placed my good hand on my stomach and spoke calmly to the horse, but her hooves went on pacing, her sweating flanks strong as a damn. My wrist sang with pain and I thought I might be sick. I tried to push myself up and cried out with the shock of it. There was a tree trunk two or three yards away, so I leaned on my elbows and tried to drag myself toward it.

"Damn fox," I muttered. "Damn mule."

"Don't move."

A woman emerged between two trees. At once I knew her — she was the same strange girl from the woods the other day. Proceeding cautiously toward the wild horse with her hands outstretched, she did not speak or click her tongue, but the effect of her presence was as though she had, with her clear gaze and steady hands. Submitting gratefully to direction, the mare stopped her twitching and came to a halt, her black eyes wide. While the woman held the sweating beast still, I watched her golden hair twisting from beneath her cap, her long face serious. Her hands were slim but too bony to be elegant. I tried to push myself up again and winced with pain, my wrist burning hot as coal.

"Don't move."

She spoke again in that low, musical voice, flickering like a flame in all the green. She was wearing the same old dress as before, the same mutton's wool cap. As she knelt next to me, I smelled lavender despite her dirty clothes. Carefully she took my gray wrist in her long white hands and I gritted my teeth. Looking around, she got up and snapped a short stick from the low branch of a tree. The woods whispered and shivered around us, and for a brief moment I thought she might use it as a weapon to strike me with. But she knelt again, ripped a length of fabric from her grubby apron, tied the stick to my wrist and bound it tightly in three places.

"Only a sprain," she told me. "Nothing is

broken."

"What are you doing here?" was all I could say. She regarded me with those curious amber eyes. "Why do you wander about the forest alone?"

"Why do you?" she said.

With my good hand I prodded my stomach to check it was still there and didn't hurt, but my corset made it difficult to tell. Her eyes traveled to my front, concealed by folds of velvet and brocade, though perhaps not to her, then flicked over my face, my dry lips, my bloodshot eyes and gray pallor.

As if she could smell the sickness on me, she said, "You are with child."

My vision blurred, the forest leaped around me, and as though she had invoked it, I leaned over and vomited on the roots of a tree. Sweat drenched my face and I wiped it with a shaking, muddied hand.

"You live at the big house by the river?" she asked.

"How did you know?"

"You told me last time. I will help you back, Mistress . . ."

"Shuttleworth. There is no need for it."

"You can't ride, and you are weak. I will take the horse."

"I'm not getting back on that stupid mule."

"You must. Here."

She made a cradle for my foot, and with difficulty I hoisted myself up. My skirts were damp and muddy, and made a mess on her hands, but she did not seem to notice or mind, and reluctantly I clicked my tongue and dug my heels in and we began at a gentle pace.

It was spring, and the trees knew it, but the weather had not caught up with them. They stood proud and green as a cavalry, though the wind bit their trunks and snapped at their leaves. It crossed my mind that when these same leaves turned orange and fell to coat the floor, I would almost certainly not be here to see it. I closed my eyes and we rode on in silence.

"Thank you for helping me," I said after a while. "I may have been trampled to offal by the time my husband found me."

"Your husband?"

"Richard Shuttleworth. Where do you live?"

After a pause, she said the village a few miles to the northeast.

"Colne is not so close. What brings you to my land again?" If I sounded peevish, I half meant it. I had not forgotten the massacred rabbits, the limp form dangling from her bloodied fist.

"I did not know it was your land."

"And if you had not been on it I might not have lived to tell the tale."

We moved on in a more companionable silence, me on horseback, she on foot. I only wondered later how she knew the way, with the trees so thick and the uneven ground showing no clear paths. But I let her lead me, happy as the horse was for someone to take charge. My wrist throbbed and my teeth were thick with sourness.

"Are you ill with the child?" she asked.

"Always."

"I can give you something to help."

"You can? You are a wise woman?"

"I am a midwife."

My heart beat a little faster and I sat up straighter. "You deliver babies that live? And the women — they live themselves?"

She looked at me strangely. "I do everything I can."

That was not what I wanted to hear, and I sighed and sat back in the saddle, a cloud eclipsing my brief moment of relief. We did not speak for another minute or so, then I asked if she had infants of her own. But her reaction to the simple question surprised me. I saw a twitch of something in her face — was it irritation? — and she kept her eyes on the ground. The knuckles in her hand holding the rein flared bone white as she gripped tighter. I had upset her. I always managed to say the wrong thing, and my shame sat heavily on me.

After the longest time, she spoke, so shortly I might have missed it. "No."

I sighed inwardly. I knew not how to speak to women my age, having no friends or sisters. Eleanor and Anne Shuttleworth were the closest I had to either, and I could hardly bear to be in their simpering, frothy company for more than a day or so. This young woman was being polite, as a poor village girl might with a gentlewoman. But for once in my life I wished for a normal conversation with a young woman, as equals, sitting across from one another at a card table or side by side in saddles.

"I have just had a thought," I announced, trying to sound merry. "I do not know the name of my savior."

"Alice Gray." She answered quietly, before adding, "The women that do not live . . . it's only when it cannot be helped. I know it to look at them."

I swallowed. "How do you know it?"

Alice Gray considered her response, and I watched her narrow shoulders in her wool dress that was slightly too big. "It's in their eyes, a giving over to . . . whatever is beyond. You know the daylight gate?"

I nodded, wondering what dusk had to do with childbirth.

"When the light and darkness are equal forces — partners, if you will — then there is a moment, very quick and quiet, where you can see the day giving in to the night. That's when I know. That's what it's like."

She sounded like a witch, and I almost said it.

"You think me full of fancy," she said, mistaking my silence.

"No, I understand. The death is inevitable, like the darkness."

"That's exactly it."

Not for the first time, I wondered what the darkness felt like when you were half in the light. I think I may have come close to it, but the pain anchored me to the earth. I watched Alice Gray's dull cap that cried out to be starched bob alongside the horse's shoulder, and imagined telling her about the doctor's letter. But like with Richard, the words would not come.

"You are young for a midwife," I said instead.

"I learned from my mother. She was a midwife. The best, actually."

I felt the doctor's words in his letter tighten once again round my neck, and with my good hand I adjusted my dirt-spattered collar. "Do you know it to look at a woman with child?" I asked. "If there is a chance she might die?"

"Sometimes," Alice replied.

Where she had been eloquent earlier, now it was as though a curtain had come down over her mood. She was not beautiful but there was some vital quality that made her interesting to look at: the long nose; the intelligent, searching eyes in a hungry face; the hands that brought life into the world. She was quickly becoming one of the most fascinating people I'd met.

I swallowed again, tightening my grip on the rein as though it tethered me to this life. "Do you know it to look at me?"

Alice Gray glanced up at me, then her amber eyes went back to the floor. "No," she said.

I could not tell if she was lying.

Back at Gawthorpe, the servants made a great fuss getting me off my horse and inside the entrance hall. As they lowered me down, I searched for Richard's face in the four or five gathered on the steps, and there were more in the windows. But of course, I thought dully as they helped me up the steps like an old duchess. He was away. In

70

all the activity, I remembered Alice, and slapped a maid's hand away as she tried to remove the crude stick and rags splint.

"I shall keep it on, Sarah," I said, as usual managing to sound spiteful rather than gracious.

How queer the servants thought me. For a whole year I dared not give them instruction — some of them were forty, fifty years my senior. Once, when I was fourteen or so, and brushing my horse in the stable, I heard one of the yard boys call me the child bride. I had stayed there until dusk, prickling with shame and afraid to come out in case they'd know I heard. When Richard asked where on earth I'd been for so long, I told him, tears smarting in my eyes, and the lad had been dismissed within the hour.

Sarah let go obediently, but not before I saw the story forming in her mind, the one she would save for the buttery. I would not have any of them come near my wrist. That's when I noticed Alice, almost out of sight, descending the front steps. I called her and she paused, framed in the rectangle of daylight, for the entrance hall with its warren of passages was very dark. The servants also came to a collective halt, regarding her with open curiosity.

"Will you come in for something to eat?"

71

My ears were growing red, and I had to clear my throat, knowing everyone was paying attention. I was never more uncomfortable in a role than as mistress of a staff of servants.

Alice looked uncertain, as though trying to determine whether I had issued an invitation or a command. But Sarah decided for her, ushering her in with an impatient tut and closing the heavy door behind her to keep the spring chill out. The lanterns flared and settled, and Alice wrung her hands.

Burning with self-consciousness, I turned to one of the kitchen girls who was standing uselessly aside. "Margery, have bread and cheese and something to drink sent to the parlor, and take Miss Gray there. I will change out of my wet things and see her there."

Alice was looking with interest at the high ceilings, the dark corners, the sconces. I tried to smile at her before going to the staircase, hoping it was not obvious this was the first time in four years I'd had my very own guest.

None of the servants offered to help me get out of my riding clothes, which, given how filthy and trampled they were, was difficult with two hands and impossible with one.

My wrist ached, and Puck sniffed curiously at my legs, and when I was undressed, out of habit I put a hand between my legs to check I was not bleeding. Almost a full half hour later I was in a clean skirt and jacket, and went down with Puck padding behind me. Voices were coming from beneath the staircase where the parlor was at the back of the house, and I pushed the door open, to be greeted to my surprise by two faces.

"Richard!"

He came to me and kissed my cheek distractedly, taking hold of my wrist. "I was on my way to your chamber — I have just arrived back — what's this about you falling from your horse, little ghost? And *what* is this invention? A fine improvisation, I must say. Miss Gray, is this your work? Fleetwood, are you hurt? I hope no one else is?"

As always, Richard's bombardment of questions made me feel dizzy, and I knew not which to answer first. Leaving my hands in his, I looked instead at Alice, whose face was expressionless, giving no hint of their conversation. The parlor was not grand, but in it Alice looked twice as poorly dressed, her dress drab and dusty against the jewel-like Turkey carpets and honey-colored paneling.

"You are surprised to see me. Did you forget I was not leaving until tonight?"

Weakly, with his help, I sat down in one of the polished oak chairs by the low fire, which thankfully was crackling cheerfully. Before I could speak, Margery brought a loaf with cheese and fruit and a jug of ale, departing with a swift appraisal of Alice and her muddy hands.

"Your hands — shall I send for water? Alice helped me back onto my horse," I told Richard, who had begun pouring ale into two cups.

"An angel of the forest," he announced, handing one to her.

Indoors, she was different — ordinary, almost, and younger, perhaps twenty-two or -three. She brushed her hands on her apron before accepting the cup and drinking thirstily.

I realized Richard was waiting for an answer from me, his gray eyes on mine. "All is well?"

He was in a good mood from his travels, as usual, light of spirit and foot and heart. Often I envied him for it. Sometimes he made me feel as though I wore a cloak of doom and gloom that would never unfasten, yet if the same one was placed around him he would shake it off as easily as a wet dog.

"All is well," I replied with a reassuring smile. *For now,* my mind echoed.

He knelt and took my free hand, kissing it then filling it with the cup of ale. "I will leave you women to talk of French farthingales while I get out of these clothes. I think I will delay my trip another day. Besides, Easter is almost here so there will not be much business to be done."

My heart sang at his words, but before I could thank him he was gone, grabbing a fistful of grapes on his way out. I watched Alice, wondering what effect my husband had on her, but she just looked tired, with her hair tumbling out of her cap and her mouth turning down at the corners. The faintest hint of lavender drifted over again. The fire cracked and glowed, filling the little room with its comforting scent of woodsmoke.

Before I could speak, she said, "What is a French farthingale?"

I almost laughed, pleased I could answer her for once. "It's a wheel you wear under your skirts at the waist, to make them wide. You have never heard of one?"

She shook her head. "How is your wrist? You will need to bind it tightly with rags."

I prodded it gingerly. "Fine. I have come off my horse plenty of times. My friend

Roger says you are not a rider unless you come off seven times, and one for luck. I suppose you come off frequently, rushing to women in childbed."

"I do not have a horse."

"Do not have a horse?" I was shocked. "Then how do you get anywhere?"

A trace of a smile lifted her lips at the corners. "I walk. Or if a rich yeoman is sending his man for me, sometimes he will bring a spare horse." I must have looked astonished, for she added, "Babies are often not quick to be born."

"I would not know." I felt her eyes watching me from across the room, burning like two rushlights. "Please, sit down. Eat."

She obliged. "I cannot stay long, I have to . . . go soon." I nodded, watching her cut the cheese delicately with long fingers, her knucklebones white beneath her skin. "This is your first child?"

"Yes," I said. I realized I sounded exactly the same as she did when she said earlier that she did not have any children. As she ate quietly, I twisted my wedding band, considering. What had I brought her to my parlor for, if not just to show her my gratitude? I thought of Richard's concern. *All is well.* For how long would it be well? And there was something about Alice that invited confidence, the way she'd tamed my horse in the clearing without speaking.

"I have lost three children," I said quickly.

She let go of the knife buried in the cheese, sitting back and wiping her hands on her apron, dusting crumbs from her fingers. I could not look her in the face, so I stared at the carpet, finding here and there Puck's orange hairs, so fine they looked woven in.

"I'm sorry." Her voice was full of kindness.

I polished one of the wooden lions on the arm of my chair with my finger. "My mother thinks I am not able to have children. She thinks I am failing to carry out my duty as a wife."

The silence from the chair opposite was thoughtful and patient. "How old were they?"

"All of them died before they were born." I pulled at a loose thread of gold in my skirt, then tried to tuck it back in. "After the first time, Richard was worried, so he hired a woman to watch over me."

"Watch over you?"

"To see I was eating right, things like that. He was worried," I said again.

"About you or the child?"

"About both of us." She nodded. "What

did the two of you talk about earlier?" I asked.

"This and that. Work."

A sting of jealousy made me sneer. "He talked to you of his business?"

"No. I work at the Hand and Shuttle in Padiham. I did not know you and your husband owned it."

"Do we?" I asked, realizing too late how ignorant I sounded. "I thought you . . . So you have two places of work?"

"Babies are not born every day. Not in Colne."

I drank again, and thought idly of the rattle Richard bought that I'd stuffed in the drawer. *Her earthly life will end.*

"How long have you worked there?"

"Not long."

"How much do they pay you?"

She took a long drink of beer and wiped her mouth. It made me hungry and thirsty, envious, even, to watch her enjoying her food and drink. My stomach growled.

"Two pounds," she said.

"A week?"

Alice stared at me. "A year."

I knew my face glowed scarlet, but I did not look away. In a whole year she made what I paid for three yards of velvet. I shifted in my seat and adjusted the rags from her apron around my wrist, which were beginning to itch. The smooth oak was cool where it met my skin.

"You said you could stop me from feeling ill?" My mouth was dry. I licked my lips. I wanted to tell her about Richard moving out of our chamber, about how in February I was sick forty times in one day. She nodded. "Can you help me have a baby? A living one?"

"I . . ."

"I will pay you five shillings a week."

The sum would no doubt send James the steward's eyebrows into his hair as he entered it into the ledger, but my grasp on money had humiliated me, so I knew any offer had to sit comfortably between generous and fair. Richard had once said that money was impossible to discuss with poor people. Alice was quite clearly poor, and — I looked at her hands for rings — unmarried. I knew what he meant.

"That's five times what I earn now," she said softly.

She reached a finger under her cap to scratch at her hair, and set her beer down gently. My stomach made a noise we both heard; I had not eaten a morsel.

"I will also give you use of a horse, so you can ride here and to the inn at Padiham.

Colne is a long way to walk."

She considered this, licking her lips and staring at the fire, then asked, "Are you further along now than you have been before? When will it come?"

"Autumn, I suppose. The last time was . . . somewhere near the end."

"I would need to examine you," she said. "You have not bled since . . . ?"

"New year. There is something else." I reached into my gown and pulled out the letter from the doctor that I'd shoved inexplicably into my jacket when I dressed. I'd kept it locked behind a small square panel in my dresser, and the key I hid between the rope and mattress beneath my bed. I unfolded the letter, smoothing it out and feeling the intimate warmth of my body heat. But Alice did not take it, and a frown had creased between her eyebrows.

"I cannot read," she said dully.

There was a sudden scratching at the door, and we both sat up straight. I stuffed the paper down the side of the chair but no one entered.

I called, "Yes?" When no answer came I got up to open it. Puck stood panting on the other side and, dropping to my knees, I let out a sigh of relief. "It's only you. Good boy."

He followed me to my chair and I saw Alice's eyes widen at the size of him.

"He is a gentle giant," I reassured her, letting him settle at my feet. "I am constantly brushing dog hairs off my skirts, but I don't mind really. Finish your cheese or he will have it."

"He is very big," Alice said.

Puck lifted his russet head when she spoke and barked once, loudly.

"That's enough," I told him.

"What is he?"

"A French mastiff."

"Was he a gift from your husband?"

Instinctively I reached to scratch his ears. "No. I rescued him from a bearbaiting pit in London. He was thin and starving, tied up in the street next to a bear warden selling tickets. I went to stroke him and the bear warden kicked him. He said dogs were useless if they were soft and I would ruin him. I asked him how much for the pup and he said he wasn't worth the rope tied around his neck. So I picked him up off the ground and said I would take him. He changed his mind then, said I was denying him a prizefighter. I gave him a shilling, and off we went without a backward glance. I named him Puck, for a character in a play Richard and I saw a few days before — an

81

imp of the forest. Not that there is anything imp-like about him."

Alice gazed thoughtfully at the spoiled beast on the Turkey carpet. His tongue was the size of a salmon, lolling happily from his jaws.

"How far he has come in life," she remarked. "I have heard of bearbaiting but never seen it."

"I find it dreadful. They are bloodthirsty people in London. Perhaps it's because they can't hunt."

We sat in a silence more comfortable than before, and she nodded at the letter in my hands. "What does it say?"

"That the next time I am in childbed I will die." Saying it aloud for the first time, I felt the tendrils loosen around my neck. "As you can see, I am going to need a miracle. God has blessed me with many things. I am not sure that being a mother is one of them, but today I wished for a wise woman and there you were. I so want to give my husband a son — he longs for it."

"And you?"

"I am his wife, and I hope to be a mother. I do not want him to be a widower."

I tried to swallow the lump in my throat. Alice was looking at me with abject sympathy, and briefly I wondered how she could:

she who was poor, and unmarried, who had two jobs and no horse, felt sorry for me. Perhaps the fine house and handsome husband and expensive clothes meant nothing to her, and perhaps she could see also that they were of little use to me, who could buy anything I wanted except the thing I wanted most: to succeed as Richard's wife, and pay him back for what he did for me, for the future he took me away from. For him, I wanted to have my stomach grow, and fill the house with sticky hands and dusty knees. While we had no children, we were not a family; we had a house but not a home. Even spending a lifetime locked up at Barton, with my mother's disapproval the first thing I saw in the morning and the last I saw at night, was preferable to the alternative. Were it not for Richard, I knew where I would be, not here, nor at Barton. I could only picture it, for I had never been. I remembered his kind face on our wedding day, how he held my hands in his and smiled as though he had been looking forward to it even more than I had. *Thank you,* I wanted to say to him that day, and the day after, and every day after that. *Thank you for saving me.*

"Mistress?" Alice was looking at me with concern. The fire spat and sputtered, and the knife still stuck out from the cheese like a dagger hurled into a tree.

I leaned forward, urgent for the first time. My desperation had been there since I'd met her, had been there for months, but now it was gushing out of me. "Please," I said. "Say you will help me." I realized I was gripping the arms of my chair, and squeezing them. "I need you to save my life, and with it another one. Help me live, Alice. Please help me be a mother, and have a child."

She was looking at me strangely, weighing me up, unsure of the purchase. Then she nodded, and it was like she had taken my hand.

CHAPTER FIVE

That night, in bed alone, I had The Nightmare. The forest was pitch-black and cold, and my feet crunched on dead leaves when I moved, so I stayed still, unable to see even my hand in front of my face. My heart thudded, and my ears strained for sound. Then the boars came. Shuffling and grunting nearby, their greedy breath hot and curious. I closed my eyes to hear better, and something brushed against my skirts. Then everything went still. A bead of sweat trickled down my face, and then the silence broke, and it began. The noises they were making were awful — high-pitched, excited screeches and barks. I started running, blindly, my hands out in front in case I hit the trees, which I never did. I was crying, and they were catching me, about to catch me, snarling and gnashing their jaws, their stabbing tusks like knives made of bone. I tripped and stumbled to the ground, covered my head with my hands and screamed. They found me, dancing around me, their fallen prey. They were hungry; they were going to pierce me, gouge me right the way through with their tusks. A ripping, shooting pain cut me in half and made me pull my knees up, but they were bound in my skirts, and I cried out.

I was in my bedroom, soaked with sweat in bright daylight. My heart was loud as a bell, my face wet with tears, but I was alone. There were no boars, and I wasn't in the forest. My breathing slowed, and my wrist ached dully. The tight rags Alice had told me to wrap around it had come loose, trailing beneath me in the bedclothes. I yawned, blinking in the sunlight, stretched and turned over.

Sitting next to the bed, watching me like a hawk, was my mother.

She waited as I tried to push myself into a sitting position. I did not look at her but knew that her mouth would be a thin line as she examined my wild black hair, my skin gray as the ashes that lay in the fireplace. Mary Barton disapproved of illness, weakness or failure of any kind; in fact she found it offensive.

Before either of us spoke, I heard the tread of Richard's boots in the passage, his coin belt jangling. "Look who is here for a visit," he announced, coming in and resting a hand on my mother's rigid shoulder.

I did look, and her black eyes met mine. Her head was bare and her collar, starched to perfection, fanned out high around her. Her white hands were folded serenely in her lap and her expression was one of great restraint. She was still wearing her outdoor cloak, giving the impression she had either just alighted her horse or was about to leave. She always felt the cold, which was why she moved out of Barton after Richard and I were married, complaining of the size of it, settling at Richard's suggestion into a more modest house farther north.

Not north enough.

"Mother," I said.

"You missed breakfast," she announced.

I licked my teeth. My breath was rank.

"I will have some food brought up," Richard said, leaving and closing the door behind him.

I pushed back the thick counterpane, climbed out of bed and went to get a length of cloth to clean my teeth, my mother watching me all the time.

"This chamber is like a pigsty. Your servants should be more attentive — what else could they possibly be occupied with?" she

87

said. When I ignored her, she went on. "Will you get dressed today?"

"Perhaps."

Standing sentry above the mantelpiece on either side of the Shuttleworth coat of arms were two plaster female figurines half my height: Prudence and Justice. Sometimes I imagined them as my friends. My mother's straight back and position in front of the fireplace set her directly in the middle of them, making her look like their third sister, Misery.

"Why do you look amused, Fleetwood? You are mistress of this house — get dressed at once."

At that moment Puck sauntered in, sniffing her skirts then dismissing her. "I cannot understand why you keep that beast in the house," she said. "Dogs are for hunting and guarding, not treating like infants. What is that on your wrist?"

I tugged at the bandage, wincing as it unraveled, and began to tie it more tightly. "I fell off my horse yesterday while riding. It's only a sprain."

"Fleetwood," she said, lowering her voice and glancing over her shoulder to check the door was closed. I could smell the sickly pomade she dabbed at her wrists. "Richard tells me you are expecting again. If I am not mistaken, you have lost three children before they came to this earth."

"I have not *lost* anything." I began to shiver.

"Then I will put it plainly. Three times you have failed to carry a child. Do you in honesty think you should be throwing yourself off horses? You are not being careful enough. You have a midwife?"

"Yes."

"Where did you find her?"

"She is local. From Colne."

"Might you have been wiser to employ a woman who came recommended from a family we know? Did you or Richard speak to Jane Towneley? Or Margaret Starkie?"

I stared at Prudence's plaster face. Her stoic gaze avoided mine, landing somewhere in the distance. I was a wife, the mistress of one of the finest households for miles around, and I was standing in my nightgown being scolded by my mother. Had Richard invited her? He knew how I hated her. I clenched my fists, once, twice, three times. "Whomever I employ is my decision, *Mother.*" I coated the last word with honey and her face, so composed at all times, betrayed a tiny flicker of fury.

"I shall discuss it with Richard," she said. "In the meantime, I want you to promise you are doing everything you can to carry this child into life. I am not convinced you are currently. More rest is required, and . . . indoor pursuits. Perhaps take up an instrument instead of galloping around like a squire. You have a fine husband, and if you start behaving like a wife and mother, God's gift will come. I did not unite our families so you could play at being a princess in a tower. Now, I expect you to dine with me. Please get dressed and meet me downstairs."

I heard her descend the staircase and prayed that her portrait would fall from its hangings and flatten her.

Richard poured a glass of red wine under my nose and passed it to my mother. It was dark as a ruby, the same color that had leaked from me three times — surprisingly beautiful in its richness, drenching the bed linen that had to be burned under the sky.

To avoid its heady scent I lifted my face to the ceiling. The plasterwork in the dining room was decorated with dozens of bunches of grapes, their vines climbing out toward the corners, entwining like lovers' hands.

"No wine for you, Fleetwood?"

"No, thank you."

Richard poured another glass for his friend, Thomas Lister, who was passing through on his way to York. We sat around the fire, which was low, and the smokiness of it was making me drowsy. Not drowsy enough, however, to miss how Thomas's greedy glance slipped to Richard's rings when he handed his friend the glass. His own bare hand flexed in response and he caught my eye, looking immediately away.

In years, Thomas was somewhere in between Richard's age and mine, and his wealth was somewhere in between a plain country gentleman and ours. He would have admitted to the first but never the latter. He and Richard had other things in common: they were both married four years, their fathers had died and they had inherited large estates with mothers and sisters to support. Four years earlier, Master Lister Senior had been taken ill at his son's wedding, collapsing during the vows and dying a few days later. Thomas's mother never truly recovered and hadn't left the house in all that time.

I found Thomas Lister a strange and rather interesting man — he did not easily make conversation, preferring to be somewhere on the edge of it. His wide eyes bulged slightly and he was very small and slim, like a woman. Richard said his build made him a great rider, that he held himself straight as an arrow.

My mother failed to mix comfortably with young people: she had a way of making them feel like infants, and Thomas stuttered a polite response when she asked after his mother. He was rescued by the entrance of Edmund the apprentice, who told Richard that a woman had arrived from one of the farms with news of a dog that had withered a ewe. In those days we kept hundreds of sheep in the fields; the soil was too wet for anything else.

There was a pause, in which Richard set his glass down. "To whom does the dog belong?"

Edmund shook his head. "She knows not, Master. She found it running around, worrying the flock. She asks you to come quickly."

Richard hurried out. People were always coming to knock at our door and tell us their tales. Richard was generous, giving them grain when their crops were down and wood to repair their houses. There were two hundred families in Padiham and just as many problems laid at our door since we'd been there.

"What takes you to York?" my mother asked Thomas. She was making the point of being a good hostess, which I was not.

"I am going to a trial at the Lent assizes," said Thomas.

"A trial?"

The logs in the hearth cracked and burned. I wondered how long Richard would be gone; it was the daylight gate, and darkness pressed in at the windows.

"For what purpose?" my mother asked, draining her glass.

Thomas shifted in his chair. "A murder trial," he said softly. "The accused is a woman named Jennet Preston."

I sat up a little straighter. "Do you know her?" I asked.

"Unfortunately, very well." A tendon jumped in his cheek. "She worked for my family for many years, but since my father died she has not left us alone. We gave her kindness and favors but she is ungrateful, always asking for more."

"Who is she accused of murdering?"

"A child."

Both my mother and I were united briefly in shock. Thomas stared grimly at the fire.

"Are you speaking for her?"

Thomas looked sharply at me. "For her? Against her. She murdered another servant's son — an infant, not a year old — brutally and heartlessly."

Before I could stop it, a memory crowded

in: a small, cold body; two tiny rows of eyelashes that would never open. I closed my eyes and forced the image away.

"Why would she do that?" I asked.

"Because she is a jealous woman," Thomas said shortly. "She failed to seduce Edward and so took the thing that was most precious to him and his wife. She is a witch."

My mother leaned forward. "Another witch?" Thomas was confused. "You have not heard of the events at Read Hall?"

"How do *you* know of the events at Read Hall?" I asked.

She shrugged one shoulder dismissively. "Richard told me."

She said it in a way that implied of course he would inform his mother-in-law of every matter of which he knew. But she had a way of drawing things out of people, of picking up on a moment of hesitation or an off hand comment and worrying it like the dog with the ewe. Richard would not have spread his friend's affairs about the county; my mother must already have heard it from someone else and no doubt questioned him while he was occupied and distracted.

"What is at Read Hall?" Thomas asked, looking from one of us to the other.

So my mother told him about Roger and the peddler John Law and the witch Alizon

Device, and he listened with great interest.

Stifling a yawn and searching for distraction, I turned my attention to the frieze that crowded the tops of the dining room walls. Mermaids, dolphins, griffins and all sorts of creatures, half-human, half-animal, fixed their attention on the center of the room, as though we were at some great mythical court. When I came to Gawthorpe the frieze was my favorite thing about the house, and I would walk round and round examining each figure and giving them names and little stories. Here were two orphan sisters who were princesses of the sea and ruled the waves; there was a lion army with their shields, primed to attack. I watched them grow darker and more mysterious as the daylight gate left and night arrived, and my mother and Thomas Lister nattered like two washerwomen. My eyelids began to droop; my mouth was dry and my back ached. Until Richard came back I would have to sit here, and there was no sign of him.

That's when it occurred to me: Richard and I would have to sleep in the same bed as long as my mother was here. She had given no sign that she had seen the truckle bed, but perhaps Richard had closed the dressing room door.

I pulled at the rolls in my hair and wondered how long until I could take them out.

"The girl is at Nowell's house," my mother was saying, her eyes shining. "He is keeping her there so she can do no harm to others."

"And she confessed?"

"So they say."

"And Nowell thinks there are others?"

My mother nodded. "In the same family."

"Heavens, Mother. Anyone would think you had been walking alongside John Law when he was cursed," I said.

Thomas was looking thoughtful, clutching his glass against his chest.

"Will you admire our mermaids, Thomas?" I asked. "Take a closer look. They are quite remarkable, designed by two brothers who carried out all the plasterwork at Gawthorpe."

Obligingly he stood and approached them, and I turned to my mother and whispered, "We do not talk of Roger Nowell's business like village wives in this house. He is our friend. Now Thomas is going to take what you told him to York, which is farther than it needed to go."

My mother's face grew sour. "I am merely informing your neighbor of what is happening under his nose. Everyone will know soon enough that there are witches in these parts. And so they should. Do they not say the women are wild here?"

"I know not what *they* say, nor do I care to. And I'm not sure wild is the same as evil."

"Very skilled work," Thomas commented politely behind us. "Extremely intricate. Quite fantastical." He seemed stirred and didn't come back to his seat. "I will set out again before it gets dark. I may call at Read Hall before my journey to York."

"Read Hall is five miles in the other direction," I said.

He reached for his cloak. "My regards to Richard."

He left swiftly, his boots echoing in the passage. There was a moment of silence, then I excused myself on the pretense of needing to go to bed.

The candles had been lit in my chamber and I stood in front of the glass to remove the rolls from my hair. It looked weak and thin, and strands fell away to the floor when I combed through it. I went to the window to close the drapes and in the glass saw Richard's outline in the doorway.

"You'll sleep in here tonight?" I asked.

"I suppose."

I turned and my heart stopped in my chest. His hands were scarlet. Blood coated his doublet and there were flecks on his face

97

and up to his elbows on both arms.

"What happened?"

"I've sent for a jug." He wiped his hands along his arms but the blood was dried. The skin around his fingernails was already turning brown. "It was a mess. If I hadn't seen the dog I would have thought a wolf had done it."

I walked over to the bed and sat on it to remove my slippers.

"That's impossible. There have been no wolves for a hundred years."

I thought about our bodies being close again tonight, his warmth next to me, spreading toward me. Maybe I could run my finger down his spine like I used to. Maybe he would turn and put his mouth to mine, his hardness inside me. Even if we never slept in the same bed again, I would never forget the soft warmth of his skin at the tips of my fingers. I thought of the secret letter, and the image vanished.

"Was the sheep dead?" I asked, turning to let Richard unlace me.

"No. I had to kill it."

"And the dog? What was it?"

"A brown mongrel. It ran off before I could catch it. I'll ask around to find out who it belongs to."

"I have hired the girl who rescued me as a

midwife."

"Oh, yes, what was her name? She is a midwife?"

"Alice. She is very experienced." I did not meet his eye. "I hope you don't mind — I've lent her a horse from the stables, for while she is visiting me."

"Not one of mine?"

"No, the gray draft mare. She is quite old now. Richard . . ." I swallowed. "Will you stay in here from tonight?"

"Many men and their wives sleep in different rooms, it's not unusual," he replied, not unkindly.

"It should be."

"Nonsense. Besides, you are already with child. It is not as though we can make another one."

But I did not hear him, because I'd lifted my smock over my head. A fine thread of scarlet was trailing down my thigh. I halted it on its path with a finger, bringing it to my mouth. I sat naked on the bed, not wanting to turn round, not knowing what to do now that the moment I had been dreading was here. Panic rolled toward me like storm clouds, and I closed my eyes and prayed.

CHAPTER SIX

I lay awake, stiff as a board next to Richard's soft snores, rising finally to walk in the long gallery while the moonlight streamed in. The house was silent, and the polished floors gleamed bright as snow. The flooring creaked under my silent tread as I went up and down, east to west and back again. I returned to bed before the day arrived. More than once I looked at the dried streak of red that had faded into my skin to prove it had happened, or rather had started to happen, and then stopped.

Alice had asked me to give her a few days to collect some herbs that would make me stronger, and it already felt like an eternity, so in the morning while everyone breakfasted, I walked out to give Puck his exercise. I could not eat because my stomach was like a bag of eels again, but with worry this time. We turned right out of the house and went along the edge of the lawn, following the river and passing the great barn and outbuildings. The dogs in their kennels caught Puck's scent and drove themselves into a fury. He sniffed around the corners and walls, ignoring them. Sometimes I wondered if he knew he was a dog. I wondered if he could remember anything from before I'd rescued him and hoped he couldn't.

"Good morning, Mistress," the farming men and apprentices said, laden with tools and ropes and things I had no idea the uses of.

"Good morning," I said, and walked on.

The house and all its buildings were soon swallowed by the trees, which closed over it like a green drape. They rustled around me and I followed the narrow road that went away from Gawthorpe, occasionally watching Puck as he explored, flitting through trees, his nose fixed to the ground.

When I was a quarter of a mile or so from the house I could see two figures approaching on horseback. I stepped closer to the trees and waited, recognizing the larger shape to be Roger. When they were ten yards or so away, he spoke briefly to the person on his right — a woman, in a plain wool dress. My eyesight was poor, but I knew it was not his wife, Katherine. Roger dismounted and approached holding the reins of his horse, which I noticed was roped to its companion. A prisoner, then. I looked up into the pale, shrewd face of the young woman, with dark eyes and thin lips. Her spindly white hands were bound in manacles, which were tied to the reins. My gaze lingered a moment too long on them, and when I looked up, she was regarding me with a hostile sort of pride.

"Mistress, I am pleased to see you out walking on this fine day. You look to be in invigorated spirits," said Roger.

"Are you visiting us?" I asked, holding my hand out to let him kiss it.

"A different kind of visit today — more an invitation for Richard, in fact. Is he at home?"

"Yes."

"Does he have free time this morning?"

"He leaves for Manchester in an hour," I lied. Richard was not going off with Roger and leaving me alone with my mother if I had anything to do with it. "His things are being prepared. Is everything all right?"

He nodded. It was strange for him to not introduce his companion, especially not to me. "That's disappointing. I am going now to Ashlar House."

"James Walmsley's home?"

"Indeed. I wondered if Richard would be interested in accompanying me — I have two interviews to conduct and would appreciate his assistance." He leaned closer. "He is going to do great things one day, your husband. Mark my words, he will be high in government by the time he is as old as I am, and I plan to help him on his way. He has the advantage of birth that I did not, and his uncle was well-known at court. At some point I will introduce him to the king, and I wish for him to have a hand in these developments at Pendle because they are important, not just for me but for him. They could further him in the eyes of the crown. I trust his opinion, as does Master Walmsley, but we shall have to get on without him today." He turned to glance back at his companion, whose quiet presence was somehow unnerving.

"I hear you have employed a midwife," Roger said unexpectedly.

I blinked in surprise. It was hard to stay present with the malicious radiance emitting from Roger's unknown companion. As magistrate, he was often carting felons around the county and sometimes took them up to the gaol at Lancaster.

"I have," I replied, wondering how he

knew. Richard had not seen him since their hunt.

Roger beamed. "Wonderful. There will be an heir at Gawthorpe before the year is out. Is it the same woman as last time? From Wigan?"

"No. A local woman."

"Jennifer Barley? She was Katherine's."

"No," I said reluctantly. "A girl called Alice, from Colne."

Then something strange happened. At the mention of Alice's name, Roger's acquaintance made a sudden movement that startled her horse. I glanced up at her, and quickly away when I saw she had not removed her gaze from my face, as though she was reading something quite fascinating. How could Roger carry on our conversation as though she was not even here?

"We shall have to arrange a gift for your confinement," Roger was saying. He looked pleased. "What to buy for the woman who has everything?"

"Who is your friend, Roger? Will you not introduce me?"

"This," he said, "is Alizon Device."

I felt as though my skin had been brushed with feathers. So Roger was parading the witch around Pendle and had brought her to Gawthorpe. There was something in Alizon's proud stare that led me to believe she knew this, and I felt a twinge of sympathy.

"Don't let the dress fool you — it's Katherine's. She has been staying with me these past few days. We are going to Ashlar House for a meeting with some of Alizon's relatives," he said jovially, turning back to his charge.

The girl did not speak, but shimmered with her hostile force. In the silence that followed, a rook cried out from the trees and a gust of wind moved the forest around us.

"Give Richard my best. And Friday sennight, you'll come to dine at Read? Katherine is so looking forward to seeing you."

"It would be our honor." I curtsied, and let my eyes flick once more to Alizon Device, who was still as a statue.

He raised his hat and mounted. I watched them go, seeing Roger's many-ringed hand rise up in farewell. Then I called for Puck and started back toward the house.

As it was the last day of Lent and Mary Barton did not care for fish, and Margery the cook always remembered, we sat down to a rich dinner of cheese pies with potatoes, fruit, bread and beer. I nibbled at crusts and crumbs but was so used to not eating I barely felt hungry anymore.

My mother disapproved of all our servants apart from the cook: she decided they were surly and ungrateful and said that it was only a matter of time before the silver and silk began to go missing. Sometimes I wondered if I lived in my own house or hers. I could tell she missed the days of her great house and large staff. Richard and I used to call her Gloriana of the Manor when she visited us after we were married, trying to direct us as though we were both her children. Until then I'd never had anyone to make fun with. We would stop up our mouths with food when she said things like: *Really, Richard, I never knew a man to wear as much jewelry as you,* and *You should have your crest put on your bottles for serving wine — it's the fashionable thing, you know — they are even doing it in York.*

On that morning she decided to take issue with the set of panels above the fireplace.

"Richard, I see you have still not had my daughter's name scribed on the overmantel," she announced. Five solid wood squares were engraved with various names of members of the Shuttleworth family, and Richard's initials were added to the fourth before we married. He meant to have a carpenter put my initials with his but had not found the time, so *R* and *S* floated on their own, waiting for a companion. It was a bruise that my mother could not stop pressing, as though the wooden panel was the only evidence of my existence and not simply decoration.

"There is no great urgency, Mother," I said.

"Is four years not enough time?"

"I will add it to my ever-growing list," was Richard's genial reply.

It was decided she would leave the following day, Easter Sunday, and we went all together to church. I might have been imagining it but my waist felt thicker overnight. I sat during the service staring at my hands folded neatly in my lap, wondering where Alice Gray was and what she was doing. All the people from the town were staring at me a beat longer than usual; I knew I looked ill. I stuck to wearing black — colors highlighted the gray of my face, which was dull as a raincloud. The addition of my mother earned us more than a few extra glances. She kept her face passive with indifference, but I knew inside she was purring like a cat.

During the service as the curate spoke, I moved my eyes over the hats and caps, looking for a twist of golden hair, but saw none.

I caught the eye of a young woman sitting a few pews across, dressed in a fine warm cloak, her globe of a stomach pressing through it. She looked at me in the bold, friendly way countrywomen look at one another, as though to say "we are one and the same." But we were not, and I looked away.

My hands were like ice, so I sat on them until they were numb. The nausea had crept back that morning, persistent and unwelcome. Colne was a few miles away and had its own parish, so it was unlikely Alice would be a worshipper at St. Leonard's. But she worked at the Hand and Shuttle, less than a mile away — dare I show my impatience and visit her there? I had invited her to come on Good Friday, but she said she could not and would come after Easter.

I saw the apothecary sitting a few pews away with his family, his well-meaning face turned to the pulpit like a growing flower looks to the light. Would Alice grow the herbs herself, or buy them from him? And if she did, would she be discreet?

John Baxter the curate had a high, clear voice that rang up into the eaves of the church, banishing darkness from every corner. *"And when Herod saw Jesus, he was exceeding glad,"* he was saying. *"For he was desirous to see him of a long season, because he had heard many things of him, and he hoped to have seen some miracle done by him."*

Up there with him at the pulpit was the new King's Bible we had bought him in London. It was the first time I'd been in a printer's, a tall building in the city that to me was as narrow as a wardrobe. In the streets outside, children carried baskets of loaves on their heads as though we were in Galilee. Inside the printer's it was a different world entirely, half-scholarly with its atmosphere of paper and ink, and half like a torture chamber with huge, groaning wooden contraptions.

"And the chief priests and scribes stood and vehemently accused him. And Herod with his men of war set him at nought, and mocked him, and arrayed him in a gorgeous robe, and sent him again to Pilate."

The new Bible had been printed last year and we bought three copies: one for the house, one for the church and one for Richard's mother. All of them were objects of beauty, edged in gold, the paper inside as thin as petals.

"But they cried, saying crucify him, crucify him. And he said unto them the third time, Why, what evil hath he done? I have found no

cause of death in him: I will therefore chastise him, and let him go. And they were instant with loud voices, requiring that he might be crucified."

John Baxter was old, his skin the color of Bible pages, but his voice carried like a much younger man's over the coughing and shuffling and mumbling of infants. My head felt light, as though I was an hourglass needing to be tipped upside down.

"For, behold, the days are coming, in the which they shall say, Blessed are the barren, and the wombs that never bear, and the paps which never gave suck. Then shall they begin to say to the mountains, Fall on us; and to the hills, Cover us."

I felt my mother move next to me, her dress crushing against mine. My corset was tight and my blood beat in my neck. My head was so empty I thought it might detach from my neck and float like feathers into the rafters.

John Baxter invited us to rise, and the crowd moved upward, carrying me with it, and the room warped and swam. Then everything went black.

The following morning, instead of waiting for Alice at the windows, I decided to join Richard on the lawn where I saw him training his new falcon. A dark cloud had lifted since my mother had left, but the old one had taken its place once again, following me around. Picking my way across the wet grass to where Richard was standing by the steps, I stopped quietly behind him so as not to frighten the bird, which was tied to his wrist by a string. Blinded by its hood, it flapped confused above our heads, driven to distraction by the scent of chicken flesh in a pouch at Richard's thigh.

If there was an art to the training of birds, then Richard was a master of it. He made a clicking noise and pulled the string so the falcon came down with it, scrambling about until it found a perch on his glove. He tossed it a bit of meat.

"I shall never know why you do this yourself and leave the falconer idle," I said. "I am surprised you still have eyes in your head."

"Because it's most satisfying," he replied easily. "Besides, she is only ever yours if you do it the long way. Loyalty is earned, not demanded." The bird took off again, getting a shock when it reached the end of the string and shrieking loudly. "This one is from Turkey. She will need no bells if she insists on making this noise."

"She is cursing you," I teased.

111

"I did not know you spoke Turkish."

"You still have much to discover about me." We smiled at one another, and my thoughts rushed again to the surface. I pushed them down.

"Something is troubling you?" Richard asked.

It would be so easy to go and fetch the letter from my cupboard. "Tell me why you have kept this from me," I would say, handing it to him. "Tell me it isn't true."

Instead, I shook my head and fixed my eyes on the bird. "Roger has invited us to dine on Friday," I said.

"Yes, he told me he saw you. He had his witch with him?"

"She was a strange creature. I am not sure what chilled me more — her presence or Roger's indifference. She must be dangerous or she wouldn't be manacled. Why would Roger bring her to our house?"

"He has made her his shadow. As long as she is in his sight, he is in the king's. I'm sure he will dispose of her once she has served his purpose."

"That's a callous thing to think about your friend."

Richard looked sideways at me. "That's an innocent thing to think about yours. That will be quite a bruise," he said, touching the blooming stain at my temple with a gentle thumb.

"It already has more colors than my dress," I said. "My pride is bruised more than anything — all those people who watched me go down."

"We shall have to lock you in the house. First falling from your horse, then fainting in church. Whatever will we do with you?"

Barrels of wine were being rolled into the bottom of the house behind us, tumbling over the stone passage that led into the cellar. Richard's attention moved back to the bird, and I followed his gaze to admire her bright talons, her gentle wings struggling against the string. After a few months of this, a dead hare stuffed with a live chicken would be used as prey, then a hare with a broken leg. By the time she went on her first hunt I might be buried in the churchyard.

The falcon shrieked and flapped above us, and between the flapping was the sound of hooves. Richard brought the bird down to his glove, and that's when I felt it for the first time: the quickening. Palpable, and yet before I realized it was happening it stopped, so suddenly I wondered if I imagined it. But I knew it from once before: it felt like I was a barrel of water and a fish was turning inside me. I gripped Richard's arm, my ears ringing, my whole body ringing.

"Fleetwood, are you well?"

"Yes," I lied. "The baby . . . I felt it moving."

"But that's wonderful!" He beamed, and I couldn't help but match his smile.

His bird flapped impatiently, and before it could take hold of my head I backed away. "Alice should be on her way — I will ride to meet her on the Colne road."

"Your wrist is well enough to ride?"

I held up my bandaged arm. "Almost like new."

In the clean air with the river on one side and forest on the other, with every jolt of the horse I felt my thoughts slip further away from my own life and further toward Alice's. There was so much I didn't know. As I walked her out of Gawthorpe, I'd inquired after her father, and Alice told me he was ill and unable to work. I wondered if they had a close relationship, or if Alice dreamed of marrying so she could move out. Poor girls were so unlike rich girls, who only had to wait in their houses for the day a husband arrived, like turkeys fattening for Christmas. Poor girls could choose for themselves, perhaps even as equals: a neighbor might catch their eye, or a shop boy they visited each week to buy their meat. I tried to imagine Alice with a man — her long white fingers touching his face, him moving a twist of gold from hers — and couldn't.

The trees thinned out and made way for the open sky, and green hills billowed around in the manner of fresh linen being put on a bed. The river rounded in front of me and I had to cut into Hagg Wood, moving out of the open and into the trees. The horse's hooves were quieter there, and after a minute or so I saw two figures ahead in a clearing — women, wearing dull colors and bright white caps. They hadn't noticed me. I pulled in the reins to slow down, when I realized one of them was Alice, and her voice was raised and angry, traveling through the trees. I slid down from my horse's back and left her where she was, crossing silently over the mossy ground toward them and stopping behind a tree, where I had a clearer view of the other woman.

She was the ugliest person I'd ever seen in my life, so much that she was frightening to look at. She was poor: that was clear. Her dress was so baggy and shapeless it looked as though she had stitched sacking together, making her appear thin and deformed. But the most alarming thing about her was her eyes: they were set in different parts of her face and not level with each other. One sat high, gazing up at the leaves of the trees around her, and the other, lower in her face, examined the roots. I could not tell how she could see like a normal person. She stood with her mouth open, letting her tongue pass over her lips as Alice spoke, sharp and low at once.

I could not hear what was being said, and as I strained forward, a movement next to me made me jump. A thin brown dog with ragged fur trotted out from the trees at the side of me, skirting past me and going toward the women, who did not pay it attention. It cut through the small gap between them and passed on into the trees beyond. The ugly woman's pet, then. I thought about turning away before I was seen, but Alice made as though to stalk off toward me and my horse, and I froze. The woman spoke in a rasped, harsh voice, saying some admonishment or other.

The dog barked far off, and the woman looked over her shoulder briefly before — chillingly — turning her wayward eyes in my direction. My skin pricked all over, and I willed my dark green dress to make me difficult to spy. She spoke once more to Alice, then lumbered off after the dog, muttering to herself.

Alice stayed for a moment in the clearing and I saw her fists clench and unclench. She rubbed the tops of her arms as though she was cold — a vulnerable gesture that made me feel guilty for concealing myself. Then she went off in the opposite direction, making directly for the river.

I could not see her horse anywhere, and did not hear hooves on the forest floor. Unsure of what to do, for a minute I watched her go, then climbed astride my horse and cantered the short distance home. Dismounting breathlessly at the bottom of the steps, I turned to look the way I'd come and after a few minutes saw her bowed form hurrying from the bank of trees east of the park. There was stealth in her stride, and grace, and authority, and she crossed the lawn in front of the house quick as a rabbit, bent into the biting wind. She wore no cloak. Her expression was dark, and she looked troubled.

"Where is your horse?" was the first thing I asked her.

Before she could reply there was the sound of a dog barking from the direction we had come. She looked back, distracted.

117

"Alice?"

The front door opened, and Richard stood at the top of the steps. "Ah, the two wood sprites are returned from the forest. Pleasure to make your acquaintance again, Miss Gray."

Alice nodded, her eyes on the ground. "You, too, sir."

"You are taking good care of my wife?"

Alice nodded again.

"Fleetwood, is your horse to walk herself to the stable?" Richard asked. I gathered myself and took the reins, ready to take her the short distance, but Richard stopped me. "Your midwife can do that."

I looked anxiously at Alice, who was out of breath and red about the cheeks, as though ill with a fever.

"Unless she objects?" Richard asked her.

With a pained expression, Alice took the reins from me. I watched her go, hunched against the animal, then gathered my skirts and entered the house.

"She does seem young for a midwife," Richard said as I moved past him into the dark hallway. The wall lamps flared in the draft as the door shut.

"She is about your age."

"I still think you should go to London. There are hundreds of midwives there, if not thousands, delivering infants every day."

"Don't make me go to London, Richard. I want your heir to be born at home." That seemed to do it, and he reached for my hand, squeezing it once. "Alice and I will be in my chamber while she examines me."

I thought I saw a low shape move behind him in the shadows of the hallway and slip into the buttery, but I thought nothing of it until I climbed the stairs to my chamber, where Puck was lying in front of the fireplace.

Ten minutes later there was still no sign of Alice, and I got up from the floor where I was stroking Puck to go to the top of the stairs. There she was, standing beneath my portrait, staring at it. She did not know I was there, and I saw the edges of her lips curve up, as though she was smiling, lost in some fond memory.

"What do you think of my mother?" I asked, startling her.

"She is very . . . pointy," was her reply, which made me grin. "That's you?" She nodded at the child in the picture.

"What were you smiling at?"

"Your face is very serious for one so small. You remind me of . . ." she trailed off.

"Who?"

But she did not answer, moving as if disturbed from a daydream, picking up her skirts and joining me at the top of the staircase. We passed the dressing room where Richard was sleeping, the truckle bed clearly visible, and I noticed for the first time her arms were empty; she had nothing with her.

"My husband wondered how many years you have," I said, closing the door behind us.

Her mouth opened wordlessly, and her shoulders sank a little. "I do not know exactly."

I stared at her. "You do not know how old you are? Well, when is your birthday?"

She shook her head and shrugged. "I have slightly more than twenty years, I think."

"You do not know your birthday?"

She swallowed. "I am afraid I have to confess something." I waited while she opened and closed her mouth a few times. "I lost the horse you gave me."

"You *lost* it?"

"I tied it outside my house and the next morning, it was gone."

Every line of her was apologetic, and I cursed silently at my own foolishness; I had not thought to ask if she had a stable, but of course she did not. I should have paid for her to keep it at an inn or nearby farm.

She mistook my reaction for intense disappointment, and breathed deeply, and said, "I will pay you back. I will work for free. How much are horses?"

"I don't know . . . a few pounds?" Her face fell. "Do not worry, it is done now, and I will pay you just the same," I said without conviction, for Richard's anger would know no bounds.

How would I tell him? Never mind. While Alice was there, we would focus on the immediate.

I asked her what she had brought, and she walked over to the dresser and began lifting up her skirts, taking little linen parcels from her pocket and lining them up on the polished top before opening them to reveal herbs of varying shades of green. With the fire full and friendly and the dog snoozing nobly on the rug, my chamber had the same atmosphere of purpose as the kitchen, and I went to the edge of the bed and sat on it, not knowing what to do.

"What have you brought?" She waved me over, and I went to look at her display. "You are like a traveling herb merchant — Richard would be impressed."

"Anethum graveolens." She pointed from left to right. *"Calendula, lavendula, camame-*

lum." I stared at her in bewilderment, and she laughed. "To you, and your cook — dill, marigold, lavender, chamomile."

"You know the Latin names? I thought you couldn't read?"

She blinked. "I can't. My mother taught me. Every good herbalist knows the proper names." She held up the first bunch: soft and feathery with fine, waving fronds. "Have your cook chop this and mix it into butter, which you can put on your meat, fish, anything."

"What does it do?"

"A lot. These petals —" she held up the delicate golden flowers "— can be dried and stirred into hot milk, or used to flavor cheese. Have the kitchen make you a hot cup each morning and night and stir this in, and it will help with the sickness."

I nodded, remembering: butter, hot milk, cheese.

"Lavender," she said. "Infuse it in some rainwater to make a tincture, and sprinkle it over your pillowcase to help you sleep, and keep away bad dreams."

She looked meaningfully at me, and for a moment I wondered if I had told her about The Nightmare. How could she know?

She lifted her apron again and brought out a tiny glass vial between finger and thumb. "I made you some already — this is the only bottle I had." She went over to the bed and, stopping up half the neck with her finger, shook it lightly over the pillows and down. Something made her pause, and she leaned farther over to examine it. "Your hair is falling out?"

I patted it self-consciously, where it barely covered the rolls beneath. "Yes."

I could not see her face, but she appeared to be thinking about something as she smoothed the lavender water over the bedclothes. A moment later she was back at my side, pushing the vial of lavender water into my hand, then holding up a fistful of a daisy-like plant.

"Like a chamomile bed, the more it is trodden, the more it will spread," I recited.

"Yes, chamomile spreads easily," she said, missing my point about triumphing in adversity. "Steep this in hot milk, too, and strain it, then it can be drunk. And the final one —" She held a narrow strip of what looked like tree trunk between her long fingers. "Willow bark. Chew on this if you have any pain — it will help."

"Where do you get all these from? Mr. Blezard in Padiham?"

"Women I know," she said.

"*Wise* women?"

"Most women are wise."

I could not tell if she was teasing me. "Are they to be trusted?"

Alice gave me a look. "According to the king? No. He has driven them into the shadows, but people are still sick, and dying, and having children, and not everyone has a royal physick. The king has muddled wise women with witchcraft."

"You sound as though you are not a supporter of his."

She did not reply, and began folding up the little squares of linen. The people in these parts had their opinions on the king but kept them to themselves for good reason, so I was taken aback by her candor. Perhaps all lower-class people spoke as boldly.

"The king is not a supporter of women trying to make their way in the world any way they can — helping neighbors, and driving off sickness, and trying to keep their children alive. And while he is not, I am not of him." She brushed her palms together and became more businesslike. "You remember each of the instructions?"

"I think so."

How glad I was that Richard or the servants had not overheard. Alice took out her pocket, folded the linen back into it, then asked to see my wrist.

"I almost forgot," I began as she examined it, pressing here and there and bending my palm backward and forward. There was no pain now. "I bled the other night. Not a lot. In fact I was not even sure it *was* blood, until I tasted it."

Alice fixed her large amber eyes on mine and once again I smelled lavender. Where did it come from? She could not have perfume; she must crush it at her wrists and neck. It was touching, really, that she made this daily attempt at femininity.

"Was there any pain?" I shook my head. She licked her lips and narrowed her eyes in concentration. "There may be too much blood in your body, which is not good for you or the infant. Next time I come, I will bring something."

"When will that be?"

"In a few days. Until then, use these as I directed, and you should see an improvement."

I went to my cupboard where I kept the doctor's letter, and took out a small cloth bag of coins, handing it to her. She asked, "What's this?"

"The first month in advance. How much do I owe for the herbs?"

"Nothing."

She held the weight of the bag in her palm, letting the coins slide around. The sound reminded me of Richard, and I glanced toward the door. I had not told him or James how much I was paying Alice — that could wait until later, until I grew bigger and he could see her tinctures were working. Then he could hardly protest.

I saw her out, waving from the top of the stairs, and went back to my chamber to rest. Usually I had to pluck my dark hairs from the pillow and toss them in the fire, met with the anxious thought that eventually they would all fall out and I would be bald as an egg. What else would this child take from me? They made fine wigs these days, but a woman's hair was as much an asset as her clothes and jewelry, and one that could not be removed. If Richard did not desire me already with my growing belly and gray skin, he certainly would not without my thick black hair that used to be shiny as a raven's coat. When I met his sisters I'd envied their fine golden heads. But black was an expensive color, difficult to dye and maintain. Black meant wealth and power.

I sat on the edge of the bed and ran my hand over the pillow, but no black threads showed on the white. Alice must have moved them. I lay down, closed my eyes and let the lavender carry me to sleep.

CHAPTER SEVEN

From the very start of our marriage, Richard took pride in showing me off. At parties, his friends' houses and local dinners, I would shine under his companions' gazes like a jewel in candlelight, always meeting his eye for approval and finding it, and shining brighter.

I was looking forward to dinner at Roger's, and shining like a jewel once again now Alice's tinctures were working. I was glad, though, she could not see me pacing my chamber building the courage to go down to the kitchen and repeat her instructions to the servants. My mother said I always cared far too much what people thought, but really I cared far too much what people said, especially when my back was turned. Thoughts were private; rumor was not, and as mistress at Gawthorpe I knew I was the subject of both. The cook listened to me with one eyebrow raised when I showed her the dill for the butter, and scattered the chamomile leaves onto the scrubbed wooden table. But listened she had, and a cup of warm milk infused with sweet chamomile was delivered to my door at night, and a special butter dish brought for me at dinnertime the next day, and for the first time I felt quite fond of the staff. Richard was still sleeping in the next room, so I hoped to shine so brightly at Roger's the truckle bed would remain undisturbed for tonight.

Friday arrived, and at eleven o'clock we were ready to ride to Read Hall. The days were longer now, and even if we stayed at the Nowells' all afternoon it would still be light by the time we left. I did not much like riding at night, when the edges of the forest couldn't be seen but could be heard shivering and straining from their roots like hounds on leashes. I had been ill for so long I couldn't recall the last time Richard and I went out visiting together, so I put on one of my favorite dresses of dark blue, embroidered with exotic birds and beetles, and a tall silk hat, with my riding things over the top. I decided to leave off telling him about the missing horse and save it for another day, because it would no doubt spoil the evening. I was determined nothing would.

■ ■ ■ ■

"Ah, the two turtledoves," Roger greeted us in the great hall, handing us each a glass of sacke. He was dressed finely but retained an element of the countryman about him in his black velvet suit and soft boots.

His wife, Katherine, made straight for me in her gown of black lace with fine gold embroidery. She was hatless, and her dress was cut very low. I was younger than her daughter, but we had mutual interests in fashions and London and the best clothiers in Manchester and Halifax and Lancaster.

"What news at Gawthorpe? We have not seen you in such a long time — Richard said you were quite ill. I hope you are recovered?" Katherine said once we had done the necessary complimenting of each other's clothes. Her emerald drop earrings shimmered in the candlelight. I had not noticed her look at my stomach, but it would have been difficult to see anything in the dark room with my dark clothes.

"Oh," I said. "Yes, I was confined for some time but now I am better, thank you."

"Roger said you went hunting with them not long ago? I was surprised — all that mud spoiling your things!"

130

"Yes, although Richard blamed me for driving the quarry away with my voice — hunting is perhaps not the best opportunity to talk with friends." I smiled.

"You are always welcome at Read — although we are a chamber short at the moment."

"Oh?"

"I will leave of Roger to tell you at supper."

At that moment one of the men in the party turned and I saw it was Thomas Lister. He caught my eye and gave a polite nod.

"Master Lister was not long at Gawthorpe, on his way to York," I said.

Shrunken old Nick Bannister, the former magistrate of Pendle, also stood with Roger, Thomas and Richard, cradling his cup to his chest.

"And Roger persuaded Nick out of *his* confinement with the promise of a few fat birds and barrels of sacke," Katherine added warmly, before asking us to sit. Thomas Lister was on my left and Nick Bannister on my right, with Roger, Katherine and Richard opposite.

"We must separate the turtles or they will be crooning at one another all night," Roger said with a wink.

I smiled, and imagined the effect that announcing these two turtledoves slept in different rooms would have.

The first course was brought out: a spread of mutton pies, fallow deer pasties, and ham and pea pottage. Roger waited for everything to be set down and served before he spoke. "Now," he said as we picked up our knives. "As you will all know, I have been investigating a series of crimes in the Pendle area. What some of you may not know is further arrests have been made after some deeply disturbing interviews." He moved in his chair and indicated for a servant to top everyone's glasses with sacke. "You may remember I told you of Alizon Device, the girl who performed witchcraft on John Law the peddler? It satisfies me to report she is now safely in gaol with her family, so the innocent people of Pendle are no longer at the mercy of the Devil's work for the time being."

"Her family are in gaol, too?" I asked.

Roger nodded slowly. "Her mother, grandmother and brother all confessed to witchcraft and popery. Many lives have been lost to the Device family — they have eluded the eyes of the law for too long."

The wizened, elderly man on my right spoke for the first time. "It is a coincidence, is it not, that Device sounds like Devil?"

Laughter broke out at the table and I waited to speak. "What did they do?"

"Oh." Roger waved a casual hand. "A horrible medley of things — dolls made of clay, spells, curses. Each of them has their own familiar spirit, which is proof enough."

"You saw their familiars?" I asked, recalling that he had never seen Alizon's with his own eyes.

"I did not need to. I know they exist. John Law described Alizon's — the dog. Her mother, Elizabeth, also has a dog named Ball, and her grandmother has kept one for some twenty years. For two decades she has had a pact with the Devil, carrying out his work across the county!"

"But if you cannot see them, how can you know for certain?" I asked.

There were a few beats of silence as everyone chewed and swallowed around me.

Roger regarded me. "The Devil only appears to those he recognizes to be his servants. They let their animals suck blood from their bodies — does that sound like a normal pet to you? Do you let your dog do that, Fleetwood?"

"Roger," Richard said coolly. "I will set my falcon on you and it will suck *your* blood."

Everyone apart from me laughed.

I took up my knife and fork and moved the food around my plate, but the fatty mutton made my stomach churn.

"What news of the Preston woman?" Katherine asked Thomas Lister, who always needed coaxing into conversation. He sat up a little straighter at the mention of his servant, clearing his throat.

"It was a blow when she was acquitted." He spoke quietly, swilling the sacke in his cup. "But I am sure she will be back before she knows it."

I was not sure I had heard him right. "Back where?" I asked. "Surely you would not have her back at Westby if you thought she killed a child?"

He set down his cup and dabbed his small mouth with a napkin. "On trial at York."

I looked around at the other guests. "I'm sorry, I don't understand."

"Well," he said softly. "Jennet Preston murdered my father."

The table went silent. The only sounds were the wind at the window and the flames roaring heartily in the great fireplace. The other guests appeared to be as confused as I was. Roger sat back and gave Thomas a paternal nod, as though he had laid bare some deep truth.

Richard spoke. "Your father died four years past."

Thomas fixed his eyes on his plate, his small frame rigid. "I did not tell anyone of the words he spoke at the time he died," he said softly. "Only my mother knows. We did not speak of it. He was terrified out of his wits."

"Of what?"

"Of Preston." He took an invigorating swig. "My father on his deathbed cried out, 'Jennet lies heavy upon me! Preston's wife lies heavy upon me — help me, help me!'" For this part he raised his voice into a high, excited cry. Everyone at the table was silent, and his ringing voice sent a shiver over my skin. "He bade us shut the doors, all the doors in the house so she could not escape."

"She was there?"

"Her *spirit* was there. He could see it, I know. After his death she was brought to my father's corpse and it bled at her touch."

"The surest sign of a witch," Roger said with confidence.

"But," I began, "if this did happen four years ago, why is she only being brought to trial now? And was brought for something else last month?"

Master Lister looked to Roger.

"Last week, on Good Friday, when all of

us good citizens were praying, a party was gathering," Roger said in a slow, revealing way. "And when all of us were fasting, as is the Lord's wish, this party was feasting on a stolen mutton. It took place at a miserable dwelling called Malkin Tower — the home of Alizon Device's grandmother old Demdike. And one of the party was Jennet Preston."

"Preston is connected to the Device family?" Richard asked.

Roger nodded once. "Because she is a witch. And what did they speak of at this gathering, other than comparing their familiars and blaspheming the Lord Jesus, for whom they should have been fasting? Why, they spoke of young Master Lister here."

I could not have been more confused. "Why?"

"Preston was plotting to kill him," Roger said simply.

Next to me, I could feel Thomas Lister shaking. He began touching all his cutlery and dishes, moving them and lining them up in a meticulous display.

Roger went on. "That is not the only thing they spoke of. The lot of them were gathered to discuss a plot not dissimilar to the one that almost unseated the king from his

136

throne not so long ago." He leaned in, his teeth shining in the candlelight. "They planned to blow up Lancaster castle, where their kin are held. To set them free."

"How do you know this?"

Roger tapped his nose and, folding his handkerchief neatly in his place, pushed back his chair to rise. "Allow me to introduce my most valuable witness."

He left the room, and a little gasp went round the table when he returned with his wide, bearlike grip around the small shoulder of a little girl.

She strode with him into the room and they stopped short of the table. She could not have been older than nine or ten, and had a pale, pointed face with wide, clear eyes. Grayish-brown hair straggled from her cap, which was newly starched, and although her apron was tied tightly, her simple wool dress drowned her. She was not afraid to look each of us in the eye, and when her bold gaze came to me I could not look away. What I found disturbing was that she was neither afraid nor impressed, her expression as smooth as a painted portrait.

"This," Roger announced, "is Jennet Device."

"A popular name among their kind," wheezed Mr. Bannister.

"Master and Mistress Shuttleworth, Master Lister, allow me to introduce you to my source of all knowledge. Jennet has been helping Mr. Bannister and me with our investigations. She is Alizon's sister."

I saw Katherine glance quickly at the girl with an expression both suspicious and fearful. She looked as though she would put another person between them if she could.

I turned to Mr. Bannister and whispered, "She is staying here at Read Hall?"

"Indeed." He breathed. "In one of the children's old chambers."

I wondered what Roger's family would think of that — I barely knew what I thought of it myself. The witch Alizon's own sister? Nobody was speaking, and the way they were looking the Device girl up and down made my skin crawl, so I spoke. "Hello, Jennet," I said. "How are you finding Read Hall?"

"Right nice," the child rasped in a strong accent.

"And how long will you stay?"

"She will stay until the trial date is set at the summer assizes."

Katherine made a small noise. "Summer? Roger, she will really stay for that long?"

"Where else would you have her go, Katherine? Her family is at Lancaster gaol and there they will stay until they are called before the Lords Justices."

His words did not seem to disturb Jennet in the slightest; she continued to look around at the guests and the room itself, her wandering gaze absorbed by the portraits, the paneling and family shields on the wall. She had surely never seen such things in her life, nor a fire as great as the one that towered above her, nor food so plentiful.

"Will you have some of our second course, Jennet?" asked Roger. "We have roast chicken and beef, and bread, and some butter that was made this morning."

Jennet nodded eagerly and was seated at the end of the table next to Katherine, who appeared no less uncomfortable. Though a trace of a hostess's smile played on her lips, it did not reach her eyes. Her earrings glittered.

"Jennet was at Malkin Tower on Good Friday and has told me all that was said — including the plot against Master Lister here," Roger declared as he returned to his seat. "There were quite a number of people present that her brother James told me of, and Jennet has confirmed all the names on the list. We work well together, do we not, Jennet?"

The child was eyeing the half-finished food at the table, and I could not help but glance at her every few seconds. Her head was so small I imagined Roger could crush it with one hand. She did not appear at all affected by the incarceration of her entire family, and I could not decide if that chilled me or made me pitiful.

The second course was brought and Roger and Richard talked of other things that interested them: the price of salt, what their cattle got at market. Jennet ate like a wild animal, with grease smeared all up her face and hands. I was still watching her when I heard Richard tell Roger he had ordered a gun, which made me look round sharply.

"A gun? Richard, you did not tell me that."

Richard glanced at Roger as if to share something with him. "Fleetwood, I hardly think I need consult you," he said. "Unless you have an expertise in guns I know nothing of?"

The table tittered, and I flushed. "Won't it go off in the house?"

"Not if it is handled correctly, which it will be," Richard said in an insolent way, and he repositioned himself more directly to Roger, indicating the topic was closed.

I tried to speak to Master Lister on my

left but he was acting very strangely and would not make eye contact. I think the presence of the child frightened him. Katherine squirmed next to Jennet and did not speak to her once.

Before long the topic came back to Roger's hunt for witches. "Let us speak of it away from the child in case it should give her nightmares," Roger said. "Jennet, go up to your chamber and I shall send for you in the morning."

The little girl slid sideways from the table without even removing her chair, she was so thin. She made no noise as she left and the moment she had gone, it was easy to believe she had never been there at all.

Roger turned back to us and grew confidential. "Her mother was beside herself when she found out the child had handed them over. I thought she would go mad before my eyes."

Mr. Bannister burped beside me and pardoned himself, covering his mouth with a brown-spotted hand. "She is a sight for sore eyes, Elizabeth Device," he said. "She'd give you a fright if you saw her — one eye set up in her head and the other looking right down at the floor."

I felt as though a bucket of icy water had been thrown over me. I stared dumbly at

Mr. Bannister, and he mistook my disbelief for fascination. "She does sound like something from a comedy play, but I'm not making it up. How she has three children by two men I'll never know."

My mouth was dry as sand. "Where do they live, the Devices?"

"Just outside Colne. A horrible, damp hovel is Malkin Tower. How folk live like that, I don't know."

CHAPTER EIGHT

"This will not be pleasant. You will need a strong stomach."

Alice took up one of the things she had set on the dresser in my chamber: a knife that folded in on itself, encased in a horn shell. For a terrible moment I thought she meant to perform surgery on my stomach, but she saw my expression and her scowl softened. "I will breathe your veins," she explained. "It is the only thing for too much blood."

She drew the dull-looking blade out of the horn handle and showed me how the point of the knife was flat, not sharp, and how a small triangle shape jutted down from it at a right angle. It was a curious-looking thing. She told me it was called a fleam, and she would place it on a vein in my arm then drive it in like a stake with the small wooden stick she held in her other hand. I had seen enough of my own blood and felt enough pain to fear neither.

Alice had appeared as mysteriously as ever, crossing the lawn in front of the house with round-shouldered purpose. She offered no chitchat, but nor did I. We'd grown easier in each other's company, however — as easy as two women can be who could not be more different. I liked her soft voice, and wondered if she read to her father by the fire. Then I remembered she couldn't read. Her voice was the only soft thing about her, though, I thought idly as she moved about the room with a brisk directness, her back straight, her neck long and equine. She'd have made a fine mistress of a house like this in another life. Probably better than I. Working in an alehouse might harden a person. Being poor almost certainly did. Still, she would leave wealthier than she arrived.

She told me to take off my jacket and layers so that my arms were bare, then pulled a chair over to the window and nodded for me to sit at it. Then she tied a length of ribbon round the top of my arm and prodded the white skin at my elbow.

"Alice," I said. "Do you think that it will have eyelashes by now?"

"Eyelashes?"

"Do you think the baby will have eyelashes?"

"What a strange question. It's hard to say."
I nodded.

"I will need a large bowl, and fresh linen and water. And a needle and some pale thread."

I swallowed and fetched them from various parts of my room, but not before turning the key in my chamber door. Richard was with James and the ledger, and Alice was standing at the fireplace looking at the plaster figures on either side.

"Are they your family?" she asked.

"No. *Prudentia.*" I pointed. *"Justia."*

"What does that mean?"

"*Prudence and justice* is the Shuttleworth family motto." I nodded at the fleam. "Where did you get that?"

She wiped the blade on her apron for a few moments, then said, not unkindly, "You take such an interest in where my things come from."

"Well, I am glad you did not ask me to find one. First, I would not know where to look. Second, I can imagine James's face if I told him I'd ordered one."

"Who is James?"

"Our steward."

"Why would you have to tell him?" she asked.

"Everything we buy goes in the household ledger he keeps, and everything that leaves Gawthorpe, whether it's beer from the brewery or chickens from the farm or midwives for the mistress."

"Even me?"

"Yes, even you."

My hand throbbed as the blood collected in it. She asked me to pass the bowl — a pretty brass one decorated with flowers, given to us by Richard's mother — and set it on the dresser, placing my arm above it.

"Are you ready?"

Before I could say yes she had driven the fleam into the crook of my arm with the wooden stick, and I yelped like a puppy as she drew it out. Warm, red blood began gushing immediately from the hole she had made. I clapped my other hand over my mouth but could not take my eyes from the grotesqueness of it. I looked like a character in a medieval tapestry scene.

"What does *prudence* mean?" asked Alice, adjusting her grip on my arm.

A light, clear pain flooded through my whole body. "Ah . . . prudence. Prudence means . . . How long does this go on?"

"Until the bowl is half-full."

"Half-full?" It was coming out so fast.

"What does prudence mean?" Alice said again.

"It means cautiousness. Proceeding with care."

"And *justice* means freedom?"

"No," I said, trying to look at anything but the bowl filling as easily with my own blood as if it was wine being poured from a bottle. My head felt as light as it did in the church, when I fainted. "Justice means fairness. Lack of prejudice."

Working as quickly as she had before, Alice pinched the skin on either side of the piercing and drove a needle through it. I looked away as she stitched it with thread, wincing every time it made a puncture.

"I will look like a cushion," I said, feeling her breath on my arm. "This will work, do you think?"

"Breathing the veins is the best way to bleed while you're not having monthlies," she said. "Bleeding can be healthy from the right place."

She washed the blood from my arm and pressed a ball of linen to it, instructing me to hold it. Puck lumbered over, curious. I pulled the pad of linen away from my arm and saw how fresh blood was leaking through the thread. Puck sniffed and licked at it a few times before deciding it was not as tasteful as he imagined.

Immediately I recalled Roger's words, *Do you let your pet suck blood from you, Fleetwood?* I almost laughed at the absurdity of it.

Alice wrapped my arm in a strip of linen and tied it before leading me to the bed and instructing me to lie down while she tidied up. The wound was on the same arm as my sprain — I had quite the inventory of injuries since meeting her, and I told her so. She smiled and closed the drapes.

"I do not feel any different," I said after a while.

"Give it a day or two," came her voice. I heard the tinkle of glass, or it might have been the pin rolling onto the floor. "If you feel no better we can try the other arm, with more blood. You still have the willow bark I gave you?"

"Yes."

She appeared in the curtain fold with a piece of cloth no bigger than my hand, and took from its folds a single green leaf. She ripped a tiny edge off it and handed it to me. "Suck this," she said. "It will stop the blood coming so quickly. But don't have any more than that, and spit it out — don't swallow it."

I lay with my hands on my stomach, sucking the bit of leaf like a farm apprentice on a summer afternoon. It seemed to dissolve on my tongue, and a sense of peace washed over me. Though I'd only known Alice a fortnight, with her here my worries seemed to fade to dying embers, only to flare up again at night. She could not promise that she would save my life. She had not promised anything, in fact. But knowing she was trying to help me, I felt safer than I had perhaps since I married Richard.

"Alice, am I safe to keep riding in child-bed?"

There was a pause while she considered. "I have not known many women who have horses, but my mother did, and she always said they could. Do you ride regular?"

"Every day," I replied.

"Then you've no reason to stop if you've always done it, as long as you don't come off. I expect for a skilled horsewoman it's as safe as walking."

"Richard seemed to think the last time that . . . it was my fault for being rough, riding around and playing with Puck. He thinks it's not good for a woman. The truth is I'd die if I had to stay indoors all the time, sitting in hard chairs embroidering cushions, though he thinks that is the safest place to be."

"Perhaps he wants to keep you where he can see you, like all husbands. Until they want you out of their sight, that is," she added more bitterly.

"I thought you said you weren't married?"

"I'm not," she said quickly. And then as though she'd said too much and wanted to change the topic, added, "Oh, I found your horse that ran away. It's back in your stable." I was too surprised to reply. "Did you hear me?" she called from behind the drapes.

"Yes. Where was it?"

"A neighbor found it grazing in a field and brought it back."

"You're sure it's the same one?"

"With the triangle of white on its nose? And a black tip on its ear? I'm sorry but the tack was gone, probably it threw it off."

Or more likely someone stole it, seeing as I'd never known a horse to be rid of its saddle, bridle, halter and reins by itself.

Before I could reply, a noise at the door startled me, followed by Richard's voice. "Fleetwood? Why is the door locked?"

I pulled open the curtains and Alice was already halfway toward me with my jacket, which I pulled on to cover the wound.

"Fleetwood?" Richard was rapping impatiently, and stepped immediately into the

150

room when I finally unlocked the door. "Why was the door locked?" he asked again, directing the question at Alice.

She looked helplessly at me, and, panicking, I swiftly glanced over at the dresser where her things had been moments before, but it was empty and gleaming as usual.

"Richard, you must understand we do not want to be disturbed when Alice is doing her work." I tried to sound soothing, but he was still glaring at Alice.

"And what work is that?"

I grasped wildly for an answer. "Feminine exercises."

There was an awful period of silence that lasted perhaps five seconds, and Alice cast her eyes down to the floor. Where had she put her things so quickly? I eyed the corner of the room and the fireplace, but there was no sign of the bowl of blood.

"Very well," Richard said finally. "Roger is downstairs, and wishes to see you. He has . . . someone with him."

"Who is it?"

I could not say why, but there had been a coolness between us since Roger's dinner. I wondered if I had irritated him by asking too many questions.

"You will soon find out." He turned on his heel, but not before his eyes searched

151

the room. "There is a strange smell in here, is there not?" His eyes lingered on Alice, then he left, closing the door firmly behind him.

"He meant the blood. I can smell it, too," I told Alice, but her face was smooth. How like a window she could be: transparent one moment and dark the next. "Will you wait here while I see which guest has arrived?"

I could only hope Richard did not mean my mother. As I descended to the bottom of the house, I thought of the curious exchange I'd just witnessed. Richard had acted as though he found Alice's presence offensive, revolting even. Well, he had chosen a woman as my companion once, and now it was my turn. But all thoughts of my husband and midwife evaporated when I turned the final corner of the staircase, for standing in the entrance hall were two figures: the expansive Roger Nowell and the parchment-thin Device child.

"Roger. Jennet." I tried not to look so startled. "What a pleasant surprise."

Jennet was not looking at me, but observing everything in her sight with her wide eyes — the oak banister, the portraits hanging in the gloom of the stairwell. She was still wearing the same old dress and starched white cap, which made her face look all the

152

paler. Without saying a word, she walked to the picture window at the back of the house.

I blinked at Roger. "Do you have business with Richard?"

"Yes, he is waiting for me in the hall. I came to ask if it would not be an inconvenience to show Jennet around Gawthorpe while Richard and I discuss matters? She has never seen such a palace and would greatly enjoy a tour."

I touched my arm where the fleam had punctured it; the linen was making it itch. I thought of Alice upstairs in my chamber, and looked over at Jennet's small silhouette at the window.

Without waiting for an answer, Roger gave me a fatherly wink and departed, his polished boots echoing on the stone floor.

I swallowed and went over to where the child was standing. "That's Pendle Hill." I pointed at the looming mass in the distance. "And this is the River Calder. Sometimes you can see salmon jumping upstream."

Her face was quite delicate, and not ugly. Her small upturned nose was spattered with freckles, and her eyelashes were long and gray. "Which rooms would you like to see?"

She shrugged, and in her raspy, broad accent said, "How many are there?"

"Do you know, I've never thought about

it. I don't know. Perhaps we could count? Though there are many more for the servants, and I don't think we should disturb them. How many rooms are in your house?"

She stared at me. "One."

"Oh. Well, then. Let's see." I showed her around the ground floor — the dining room, the buttery and servants' working rooms where the study was. In the great hall, I pointed up to the gallery and told her how minstrels and players sometimes came to perform, and we would watch from below. She paced around mostly in silence, occasionally asking who was in a portrait or why we needed swords. The mermaids and mystical figures in the dining room appeared to fascinate her, and she examined each one with her hands behind her back, like a miniature Roger. Then we went to the outbuildings: the great barn, which I told her was one of the largest in the county, and the stables and farm offices. Sure enough, as we walked past the stable doors in the yard, and the stable boys and apprentices nodded and wished us good day, I saw the gray mare with the white triangle on her nose and black tip on her ear chewing hay languidly in her stall. I gave her a pat, and wished she could tell me where she had been.

"Are you enjoying staying at Read Hall?" I asked as we returned to the house. Jennet wanted to see upstairs, and after a moment's hesitation I agreed.

She shrugged again. "It is not as big as this house."

"But Roger and Katherine keep a lovely home. I'm sure they are looking after you well." I wondered how Roger could keep her one way and her family another, taking responsibility for one and disposing of the rest.

Jennet had turned on the stair to face me. "Can I live here instead?" she asked. She left one hand on the banister, like a little lady of the court.

I opened and closed my mouth a few times, disarmed by her forthrightness. "I'm afraid that's not possible. You are a guest of Roger's."

Her stare was so intense she could have frozen blood, giving me the oddest feeling that I had said the wrong thing, and would regret it later. Then she turned on her heel and continued her climb up to the top of the house.

After her request, I was embarrassed to show her all the empty bedrooms, made for guests that never stayed. "Sometimes my mother comes to visit," I lied. "And Rich-

155

ard's family, who live in York. He has lots of brothers and sisters, and I have none." We were back at the staircase now.

"Who is that?" She was pointing at the Barton family portrait.

"That's my mother and me."

"Why do you have a bird on your hand?"

"That was my pet, Samuel. He didn't live for very long. I kept him in a cage in my room."

"Why does your mother have no bird?"

"She did not have a pet."

"My mother has a dog." I thought of the ugly woman Elizabeth Device, who I'd seen in Hagg Wood with Alice, and the brown dog that had slipped past me, and what Roger had said about her familiar spirit. Surely it was nonsense — I'd seen the mongrel with my own eyes and there'd been nothing devilish about it. But she had turned to me when it passed her . . . My skin pricked at the memory of her eyes.

"What is its name?" I asked.

"Ball."

"That's a strange name for a dog. Do you have a dog?"

"No, mine hasn't shown itself yet."

What a strange child she was. "I have a large dog named Puck. He is somewhere in the house," I said.

"Does he talk to you?"

"No, but we understand each other."

Jennet nodded. "My sister has one, too. And my grandma has a boy."

"A *boy*? You mean a son?"

"No, a boy. His name is Fancie. He wears a coat that is brown and black and sometimes he comes to our house and they go for a walk."

"Oh, you mean a dog."

"No. He is a boy. She's known him twenty years and he's never grown up."

I couldn't help but stare at her. "Have you told Roger all this?"

"Oh, yes. He is very interested in my family."

We stood in an awkward silence, looking at my portrait, then Jennet mounted the last of the stairs and I showed her the long gallery. It was a bright day, and the floor had just been polished, so the windows reflected onto the wood like the sky in a lake. I felt that Jennet was growing bored with her tour, though her gaze continued to rove over every cupboard, every chair, as though she was a merchant assessing it for sale. "What's that room?" She pointed once we were back in the tower staircase.

"That's my bedroom."

"Can we go in?"

I laughed nervously. "Not today."

"Is someone in there?"

"No."

After a pause, she nodded and began her ladylike descent. My palms were slicked with sweat, and my heart had begun beating a pattern in my chest. Did she know Alice if Alice knew her mother? It would probably have been harmless to introduce them, but I did not want to ambush Alice, because I had a peculiar feeling that Jennet Device was dangerous, and I could not say why. How ridiculous that sounded, though — she was a child.

I took her into the hall and she scampered over to Roger like a granddaughter. He and Richard were sitting on either side of the table with papers spread between them, and Roger was pouring the dregs of a jug of wine into his cup.

"Did you enjoy your tour, little one?" he asked. Jennet nodded. "Fleetwood, you are looking better every day." I smiled and nodded. "Richard," he went on. "Might I trouble you for a mouthful of something before I begin the journey to Lancaster? Is there any of that chicken pie your cook makes going spare? I wouldn't turn down a crust of that. Would we, now?" He winked at Jennet, who was standing behind his chair like an attentive servant.

"Fleetwood, would you mind asking the kitchen?" Richard asked.

"Of course." I curtsied and went back through the house, feeling chilly even though almost all the fires were lit. The kitchen was a part of the house I rarely visited. Along the length of it was a long, low table covered at intervals with flour and pots. Baskets of vegetables stood on the floor and the open range glowed and threw warmth around the room. Waste Not Want Not was spelled in stone letters the size of a forearm above it, a reminder left by Uncle Lawrence. A rabbit hung framed in the window, swinging gently. The kitchen staff regarded me in the way I'd grown used to: a quick glance, then away.

"Barbara?" I called to the large-framed woman at the table brushing pies with egg yolk. She had not noticed me enter, and my voice was so small in the clangs and clatters of the room, one of the younger servants had to call her. I passed on Roger's request, and she went off to the larder to fetch some things to wrap in a parcel. As usual, the kitchen was busy with purpose, and I watched various servants roll and chop and brew.

As she handed me a warm folded cloth

stacked with cold pies and meats, I lingered for a moment, then said, "Thank you for carrying out my instructions with the herbs so well. The butter is delicious and the chamomile milk sends me straight to sleep."

A smile swept her red face. "You are most welcome, Mistress. I am glad to see your cheeks fattening. We are almost finished with the stock you gave me, so I can ask James to order more?"

"No," I said quickly. "I will have my midwife bring more."

I thanked her and turned to go, but she said, "Mistress? Is it true the witch child is at Gawthorpe today?"

"If you mean Jennet Device, she is a guest of Roger Nowell's."

A few of the servants nearby had their ears pricked.

"I have no mind to look at her," Barbara went on. "They say she is the Devil's daughter."

"I am sure there is no truth in that."

"I'm sure Mistress knows what she is doing opening the door to such folk, but I hope she doesn't bring a curse to this house. Just this morning the milk began to turn. Fresh from the farm, it was."

Wishing to end the conversation, I nodded and turned, but Barbara called me back at the door, her voice raised. "That midwife of yours," she said. "Where's she from?"

Impatient now, I replied, "Colne."

Barbara's mouth turned down at the corners. "I ain't never seen her before, and my sister's a midwife. You might have asked down here if any of us had someone to recommend."

"Yes, well, it was Alice's idea to introduce the herbs to my diet, and they are working very well." The tips of my ears were hot, and I felt a blush creeping up my neck. Did servants usually question their mistress's employment decisions? Did they advise on whom to invite into the house? "Thank you for this."

I tripped on the way out, no doubt creating a stifled ripple of laughter in my wake. By the time I reached the hall, I was flustered and irritated, my goodwill toward the household soured once again. The two men were standing now, clearing the papers between them. Jennet was crouched at the fireplace, looking up into its corners — she could stand comfortably in there, like I could in the fireplace at Barton when I was her age.

"This is the list for Nick Bannister," Roger said, separating a sealed document from the sheaf in front of him. He tossed it onto the table. "I have a copy at Read, but as I'm away he will call here to collect it." Richard nodded, sliding it toward himself and tucking it into his waistcoat. "Don't get too close to that fire, Jennet. Fire is for stew pots and heretics, not children."

"And witches?" the child asked.

"In His Majesty's homeland they are thrown on the fire. I am of the opinion that England should follow in Scotland's lead, but unfortunately the penalty here is the rope. Perhaps His Majesty can still be persuaded to change his mind. Now, we must be on our way to Lancaster."

She shot up. "To see Ma?"

Roger glanced at me, indicating I hand him his parcel of food, and I crossed the room. "Your mother is still at the inn where they don't allow children. Thank you, Fleetwood."

"What about Alizon? And Grandma?"

"They are there, too. You will see them before long, in a grand room in a castle with lots of important people who will ask you questions about them. And you remember what to say, don't you? Everything we talked about?" She nodded, unfolding the cloth to sneak her hand in and pinch a piece of pie. "This one has a belly bigger than her eyes. Well, we'll be on our way."

Richard saw them out, and I watched Jennet follow them into the passage, quick and soundless as a shadow.

Alice was sitting quietly by the window in my chamber, looking out at the hills. "Sorry I kept you in here so long," I said, closing the door behind me. "I hope I've not kept you from your work at the alehouse?"

She shook her head. "I start later on. Did I hear a child's voice?"

I licked my lips, deciding. "My friend Roger Nowell brought a child named Jennet Device. Her family is awaiting trial at Lancaster, accused of witchcraft." I watched her face for a flicker of recognition, but none came — her face was blank and smooth. I waited a beat, then said, "Do you know them?"

She stood, brushing down her skirts and tucking the chair back against the wall. "No," she said. "I don't."

I'd lost count of the nights Richard had slept in the room beside mine, so much that waking up alone was beginning to feel normal. Thanks to the lavender tincture on my pillow, I hadn't had The Nightmare, and my hair had stopped falling out at such an alarming rate. I found Richard eating breakfast in the dining room, and took my seat

163

opposite him, accepting a roll and some honey and breaking it into pieces.

"Richard," I said once the servants had left the room. "I have been feeling much better lately. Might you consider moving back to our chamber?"

He read his correspondence for a moment or two longer, then looked up. "What was that?"

"I said I am feeling much better, and I wish you would join me in our chamber. I haven't been ill in almost a fortnight."

"That's wonderful news."

When he continued reading and chewing and it became clear he would not respond to the other part of my statement, I remembered what had bothered me that morning. "I can't find my ruby necklace, the one you gave me when we had been married a year."

Now I had his attention, and he folded the letter he was reading and tucked it beneath his plate. "Oh? Where do you keep it?"

"In the cupboard in the wardrobe. I looked for it last night and again this morning and seem to have misplaced it. I can't remember when I last wore it."

His gray eyes were thoughtful. "Your midwife spends a lot of time up there, does she not?"

"She does, but she would not have taken it."

"Would she not?" he asked lightly. "Does she have plenty of her own?"

I ripped my bread roll into tiny pieces and put one into my mouth. "I know she would not. I trust her."

"You seem to trust her much more easily than Miss Fawnbrake."

I did not reply. I had no doubt Richard had not taken kindly to Alice because she was direct and indifferent, and did not have an interest in smiling and indulging him like the other female servants.

"I will go and look again," I said, pushing my plate away and leaving before he could protest, trying to ignore the creeping feeling of doubt that plucked at my thoughts like a needle. I turned my room upside down that morning, and looked in all the guest rooms and cupboards that I had keys to. Although my most precious jewelry was locked away, I kept the keys in a vase on the mantelpiece in the wardrobe — not the most discreet of hiding places. The rest of my jewelry was as it should be — my favorite opal rings, the velvet and pearl choker, the emerald drop earrings given to me by my mother on my thirteenth birthday.

Hot and bothered, I went downstairs to

ask the chambermaids if they had seen it recently, when I heard a commotion. At the last turn of the staircase, I almost bumped into Richard flying toward me, looking thunderous. "Have you found it?" he demanded.

"No, I . . ."

"That necklace was my father's sister's," he fumed. "He gave it to me when she died. It's an insult to his memory. It belongs in the family."

"I'm sorry," I faltered, but he shook his head. That's when I noticed the servants flocking out of doorways and passages toward the hall, throwing us nervous glances.

"Come with me, we will put an end to this." He took my hand and pulled me in the same direction, and I was alarmed to find the entire household gathered beneath the high ceiling: fifteen or twenty people, and one I was not expecting.

"Alice!" She glanced over at me, and her face was anxious. In her hands she had a parcel tied with string: more herbs, as she had promised to bring when I told her the kitchen was low. There were high spots of color on her cheeks, and her golden hair fell more untidily than usual around her face, as though she had hurried here.

Richard had left my side, and was climbing the narrow stairs up to the minstrels' gallery. Clearly he was about to make an announcement. "My wife has informed me a precious ruby necklace has gone missing," he declared. "This is the first time anything like this has happened at Gawthorpe, and I am loath to suggest one — or some — of you might know its whereabouts, because you are a loyal staff." As I watched him speak, sweat pricking at my armpits, I felt several pairs of eyes on me. "There is every possibility it has been misplaced, but Mistress Shuttleworth has assured me she has checked every usual place. Now, that necklace was given to my father," he went on, his tone melting from stern to appealing, which always made the servants melt in turn. "It is very important to me that we find it. I will ask the chambermaids to carry out a thorough sweep of the rooms, and everyone else their usual habitats. This time tomorrow I would like it placed in my hands. I will ask no questions when it is."

A few of the servants straightened in approval — he'd even called the stable boys and carter in, I realized. *Why not the farm apprentices, too?* I thought in exasperation. Then I noticed someone had raised a hand: Sarah, one of the bolder chambermaids, who liked to bask under Richard's warm light. And who, I'm sure, took delight in the fact he was sleeping alone, and possibly even imagined going to him in her stockinged feet at night.

"Sarah?" Richard nodded, indicating she speak.

"I'm sure you know those of us who've worked here such a long time would bring anything we found to you or the mistress straightway," she said. "So maybe you should look at those who haven't worked here so long."

A ripple of interest broke across the room — half surprise, half amusement at her brazenness.

"What makes you say that, Sarah? Might you know something you wish to share?" Richard's tone was inviting. I imagined them alone together, then pushed the thought away. He was a good businessman, skilled at getting the deal he wanted. Nothing more.

I glanced at Alice, who was shifting her weight on her feet. She was not looking at Richard, but directly at Sarah, and the tops of her ears were red. "All I'm saying is," Sarah chattered on in her girlish, broad accent. "It might not be a coincidence that someone new starts working here and two minutes later the Mistress's jewelry goes missing." The two or three young girls standing next to her were shining with barely concealed glee.

"The saucy baggage!" muttered an older voice from over my shoulder.

"Thank you, Sarah, that's enough. While there's no need to throw accusations around, I trust my household's loyalty in the main. Some, however, could be more demonstrative with their allegiance."

Did he look pointedly at Alice? But when I snapped my neck around to see the subject of his gaze, Alice's face was hidden by a wide shoulder, and Richard was moving toward the staircase. "I will leave it with you. Remember, noon tomorrow, that necklace will be back in Fleetwood's possession. That is not a request."

As the hall filled with chatter and the servants filed out, I went to Alice and took her arm. "Will you come upstairs?"

She shook me off. "I don't think I will." She handed me the package, shoving it in my arms. The scent of herbs and lavender drifted up, but now the strength of the mingling scents was making me feel sick.

"Why not?"

"I have brought things as you asked. I can't see what else I am needed for."

"The parlor, then. I will have the kitchen send up some . . ."

"No, thank you. I need to go to the Hand." Her voice had lost all its softness.

The hall was quiet now, with the last footsteps squeaking in the passages. Richard's ancestors watched keenly from their portraits on the walls, and all the while Alice was glaring at me.

"I hope you don't think I was accusing you of theft," I said, trying to coat my words with ridicule, but it came out as pleading.

"You have nice jewelry, but I'm not sure any of it would suit me. I trust you aren't in need of my service any longer?"

"Pardon? Alice, no, you can't leave. I know you didn't steal it." *Do I?* I remembered her closing the drapes around me after she drew my blood. How, an hour after I left her, she sat thoughtfully at the window in my chamber with her straight back and fine angular features, as though she was posing for a portrait. But buried underneath was another thought: What did she do with my blood? There was a whole bowlful of it, and when Richard demanded to be let in it was gone. Had she thrown it on the fire? I'd heard no sizzle of burning liquid, no stench of burning blood. Now was not the time to wonder: Alice was watching me, and I knew my face

170

betrayed my doubt.

"I must go," she said hotly. "I cannot work where I am not trusted."

And before I could move she had slipped into the passage; by the time I reached it she was at the front door, hauling it open and flying down the steps, barely avoiding a collision with the figure dismounting his horse at the bottom.

"Mistress Shuttleworth!" said Nick Bannister, turning to watch Alice's narrow form grow smaller.

"Nick," I managed to say, catching my breath. I felt as though I was coming apart; something terrible had happened, and I had no idea what to do about it. Over a stupid necklace that meant nothing to me!

"You look as though you've had a fright — who was that woman?"

The magistrate approached hesitantly, placing a wrinkled hand on my arm where the fleam had been driven in. The wound smarted at his touch, and I withdrew it, stammering my apologies. In just a few days it had almost sealed itself into a neat scar the shape of a crescent moon. All I could see of Alice was her white cap bobbing toward the edge of the forest — she had not gone to the road via the outbuildings, but straight into the trees.

"Mistress, are you quite well?"

I sighed, and felt the chill wind creep its fingers down my gown. My stomach pushed at my corset, and it would not be long before I could no longer wear them. "Yes, quite well, thank you, Nick. Are you come to see Richard?"

"Only if he is available. I am here to collect a message Roger left when he was here last."

"Yes, I know it. I will find it for you."

I would not ask Richard; I did not even want to look at him. Nick followed me into the house and I instructed a passing servant to see to his horse. James's study was only a few steps from the front door, and he was out for the day with the bailiff. As though sensing I was upset, Puck found me and came to me, pushing his wet nose into my hand.

"Forgive me, Nick, what is it I am looking for?"

"Perhaps Richard knows its whereabouts . . ."

"No. I can help you," I said, more sharply than I realized. "Richard has done enough for today."

I pushed open the door and went to the large desk in the center of the room. James kept a neat office, with only a jar of quills, a single bottle of ink and a neat stack of parchment on its surface. Behind the leather chair was a shelf containing several bound household ledgers, dating back twenty years to when Richard's father first began to keep the Shuttleworth family records. I searched the stacks of bound letters organized and filed in some unknown method, remembering how James had brought me the neat parcel of correspondence about my failed pregnancies. A rage was burning inside me: Richard did not think it prudent to inform me of my impending death, and now he had removed from the house the only person I could trust to save me. I realized I was shaking, and hot tears were blurring my sight. I sniffed, and Nick cleared his throat.

"Fine beast you have, Mistress," he said.

I wiped my eyes and scanned the shelves once more, finding what I needed: a square letter sealed in wax with the Nowell crest. I turned it over to find Nick Bannister's name written in Roger's cursive script, and handed it to the shabby little man stroking my dog.

"Thank you." He nodded. I know I had made him uncomfortable, and he was looking for something to say. "Nasty business, this."

"What is?"

"These Pendle witches. Trust Roger to root them out, though. I doubt he shall ever retire from the king's service. I said to him — Roger, have this last hurrah and then live comfortably. Let some youngblood take over, like your Richard. He trusts your man, you know. Hopes he'll carry on his work one day, as justice of the peace."

"Yes," I said dully.

"Roger doesn't do things by halves — he's not content with sending a whole family to trial, oh no. He wants the glory days back — he wants his name in the London press. I swear he's after a knighthood. He is already known at court, but he won't stop there. You know him as well as me."

I wondered how far Alice had got, whether she had reached the alehouse yet. Whether I should have gone after her, and how soon I could.

"Best get them all, I said. There can't be harm in questioning them."

"Questioning who?" I was being awfully rude, but wanted Nick to finish his monologue and go, so I could think about what to do. Perhaps in the months it took for me to grow, Alice's temper might cool, and she could be persuaded back? If Richard was in the house, that was unlikely.

"The gathering of witches at Malkin

Tower. He found quite the rats' nest there. Not just the Devices but friends of theirs, the ones talking about killing Master Lister, and blowing up the gaol. There are a few local names on it. No doubt this will cause a scandal in the community. Who would have thought, so much Devil's work in this wet little corner of the land? And on Good Friday — ha. It won't be a good one for them, not now."

"You have the list there?" I nodded at the paper in his hand, something in his words making me curious. "What does it say?"

Relieved by my interest, he asked for a knife, and I found one in the top drawer of James's desk. He sliced open Roger's scroll, letting it fall and holding it at arm's length to read the words.

"Jennet and James Device said they rode off on white foals after the meeting, and Jennet Preston bade them come to her house in Gisburn for their next meeting in a year's time. Preston brought her familiar to the meeting: a white foal with a brown spot on its face."

I felt my heart pumping in my chest. "The other people at the gathering on Good Friday — who were they?"

It took an age for the elderly man to find them with his cloudy squint. "Let me see . . . ah, yes, here we are: *the wife of Hugh*

Hargreaves of Barley; the wife of Christopher Bulcock of the Moss End, and John her son; the mother of Miles Nutter; one Mouldheels, of Colne, and one Alice Gray, of the same."

CHAPTER NINE

The Hand and Shuttle was a short distance from the river before the road split to go north or west. I had passed it many times before but barely given it a glance. As I tied my horse in the yard and saw the wooden sign on the side of the low building, the thought arrived that its name of course came from mine. Above the mantelpiece in my chamber was the Shuttleworth coat of arms in plaster: a shield of three shuttles, with a hand rising from it grasping a fourth, and the same symbol was carved here.

The place went silent as I stepped through the door, and what felt like a hundred pairs of eyes came to rest on me, even though I wore one of my most modest outfits with a black wool cloak, and a simple black hat with a gold band. The place was small and low ceilinged. A few groups of men sat around what looked like creepie stools laden with jugs, their faces hard and blank. A man behind a partition like a stable door waited to see what I would do, perhaps thinking I had walked into the inn by mistake. I moved toward him.

"I must speak with Alice," I said.

He had a ruddy face, and his mouth stayed open when he was not speaking, displaying unpleasant teeth. "Alice . . ."

"Alice Gray," I whispered. "Is she here?"

He nodded dumbly. "I'll fetch her, Mistress. Might you want somewhere more private?"

"Thank you."

I followed him through a curtain of cloth and he led me through a narrow, dimly lit passage to the dining chamber, which was empty. The whole place was cold, with no fires lit, and stank like the brewers at Gawthorpe. I pulled my cloak around me and went to the window that overlooked the yard, where barrels were being rolled into the storehouse. I recognized them to be the ones from the house, stamped with the Shuttleworth crest. So the landlord was our tenant and we sold him the ale. Before I could think about what this meant, through the open door I heard footsteps in the passage, and raised voices.

"Stop coming here."

It took a moment for me to recognize it as

Alice's voice. I placed a protective hand on my stomach and stepped into the doorway to look out. At the end of the passage was a dark-haired young man, whose grubby shirt and threadbare trousers did not detract from how handsome he was. He looked almost foreign, like a pirate or a prince, with black hair and tanned skin and fine, dark eyes. Alice was standing with her back to me, her hands on her hips.

"You think you can just leave me?" he demanded.

"Leave a horrid drunk like you, why on earth would I do that? Go home."

"There is nothing for me there, not now." He looked as though he might cry, his face crumpling.

At that, her shoulders sank, and she held the tops of her arms like I'd seen her do in the woods. I drew back in the doorway in fear they should see me. When she spoke next, her voice was thick. "We have to put it behind us."

"Easy for you to say, with your work and your new . . . *position.*"

"Get out, will you."

He pushed his face into hers, and his dark eyes shone. "I can ruin that for you, if I like. I could tell them things . . . People have been asking."

179

"Leave me alone!" she shrieked, and the hairs on my neck stood up. "Don't you dare come back."

With a final withering look, he stumbled down the passage, past me and out into the yard. The distinctive smell of ale clung to him. I took a few hesitant steps to where Alice was standing facing away from me, hugging herself.

"Alice?"

She spun round, her face a paler shade than usual. Her eyes were large and fearful — more fearful than I'd seen her earlier in the hall full of servants. "Fleetwood. What are you doing here?"

I took her hand and led her into the room. "Will we be heard in here?"

"Who by?"

"Anyone."

She shook her head, and I closed the door. "Who was that?" I whispered, my voice trembling.

She shook her head. "No one. If you've come about the necklace . . ."

"No, I haven't, forget all that. Alice, I read a letter just after you left, from Roger Nowell to Nick Bannister. Do you know either of them?" She shook her head again, and her face was so open and confused I did not think for a moment she was not telling the truth. "Well, Roger knows you, or he will. Alice, how do you know the Devices?" Alice swayed like a felled tree and had to grip the back of a chair to stop herself. "How do you know them, Alice? How?"

"I do not know them."

"What were you doing at their house on Good Friday? They are accused of witch-craft, Alice. They are almost sure to be executed — all of them. The grandmother, the mother, Alizon . . . The youngest daugh-ter, Jennet, she is staying with Roger, telling him everything."

Her eyes darted in front of her as though she was trying to see something. "I . . ."

"Alice, you have to understand. Your name is on a list — a list that is in the hands of a very powerful man who makes the law around here. You will be arrested, and almost certainly arraigned for witchcraft."

All the color drained from her face. I thought she might fall, so I ran to her, hold-ing her by the arms and sitting her carefully in a chair.

"I am . . . I will be arrested? And ar-raigned . . . but what does that mean?"

I swallowed. "It means you will face trial at the assizes. Lent has happened, so sum-mer, perhaps."

"Trial," she whispered. "But witches are

hanged."

"*Most* of them are." I knelt before her, and took her hands in mine. "But you have not yet been arrested, and there is time to change Roger's mind. Alice, you *must* tell me what you were doing with the Devices at Malkin Tower. I can help you. Richard can help you."

Still frozen in shock, she ever so slightly shook her head in disbelief. Then she balled her hands into fists, shoving them under her armpits like she was cold. "Who gave him my name? Elizabeth Device?"

"Her daughter, Jennet, I think. What took you there, Alice? You have to tell me so I can tell Roger he has it wrong."

There were footsteps in the passage; my heart pounded with them until they went away, and Alice looked up briefly, distracted with fear. More barrels rolled around outside.

"*Was* he wrong?" I asked.

After what felt like an age, she sat up straight and tucked her hair beneath her cap. Her wide mouth was solemn. "I do not know those people," she said.

"You have to understand they will think you do if you were there. They will see you as a witch."

She bit her lip and blood bloomed under

her tooth. The pink tip of her tongue came out, serpent-like, to lick it.

"Tell me. I will tell Richard and together we will go to Roger and tell him he has made a mistake."

She was not looking at me, her gaze somewhere beyond. "No. I do not trust him. And you should not either."

"Trust who? Roger?"

She closed her eyes and rubbed at them, as though she was suddenly very tired.

"Richard?" I said. Her fingertips covered her eyes. Her mouth remained closed. "I can't trust Richard? My husband?" I rose to stand, but my meager height meant I was only a head or two above her. "Is this because of what he said about the necklace? He knows you didn't steal it — he was just angry."

Something was starting to make me tremble and I realized it was fear. I wanted to prize her hands away from her face and make her look at me. "I do not think you comprehend how much danger you are in." My voice shook with emotion. "Roger is witch-hunting. He is collecting women like cards at a table. I have come to warn you, and offer my help. If you want it." I turned to go. "I would advise you stay away from Colne for now."

"But that is where I live."

"And that is where they will look for you. You should stay with a friend, or family. Roger and Richard know your name, do they not? It won't take them long to realize you're the same Alice on Roger's list."

"Then why have they not burst through the door to arrest me?"

"Because they do not know you yet, and I will not lead them to you."

With that she made a noise that sounded like a scoff.

I reached for the door handle. "I will go home and explain everything to Richard, and he will go to Roger."

"You adore your husband." Her voice rung out clear in the cold, empty room.

"Of course I do. What do you mean by this?"

"Do not go to Richard."

"Why?" Hot fury bubbled up again. "Do you not comprehend how much influence my husband has? Are you saying you do not *need* our help? That you will somehow get through this on your own? Alice, your *life* is at stake. Roger will not be made a fool of in front of the London justices if I know him at all. He made a list for the former magistrate Nick Bannister, and *your name is on it.* What of this do you not understand?"

184

Again she put her head in her hands. She had aged ten years in one afternoon.

"Alice, are you listening to me? Do you not trust me?"

"Yes, I trust you," she said. It was a small triumph, and despite my anger, her words glowed in my chest. They'd never been said to me before, or needed to be.

"But you don't trust Richard? What is this?"

Very slowly, she turned her face slowly to look at me, as if it was causing her great pain. "The ledger," she said.

"What?"

"The ledger your steward keeps. Everything you buy and everything that leaves Gawthorpe goes in there, you said. Is that right?"

I nodded, bewildered.

"Look at the ledger."

"But . . . how do you know what's in there? You can't read."

In her wide amber eyes there was an inexplicable sympathy. "I don't need to read things to see them."

I went straight to James's study. Even though the fire was lit, I was cold as stone and my teeth chattered in my head as I drew out the thick book bound in calfskin. In his neat handwriting was a list of everything bought and paid.

March: two loads malt; rundlet of sacke; three great salt lings delivered to Thomas Yate in London . . .

What was I supposed to be looking for?

April: Michael Thorpe to Colne with bacon; half a year's rent for Ightenhill Park; the carriage of a gun down from London.

Could it be the gun? I knew about the gun!

Mr. William Anderton to bring marriage license from York.

I paused on this, my finger holding the place. Why would anyone at Gawthorpe need a marriage license? No one was betrothed, as far as I knew.

That's when I noticed a word so familiar to me I had overlooked it altogether:

Sweet soap to Barton.

Coals from Padiham pit to Barton.

Chickens bought at Clitheroe to Barton.

Barton.

Barton.

It had been my name and also my home. But nobody lived there: it had been empty since my mother and I moved out four years before.

"Mistress, here you are." James stood in the doorway, his usually composed face a mask of concern. "Was there something you needed?"

"No, James, thank you."

I slammed the book shut and moved around the desk, embarrassed. But when I brushed past him into the passage, suddenly the rage returned: How was *I* doing something wrong by looking at my own household ledger? Why *shouldn't* I care how the property I'd brought to this family was being kept, as though none of it was my business? Something told me I had to be careful. I'd left Alice in that dank little room at the alehouse and they were my parting words to her. "Where will you go?" I'd asked, and she had shrugged, and stared only at the empty hearth. I'd been too consumed to offer my help, and galloped the short ride home in a fog of my own turmoil.

"The master has been searching for you," said James. That's when I realized his usual composure was absent; he was very pale, and grave.

"Is something wrong?"

"One of the servants has been taken ill — Sarah, the chambermaid. Richard has asked me to send for the doctor."

"Very well. What is the matter?"

"She complained of a headache, and now is in a fever. She is delirious and asking for

187

her mother."

"Then send for her mother. Or can she be sent home?"

"I think it might be best, once the doctor has seen her. In case it's catching."

I frowned. There was far too much in my head at once, with supplies being sent to Barton and servants being struck down with illness and Alice's association with the Devices, and the ruby necklace. More had happened today than in a year.

"She seemed fine earlier," I thought out loud, remembering how she'd spoken up in Richard's household meeting. Then I remembered Alice's anger when the room emptied, and my stomach sank. I prayed silently that the sweating sickness or some other deadly disease had not come to this house.

The passage outside was dark, and James's study was friendly and warm, and a twenty-mile ride that I had no wish to make lay ahead. But it had to be now.

"James, I need you to do two things for me — have my horse saddled, and pass Richard a message."

"The master is due to return any moment . . ."

"The message is this — I am going to Colne to take a room at an inn there, and

188

try to persuade Alice to return as my midwife."

He looked at me in astonishment. "But, Mistress . . ."

"I feel as though Richard handled the necklace business quite poorly — you were there. You saw it. But of course you won't tell him I said that. I am afraid he has cost me a skilled midwife who I trusted and liked very much, and I will have no one else deliver my child. Tell him what you will. The real reason, James, is that I cannot stand to look at my husband for the way he treated the staff. You are all loyal and precious to me, and I hope you won't think badly of him for it. That is why I am taking a room there, just for tonight. I think there is an inn called the Queen's Arms there. That's where I'll go. Please tell him not to follow me, and I will be back in the morning."

After a moment's hesitation, he nodded smartly. "Yes, Mistress."

I turned, and then, as though I'd just remembered, half turned back, hoping my face was hidden in the darkness and did not give me away. "Oh and, James? How are things at Barton? All in order?"

His face fell at once, and he went quite gray. It was all I needed. He opened and closed his mouth a few times like a fish while I waited calmly. "Might you need something fetched from there, Mistress? It has been shut up for . . ."

"Four years, has it not?"

His mouth closed. His Adam's apple quivered as he swallowed his words. "Yes, that's right."

"Very well. I will get my cloak."

I arrived shortly after night fell. There was no moon, only clouds, so everything was black, but I saw the vast shape of the house lurking ahead, and warm light burning merrily in a room on the ground floor. I had not wanted to come back here ever. I did not want to see the chamber my mother and I shared. I did not want to see the parlor where my childhood ended in the time it took my mother to fetch something. I did not want to see the creaking staircase, the high, cold ceilings or the empty cage where I had found Samuel dead one winter morning after he'd been left too close to the fire.

I dismounted a few hundred yards from the house when a noise, or rather a presence made me turn my head, and something very low and slim crossed the grass to my right. It was no more than a silky shadow, but it paused, its brushlike tail straight out

190

behind it: a fox. It froze, still as a statue, and we stared at one another, and my skin tingled. But then it bolted and disappeared in the blackness, and I carried on alone, stumbling on the front steps and cursing the clumsy pattens that protected my slippers. I flung them off and they clattered to the ground.

The entrance was dark, and that old chill caressed me at the door "Hello?" I called. I dared not — could not — think of what, or who, was in the room I knew to be the great hall. At worst it might be a vagrant — or would that be best? The door opened with no resistance into the entrance hall, and in my slippers my feet were almost silent. The only sound I could hear was my breath ragged in my chest and my blood pounding in my ears. I walked blindly in the dark, my hands out in front of my face, to where the door for the great hall was, feeling my way along the walls. I tried to ignore the thought that I might touch the face of a person waiting for me in the dark. After combing the walls from top to bottom, I found the handle I'd been searching for and pulled it.

A warmly lit scene met my eyes. The sconces were glowing around the walls, and the glass above the fireplace cast light back into the room that reflected again off the chandelier. At the great fireplace that measured ten feet across — the one I used to walk around inside and be scolded for when my slippers were ruined on the ash — a woman was seated. I felt as though I was dreaming, floating, as I approached her, for she did not seem to get any closer. She noticed me, and stood. She was older than me by a few years, and her dark head was uncovered. She looked very afraid, and I did not understand, and then I did, and my heart fluttered and stopped.

A noise in the passage behind me should have startled me, but did not, so when James appeared behind me, breathless and steaming from the gallop from Gawthorpe, I barely reacted. My eyes were fixed on the woman before me, because her cloak had fallen open when she stood. Her stomach was round like mine.

The floor tilted. The stone flags rushed to welcome me as their old mistress, and I was grateful for their embrace as my world came crashing down, and my body went with it.

■ ■ ■ ■

PART TWO

■ ■ ■ ■

WESTMORLAND
(NOW CUMBRIA),
MAY, 1612

"Laws [are] like cobwebs, where
the small flies are caught but the great
break through."

SIR FRANCIS BACON

CHAPTER TEN

The cushion cover I was embroidering was so dreadful it looked as though a child had sewn it with its eyes closed. But nobody said so, and I decided that when I finished it I would give it to my mother's cook, who, with Alice's herbs, was feeding me the most delicious food I'd tasted in my life. I knew she took pleasure in watching my cheeks fatten and my stomach grow. I began by stitching the plants Alice had laid on my dresser: the lion's mane–like marigold, the tiny buds of lavender. If Alice noticed, she didn't say anything, but she was not interested anyway — she was spending hours at a stretch outside on her hands and knees in the soil, coming in with her hands and dress dirty and washing them with the jug in the chamber that we shared.

James had escorted me back to Gawthorpe, through the wind and rain, and as soon as I reached my chamber there I locked the door. It stayed locked for a full day and night, and I grew used to the sound of Richard pounding at it because it was difficult to mind anything with my stomach so empty. Prudence, Justice and I waited, for what, we didn't know, but then late on the second day, when I began to think seriously about having my fire lit and some food sent, one of the chambermaids came to the door and said there was a messenger arrived from my mother. Through the keyhole I told her to pass on to the messenger that I wished to be left alone, and her voice became more anguished as she returned and introduced a male voice I did not know.

"Mistress Barton wishes me to inform you that a caroche is waiting outside Gawthorpe," the voice said. I waited. "She asked me to pass on that it will not leave until you are in it," the messenger said.

"Then it will be there until it rots," I said from my bed.

The man cleared his throat. I wondered who else might be standing with him in silence. "Mistress Barton is inviting you to stay with her at Kirkby Lonsdale. She thought you might wish for a change of scenery." There was a deferential pause. "I am to wait here until you are ready."

I stayed where I was for quite some time, sprawled in and out of the bedclothes. Eventually, my voice choking, I said, "Are you there, Richard?"

After a pause, the messenger said, "I am quite alone, Mistress."

With an almighty effort I dragged myself off the bed and went to look at the keyhole. All I could see was a clothed thigh and sword sheath. I went back to the bed. Even after a day and night, I still had not been able to comprehend the scale of betrayal. It began in my bed and spread down to the brewery that was sending beer; the study, where our loyal servant James committed each individual blow to ink. It had traveled to the Hand and Shuttle, where I assumed Alice had heard of it. And it even seeped into my past, spreading its stain on my already unsentimental childhood. That was almost worst of all: that Richard was keeping his woman in the house I grew up in, that was handed over to him like a parcel the day we married, because he knew I would never go there again.

That was when the thought occurred to me: Did my mother know about the dark-haired woman with her full belly? As the afternoon wore on the question hummed in my ear like a fly, and then I heard Puck barking on the other side of the door. He scratched and whined outside it, and I realized I had not given him a thought, concerned with only myself. I went to sit at the door.

"Puck," I said in a small voice. "Puck, stop. I am here. I am here."

Tears streamed down my face as he howled, a sound that felt as though it was ripping me in two, and no matter what I said he would not be quiet. The need to hold him overwhelmed me, so I turned the key in the lock and he fell inside, knocking me onto the floor. His huge tongue wiped at my face and I could not help but laugh as he climbed all over me, whining and panting and making noises of pure pleasure. When he had quite finished I pulled myself up to sit. The messenger stood away from the door, waiting diffidently.

"I will come but only on my terms." He bowed graciously, then stood up straight, expectant. "I will bring my dog. And there is somewhere we must stop on the way."

"Should I send for a servant to pack your things?" he asked.

"I will pack them myself."

During the journey north, Alice and I came up with a plan. So Roger could not find her, she had left her position at the Hand and Shuttle, telling the landlord her father was ill, and needed caring for. I waited a few streets away in the carriage, so as not to be seen. When she climbed in I asked if there was anything she needed from home, and she said no. There was a nervous urgency about us both, because she was running away in all but name. We decided she would come to my mother's as my companion Jill, which she told me was her mother's name.

As we waited at an inn yard while Henry changed horses, the smell of supper cooking and meat roasting wafted in, and I asked if she would like anything to eat. She shook her head. It was a pleasant May evening — warm and still — and we listened to the sounds of the yard, of horses' hooves and people chatting and going about their normal lives, with the curtain drawn across the carriage door so nobody could see in.

"You said your mother was a midwife," I said. "Is she . . ."

"She died."

"I'm sorry."

"It was years ago." Alice sat very straight, had good posture even without a corset.

"What did she die from?"

After a moment, she replied. "She had a fever. She was ill for a long time, then that carried her into the next life. There was nothing I could do."

"Did you learn about herbs from her?"

She nodded. "She had a garden . . . her kitchen, she called it, because we did not have one. She grew things to eat, herbs . . . I try to keep it going because I know how she loved it. She told me the names of everything. We would go out walking and she would show me things and tell me what they could do. She said it was useful for a woman to know, for a wife and mother to keep her family together in this world. She loved to think of me with a family," she finished softly.

"Where did she learn her trade?" I asked.

"Where does any woman learn it? By doing it, I suppose. She and her friend did it together, they would go where they were needed. Mouldheels, they called her friend Katherine, because she took so long over everything, making sure it was all right. She always folded her map away properly even if the mother was screaming to high heaven."

"And you would go with them?"

Alice nodded and smiled at some private memory.

"How many babies have you birthed?" I asked.

"I don't know . . . twenty? Maybe more?"

Her answer surprised me — I had thought her more experienced, but then I hadn't asked. After a while I asked if her father would miss her while she was away.

She thought about it, then shook her head. "No. What I do, perhaps, but not me."

"What do you mean?"

"Cooking. Feeding the chickens. Keeping the house. Earning money." Her voice was flat.

"You never thought of marrying and having a house of your own?"

Her face darkened suddenly, a cloud over the sun. She appeared to consider her answer, then said, "There is no difference in it, really. It's the same life for a daughter as it is for a wife — just a different man telling you what to do."

"I suppose you are right," I said. "But you would have infants of your own. Every woman wants that, it's our purpose in life."

Alice lowered her eyes. "Children are more trouble than they are worth."

It was a strange answer, especially for a midwife.

Henry climbed up onto the roof, jolting us in our seats, and we set off again. When she did not speak, I thought I may have offended her, until a few miles later, when I began to doze, and I heard her say in a quiet voice, as though to herself, "I have never been in a carriage before."

Darkness had fallen when we arrived. I had time to prepare myself because the ride up to the manor was steep, and I had to press my feet against the seat opposite to prevent sliding down. Set up high, the park stretched to the top of the valley where rocky debris and heather met the sky. The manor itself sat on the side of a hill in the midst of a copse of thick woodland. Puck was asleep, as was Alice. She was an odd sleeper and still somehow looked alert, her neck long, her face impassive, as though she had just closed her eyes.

The carriage drew up and I climbed exhausted from it, dog-tired after my second long journey in as many days. Puck dropped to the ground behind me, yawned and stretched, and Alice after him. Henry unloaded my trunk and the wide front door opened at the top of the steps, spilling light onto our strange party and framing the clear silhouette of my mother.

"Fleetwood," she said, her thin voice carrying into the night. "I thought you would never come."

I glanced at Alice and together we ascended the steps.

The house my mother lived in was owned

by the Shuttleworths, bought by Richard's uncle some two decades before as a place to rest or hunt on the road to Scotland. I had been once before, when my mother was ill with a bad chest and Richard persuaded me to visit.

I decided I would get straight to business. Before my trunk had even been set down on the stone flags of the entrance hall I turned to face my mother. "Did you know of Richard's woman?"

"Of course I knew, Fleetwood. Now get inside before you are dead on your feet."

Though she'd only confirmed what I suspected, still I felt as though she had driven a sword through me, then pulled it straight back out again.

Alice took my arm and almost carried me through carpeted corridors to a snug room that was sparsely furnished. There were no books, vases or jugs, just bare surfaces, as though they were waiting to have their things replaced after dusting. Mary Barton had always taken a Calvinist approach to furnishing, but here the carpet needed replacing, the fire sweeping, the windows washing. She took her seat by the fire and indicated I take the one opposite — even these were old and tired. I wondered if the furniture had been updated since Richard's uncle bought the place twenty years ago. But it was warm, and a low coal fire burned in the grate. There was a mildly unpleasant smell, cloying and meaty, and it took me a moment to realize the candles put about the room were tallow, not wax. Burning animal fat slid down their sides, and I wondered why on earth my mother did not use wax, but did not ask.

"My midwife will need a chair," I said.

My mother stared at me, then looked Alice swiftly up and down before rising and striding from the room. Alice was taking no interest in her surroundings, staring absently at the threadbare carpet at her feet. My mother returned with a servant behind her carrying a sturdy chair, which he set against the wall before bowing and quietly closing the door on his way out.

The room was completely silent as we all waited for the other to speak. It did not take long for me to lose my temper. "You invited me to travel forty miles but have nothing to say?" I snapped.

No matter how rude I was, her face remained inscrutable. She was white as chalk and I noticed she had more lines at her eyes and lips than the last time I saw her.

My mother sighed deeply, closing her eyes. "I hoped this day would not come," she said.

"Did you think I would not find out?"

"Yes," she said simply.

"Why? Why would you not tell me if you knew? Richard has betrayed me, he has *broken* me and our marriage, and you knew. My own mother!"

"I was trying to protect you," she said slowly. Her white teeth flashed and her eyes were dark.

"How can I trust you? I cannot trust anyone. Not one person," I said. *Apart from Alice,* added a voice in my head.

I started to cry, and my mother watched, her expression awful, as I held my face in my hands. "I hate you!" I screamed at her. The sound ripped through the small room, bouncing from the wooden walls. "I hate both of you. You have both betrayed me."

She let me gather myself and I slumped back in my chair, a sullen child again. My breathing slowed and I wiped my face dry.

"You will stay here," my mother said eventually.

"Until when? Until *she* has the child?" I asked.

"What child?"

Understanding dawned on my mother's face. She reached for the arm of her chair with one white hand and her impossibly pale face turned paler. "She . . ."

"She will have his child," I said.

She closed her eyes. "The stupid fool," she whispered.

I did not know who was the fool, or if we all were.

"And you know she is at Barton?"

My mother nodded. Perhaps absently she flexed the finger that held her plain gold wedding band. I saw her mind working. From the corner of my eye I was aware of Alice, frozen as a statue in ice. My mother had not asked her name or even acknowledged her existence; we may not have needed a false name after all, because it was likely she would never be asked it.

"Do you know her name?"

"Judith Thorpe."

"How did you come to know?"

"It is not important."

"It is to me."

"What *is* important is that you succeed in carrying this child, as you have not done before."

My stomach dropped. "Why?"

She licked her teeth. "Fleetwood, listen to me. If you do not produce an heir, she will."

Her voice rang clear in the room, and we stared at one another, understanding one another for possibly the first time in our lives. I felt suddenly cold all over.

"But she is not his wife." Alice spoke, surprising us both.

"An illegitimate child is as good as an heir," my mother said darkly. "They may not be able to inherit directly but a man can bequeath all kinds of things to his bastard — estates, land, property. Especially if there are no others. The only other way a bastard can be legitimized is if his father and mother marry," she added dismissively.

James's writing swam before my eyes: *Mr. William Anderton to bring marriage license from York.* I covered my mouth with my hand.

"He means to marry her. He knows I am to die."

"Die?"

I told my mother about Dr. Jensen's letter; the order of a marriage license I found in the ledger. I was shaking so violently I might have been fitting.

"Fleetwood!" My mother was shocked and appalled as I twitched and shivered, apparently having lost control of every limb.

Alice shot up next to me. "Have you *rosa solis*?" she asked my mother.

"What is that?"

"Brandy and cinnamon. Have it made for her, it will help."

My mother fled from the room and Alice took my hand in hers: pink against gray. Presently my mother returned with a servant bearing a tray on which was a pewter cup. Alice took it and handed it to me, and the pewter clattered against my teeth as I choked back the drink. It fired my throat and warmed my insides, and gradually the shivering slowed to a gentle twitch. My mother replaced the cup on the tray and asked for bread and wine to be brought.

"Mistress," the servant said softly. "There is no more manchet, just cheat."

"Bring it whatever," my mother snapped. Then she turned to Alice, and her dark eyes were interested. "What is your name?"

"Jill, Mistress."

My mother nodded once, to indicate both approval and dismissal, and returned to her seat before me. My head was thick with thoughts. I felt the child in my stomach move as though reminding me it was still there. It felt like when a carriage ran over a dip, not entirely unpleasant, and I cupped my stomach with my hands and rubbed as though to warm it, remembering those words that were now as familiar to me as my own name: *Her earthly life will end.*

CHAPTER ELEVEN

Alice and I shared a room at the top of the house because it was warm — the start of summer had not yet reached this far north. She was on a truckle bed brought in and set next to mine, and she slept in a peculiar way, curled round on the mattress, without using the pillow. I knew because I barely slept. Not wanting to wake her with my rolling and creaking, I eventually got up and sat at the window.

All I could think of was Richard's woman. The more I tried to picture her the less clear her face became, but I was sure I had never seen her before that moment, that she was not someone I had met before. I wondered if she slept in my old bed at Barton, and if Richard did, too, when he was there. All the times he had gone away and kissed my forehead, and I had watched from a window as he departed on his horse. Halifax, Manchester, Lancaster, and farther: Coventry,

London, Edinburgh. But really: Barton, Barton, Barton.

Tears came easily now, and I tried not to sniff too hard or make much noise. I could not imagine going back to Gawthorpe but I could not stay here either, forever a guest in my mother's house. I was stuck in the mud, and sinking. But for now I was sitting at the window looking out, and while it was still dark I would not think of the next day, or the day after that. And I was still alive, and my child, too, for it was squirming like a newborn kitten now, and I felt it all the time — I was never truly alone. Then I realized that if it was born, and if I lived and became a mother, I would never be alone, and the thought came like a ray of warm sunshine on my face. I may have lost Richard — or a part of him — and my marriage was no longer what I thought it would be, but I would have a friend.

I turned to look at the sleeping form of the woman who was my only means of achieving it. Her golden hair fell down her back, and her chest rose and fell peacefully. I thought of the man who'd upset her in the Hand and Shuttle, how she'd said children were more trouble than they were worth. I felt as though she was the first person I could call a friend, but how much did I really know about her?

As though aware in some part of herself that she was being watched, she shifted in her narrow bed and whimpered. I watched her settle again, then she stiffened, her hands scrabbling at her covers as though searching for something. "Leave her," she whimpered, so quietly it wouldn't have woken me if I was asleep. "No, don't touch her! Leave her."

Her face was a mask of pain, contorted in agony, and I froze with alarm, unsure of whether or not to wake her. But as suddenly as she'd begun, she melted into peace, her body relaxing and her face smoothing back into sleep. Clearly I wasn't the only one who had nightmares.

I sat with my hands on my stomach and watched the inky-blue sky grow darker before it got lighter, and it was only when the birds began to pierce the silence that my eyes grew heavy and I climbed back into the bedsheets, which were cold.

Breaking our fasts that morning, we made a somber group. Alice went as though to eat with the servants but I insisted she sit with my mother and me, and when she refused I pleaded. Neither she nor my mother were happy about it and sat with their faces pinched as their eggs were set down in front of them. The bread was brought, but it was different than what I was used to, and I remembered what my mother's servant had said the night before, that they only had cheat flour, made of bran, not wheat.

I scratched at my clothes and cap where they felt tight and yawned. Alice was nibbling at a boiled egg, and I took one from the bowl and held its warm weight in the palm of my hand. Against the thick white of it, my skin looked yellow.

"Fleetwood, is there something wrong with your egg?" my mother asked.

I bit into it and found it surprisingly delicious: salty and solid, not like the trembling, watery things my kitchen served in their shells. I had to put it down to scratch my arm, rubbing the material of my dress hard where I could not touch the skin.

"Fleetwood," my mother said. "Do you have lice?"

I thought I might, although I hadn't seen any. It felt as though I was being tickled very softly and finely all over, from my ankles to my ears. I scratched at my neck, my face, my wrists and my stockings: anywhere I could reach. "Perhaps I do," I said. Poor people got lice, unclean people, not me, who rubbed myself with linen every day and dabbed oil of roses at my wrists and throat.

"Eat your breakfast," my mother said. "If only you had the appetite of your midwife."

Alice colored and paused buttering her bread, setting the knife down slowly.

"I prefer manchet to this cheap stuff," I said to make my mother color in turn, which she did. But I was lying: the seed loaf was warm and nourishing, and delicious with the homemade butter.

The itching started up again and my knife clattered to the table as I sprang up to relieve the backs of my legs.

"Fleetwood!"

"I don't know what's wrong with me." I stuck my fingers down the back of my dress, but as that brought relief my arm tingled where I'd rubbed it a moment before.

"Control yourself, you are causing a display."

"This has not happened before, and the moment I come to stay with you I itch from head to toe. Do you wash the bed linen, Mother?"

"Of course it is washed, don't be absurd!"

"I need to get out of this dress." I stalked from the room and wished my dress could fall away like a cloak, but it was a fussy one with ribbons and Alice had helped me get into it that morning. I stopped in the doorway. "Jill, will you help me?"

She looked relieved to abandon breakfast and followed me out of the dining chamber and upstairs.

I was impatient as she unlaced every ribbon and lace that she had tied not half an hour before. "Hurry, please!"

The gown fell down around me and I stepped out of it, then my corset had to come off and the French farthingale be pulled from my hips. By the time I could sit down to untie my stockings, I was shoving up the sleeves of my underclothes to tear at my skin with my nails. I reached under my nightgown to get to the flesh at my stomach, which was hard and smooth where before it was doughy. I pulled a pin from my hair and used it to scratch down the back of my neck.

Alice watched, scratching the nape of her neck thoughtfully as I contorted myself in front of her. "Perhaps a bath would help?" she suggested.

A tub was brought and jugs of water from the kitchen. Then a chambermaid knocked on the door with a slice of soap, which was soft and black and homemade, not like the solid white cakes we bought. I did not know how to ask Alice to turn away as I un-

216

dressed, but she did anyway. As everything fell to the floor, I half expected to see tiny black things crawling up and down my flesh and in and out of my clothes, but there was nothing. My skin was white all over, not flaming red as it felt. I started to laugh. Alice half turned from her truckle bed. "What is it?"

"There's nothing there. No lice. No rash. I must be addled."

I lowered myself into the water and splashed it all over, extinguishing the itching like so many little flames licking my skin.

"Would you like me to leave?" Alice asked from where she was facing the wall.

"No, stay," I said.

She lowered herself onto the truckle bed and kept her back to me, folding her legs beneath her.

The water settled and I stared down at my stomach, which was much bigger than the last time I'd bathed. I couldn't see the coarse black hairs below it. I moved the soap all over my skin, making it slick as an eel, and the itching dulled. I filled the jug and tipped it over my head, lathering my hair so it tangled into a knotted mess. The water lapped gently around me and I sighed.

"Alice, have you heard of familiar spirits?"

I heard her weight shift on the bed. "Yes,"

she said.

"Jennet Device told me her mother had a dog, and I saw a dog with her when you were . . ."

Alice went still. "When I was what?" I swallowed. She turned and looked straight at me over her shoulder, her eyes bright and clear. "When I was what?"

"Alice, do not look." I attempted to cover myself in the tub, but her gaze did not stray from my face.

"Were you spying on me?"

"No."

"When?"

"I . . . I went out riding to meet you. I saw you with her in the forest."

She turned again to the fire and reached for the iron poker, pushing it into the splintered coals. "What did you hear?"

"Nothing."

"Why did you not make yourself known?"

"I . . . I was afraid. Of her. Of the woman. Elizabeth Device."

"Why?"

"Her eyes. They frightened me." How awful she had looked when she'd turned toward me, staring wildly in different directions. "Her daughter, Jennet," I went on. "I cannot fathom why Roger believes everything she tells him. How can he? She is just a child." As I said it, I thought of myself, and how I'd told no one about what happened to me, knowing no one would believe me. But that was different — Jennet's stories were full of magick and spirits, like a tale told to a child to get them to sleep.

"Maybe he wants to believe it. Maybe he is telling her what to say."

"Roger would not do that."

"How do you know?"

"He is a good man. He has been good to us." As my words rang out in the room they sounded hollow. Did Roger know of Richard's woman? That would be a betrayal twice over, and worse even than my own mother's. He called Richard and me *the turtledoves.* Either he was ignorant or cruel.

"Alice, I am sorry for spying, I did not mean it," I said after a long silence.

My thoughts were becoming too much for me; I needed to separate them like threads and follow each of them in turn. I thought Alice hated me and watched her pick at something on her skirt. Her old dress badly needed mending and washing and her cap starching. I decided I would have it done here. I wondered when the last time she bathed was, if she longed to scrub herself clean. "Alice, would you like to bathe?"

"No, thank you."

"I can have more water sent up."

She bristled. "Do I smell badly? Do you think *I* have given you lice?"

"No, of course not. There are no lice. I imagined it . . ." I saw the white pile of my underthings on the floor and watched them again to see if they crawled. "Alice, do you think my skin looks yellow?"

She glanced dismissively at me. "I couldn't say — it does not look healthy, but then it never does."

She was full of resentment, and for the first time I did not know if I'd been right to bring her with me. Something had shifted in her the day I accused her of stealing my necklace, which was still missing — though she had brought no luggage to my mother's, so if she did have it, she might have hidden it. But if she was not responsible, then she had every right to act off with me. Still, I was used only to being deferred to, and she treated me almost like an equal. Yet I realized I did not mind.

I scooped water over myself once more, then stood up, meeting myself in the mirror at the dresser. My hair was wild, bunched up around my ears like a bird's nest. My paps were full with dark rings around the nipples, the buds of which were also dark. Shadows hung beneath my eyes, which were a dirty white.

I pressed myself with clean linen towels and wrapped a bath sheet around me to sit on the bed. Alice had not moved from where she was. I thought about where she might want to be: it was not here, but instinct told me she did not pine for the place she had left either; impossible anyway, now it was unsafe. Perhaps it was somewhere I had not pictured her where she felt most comfortable: in a lover's arms beneath old sheets, or sitting comfortably with her father outside on a warm spring evening.

"Alice, tell me," I said as I pulled a clean smock over my head. "Am I keeping you from your father?"

"No."

"Or anyone else?" I said. She shook her head. "The man in the alehouse . . ." I hesitated.

She looked sharply at me. "You saw him?"

For the second time I'd admitted to spying. I colored slightly, and nodded. "Just in the passage as he was leaving. Did he upset you?"

"I don't want to talk about it." She turned so I could not see her face.

I combed my hair and picked up my corset wrapped in pearl-colored silk, rapping it lightly with my knuckles. I decided I would wear my gown without it today; I could not bear to bind my stomach again.

Alice saw me playing with it. "Do you ever tire of wearing clothes you cannot put on yourself?" she said.

"No," I said truthfully. "I only dress once a day. Apart from today."

We smiled at one another, and I knew I was forgiven.

A knock came at the door and someone collected the bathwater while another servant brought sugar biscuits and hot milk, which I shared with Alice. She said that she had eaten better in twenty-four hours than she had all year. We sat eating the biscuits and feeding crumbs to Puck, and with sugar crystals on my lips and my hair clean and soft and my gown fresh, it would have been easy to forget why I was here, but I couldn't quite manage it. The reason Alice was with me was because I was growing heavy with child, and the reason *I* was here in this bright, airy chamber fifty miles away from my own was because my husband had another woman. It was all such a mess, but somehow it didn't feel completely hopeless. Not yet anyway.

Before long my mother came in, and made no attempt to hide her displeasure at the sight of Alice sitting on her bed, her legs tucked to the side of her, a cup of milk resting on her skirts that were dusted with sugar. My mother did not knock; she preferred startling people, as Alice was now, coloring slightly and sitting properly.

"Will you dress today, Fleetwood?" my mother asked.

"Perhaps." I saw her eyes flick momentarily to my stomach, which was more pronounced in just my nightdress with no layers of silk or velvet or wool piled over it. "Have you no wood for the fires? We are like two servants hunched over dying coal embers."

Her eyes shone very black. "We keep a good economy in this house. If you prefer a wood fire I can fetch you an ax."

We glowered at one another, then she left, closing the door firmly behind her.

"No wood, no wheat and no wax candles," I thought out loud. "I am beginning to think my mother is growing cheap in her old age."

Alice prodded the ashes in the hearth with the iron stoker. "How does she get her money?" she asked.

"I had never thought about it, but I suppose . . . from us."

A bird sang in the canopy of trees beneath the window, sweet and clear. *Us.* I had always known that word to mean my husband and me, but all along he had two versions. Which one did he think of first? I slid my wedding band off my wet finger and slipped it on again. Off, on, off, on.

"You grew up here?"

"Here? No. I grew up at Barton."

"Barton? But isn't that . . ."

"Yes."

Her eyes were wide. "Your husband keeps his mistress at your house?"

"I don't see it as mine, but yes."

"Why not?" I felt her golden eyes on my face.

"It was not a happy place."

She let out a laugh, curling her feet beside her once again. "How can a manor house not be a happy place? Did you not have fancy gowns, and fine food, and servants?"

I did not smile. Earlier she had allowed me a glimpse into her life — a keyhole's worth, but still a glimpse. She waited for me to decide how much to tell her, her clever eyes never leaving my face. I sighed, and crossed my legs to mirror hers.

"My father died a few years after I was born. I don't remember him. Then it was just my mother and me. I had no friends or cousins or anyone to play with, apart from my bird, Samuel. One day I left his cage too close to the fire and he died. He was the

224

only friend I had. I was a miserable child. Whenever I misbehaved, my mother threatened to send me to my husband. I should have got another pet, something to keep me company, but I didn't."

"Your husband?" Alice asked suddenly. "You mean Richard?"

"I was married before Richard."

Before I could stop it, the memory that I fought so hard to forget leaped into focus: the parlor, my mother's skirts disappearing around the corner, my husband's deep, cracked voice, "Come to me, Fleetwood." His large hand reaching under my dress.

"You were married *before*? So you were . . . you are divorced?"

"Heavens, no. The marriage was annulled so that I could marry Richard." I sighed. "My mother decided the Bartons and the Shuttleworths made a better match. If Richard had not agreed . . . I would still be wed to Master Molyneux." I had not spoken his name aloud in such a long time, but quite to my surprise it had no effect on me. It sounded like any name. "And I do not think he was a good man."

Alice was quiet and thoughtful. "How old were you when you married the first time?" she asked.

"Four."

Alice was shocked into silence. Then she said, "How old was he?"

"About thirty."

"How awful," she whispered.

"I only met him twice. Once at Barton, and the second time at our wedding. After that, my mother took me home to live until I was ready to be his wife. Thankfully that day never came."

There was pity in every line of Alice's face, and something else: a grave kind of understanding, as though she, too, knew what went on in the world, and had seen some of it.

"Why do you look like that?" I almost laughed. "Did you think I could choose a husband? Catch someone's eye in the alehouse?"

"I suppose so."

"The thing is, if I could, I would still have chosen Richard."

"You must love him a great deal."

"I do," I said simply. "He rescued me from a different future, and gave me a new one. I had no say in the matter. But you — you are lucky. *You* can choose whomever you like."

She gave a small smile. "I have never been called lucky before."

"Do you meet lots of men at the inn?"

"Drunks, plenty."

"A world of choice, then."

We both laughed, and there was a comfortable pause. I wondered if this was what friendship was like.

"I can't imagine going home," I said after a while, growing serious again.

"What will you do?" Alice asked.

"I have no idea." I twirled my wedding band round and round. "Do you want to hear a story?"

"Yes."

She was almost like a child, with her knees pointing out and her elbows pressed into them.

"I do not know where it came from but people in the village at Barton, where my house was, say that a wild boar was running around causing havoc in the forest. My father offered up my hand in marriage to the person who could slay the boar. A hunt followed, and on St. Lawrence's Day, the eldest Shuttleworth son slew it. There is an inn on the site called The Boar's Head, and I'm not sure which came first, that or the story."

Alice was confused. "But your father died before you were . . ."

"It's just a story," I said. "And do you know the best part? I am terrified of boars."

227

"Why?"

I shrugged. "I have nightmares about them chasing me. I must have heard that story when I was a child because I've been afraid of them for as long as I can remember. The Barton family crest is three boars. I cannot bear to have it anywhere in the house, though Richard insisted we put it above the hearth in the great hall, should guests forget my lineage."

I had not told anyone but Richard so much about myself, and felt slightly exposed. Alice was quiet.

"I bet you are not afraid of anything," I said.

"Of course I am," she said, and she pulled at a loose thread in her apron. "I am afraid of lies."

That night, in the early hours, I woke suddenly. The room was black, with the candles burned down and their smoke not quite escaped. Something had woken me — a noise or a movement. It might have been Puck — he had taken to sometimes sleeping in the room with us. I closed my eyes and tried to get comfortable beneath the counterpane, but could not dismiss the feeling I was being watched. I pushed off the bedclothes and crawled to the edge of the bed to look over at Alice's truckle bed, letting my eyes adjust to the darkness. The white linen glowed faintly in the moonlight, empty of any shape sleeping on top. The narrow bed was empty.

A breath of noise stirred behind me, and I knew immediately there was someone else in the room. I turned slowly, searching here and there in the dark, and almost jumped from my skin to see a tall figure in a white nightdress standing directly beside my bed, where my head had been. A scream died in my throat. "Alice?" I whispered, unable to even hear myself over the rushing in my ears.

She did not move, apart from swaying slightly, giving her the strange impression of laundry drying in a light breeze. I could not see her face.

"Alice," I said, louder. "You are frightening me."

Making no noise, she walked back to her bed and climbed into it. It took so long for my heart to stop racing, the edges of the window were light by the time I went to sleep.

"Do you remember what happened last night?" I asked her in the morning as she scrubbed herself with linen. She stared at me. "You were standing over my bed."

"Was I?"

"Yes, you frightened me. I thought my heart would stop." She appeared surprised, and told me she did not remember. "You rose from your bed while in a fast sleep?"

"Yes, but only since . . ." She stopped, and began scrubbing again.

"Since what?"

"Nothing."

A few nights later, I woke with that same feeling again, and she was there, ghostly and moonlit, and then again a few nights after that. It always unsettled me, because I could not see her face, and was almost glad, because I did not know what I would find on it.

The easy way she took up the position made me wonder if it was something she had done in wakefulness. Could she have been dreaming of watching her mother in her sickbed? Or was she dreaming of the forest, feeling the leaves and mud beneath her feet and the birds in her ears? I never did find out, because she could never remember. That's what she told me.

The cook at my mother's house was a woman named Mrs. Knave, and it was thanks to her that after a long winter of hibernation, my appetite returned. She fed me apple pie, bread and butter, biscuits, gingerbread and marchpane. At mealtimes we had flaky salmon with creamy parsley sauce, oyster pies and beef that was soft and pink in the middle. There were fluffy potatoes and buttery carrots and cheese pasties that burned my tongue. Each night I had *rosa solis* — brandy with cinnamon — and the color slowly returned to my hollow cheeks. I hadn't been sick once. After my conversation with Alice about my mother's housekeeping, without consulting her I had the coal in the fireplaces replaced with wood and the tallow candles with wax, instructing the suppliers to bill Richard directly.

One morning the movement in my stomach woke me before it was full light. I lay with my hands on my rounded stomach, taut as a drum skin, thinking how strange it was and listening to Alice's steady breathing. Dr. Jensen's words came back to me, as they always did in the small, lonely hours, so I slipped out of bed and went to the window. The sky was a beautiful deep blue but the forest of trees that surrounded the house was still in shadow. Beyond them was the village.

The chamber was warm and the air stale, so I found my cloak and put it on over my nightdress. The passage outside was silent, my mother's chamber door closed at the far end. I went quietly down to the kitchen, my mouth parched for a ripe pear or juicy apricot. I found a pear in a basket on the floor and went to the back door, turning the key to step outside and eat it while dawn broke and birds sang above me. The juice coated my hands and chin and I stood beneath the wide sky, thinking about everything but wishing my mind was still. My stomach rolled and tiny fists and feet pummeled and kicked.

"Good morning," I whispered. "Shall we watch the sun rise?"

My skin itched again and I scratched distractedly, my attention caught by something at the edge of the bank of trees. It was an animal, weaving in and out of the trunks. In the morning light it looked the same color as Puck, but he was fast asleep on the Turkey carpet. I stood still against the wall and watched it come all the way around, looping through the trees as though making for the house without wanting to be seen.

It was a fox. It held my gaze as we each waited for the other to move first, then a large bird, a rook or raven, burst out of the treetops and flapped cawing into the morning. By the time I looked back, the fox had gone, but something about it pulled a thread in my head somewhere. It wasn't until I went back upstairs and found Alice in our chamber making her bed that I realized what it was. She looked up when I came in, and I saw it: her eyes were the same color as a fox's, like coins in the sun.

Chapter Twelve

Two letters arrived at once: one for me, one for my mother, both from Richard. Even though it was only a piece of paper, I felt that somehow he had arrived at the house, barging in where he was not welcome. His slanted handwriting always looked rushed no matter if a letter took him all afternoon, and there it was, spelling out my name. While my mother pulled hers open straightaway, I put mine in my pocket.

Alice was in the garden. She had also been spending time in the woods, searching for plants she could grow in the kitchen garden, and I'd often look out the window to see her kneeling on the soil, her skirts bunched underneath her, her white cap bobbing among the green. A few days after the itching started, I watched her go from the garden to the kitchen door with a fistful of flat green leaves, then bring them to me in my chamber. She told me to rub them on my skin where it itched, and soon after it stopped altogether and my skin grew milky again.

"When I met you, you said children are more trouble than they are worth."

I was standing outside watching her at work in the soil. Dirt streaked her face where she'd moved her hair from it. She sat back on her heels and wiped her cheek with the back of her hand, warm from her industry despite it being a chill spring day. "And here you are planting a bed for one that is not yet born," I considered aloud. "I wonder if you are afraid of having them, knowing what you do about the delivery of them. Usually midwives are old and past their childbearing years, or those I have seen are."

"Perhaps."

She seemed thoughtful and distracted at the same time. I watched her pull up a weed and toss it in her basket, and decided to go in, because the fresh breeze was no longer pleasant, but then she spoke.

"How many children do you want to have?"

I wrapped my arms around myself. "Two," I replied. "So that they would never be on their own like I was."

"A boy and a girl?" she asked.

235

"Two boys. I wouldn't wish a girl's life on anyone."

Richard's letter stayed where it was in the pocket of my gown, and though I forgot about it, my mother decided that two days after his word came was the appropriate time to discuss it. I knew it was coming from the way she set her spoon down; I could see her tasting his name in her mouth.

"Fleetwood," she said. "Have you thought about when you will go back to Gaw-thorpe?"

"No."

"You have not thought about it?"

"I have not."

"Tell me, then —" My mother sipped at her spoon of meal and honey. "What have you been thinking of?"

Until that moment I had not noticed a copy of the Bible lying next to her hand. She saw me looking at it and lifted it, open-ing it at the ribbon marker. "While we eat, let us consider the gospel according to Luke. *Judge not, and ye shall not be judged. Condemn not, and ye shall not be condemned. Forgive, and ye shall be forgiven.*" She set the book down and took up her spoon again. "What do you think to that passage, Fleetwood?"

I pretended to consider and licked my teeth. "I think that it is remarkable how with his Bible, the king has a presence in every household, and on every bookshelf. He endorses not condemning, yet seems to do little else. Papists, witches . . ."

"The king has not *written* the bible, Fleetwood. This is the word of God. The king writes about witches in his own publication."

"He does?"

She got up and left the room, coming back a few moments later with a slim volume bound in black calfskin, which she handed to me. I pushed my bowl away and lifted the soft cover. The word *Daemonologie* was printed below an ink depiction of the Devil. Flames licked his body and great wings expanded behind him. I looked up at my mother, who indicated for me to read on. "Written by the high and mighty Prince James," I said.

Alice was looking at the book in my hands and I remembered she could not read. I turned the page and followed the king's words.

"What does it say?" Alice asked.

"*The fearful abounding at this time in this country of these detestable slaves of the Devil, the witches or enchanters, has moved me, beloved reader, to dispatch in post this following Treatise of mine . . .* He has written a book about witchcraft?" I asked my mother, leafing through what appeared to be a very thorough treatise.

"Twenty or more years ago, a ship he was traveling in to Scotland was cursed by witchcraft. He put around a hundred witches on trial for treason. There are witch trials held there twenty times a year. One of the stable boy's distant relatives was executed not long ago; here in Westmorland we are not far from the border. Your friend Roger Nowell is only catching up with the times, Fleetwood. The execution of heretics is nothing new."

Nick Bannister's handwriting came to my mind: *Alice Gray, of the same.* It had been easy to put from our minds this far north, or at least it had been for me. I wondered if the child Jennet was still at Read Hall.

"But the definition of witch is new." Alice spoke from the end of the table, making me look up in surprise. "These are peaceful people, carrying on as they have for centuries," Alice went on. "It's only since the king came to the throne that people became fearful. Have *you* never needed the help of a wise woman?"

My mother shimmered with hostility.

"How dare you address me in so insolent a manner in my own house? Are you a midwife or an authority on politics?"

I gave Alice a warning glance. A flush was creeping up her throat.

"Jill merely means that perhaps not all those accused of witchcraft are guilty," I said quickly.

My mother had turned red as a nettle rash and turned her full force on Alice. "You defend these Devil worshippers? Who use blood and bones and hair to carry out their sorcery? What is peaceful about that? They are godless people."

Her words stirred a memory in me: my hair swept from the pillow; a bowl of blood disappeared. I glanced at Alice, but her eyes were on the table — she appeared to know she had spoken out of turn.

"Enough of this," my mother spat, straightening her napkin on her lap. "Let us return to the matter in hand — when you will return to Lancaster, and to your husband. You have had time apart, and now it is only right that you go back. You are a wife, and wives live at home, not with their mothers."

"What if Richard has moved that woman in?"

"He would do nothing of the sort."

"So I suppose she will go on living at our house?"

"Where else would you have her? She is not in your parish, not in your way. She is out of sight and out of mind."

I threw the king's book onto the table. "She is not out of *my* mind. She might be yours but it is not *your* husband who has a woman. How can you defend her? And him? If he is such an angel, why does he have you furnishing your house like a yeoman's wife? You would defend him if he had you use rushlights!"

"I am content with my lot, as you should be yours," my mother snapped. "That nasty temper of yours is no doubt what drove him away."

"What drove him away is his need for an heir, and his wife not being able to give him one." My eyes stung and my throat was tight.

"Fleetwood." This time my mother's voice was not so unkind. "Do you think Richard is the first man to have a mistress and a bastard?"

The ghost of an itch sent my fingers to my scalp, my neck. "Next you will tell me that Father had twenty."

"Of course he didn't. My father did, though."

I stared at her.

"My father had three wives, and all of them had his children by the time they were married. When his first two wives died the next set was ready to move in. Not me," she said quickly. "But I had many brothers and sisters. His will was ten pages long — he left something to all of us."

"So you are telling me," I said slowly, "that if I die, this woman will easily take my place and move her children in, and nobody will remember me at all?"

"The things that come out of your mouth!" my mother cried. "That is not what I am saying. While you can have children, your place in the family is safe. Deliver your husband's heir and nobody will give a thought to this other woman, just as nobody gives a thought to the hundreds of other women and their bastard children in homes all over the country."

Her chair screeched against the flooring as she forced it backward and strode from the room. I waited until her feet were on the stone flags outside, then I took the king's book and threw it at the wall.

But *Daemonologie* turned up again later that day on Alice's bed. I asked her about it when she came in from the garden, her palms dirty. "I thought you could not read." I pointed to it.

"I can't," she said, pouring water from the jug into the bowl on the dresser. "I wanted to look at it. Would you read it to me? I want to know what he says. The king."

"Why do you?"

Brown water lapped the sides of the bowl as she rubbed her hands and wrists. "Please," she said, and then, "I spoke out of turn with your mother. I should not have been so bold."

"Think not on it," I said. "I don't."

I sighed and sat down on the end of Alice's truckle bed, reaching for *Daemonologie* and leafing through it. "How odd, it's written in dialogue." Alice looked blankly at me. "Dialogue, like what is spoken in plays."

"I have never seen one."

I opened it at chapter three. *"Epistemon says: I pray you likewise forget not to tell what are the Devil's rudiments."*

"Rudiments?"

"I mean either by such kind of Charms as commonly daft wives use, for healing of forspoken goods, for preserving them from evil . . . by curing the worm, by healing of horse-crooks, by turning of the riddle, or doing of such like innumerable things by words, without applying anything, meet to the part of-

fended, as mediciners do."

"What does it mean?"

"Doing things by words without applying anything. Curses," I said. "Healing things or maiming them from afar. I find it hard to believe the king found time to write this when he was ruling Scotland."

"I don't understand why he would write a book about it. But then, if I could write a book, maybe I would," Alice said.

I laughed. "You? Write a book? Women do not write books. You'll have to learn to read first and that might be a lifetime's work."

"If you can write a letter, why not a book?"

"Alice," I said gently. "It's not what is done." I had a thought. "Have you seen your own name?" She shook her head. "Would you like to?"

She nodded, so I took out Richard's letter, still wrapped in ribbon, and brought a feather and ink from the desk in the corner of my mother's room. I sat down beside her on the truckle bed. In one quarter of the paper, bordered by ribbon, I wrote Alice's name and blew on it to dry the ink before handing it to her. She smiled and took it from me, holding it up as though it shone in the light.

"What does that say?" she asked, pointing

to the letters curling up around the red ribbon.

"That's my name."

"Why is it longer than mine when they
take the same time to say? Fleet-wood.
A-lice."

"That isn't how it works," I said. "Each of
those things is a letter. *A-L-I-C-E.* They each
make a different sound, but when you say
them altogether they sound different again."
In the top right-hand square I wrote her
name in separate letters then handed her
the pen. "You try."

She gripped the feather in a way that
made me smile. "No, like this."

I showed her. In a shaky hand, she copied
the *A* in a new square followed by the other
letters. I burst out laughing when she
showed me.

"What?" she demanded.

"The way you've written it with the *A* so
far away, it looks like *a lice.*"

"A *lice*?"

"If you separate the *A* from the rest of the
letters, your name becomes *a lice.*"

"What?" She screwed her face up in such
a way that I could not help but laugh. Then
she began smiling, and before long we were
rolling about like two daft milkmaids,

clutching ourselves as tears ran down our faces.

"Get the *A* right first," I told her. "Then the other letters after."

That night as Alice untied my gowns and corset, I saw the paper on the desk with the quill lying next to it. Richard's words remained wrapped up and unread, and in the one remaining corner a little army of *A*s traveled across the page, like an infestation of lice. An infestation of Alices. It made me smile.

CHAPTER THIRTEEN

The window of the chamber Alice and I were staying in overlooked the front of the house, as well as the approach uphill, and the woodland on either side that was thick with partridges and pheasants. One morning I heard hooves outside, and thought Richard had finally come. But standing at the casement, peering through the glass, I saw a young woman — wearing a beautiful green gown with a waist I could only dream of — dismounting her horse, while another, plainer woman in scarlet waited beside hers. I gasped as I recognized them.

"Richard's sisters are here," I told Alice, choked with panic.

I'd got up late that morning, feeling hot and lazy, and had only finished breakfast in my nightgown. I jumped back from the window and began putting my hair in rolls. My mother had gone to the village, but I had not been listening when she told me, and did not know when she would be back, so I would have to be hostess.

Mrs. Anbrick the housekeeper came to the chamber door and rapped smartly. "Mistress, your sisters-in-law have come to pay you a visit."

The housekeeper was a warm, pleasant woman with soft skin and twinkling eyes — how she and my mother rubbed along together I had no idea. Now her tone was excited, impressed, even: visitors were rare at this house. I thanked her and when her footsteps had died away, I turned to Alice, keeping my voice low.

"Do not show yourself to them. You would be wise to stay in here."

"They don't know who I am, do they?"

"No, but they are dreadful chatterers and have noses for rumor like hounds, so stay out of their way." I closed the door behind me.

Eleanor and Anne were seated in my mother's parlor, which was always chilly. But there was a pleasant view of the old-fashioned knot garden at the back of the house, the purpose of which was more functional than stylish because only the hardiest flowers survived on these high, windy fells.

Both Richard's sisters shared his fair hair

and clear gray eyes, but Eleanor was pretty and Anne plain. "Fleetwood!" they cooed as I entered. Both immediately noticed my stomach, where my sleeveless gown parted around the cloth of silver stretching in a sphere. We kissed and I sat at the window with the sun on my face.

"We heard a rumor you were here, and it was true!" Anne said saucily. "And without Richard?"

"Yes, without Richard." I tried to force a smile. "From whom did you hear?"

"We were staying with friends at Kendal — do you know the Bellinghams of Levens Hall?" I shook my head. "One of their servants is cousin to one of yours here in the kitchen. We did not dare believe it when she told us you were staying here for the summer, but how many women are called Fleetwood Shuttleworth? And here you are! All alone?"

"All alone." Relief allowed me to sit back more comfortably. I had not rubbed my teeth and there was still the sour taste of morning in my mouth.

"Not for long." Eleanor indicated my stomach. "You are a funny little thing, staying away from your husband when you are about to have a baby. I suppose wives of the gentry can do what they like around here."

She gave a little tinkling laugh. To listen to her, you would think she'd lived all her life in one of the London mansions, when York was only the next county along. Before I could ask what else the servant had said, she went on, "How very exciting — a new Shuttleworth heir. Are you prepared? Do you have a midwife?" I nodded. "Well, you shall have to pass her on to me when you are finished. I did make a hint to Richard in my last letter, but nothing was confirmed then. I am to marry before the year is out!"

I made a delighted face. "That's wonderful news — who is your husband?"

"Sir Ralph Ashton."

Both Anne and Eleanor were older than me. When Richard and I married I had been thrilled to spend six months with them in London, but after thirteen years on my own I was not used to being spoken to, petted and teased at all hours of the day. All my life I had wanted sisters, and as soon as I got them I could not wait to be rid of them and their chatter and darting little hands and boundless inquisitiveness.

"Fleetwood?" Eleanor chided. "I said the wedding will most likely be at Michaelmas. Will the baby be born by the end of September?"

"Perhaps."

I wondered what they knew of Judith, if anything, but before I decided whether to ask, Mrs. Anbrick brought a jug of sacke and three Venice glasses. She looked approvingly at our little feminine party, pleased that the house had opened its doors to society. I poured a generous amount into each of the glasses and toasted to Eleanor's marriage. Anne was smiling but I could see that really she was downcast, with no husband arranged. Like Alice, I could not help but think her lucky. I drank deeply; the sacke was sweet and burning at the same time.

"Fleetwood, why *are* you here without Richard?" Anne asked, wearing a thin smile and shifting in her dress.

With their pale faces turned to mine, and their white ruffs gleaming in the sun, they were like two daisies.

I reached down the back of my ruff to scratch. "I . . ." Suddenly the baby kicked, and my hands flew to my stomach in response.

"Is it the quickening?"

"Yes."

"Can we feel?"

I was too surprised to say no, and within a moment four small white hands were pressed to my gown. I moved uncomfortably, wanting to pick their palms away.

"How wonderfully strange," they said, their eyes wide and staring. I willed the child to be still, and it was.

"How is your mother? She will miss you, Eleanor, when you leave Forcett."

"Yes, she is quite well but visits less often now," said Eleanor. "I expect she will pine for me, but Anne will still be there, of course."

"What news from York?" I asked.

"Nothing much of interest. Not like in Lancaster."

"What do you mean?"

"You will know all about them of course — the Pendle witches? They say there will be a trial and upward of a dozen hangings. The servants at Levens say it will be the most this county has ever seen. You must have heard something of it."

I swallowed. "Something, yes."

I thought of Alice upstairs, bent over the cupboard with her quill. We had no parchment so she had been practicing inside my mother's copy of *Daemonologie,* and having mastered her first name was inking her surname.

"Well, what do you make of it?"

"I would not know because I have been

here. And I pay no mind to servants' chatter."

That made Eleanor flush, and Anne gave a shudder. "I wonder what they look like. I am glad we do not have witches in York, I would not sleep in my bed."

Eleanor gave a high, tinkling laugh. "I do not think *you* are in danger, Anne. They only seem to curse each other and their filthy neighbors. Apparently they bury cats in their walls and prick babes to drink their blood. And Lancaster is positively full of them, by the sound of it. Are you sure you wish to return, Fleetwood, and raise your son there?" Eleanor teased.

"They murder *children*," Anne said gleefully. "And they're said to have animals that are the Devil in disguise."

"Like toads and rats and cats!" Eleanor shrieked and they writhed with giggling.

"Do you know a woman named Judith?" I interrupted them.

"Judith? No, is she a witch?"

I did not answer and filled our glasses again. The sacke was going down easily and making me feel loose-tongued. "Shall we walk around the garden? It's quite warm out."

The truth was I could not bear another moment sitting in that room with them. The three of us stood, and I realized that I was giddy. I led them outside, where the sky was blue and the air warm and windy. We walked around the side of the house, and Eleanor picked a fistful of flowers and held them at her breast. "Do I look like a bride?" she asked.

"The most beautiful bride I ever did see!" said Anne.

They flounced in their skirts, pirouetting in circles, but Anne stopped when she saw me, for I was not laughing or playing along. "Fleetwood, you are different, you know," Anne said. "I cannot think exactly why, something about you is more . . . *something.*"

"Eloquent as ever, Anne." Eleanor snorted like a pig.

"In what way?" I asked.

"You have always been quite melancholy really. But now you seem to . . . carry it better."

"Melancholy?"

"Yes, a little mournful and sad. But now you seem different, older somehow . . . more *knowing.*"

"I wish I was not *knowing,*" I muttered. "I would rather not know."

Eleanor looked blankly at me. "Know what?"

There was stillness around us; the wind had died for a moment, and I felt quite light-headed from the sacke and the bright sunlight and the green hills leaning all around.

"About your brother," I said, my face innocent. Anne had stopped too and they were both looking dumbly at me. "And his other woman. About the infant she is expecting. You did not know?"

The pretty bouquet fell from Eleanor's hands, splaying on the path. Their faces were identical masks of shock. "You aren't serious."

"I saw her with my own eyes. She is at Barton, at my father's house. That is where he keeps her."

A flock of birds flung themselves from a group of nearby trees, their wings cracking above us. I had sowed the seeds, and now they would grow whether I liked it or not.

"You are sure about this?" Anne asked, her face pale.

"Quite sure." I swallowed.

"But you have only been married . . ."

"Four years."

I was seventeen, but for all I'd been through might have been twice or three times that. My husband already had a lover, but I was no old matron, with graying hair and wrinkles at my eyes. I thought I was younger even than her, and in my mind she only grew more beautiful. The baby I'd wanted to give as a gift to Richard was now a much more precious commodity: it secured my place in the home, and in the family. Without it, I would be an ornament, a wife in name only. I knew this now. If this baby died inside me like the others, I may as well move permanently into my mother's house, for I would be less than useless. The thought of that made a hard kernel of dread in my stomach. I had to have Richard's child to secure my future, for if it died, I may as well die with it.

I pondered all this while we walked twice more around the garden in silence, with Anne and Eleanor making uncomfortable little comments about the inclement weather, and how Westmorland was so far behind York with its fashions, and had any of the Bellinghams had a new frock made in the past five years?

They did not stay much longer, and said they would not wait for my mother to return, but would go and collect their steward from the inn in the village and start on the journey back to York. But as we were walking to the stables, we passed the kitchen door at the back of the house, and it opened, and suddenly there stood Alice.

Her mouth was a little O of surprise, and she had a basket on her arm, and an old apron over her clothes. We stared at one another for a long moment, and Anne and Eleanor noticed something was odd, for usually servants went unnoticed and unacknowledged.

"Who is this?" Anne asked.

I licked my lips. "No one. Alice, go inside." I gave her a tight smile, and moved to continue on our path. Only when she did not move did I realize what I had said. I felt as though I'd missed a step, and the ground beneath me tilted, then righted itself. After a moment, Alice retreated, and the kitchen door closed.

Dread grew in my stomach, twisting and sliding like an eel in murky water, and I dared not look at Anne or Eleanor, for I did not know how much or how little they knew. What I did know was that I had to act as though nothing had happened, and Alice was no one, which was difficult with my skin turned white and my heart racing. "Do you know, I am suddenly very tired," I said weakly. "Shall we get your horses? I think I need to lie down."

Once they'd said their hurried goodbyes and went off down the windy slope, I went back into the parlor, where I finished the jug of sacke. Something had gone badly wrong, and I could not tell how badly. I had been foolish to tell them about Richard; it would do nothing for my position, and everything for his temper. And exposing Alice like that . . . They could not know she was the same Alice Gray, whose name was on a list in the next county, who may or may not be wanted for inquisition. Could they?

By the time I went upstairs to my chamber, I was drunk and it wasn't even noon. Alice was nowhere to be seen, so I sat on the edge of the bed and kicked off my slippers. Richard's sisters and mother — if she didn't already know — would surely have something to say to him about Judith, and he might be even more furious with me. Probably I would be the talk of York as well as Lancaster, my name mentioned in great halls and dining chambers and carriages. Well, I was more furious with him than myself, because all this was his fault, and my mother's, too, knowing what she did about Judith and keeping it from me, and pressuring me to produce a child, as if I did not want to, as if I did not know how important it was. I used to think I was letting everyone down with my failure, but as

I lay on the bed with the warm light pouring in, I realized everyone had let me down.

Not quite everyone.

I must have fallen asleep because I felt something damp being pressed against my face. When I opened my eyes Alice was standing over me with a bowl and cloth. "I thought you had a fever," she said.

My tongue was dry and I still had the dizzy feeling from earlier. Sweat gathered at my armpits.

"I drank too much sacke," I said. The child inside me was still, too, lulled by the sweet wine.

Richard's sisters' words echoed in my ears: *in Lancaster plenty is happening.* "I am worried," I said, sitting up. A small frown threaded between her eyebrows, and her eyes were troubled.

"About earlier, in the garden?"

"Yes. I said your name. I'm sorry. I don't know if they know . . . I don't know *what* they know. Or more worryingly, who they will tell."

"But there is nothing to tell. They would think nothing of you talking to a servant."

"Only if they did not know who you are. Oh, why could I not remember Jill? I wish I could sew my mouth shut."

She swirled the cloth in the bowl, and her

expression was uneasy.

"Alice," I said. "My mother will be back anytime, so I must ask you this now. I want you to tell me what you were doing with Elizabeth Device."

Her hand stopped on the water, her fingers balancing lightly on its surface. As well as her usual scent of lavender, though I never saw her with it, there was an earthy scent, too, of soil and things nourished and growing. "I would not ask if I did not think it important."

After a pause, she went to the court cupboard and set the bowl down on it. With her back to me, she sighed. "Do you remember when we sat in your parlor and you asked me where I worked, and I told you the Hand and Shuttle? And you asked me how long I had worked there and I said not long?"

"Yes."

"I'd been there about a week."

I waited, hardly breathing.

"And do you remember when you caught me with the rabbits the first time we met?"

"Yes."

"I really was lost. I had just started work at the Hand and Shuttle and was finding my way."

She did not look at me, and I watched her

long neck, her narrow back, as she spoke to the wall.

"Before that I used to work at an alehouse in Colne. One morning I was walking to work and I came across a man lying on the ground. It was a quiet road and there was no one else around. He was a peddler — all his things were cast all in a trail behind him, pins and needles and scraps of cloth, as though he'd staggered about dropping them. I thought he was dead, but he was alive, muttering and mumbling. One side of his face was collapsed, like it had melted, and his eye wouldn't open. I'd seen it before with my mother."

I could not breathe; the air in the room was thick and I tried to swallow but there was a lump in my throat.

"I helped him to the inn and the landlord helped me put him upstairs in a chamber and called a physick. The man kept muttering on about a black dog and a girl he'd met on the road, but his speech was slurred and we didn't know what he meant. Then later that night a girl arrived."

"Alizon Device," I whispered.

Alice had both hands on the court cupboard as though steadying herself. "She was in such a state, sobbing and begging for forgiveness. I did not know what she meant

260

until she spoke of cursing a peddler that same day. She was filthy, like she'd spent all day tramping about in the rain. I asked her to come in and get dry but the landlord would have none of it, telling me she was a beggar and he didn't let her sort in. He told her to make herself scarce. Before she went, she told me her name was Alizon and she would come back tomorrow to check on the man."

"And did she?"

Alice's cap bobbed up and down. "And the next day, and the day after that. But Peter the landlord wouldn't let her in — said she was trouble. By that time the man had woken up, and I could make out that his name was John. I sat with him, giving him beer and food and wiping his mouth when it fell out. His face was still all melted, like only one side of it worked. I don't know if it will be right again. He got some of his speech back and told us his son's name and to write to him, so Peter sent a man.

"One day I was sitting with him on my own and the girl had been again that morning as usual, standing in the yard wringing her hands and crying, asking to see him. She was distraught, kept saying that it was all her fault. I decided to tell him that she was there to beg for his forgiveness, and asked did he want me to let her in, and he nodded.

"Peter was out so I had to look after the customers. So I went down and told her to be quick. I stayed downstairs. Not long after, she came running through again, so I went back upstairs to see John and he was in such a state, sobbing and shaking and pointing at the door. She's a witch, he were saying over and over."

At this point Alice walked to the window and looked out. The sound of the moor drifted in through the glass: a lonely wind whining at the casement.

"Then what happened?" I asked.

"He told me that she had a black dog with her, the same one she'd had on the road. But I hadn't seen one, I didn't know what he was talking about or if he was dreaming. Then someone else turned up — the girl's grandmother. She made the whole place go cold, she did. Everyone felt her coming in. Everybody knew who she was."

"Who was she?"

"They call her Demdike. She kept to herself most of the time but local folk knew her. I'd seen her around, heard what people said about her."

"What did they say?"

"That she's an eccentric, a witch, she's

this, she's that. Stay away from her, they said. But she wasn't there to see John Law. She was there to see me."

"But why?"

"Alizon must have told her that I'd found John and was looking after him. That's when she started threatening me. She told me she'd put a curse on me if I didn't lie for Alizon. She wanted me to say I'd never seen her, that the old man was making it all up, that his mind was weak and he couldn't tell up from down.

"But Peter had already written to John's son, and Master Law arrived not long after, from Halifax or somewhere. John told him he'd forgiven Alizon, that he was a God-fearing man who believed in forgiveness and that's what God wanted him to do. He's a good man, John Law. But his son Abraham wouldn't hear of it. He sent for Alizon and questioned her. Demdike came with her and they put the shivers in him, I think. Demdike was denying everything, screaming and spitting all over the place, and Alizon was crying, and I just stood there not knowing what to do. And the son turned to me and said have you seen these women here before? Did this girl curse my father?

"I couldn't speak, and John was squealing like a pig in the corner, and Abraham was red in the face and looked like he was about to kill someone, and I was frightened. So I said yes, I'd seen them.

"He tried to make them break the curse but Alizon couldn't, and Demdike said only the person who'd put it on could take it off. So that was that, and Abraham sent for the magistrate, and Peter asked me to leave because of all the trouble I'd caused." Her voice was thick. "I worked there for nearly ten years. He knew I was a good worker so he found me a job at the Hand and Shuttle. His brother-in-law is the landlord."

My mind was empty. My thoughts were still. I stared at my stockinged feet, small and dainty in white silk. Alice did not speak, and we were silent for a long time, until a thought came to me. "But how does that involve Elizabeth Device? What were you doing that day with her in Hagg Wood?"

Alice sat on the truckle bed behind her and kept her back to me.

"She came to the Hand and Shuttle one night. Somehow they found out I was there, I don't know how. Alizon and her grandmother had been arrested. People were giving her funny looks when she came to see me. Well, you've seen her. I was afraid I'd lose my job there, as well, so I said she had to leave. She asked me to go to her house that Friday, said she was having some neighbors round to talk about what they could do to help those that'd been arrested. She said I had to help, that I was . . ." Her voice shook. "She said I was the reason her daughter and mother were in gaol."

I shook my head but Alice couldn't see. "She was desperate . . . angry. I could tell she just wanted to do something. And I wanted to help. Like a fool I went. I had to do something to stop them turning up at work and getting me in trouble. And even after that, after I went to Malkin Tower she was waiting for me near your house in the forest. I cannot escape them." There was real fear in her voice, like when she whimpered in her sleep.

"But what happened at Malkin Tower? What did they speak of?"

Alice shrugged. "We ate a meal and they talked about how they could help Alizon and Demdike. It was just a meeting of people who knew the family, neighbors and the like. Apart from me and one other person."

"Who was that?"

At this, Alice bowed her head. "Mould-heels. My mother's friend Katherine."

"Why did she go?"

"She was with me when . . ."

We both jumped out of our skins when the door flung open and my mother swept in, her face hard with displeasure. "You did not think to send someone to the village to fetch me?" she commanded.

I sighed. "Richard's sisters did not stay long. They were traveling from Kendal back to Forcett."

"How did they know you were here?"

"A servant here is cousins with someone at the house they were staying."

Her black eyes were penetrating. "What did you tell them?"

"Nothing," I lied.

The silence that followed demonstrated that she did not believe me. "Supper is almost ready," was all she said, and she left the door open behind her.

I went to close it quietly, and crept back toward Alice. All the questions I could have asked were ripe, hanging in the room; I could have reached anywhere and plucked one easily, but I chose the first one that came into my head, from the last thing she had said.

"Alice, you said Mouldheels was with you when . . . what?"

Alice was silent, and the wind rushed down from the moor, sounding almost like a child crying. Then she covered her face with her hands.

"Alice! What's the matter?"

"I cannot speak of it," she whispered. "I cannot bear it."

"Whatever it is, it cannot be so bad."

But she would not tell me, and I could feel the waves of irritation from my mother lapping at the door. The last thing I needed was another afternoon of combat. I felt troubled as I went downstairs to dinner, as though something apart from the wind was pressing in at the windows, wanting to be let in.

CHAPTER FOURTEEN

That night I had The Nightmare. I woke, crippled with fright, to a candle at my side, a familiar but frightened face behind it. My legs were twisted in the sheets and I was wet with sweat from my hair to my legs. I was so scared I thought my heart would leap right out of my chest, and Alice sat with me until my breathing slowed and the shadows at the corner of the room grew less frightening. I hoped I had not been screaming, but an alarm in Alice's eyes and a tightness in her jaw made me think I had.

"It's all right now," Alice whispered. "Was it the boars?"

I nodded, and gasped, and that feeling of dread arrived again, and I checked between my legs for a trickle of blood. But they were dry, and Alice went back to bed, and eventually her breathing slowed, too. We had been at my mother's for a month, and in all that time I'd been free of The Nightmare.

Since that breakfast my mother had not mentioned my going back to Gawthorpe, and neither had I, but I should have known her better than that. Perhaps if I had the plaster figure of Prudence with me in my chamber I might have remembered to exercise it once in a while, but my old friend remained in my chamber at Gawthorpe, gathering dust.

I was sitting in the kitchen with Mrs. Knave eating biscuits hot from the oven when Mrs. Anbrick came to tell me some-one was here for me. I'd known it from the moment I woke up: a change in the atmo-sphere, a shifting sense of unease in my stomach. My time was running out.

"Who is it?"

I did not need ask. The black skirts of my mother entered the kitchen before she did, smooth as a fish gliding in a pond. Her face was set for battle. "Fleetwood, come out of the kitchen now," she said. The dread stirred in my stomach, stuck me to the chair.

Mrs. Knave bowed her head, her chubby hands brushing awkwardly at her apron. I fixed my mother with the coldest look I could summon and stepped past her, re-membering how she'd untied Richard's let-ter, then kept the contents to herself. I had not thought to ask her what he had said, and his letter lay unopened still on the desk in my chamber.

"You cannot avoid him forever, Fleetwood," my mother's voice rang behind me in the hall as I went to wait in her parlor. I had decided I would not speak to her again.

I sat shivering even though the room with its high, narrow window was close and stuffy, even with no fire. Dust danced around in the watery beams of light, and a chessboard lay on a stool by my chair. My mother sometimes played chess with the housekeeper and sometimes with herself. It was something she had always done, but for the first time I realized how sad that was, with her alone in this room and me upstairs. Well, she could have asked me if she wanted to play: I would not feel sorry for a woman who chose so often to be alone. I drew my sleeveless robe around my stomach, put my hands in my lap and waited.

Puck came in first, greeting me with his tongue when he saw me and coming to sit beside me. My mother came in next, her pattens clacking on the stone flags, with a deeper, heavier tread of soft calfskin boots and that familiar jangle of coins behind her.

"Fleetwood." I heard him and saw him at the same time. His earring caught the light and his clear gray eyes shone. He looked first at my face, then my stomach. *You are still with child,* I heard him think. I had forgotten how conversations could be held in silence when you are married, when you know the flesh and bones and touch of someone and could know them in a dark room. Why not their mind, too? My mother looked blinkingly from one of us to the other.

"You look well," Richard said.

I said nothing.

"Fleetwood?" My mother spoke.

"You may go," I said coldly.

She looked appealingly at Richard but his gray eyes were fixed on my black ones as intensely as if I might disappear at any moment.

She closed the door. I did not hear her pattens in the hall, so after a few moments I said, "Mother," and she went clacking off.

Richard took the seat opposite mine and to both our surprise, Puck gave a low growl and then barked.

"You have turned the dog against me, too?" Richard said in a light way, but his eyes were sorrowful.

"He has a mind of his own. He has eyes and ears. Perhaps he saw and heard more than I did."

Richard swallowed and removed his black

271

velvet hat, offering it to Puck to sniff as a sign of peace. "Remember me, boy?" I wished I didn't but I felt doubly betrayed when Puck went to him, nuzzling into his hand and grinning broadly. "There we go," Richard said softly, rubbing him all over and patting him in the hard way he did.

"I forget how long a journey it is up to these parts," he said eventually, resting his hat on his lap.

"You do not mind when you have a hunting trip."

"I did not say I mind."

"Your journey did not take a month, though," I said. My boldness surprised us both, but Richard more. He opened his mouth, then closed it, changing position in his chair.

"No. I had some business to attend."

"That came before your wife? How could you do it, Richard?"

"I'm sorry. Come home, please."

I pressed at my eyes and remembered the last four years: us riding together, shopping together, lying together, laughing together. It felt like a lifetime of happiness.

"Gawthorpe is not the same place without you. It's our home, we should be there together."

"You are never there!"

"I am. I want to be there, with you."

"All these secrets, Richard. And lies." I remembered Alice's words: *I am afraid of lies.* Now I knew what she meant: lies had the power to destroy lives but also create them. "I am happy here."

"Happy? With your mother? You cannot stand your mother." He did not lower his voice. "What is there for you here apart from idle servants and dusty rooms?"

"If they are dusty it's because you do not give my mother enough money," I whispered. "Something I would never, *never* have suspected seeing as I brought most of it to this family."

He reached into his pocket for his purse. "How much more does she need?"

"How much do you pay for your mistress?" He sighed, drawing open the bag and setting some coins on the mantel, as though he was paying my lodgings at an inn. "That is four women to pay for now, is it not? Two mothers and two wives? I suppose it's no coincidence that standards slipped here when you added another household to your stable. Did you know the poverty you were keeping my mother in?"

"Of course not. If she needs anything, she need only ask. I will make it right. Perhaps James made some adjustments to balance the books that I was not aware of."

"Then I will ask James why he has been sending sweet soap to Barton while my mother's staff make hers by themselves."

A smile played at the corners of his lips, and I knew he was amused that I was defending my mother, and my chest churned with rage. But I did not smile, or speak, only waited with my hands clasping the arms of my chair. He could not tease me into forgetting he had taken a month to come to me.

Dressed in his fine black velvet robe and doublet he must have been warm, and I could see the sweat on his forehead. "I have come to bring you home," he said finally. He was not used to me disobeying him. I was not used to disobeying him.

"How long have you kept her?"

He pinched in his cheeks, then exhaled, blowing out his mouth as though I was testing him. "Not long."

"How long?"

"A few months?"

"So she is fertile, then. Success at last — a prize breeder. And you the sire of a fine calf, which is more than your wife can give you."

"Don't make yourself ridiculous. People are not cattle."

"Women and cattle are very similar, actually."

"You are being absurd."

The chessboard caught my eye and I lifted an ivory pawn, holding it up to catch the light. I recognized it immediately as being my father's set from Barton. I set it back in its place and saw it was before the queen. Using the pawn I bumped her off, sending the piece crashing to the floor where she rolled on the threadbare carpet.

"Will you have me executed, like the king?" I said.

"Fleetwood, I *care* about you. Do you think I wish to see you so ill? Every time you have carried a child you have almost died, and it is my fault for making you that way. I did not mean for this to happen — I turned to Judith as a way to stop it from happening, to protect you."

"To protect me? Keeping your mistress in my house was to protect me?"

"You hate that house, I knew you would never go there."

"And you were right. You know me better than anyone, Richard. Except you forgot one thing — that I could read, and you thought I would never go in James's study and find out all the things you had written down. They were there for me to see all along."

"How did you know to look in the ledger?"

My heart began to beat faster. "I needed to check something."

"What?"

"An order of linen. It is not important." I tried to act dismissive but he was a hunter, and he had caught the scent. His eyes narrowed.

"Who did you come here with?"

"No one."

I stared him down, and he did not like what he saw, for he said, "You have changed, Fleetwood." I waited, but he said no more, only impatiently, "Are we not to be given refreshments?"

I did not speak, and turned my face to the gray window.

Richard shifted uncomfortably in his seat. "Roger came not long ago with a parcel for you." I watched him from the corner of my eye. "The ruby necklace."

"The one that went missing?"

"His maid found it at the bottom of Jennet Device's bed. She is a schemer, clearly."

"She is a thief. But she had no opportunity — I did not leave her for a moment." But then I remembered my journey down to the kitchen for Roger's cold pie, and my heart sank. "Did she leave the hall at any point?"

"I suppose she must have."

"I suppose you apologized to the servants?"

A flicker of shame crossed his face, and as we sat in furious silence, the other events of that day flooded back to me — how so much had happened. "And the chambermaid Sarah — how is she?"

"Not recovered, but better. The doctor arrived in time. She is still being cared for by her mother."

"Are you sleeping in our chamber?"

He shifted again. "Yes. I have brought our carriage here, for you to take back to Gawthorpe. I have some business with my agent on the border, so I will go on to Carlisle before coming home. You can leave tomorrow."

I thought of Alice, upstairs resting on her truckle bed or kneeling in the garden or walking through the woods. I thought of what might be waiting for her if we went back. "I cannot come back."

Something seemed to stir in Richard, and he spread his fingers wide, his rings glittering, then clenched his fists. He licked his lips, picked a bit of fluff from his sleeve. "As sorry as I am, my patience is wearing thin. No man wants an unruly wife. There

is a fine line between being tolerant and being made a fool of."

Tears sprung in my eyes, hot and angry.
"And I suppose you have not made a fool
of me? I am no different from one of your
precious falcons. You have me on a leash,
then with a flick of your wrist I am back at
your arm."

At last he had the modesty to look ag-
grieved. Even as I spoke, I knew I was acting outside the boundaries of womanliness,
of wifeliness. I did not have a beautiful face
nor the manners to go with it. It was hardly
a surprise he left our bed and with it our
union, I thought miserably.

"It is time for you to settle into your new
role," was all he said.

"As a neglected wife?"

"As a mother."

"I wish to stay here a little longer."

At that moment, as though she had been
waiting for her name to be mentioned, there
was a sharp knock on the door and my
mother came in.

"You have readied her things?" Richard
asked. She nodded, and glanced once at me.

"I will not go," I said.

Light and thin as a knife through butter,
my mother's words sliced me in half. "You
will not stay here while your husband needs

you. It's time for you to leave."

I stood up from my chair and drew myself up to my full, unimpressive height, and said coldly, "If that is your wish, so be it."

Richard went farther north on his horse, and I went to my chamber, and by the time I had reached the top of the staircase a plan had formed in my mind, and I immediately relayed it to Alice. "You can return to Gawthorpe with me, as my midwife and companion, and those are the terms on which I'll forgive Richard."

But Alice looked unsure, and twisted her cap in her hands. Her hair was a mass of sprung gold, coiled and twisted like a lion's mane. "Does he ask for forgiveness?" was all she said.

"He betrayed me. Alice, come back with me and I will see to it. I'll see that your name is cleared — that will be my price. Richard will meet it. We will go back to Gawthorpe and have you a bed made and in a day or two Richard will arrive home and I will lay out my terms. That for me to stay, you must stay, too. I cannot deliver this child without you."

Doubt was written all over her face, but I knew my husband. I thought I knew everything.

We packed our things — or I packed mine, because all Alice had was what she wore. She had no trunk, no wedding ring, no husband calling her home, no sisters-in-law to pay calls on. No child in her stomach, no heir to produce. She could go anywhere, anytime, and if she had wanted to I would have let her, even when I knew I needed her more than anyone. But she climbed in the caroche beside me, just as she had on the way here. I decided I would give her a horse again when we got home — never mind the business with the other one, for I knew now that I trusted her — and she could ride to visit her father when Richard agreed my terms, and tell him she'd found a permanent position. But what would we find at home? For the first time since Alice told me her story, I thought of the Pendle witches and what would become of them. Perhaps Roger had not been able to build a case against the people at Malkin Tower; perhaps he was satisfied with the Devices and their neighbors, and tossed Nick Bannister's list in the fire.

I held my stomach, and as the carriage rocked on the uneven road and my child bucked and rolled with it, I wondered how anyone could consider coaches safer than riding. Puck whimpered at my feet, tired of the constant motion, for the journey was long. I told him we would be home soon, and I would have milk and bread brought for him, and he licked my hand with a comforting tongue.

I lost interest in my surroundings after a few hours; the sky grew more gray, and the rain fell very lightly, making everything dull again. Alice's eyes were closed, her head tipped back against the seat. I wondered if she was really awake, worrying like I was about what would happen when we were back. Even my child, who often made sleeping uncomfortable, was still.

The last part of the journey became a race against the creeping dark, and eventually I felt the carriage slow and turn into the approach to Gawthorpe. The darkness had a blacker quality here, with the woods dense on both sides. The horses' hooves clattered on cobbles: we were at the barn and outbuildings. We slowed to a stop and I heard the coachman tell someone in the yard he was instructed to take me direct to the door. By that point, thick with sleep, I'd forgotten Alice was there. We'd spent so much time together I no longer knew what it was to be on my own. The carriage was so dark I could not tell if she was awake, and I longed for my bed. I would put Alice in the room next door where Richard had slept, so that when he arrived home he might share our bed again. Perhaps he and Alice might become friends, with the necklace mystery resolved.

We slowed to a stop. The horses exhaled and shook themselves. The coachman moved around above us, then I heard his feet hit the ground. I moved first, but the carriage door sprang open before me and I almost tumbled out.

Richard was standing there. His face was hidden in shadow, and before I could speak or even exclaim in surprise, he took my wrist and helped me out. My feet hit solid ground, and I heard Puck jump out behind me, and then two things happened at once: Alice stepped out of the carriage behind me, and I saw Roger Nowell standing at the top of the steps.

Neither he nor Richard had spoken, and I could not see their faces properly in the darkness. The torches flamed on either side of the doorway, twisting this way and that. I felt as though someone had poured cold water down my back. "Richard, what are you doing here?" I said. He still had hold of my arm.

Roger's voice came from the steps. "Alice Gray, you are under arrest for the murder by witchcraft of Ann Foulds, daughter of John Foulds of Colne, and will be a prisoner of His Majesty until your time of reckoning." In a moment he was upon her, moving quick as a shadow.

"Roger!" I cried. "What is this?"

But Richard began to pull me up the steps to the open door. I twisted wildly, trying to shake him off. "Alice! What is this? Roger, Richard, tell me at once. *Alice!* Get off me."

I pushed him with all my strength and ran down the steps but he took hold of me once again, locking my arms behind me.

"Fleetwood!" Alice cried, her cap and face the only visible things in the glow from the torches.

Roger's dark bulk was forcing her back into the carriage. She was sobbing, and frightened, and disappearing before my eyes, but I could still hear her, saying "no, no, no."

One of the horses whinnied in fright, straining against its harness. Then I was in the house, and Richard was closing the door with his free hand. It thudded shut, and I was inside, and she was out.

■ ■ ■ ■

PART THREE

■ ■ ■ ■

"A man also or woman that hath a familiar
spirit, or that is a wizard, shall surely be
put to death. They shall stone them with
stones. Their blood shall be upon them."
LEVITICUS 20:27

CHAPTER FIFTEEN

Richard dropped me like a hot coal and disappeared down the passage into the great hall. I threw myself at the door and felt for the handle, pulling it open to see the carriage moving away, out of the pool of torchlight. I ran down the steps, almost falling over my trunk that was lying at the bottom of them, and raced to catch up with it, shouting her name at the window, but the drape remained closed. "Stop!" I called. "Stop!"

The coachman remained facing indifferently forward, hunched over the reins. I fell back as it picked up speed and watched the night swallow it whole, the sound of the wheels and horses' hooves growing fainter. The trees shivered around the clearing — it was a cold night for July. It was always cold here.

I stood for a long time in the blackness until the chill soaked right through to the deepest parts of me. My body felt as though it was submerged in water, anchored to the ground, my gown impossibly heavy. Two boys lifted the trunk behind me and carried it into the house.

I had led her right to the center of the web, to where the spider was waiting.

I found Richard in the great hall, waiting for me at the empty fireplace. All I could do was stare at him. "You tricked me. You lied to me!"

"And you tricked and lied to me."

"How so?"

"You told me the girl was not with you."

"You laid a trap — you had us ride into it. How *could* you . . ."

"Alice Gray is wanted for a crime. Whether she was arrested here or at your mother's, it matters not."

"It does matter. Who told you she was there — your sisters?"

"No, your mother. Inadvertently, of course. I'm not sure even she would betray her own daughter. She wrote to me and spoke of a lively young midwife named Jill, who you had brought with you. She wanted to know if Mistress Starkie had recommended her. You might do better to cover your scent next time. I thought you were a skilled huntress."

I breathed in deeply, and out, trying to control my anger. "Why has Alice been arrested?"

"I do not know all the details."

"Roger said she murdered a child? What nonsense."

"You know that, do you?"

"Of course I do. She would not harm a fly."

"Then she will have nothing to fear."

"Roger is on a quest for power," I said. "He is only doing this to appease the king and display his authority like some painted peacock. He does not care about the consequences, that people's lives are at stake. How many more *witches* has he found since I've been away?"

"I don't know."

"How many?"

"About ten. It has not been difficult for him. They are giving him the names, thinking it will buy them their freedom. They are doing the accusing, not him."

"We must do something."

Richard's temper boiled over. He had been pacing in front of the fireplace, and now he fixed me with the full force of his wrath. "We must do *nothing,*" he cried. "You have done enough."

I thought back to that rainy day in April when Roger and I stood in the long gallery. *Shame on him who thinks evil of it.* I reached for a chair and held the back of it, reluctant to do something so domestic as sitting down.

"You have left me without a midwife," I said eventually.

"There are plenty of others, Fleetwood. I do not know why you insisted on using some local slattern who may or may not have killed a child — is that who you want delivering our child?"

"Yes."

"We will send for another one."

"I will not have another."

"Then you will die. Is that what you want?"

"Perhaps. It's what you want."

"Don't be so ridiculous."

I gripped the chair harder. "Alice is not easily replaced. Tell me, Richard, why are you allowed to keep a woman and I am not?"

Blood pounded in my ears. My knuckles were white. I waited. When he didn't say anything, his face tight and furious, I went on. "Alice Gray saved my life, not just once but many times. When I itched, she brought me plants to rub on my skin. When I was

290

sick, she made me tinctures. She kept me company when I was at my lowest. She planted a garden for my health."

"Sounds like a witch to me," Richard said bitterly. "How else would she know those things?"

"She is a midwife, like her mother before her. Are you like the king now, thinking all wise women and poor women and midwives are carrying out the Devil's work? Why, he must be the largest employer in Lancaster."

I suddenly felt very tired, and had to sit. My gown was dusty from traveling, and part of my mind was still in the carriage with Alice and Roger, journeying into the darkness. My head ached with it all.

"Richard, where will Roger take Alice?"

"Perhaps Read Hall. Perhaps straight to Lancaster."

"But the assizes aren't until August."

I heard his boots on the flags and the next thing, he was kneeling beside me, his gold earring glinting in the candlelight. "Forget Alice," he said. "You have done enough for her."

"Forget her? I have done nothing for her! What can you mean? The only thing I *have* done is lead her directly to the trap you set for us."

"It was not a trap. My only concern was

291

your safety. Once I heard who Alice was I acted straightaway, of course I did. What has *happened* to you, Fleetwood? You are a different person since she came along."

He sounded so hateful. I wiped my nose with my sleeve and wanted desperately to lie down.

"I want to go to Read Hall," I said.

"You will do no such thing. It's late," Richard said.

Again, I was thwarted, bound by my invisible leash. It was strange: I was sitting in my house with my husband and dog, but had never felt more wretched. For a long time they had been enough, but now I felt like a visitor in my own life. I looked around at the dark windows, the shiny panels and the gallery where players and minstrels performed in happier times. There were the coats of arms above the fireplace, mine included; there were the pair of doors so two people of the same rank could enter at the same time. Was this really my house?

Richard helped me to my feet and I kept one hand on Puck's head to go upstairs. The staircase was dark, and I was already half-asleep.

So much had happened since the last time I was in my chamber it felt like a new room. I stared at the bed I designed as a fanciful young bride, with its frame decorated with knights' helmets, crowns and serpents. In the center, two crests were carved in one: the three shuttles and the mullet for Shuttleworth, six martlets for Fleetwood. I had refused to use the Barton crest.

Richard slept next to me that night, whether in solidarity or guilt, it did not matter to me. Puck slept on the floor at the foot of the bed, snoring loudly, and for once Richard did not complain. I stared for a long time at the canopy, and my thoughts raced from one side of my head to the other. Alice was accused of killing the daughter of a man named John. Had the child died in birth while she was delivering it? Or could it be a tale, borne of revenge from the tongue of Elizabeth Device? Perhaps John Foulds was a friend of Roger's with a long-dead daughter in the churchyard, made richer for agreeing to pedal his lies.

I waited for sleep, and knowing there was no curled figure at the foot of my bed, it did not come easily.

The next morning I took my time getting ready, washing properly after so much time on the road. I soaped my hair and combed it, letting it dry down my back before I dressed. Prudence and Justice watched vacantly as I got into my things: I had little need for a maid now I did not wear a corset. I took a clean collar from my wardrobe and a pearl headdress and fixed them in place. I tied my silk stockings above and below my knees even though my swollen legs kept them up easily, and I put on my slippers. A dab of rose oil went behind my ears and at my wrists, and I rubbed my teeth with linen and spat into the used bathwater that was scudded with sweat and grease and dust from traveling. Then I opened the door for Puck to go with me to breakfast.

I was still tired and sick from my journey, and all I could think of was Alice. The food here was bland and I picked at it, thinking of the cherries and gingerbread and butter pies we'd eaten at my mother's. Everything was duller here.

On the other side of the table Richard breakfasted with his Turkish falcon on his shoulder like some mythical knight of the realm. If he was trying to provoke me after I'd compared myself to his bird, it was working. I watched him, not touching my plate. He seemed cheerful and occupied, oblivious to my presence. Perhaps he had grown used to my absence, like I'd had to with his.

I swirled my spoon around in my oats and

pretended to sip my beer. "I wish you would not bring that creature in the house." Though I'd attempted to sound concerned, it came out spiteful. The bird regarded me with one serpent-like eye.

"I am getting her used to me. She likes to see where her master lives — don't you?"

"What if it breaks free of its leash and flies up into the rafters?"

"Be ever well in blood, for otherwise she will not long be at your commandment but make you follow her." I stared at him, and he grinned. "The first rule of falconry and hawking. All it takes is a bit of meat to coax her down."

"What if that bit of meat is a servant's finger?"

Richard winked; he was in a careless mood.

"I will go to Read Hall this morning," I announced.

"To see Katherine?"

I licked my dry lips. "Yes."

"I won't join you. I have leases to draw with James."

"What for?"

"I am buying up some land left by a farmer. Do you know, his son said he buried a cat in the wall of his house when he built it?"

"Why would he do that?"

He shrugged. "To ward off evil? These local folk can be very queer. Glass windows would do it just as well."

I realized he'd made a joke and forced my face into a smile. He had given me an idea.

I rode slowly on horseback to Read, taking my time, glad of the fresh air and space to think. Passing the same old dwellings and farmhouses on the same old roads, I saw face after face, all of them wearing their hard lives like a hood. Everybody went trudging along, their heads wrapped, their shoulders hunched against pain and illness and grief. Their houses were made of mud; their backs stooped from work. I hoped they had moments of brightness in their lives: I hoped they bit into cherries and felt the surprise of the stone. If they built a playhouse here, there would be no need for witch-hunting. Perhaps I would build one.

The sky was white and the land green, and once you grew tired of looking at one or the other there was not much else to see on the road to Read. I drew up to the house, and apart from a boy carrying hay to the stable, there was no one about. I gave him my horse and went to the door, knocking and waiting what felt like a long time before knocking again. When the door opened, I expected to see Katherine but no one was there — then I realized the person who opened it only reached my chest, and I looked down into wide, watery eyes.

"Jennet," I said, trying to hide my surprise. "I am here for Master Nowell."

The little girl stared. " 'E int home. 'E's gone," she whispered. Her skin was so pale it was almost silver.

My stomach twisted. "Gone where?"

"Jennet?" came a voice within the house. Katherine appeared behind her. Her green eyes were wide, her face tighter and thinner than when I'd last seen her.

I swallowed. "Hello, Katherine."

"Fleetwood." She wrung her hands together and stopped a few feet short of the door. "Jennet, get away from there, I told you not to answer the door. Get upstairs now." Although her words were scolding, her voice was desperate.

The child leaped away and disappeared into the house.

"Katherine, is Roger home?"

"No, he's gone to Lancaster."

"With Alice?"

"Alice?"

"Alice, my midwife, Alice."

Katherine blinked, her white hands clutching at each other. "I don't understand.

Would you come in? I'll fetch some wine . . ."

"No, thank you. I need to know if Roger has taken Alice to Lancaster."

"He went out last night and hasn't returned — he told me that's where he was going."

So he didn't put all his charges up in his house like an innkeeper. Just the ones he wanted something from. I took a step back and sighed, thinking of what to do. "Do you know a man named John Foulds?"

Her face crumpled in confusion. "I'm afraid not. Should I?" I shook my head. "Roger said you were with your mother in Kirkby Lonsdale for a spell?" Katherine asked pleasantly. "Was it . . . enjoyable?"

"Very. I have to go. I'm sorry, Katherine."

She wavered at her door like a woman on the edge of a drop, as though she might jump and come with me. "Don't go. You've just arrived! Stay for dinner."

I called goodbye again and went straight to the stable, where my horse was still drinking from the trough. I waited for it to finish before going back the way I'd come.

My head was thick with trying to understand how I'd got us into this mess and how I could get us out of it, and the ride back to Gawthorpe was a slower one. I dismounted and stood in the yard with a frown on my face, my hands still holding the reins. But there was something I needed from the house before I went on the road again.

Richard was in the great hall with James, surrounded by papers. "You are back early," he said. "Was Katherine well?"

"Fine," I said absently. "I am looking for the dog. Have you seen him?"

James cleared his throat and told me he'd last seen Puck in the parlor.

"I am going riding."

"Is that wise?"

"Alice said so, and she has not steered me wrong thus far." I held his stare. "I'll be back in a few hours." I would be much longer than that, but far away enough for them not to be able to do anything about it.

Richard's face was half amused, half annoyed. "Do you know, James," he said to the steward, "I wonder if the king has some sense in wanting to tighten the reins on Lancaster's women. They are lawless, are they not?"

There was a hint of malice about him as he looked closely at me. I'd seen the same glint of it at my mother's in the moment he decided he would tell me what to do, for the first time in our marriage. Now he was exercising his authority like a muscle, testing my limit and his, and never failing to remind me who was master.

"I know not, Master," James replied soberly.

"They are wild, are they not?" he asked me.

"They are also harmless," I replied carefully.

"And who will be the judge of that?" Richard did not look away, so I smiled clumsily and left the room, but before I disappeared he called me back. "I am on business in Ripon today and will be away for the night."

I paused with my hand on the door. "When will you be back?"

"Late tomorrow, or the morning after. But worry not — James will be here to keep an eye on you."

I wished him a successful trip and went to find the dog. With him away, I could flap about on my leash, and when he was at home I would return to his arm. James did not concern me, for there was nothing he could do apart from tell tales when Richard got home, and by then I'd be installed in my parlor amusing myself like a good little wife.

I found Puck in a warm spot beneath the window and roused him from his nap to go with me. Walking across the bottom of the staircase, I felt the presence of my mother's portrait at the top of the tower, as though she was standing on the gallery looking down at me. I shuddered and stepped back out into the chill morning with my dog at my side.

CHAPTER SIXTEEN

It was market day in Padiham, and the village was thronged with horses and carts and people. I rode into the stable yard at the Hand and Shuttle, barely registering the curious glances that fell on my dog and me. I took him inside with me and asked a young boy with a rag in his hand for the landlord. He went off down the corridor I walked down not so long ago, before Alice told me to open my eyes. Now I wished I could close them. The same man as before with a ruddy face and rotten teeth appeared, his expression lively and inquisitive. "I did not introduce myself last time I was here," I said quietly. "My name is Fleetwood Shuttleworth. I live at Gawthorpe Hall."

"I know who you are," he replied, not unpleasantly. "I'm William Tufnell the landlord."

That was when he noticed Puck at my side and almost jumped out of his skin. "No dogs allowed in here, Mistress, I'm sorry. Even yours."

I nodded, glancing around and noticing the fireplace Alice would have swept and the tables she'd wiped. "I won't take a minute of your time. I only have one thing to ask," I said. "Have you ever heard of John Foulds or his daughter Ann?"

He looked blankly back at me. "No one of that name in Padiham. And if he's got a hand to lift a tankard he'll have been in here."

"There is an inn in Colne, the Queen's Arms?"

"Aye," he said warily.

"I believe one of your employees came from there to here, looking for work."

"My brother-in-law passed on a girl, aye. She's not here anymore, though."

I regarded him coolly and nodded. "What is your brother-in-law's name? Is he the landlord?"

"Peter, Mistress. And yes."

The Queen's Arms was on the edge of the village a few miles upriver, and I imagined Alice helping a feeble and petrified John Law along the pack road and into the doorway. It was a small inn, no bigger than an alehouse, with the same smell of damp beer once I crossed the threshold. The place was empty, the benches and tables were old but well scrubbed, and there was fresh sawdust on the floor.

I left Puck outside, tying his leash to a post. A woman with a broom stood in a doorway behind the bar, talking loudly, telling a story. I waited for her to finish, my hands clasped in front of me.

The woman realized she was being watched, as anyone does after a while, because the skin sees things the eyes do not. Her mouth fell open in a rude way. "Can I help you?" She looked me up and down, clasping the broomstick in her red hands.

"My name is Fleetwood Shuttleworth. I am looking for Peter the landlord."

She could easily have called, but she went through the doorway and I heard her whispering. A moment later, a great barrel of a man with a shock of white hair stepped through the door. He was so large I felt his boots hit the packed earth floor. "Can I help?"

"Are you Peter, who employed Alice Gray?"

"If I had a feather in my hat for every person came in here asking for Alice Gray, I'd look like a chicken. What's she done now?"

His choice of words surprised me. "She has done nothing. I wondered where I might find her father."

"Joe Gray? What do you want with him?"

"I wish to speak with him."

"He don't say much worth listening to." I waited. "He lives about a half a mile that way, along the woolpack trail then right, a little way up where the trees stop. What'll you want with him?"

"That is my business. Who else has been asking for Alice?"

"Oh." He waved a large hand. "Some magistrate, t'other week. I said are you sure you've got right person? Before that all't'remnants of society, some right creatures in here all hours. God knew what they wanted with her."

"You mean Demdike? And Elizabeth Device?"

"Demdike, aye. It means demon woman, did you know that? Two families around here have been locked away for witchcraft now, would you believe — the Devices and old Chattox and her daughter. Some folk were telling me they're neighbors at war with each other, both of them in with the Devil. And that little'en who was here a few month ago, asking after that poor boor she'd cursed. Good riddance, the lot of them. I'm not having their sort in here — folk won't come if they know witches have been in. That's why I had to let Alice go, they were always asking after her. Years, she worked for me. But she were scaring the customers, that ugly wench who kept coming in."

"So you let her go," I said coldly.

"She were caught up in it, rightly or wrongly."

"All she did was bring that poor man back here."

"I wish she hadn't bothered. Brought me nothing but grief, he did. Wailing and weeping about dogs in his room and needles and curses. He's the one needed locking up but she begged me to let him stay."

I looked around at the empty tables and chairs, the full barrels waiting to be drained into men's bellies. He had a business to run, and there might have been some truth in what he was saying, but he was wrong to get rid of Alice, because in doing so he'd implicated her of wrongdoing.

"Do you know John Foulds?" I asked eventually.

"You want him as well, then, do you? She has bad luck with men, does Alice, what with her old dad and John Foulds."

The hairs on the back of my neck stood up. "I beg your pardon?"

"He comes in here, now and again. Well, he used to until . . . He's not been in a while. I don't know where he is."

"Until what?"

Peter reached round to scratch the side of his large belly. "His daughter died not long ago. How long would it be now, Margaret? Six months or so, I reckon."

"And he and Alice . . ."

"Well, they were courting. He'd been married before — his wife died. She kept her cards close to her chest did Alice, never did let on much. But they never did marry. You'll not find Alice around here anyway, sorry to disappoint. If you're asking her dad he might not have much idea either. You could try at the Hand and Shuttle, that's where she works now, in Padiham."

"What does he look like?" My mouth was dry; a cup of beer would have been welcome.

"John? Dark hair, tall. Handsome chap, until the drink takes hold of him, eh, Margaret? I've seen you having a look." Margaret rolled her eyes and slapped his arm.

So the man who'd upset her in the passage at the Hand and Shuttle was John Foulds. The idea that Alice had murdered his daughter was impossible. And she his lover? He had a fine face, but idleness and

307

wastefulness radiated from him like light from the sun.

Soon news would get out of Alice's arrest and Peter's tables would fill up again with people wanting to know. I thanked Peter and his wife flatly, and before I went to get my horse I looked up at the little windows on the second floor of the inn. I wondered which one John Law the peddler had looked out of from his sickbed, if he had at all.

The road at the side wound down to Colne one way and ran out into open fields and copses of trees on the other. Birds sang around me, and the joyful chorus they made rang empty in my ears as I rode slowly away from the town into wide green pastures. The road was muddy underfoot, and my horse's feet were unsteady. Puck padded heavily beside me, and in the quiet and clear air I had time to think.

I knew so little about Alice, and she knew so much about me. She told me once that she came close to marrying, and that must have been John. She missed her mother dearly, and found a kindred spirit in her old friend Mouldheels. She did not speak often of her father, and when she did, it was not with warmth. All these little things I knew, but they were like details at the corners of a picture: I could not see the full thing.

The road cut through a wooded area, with trees as tall as houses. I shivered as I thought of John Law meeting Alizon on this same path. It was darker here, and noisy with the rustling of the leaves and calls of the birds. I kept my eyes straight ahead until it opened into wide fields, trying to shake off the feeling that I was being watched. Just as Peter had said, the land began to rise up on the right, and a low, dark house squatted on the hillside. A mud track led up to it, so we squelched through, trying to avoid the worst of it. A thin thread of smoke drifted briefly out of a chimney into the air, only to be carried in all directions by the wind. The house was not much taller than I was, smaller even than the buttery at home. It was made of wattle and daub with a thatched roof, and the windows were not glazed but had shutters that were open to let the light in. A low wall surrounded the cottage, and flowers lay dying or dead in their beds. A few colorful heads peered from beneath the weeds like lanterns. I remembered Alice talking of her mother's herb garden and thought it must be round the back. The house was exposed on the hillside: it would have been difficult to protect growing things from the wind and driving rain here.

I rapped smartly on the door and a few moments later it opened. Joseph Gray was older than I expected: older even than Roger. Or it might have been that he looked that way because he was poor. Hunched over, he gave the impression of constant movement even when he was still: his body shook and his mouth worked, speaking silent thoughts. His cream-colored hair was tinged with gray and hung in spirals like Alice's down to his shoulders. His eyes were a clear blue, and he was thin. His clothes hung off him and looked as though they needed leaving in lye for a week. "Mr. Gray?" I said. "I am Fleet—"

"I know who you are," he muttered. "She worked for you, didn't she? Come in. I suppose you've got summat to tell me."

It was very warm in the house: the fire in the middle of the room burned as merrily as if it was December, not July. The rising smoke escaped from a hole in the center of the roof of the cottage, and I thought how cold and drafty it must be with an opening to the weather. Two low beds stood on either side of the fire — one unmade — and lengths of cloth hung over the earth walls that would no doubt be damp and cold to touch. A table, two stools and a cupboard were the only furniture. By the fire on the rush-covered floor lay some pewter pots and pans that looked used but not washed. So Alice and her father cooked, slept and lived in this house full of holes that the wind whistled through all hours.

"I suppose you're here about the nag?" Joseph spoke.

"The nag?" I asked.

"The nag you give our Alice. You've got it back though now so I don't want no trouble."

I stared blankly at him. "The horse I lent her, that went missing?"

"Aye." His mouth did not stop moving even when he was not speaking and I wondered if he was chewing tobacco. I had no idea what he meant, and said so. "I gave the money back. And was she grateful? Was she fuck."

He ambled over to his bed and sat on it. I remained where I was, struggling to breathe in the oppressive heat from the fire. Joseph licked his lips and picked a tankard off the floor, examining its contents and throwing them into his mouth.

So that's what happened to the gray draft horse: Alice's father had sold it. And she, somehow, had got it back. My chest felt heavy suddenly, and for a brief moment I felt overcome with emotion. But I straightened my skirts and continued. "Mr. Gray, I am not here about the horse. I have it back now, so no matter. I am here because Alice has been arrested by the magistrate Roger Nowell, who seems to be under the impression she has murdered a child."

His eyes were glazed and vacant, resting on the fire, and after a few seconds he pulled them with difficulty toward me. "Eh?" he said.

"Mr. Gray, your daughter is in a great deal of trouble. I will do everything I can to help her but I thought you must know about these fatal claims. She has been taken to Lancaster gaol to await the assizes next month, but it can't get that far. I won't let it. Mr. Gray, are you listening to me?"

"Bet you don't even need that horse, do you? What's one more nag to you? Bet you have a whole stable of 'em lined up like soldiers, waiting to be called to attention." He gave a half-hearted salute and again tipped his grubby tankard into his mouth, though it appeared to be empty.

"Mr. Gray! Are you listening to me? Your daughter is accused of being a witch and is in gaol. Do you know anything about this?"

He burped. "Guess she'll be going same way as her mother, then." He drew a line with one finger along his neck.

My mouth fell open. "She could be hanged, and you don't care? You have no interest in helping her?"

"What I have an interest in . . . is . . ." He lost his words and grew vacant again. "Where is my ale coming from? Cos it int from her! Or that closefisted bugger Peter whatever-his-name-is. He is only down the road, but now I have to go farther cos he won't serve me. I'm an old man, Mistress What's-Yer-Name."

The heat was so intense, the fire blinding and Joseph Gray so infuriating and strange, I felt I couldn't stay for a single second longer in his hovel. But I had come for a reason, and I owed Alice everything. I moved slowly to go to the unmade bed in the dampest corner of the room. Even the great barn at Gawthorpe was warmer, and drier — no wonder she had taken so easily to the idea of going with me to my mother's.

There was something lying on her bed — a bundle of rags, though it might have been something a cat dragged in. I lifted its damp, lifeless form — not a creature, but old wool, crudely sewn. Made as though from a handkerchief, it appeared to be a human form, stuffed with hair, with a head, and two arms and legs. There was a curious mass attached to it, and though the smoke and the heat were overwhelming, my skin went cold when I realized it was the figure of a child bound with hair to a woman. Black hair. I remembered the strands covering my pillow, and how they disappeared. Inexplicably, my eyes filled with tears, and I set the poppet back on the bed. There was the faintest scent of lavender, then it disappeared.

"Mr. Gray," I said, going back to where he sat jerking and muttering. "Alice told me about her mother. Jill." I waited for a response, and something stirred in his blank blue eyes. His head snapped as though he was dreaming. "She misses her very much, as I'm sure you do. You have already had one member of your family taken away — would you not do everything in your power to stop it happening to Alice? She is the only family you have."

He was staring wildly at something I could not see. With difficulty, I crouched down, my skirts bunching around me. "Your daughter has been very loyal to me, and helped me greatly over the past months. I am sorry that I took her away from you," I lied. I was not sorry that I had taken her from this damp, smoky cottage on its lonely hill, nor from her useless father or brutish employer. Not one bit.

"I will help her. She has helped me and now I must return her kindness." The smoke was stinging my eyes; perhaps Joseph thought I was moved to tears, when really I was full of a terror I had never known. I wished for sadness: that was easy, and came with things past rather than uncertain things ahead. "Mr. Gray," I said again.

His bland gaze cleared and he focused again. His lips parted and I thought he would speak, but he showed all his brown teeth, and it was a moment before I realized he was laughing. "They burn witches, don't they?" he wheezed, pointing at the fire.

"What?" I stood, even more alarmed.

He pointed at my skirts. "They burn witches!"

Flames were licking the bottom of my gown. Puck began barking, and horror hit me with such force I was almost blind with it. I ran to the door and flapped my skirts desperately in the open air, and the flames seemed to falter but did not go out. I looked around in desperation for a trough, any- thing, and found an old bucket against the wall filled with rainwater. With Puck bark- ing and tearing around me, I tipped the whole thing over the side of my gown, and as the brown water puddled around my feet I looked for the bright flames, barely visible in daylight, but they were gone.

Inside, Joseph Gray was laughing. I stood there panting, and Puck was circling with his back to me as though fending off an invisible army, his jaws snapping and his barks echoing down the hillside. The wind pulled at me from every angle and drew fine, dark threads of smoke away from my ruined gown. The ruby red of my skirts had gone black and gaped in a horrible wound. I don't know how long I stayed like that, but Joseph Gray did not come out, and it took me a long time to stop shaking enough to climb onto my horse. When I was up, I broke into a canter, with Puck streaking behind me, and I could not have gone faster if I was running from the Devil himself.

That night, something visited me in my chamber where I slept alone. I woke up because I felt warm fur brush against my hand. It was pitch-black, and all I could hear was my own breathing. I felt a weight shift on the bed somewhere near my feet. My breath died in my throat, my ears sang, my skin prickled. It moved again, as though getting comfortable. I imagined Joseph Gray standing in my dark chamber with a dead rabbit hanging from his dirty fist.

I closed my eyes and willed my heart to

stop hammering.

It was only a dream. I knew it was not. I felt the weight disappear from near my legs, then there was the softest, slightest sound of something landing on the floor. It was too light to be Puck, too silent. I knew it was not Puck. My hands stayed where they were on top of the bedclothes, frozen. I knew there was something in the room with me just as I knew there was a child in my stomach and Richard was not beside me. The child kicked.

I can feel it, too. I waited: either nothing would happen or I would die of fright. Though everything was black, I saw it move toward the door, and then it was gone, though the door was shut. I *saw* it. Black has different shades, just like white.

Earlier, I'd crept into the house and hurried upstairs wrapped in my cloak like a smuggler. After shoving it into the wardrobe, I'd gone to my chamber and noisily pretended a candle had fallen, burning my dress. "Oh!" I shouted, hearing myself and almost believing it. "Oh, oh!" I blew it out so it would still feel hot and placed it on the floor by my feet. "My gown!" I cried when one of the chambermaids came in.

She was frightened; she probably thought I was losing the child. She guided me to sit down, and I puffed and panted and pretended I was scared, which wasn't difficult: all I had to do was think of Joseph Gray's wide, glassy eyes and his house, which was like something from a nightmare.

I lay awake as my sweaty face dried and my heart slowed and the child inside went back to sleep. I thought of Alice. My nightmare happened when my eyes were closed. Alice's was happening when hers were open. Her father's words came to me in the darkness: *They burn witches, don't they?*

I tried to picture Alice as a child, growing up in that drafty house with her strange father and kind mother. Though I'd met two people from her life, I had no better understanding of her, the girl who did not know her own birthday and could not spell her name, but who had a masculine intelligence, and knew the properties of everything in the earth, and bargained sold horses back like a tradesman. I closed my eyes and prayed she was safe.

CHAPTER SEVENTEEN

The next morning I rose in the moments before sunrise and dressed quickly in the near dark, trying not to come across any servants. I unlocked the front door and slipped outside, closing it gently behind me and pocketing the key. The summer morning was before me, and I would have thought it glorious in another year, another lifetime. I yawned and watched the trees rustling awake, then I went to the stables. The cattle were lowing in the great barn, eager for their feed. The river sighed behind the house. I had to walk much more slowly now, so I noticed these things. One of the stable boys was dressed, a bucket in each hand, and I sent him to saddle my horse. When he came back, I thanked him, and told him I had a message to pass to him.

"Please go and find James later, and tell him I will be out all day, and he is not to tell the master about it when he returns.

Tell him if the master finds out, I will throw his precious ledgers on a fire and he will have to rewrite them from memory. Can you remember that?"

The boy, whose name was Simon, and who was probably only three or four years younger than me, nodded gleefully, thrilled at the prospect of delivering a threat to his superior.

I strapped on a pack of food I'd taken from the kitchen and wrapped in a napkin: bread smeared with honey, cheese and grapes, with biscuits for later, and before the light had come up fully I was on the road north. If Richard was back tonight, I would need to be back, too.

Several hours later, I welcomed the sounds of a town thronged with people and sellers and animals. It was a bright summer's day, and warm, and the way uphill to the castle was slow, for the streets were crammed with carts and carriages. Before I reached the gatehouse I looked back behind, where the town was spread far below, down a steep, winding street. Buildings were crammed in everywhere, with the hills rising up in the distance hemming in the town. From the castle, you could see everything: every window and cobble and pair of lovers and hungry child. On my horse I approached two helmeted guards standing with swords at their thighs like suits of armor. "I am here to visit a prisoner," I said. They regarded me lazily.

"Name," one said.

"Mine, or the name of the prisoner?"

Though he had all the time in the world to gaze at the skyline and feel the weight of the sword at his hip, he looked at me as though he did not have a single second to spare for me. "Your name."

"Fleetwood Shuttleworth, of Gawthorpe Hall near Padiham."

He looked me up and down, taking in my swollen stomach. Then he turned and was gone under the great yawning gate. My back ached and my legs burned from the long ride, and if I dismounted I thought I might never get back on the horse again.

Just as I did not think he would come back, he came striding out with a plump, slightly younger man with black hair, who was dressed finely in soft black boots, breeches and a black doublet with silver buttons fastened over his well-fed belly. Wide sleeves billowed at his wrists. "Mistress Shuttleworth?" he asked politely. "Should I be expecting you? My name is Thomas Covell. I am the coroner and keeper of the castle."

I decided to stay on my horse to keep the advantage of height. "I am here to visit Alice Gray, Mr. Covell, if such a thing is possible?" When he looked no more enlightened, I said, "She was recently arrested by Roger Nowell, who is a dear friend of mine. I was in the area and wanted to . . . inquire after her welfare."

Clearly prisoners' visitors were not a daily occurrence at the castle gatehouse. Mr. Covell was intrigued and suspicious in equal parts. He placed his fingertips together. "Ah, we do not permit callers at the castle, I am afraid to say." His eyes slipped to my stomach. "Especially under certain circumstances — the prisoners can get quite excited by it, and it does no good for their dispositions."

I swallowed. "Mr. Covell," I said. "I have traveled a long way — over forty miles." His face was impassive, as were the two guards on either side, gazing into the distance, reminding me of my bedfellows Prudence and Justice. I realized I may be able to exercise one if not the other. "My husband, Master Shuttleworth, would be very disappointed to hear I had been turned away, especially considering his late uncle Sir Richard's generous contribution to the crown not fifteen years ago — that and the fact he was chief justice at Chester, and knighted at court. So I am not sure that my late relative would look with agreement at his nephew's wife being refused entry. I would hate to have to take the matter further."

At this, Mr. Covell's eyes swiveled in his head, coming again to land on me with his eyebrows so far up they almost disappeared under his hat. He opened his mouth and closed it. "What is the name of the prisoner you seek to visit?" he asked.

"Alice Gray. She was brought here not two days ago."

Thomas Covell regarded me again coolly, taking all of me in from my hat to my rings. His fat chin wobbled and he sighed. "You have two minutes. I will have one of the gaolers escort you."

And so I passed under the gatehouse, just as Alice had two days before me, and thousands more would after me. There was only one way into the castle, and one way out.

Leaving my horse tied behind the gate-keepers, a thin, wheezing man with a pointed face like a rat took me across the castle yard — but not the way I was expecting, toward the main part of the castle. His gait was very wide, his legs sprouting from his hips, leaving a large space in between his feet, so he walked with difficulty, but also like a man determined not to show it. "What'n'ya want wi'these wenches, then, eh?" he said conversationally as we followed the interior wall of the castle.

I ignored him and stared up at the height of the stone, feeling the chill of the place even though it was a warm summer's day.

I was not expecting us to stop so suddenly, and not outside: we were next to a low arch at the foot of one of the towers, covered by an iron gate. But the door did not lead out to the other side of the castle walls — the blackness inside meant it only went one way: down. I frowned. "Why are we stopping?" I asked.

"This is the Well Tower," said my companion through a gummy smile.

"I don't understand. Alice Gray will be in a cell awaiting trial. Can you take me to her, please?"

"She's in 'ere." He pointed at the arch that was so dark I could see why it was called the Well Tower — it was like looking into one. I could not see beyond one or two steps; it was as though a black curtain covered the rest. The gaoler extracted a large bunch of keys from his hip and spent a long time considering each one, as slowly the absolute horror of what I was seeing dawned on me.

Behind this gate, in this hole, was Alice. I had never been to a gaol and did not know what a cell might look like, but this was not a cell. It was a dungeon from a legend. It was as though the sun had gone out: all the heat and light left me, and I stood shivering, staring at the entrance to hell itself.

A curious noise came from somewhere behind the gate, and I realized it was a bird chirping. Hopping from one spot to another on the top step was a robin, trapped behind the gate. It might have been small enough to get through the bars, but it was asking for us to set it free.

"Bloody stupid vermin," the gaoler muttered, unlocking and pulling open the gate. The robin froze, its freedom granted. "Get out of it." He kicked at the bird and it went soaring up over our heads, over the walls and away.

I reached for the cool stone wall to steady myself.

"Int nowt to be scared of, you wanted to come, didn't yer?"

No. I did not want to go down there for anything, not even Alice. But I had to, because I could come out again, and whoever was in there could not.

It was like going down steps into black water, so dense was the darkness. They went down and down into the earth, and at the bottom was another door of solid wood, or iron — it was too dark to tell. The gaoler closed the gate at the top of the stairs and locked it, and when I heard the clang and the key turn behind me, every nerve in my body was set jangling, and my head was light with terror.

"Stand back," he wheezed, turning another key in the door at the bottom. "Or the smell'll knock you out."

I went back up a few steps, my pattens echoing on the stone. I still thought I might faint so I kept one hand on the damp wall. I heard the gaoler's barking on the other side of the door, and waited, and then a pale face appeared at the bottom of the steps, and a slim body slipped through the doorway.

"Alice."

I was ashamed to say I started crying: me, in my fine clothes with my stomach full of cheese and bread and my horse waiting for me outside the walls. She did not cry. I had not seen her in two days but it could have been years: she looked so different. Her long face was whiter than the moon, and there were shadows under her eyes that were not there before. She blinked furiously as though the dim light of the staircase was blinding. Her dress was filthy and looked damp, and her cap was streaked with dirt. Dark blood spotted the front of her dress and no doubt the back where she sat.

She said nothing, only held herself weakly against the wall, as though she had no strength. The gaoler appeared at her side, closing the door, and I heard shrieks and cries of protests from behind him as what must have been the only light was shut out. He was right: the smell was incredible. Alice had used to smell of lavender, and clean her hands in a porcelain bowl, and now she lived in a cesspit beneath the earth.

"Who else is in there?" I breathed.

"All of 'em," the gaoler wheezed. "All the witches awaiting trial."

"How many people?" I asked Alice.

"I do not know," she said. "It's too dark to see anything." Her mouth was dry, her tongue peeling from the roof of her mouth as she spoke. The black pupils of her eyes were large as marbles.

I had traveled for hours and I could not think of a single thing to say. In that moment, I think I would have given the child in my stomach for her freedom.

The gaoler looked from one of us to the other, disappointed. "Well, this is quite the reunion, is it not? Do you have nothing to say to one another?"

"Do you have food?" I asked.

"A little," she said.

When the gaoler looked away to sort his keys, she shook her head. I wished he would go away and lock himself in that infernal pit — how did the man live with himself?

"I will help you," I said. My voice echoed on the walls. It sounded pathetic, like something a child might say.

Alice had stopped blinking so rapidly and her gaze was now vacant.

"They got Katherine, as well," she said, her voice thick.

"Who?"

"Katherine Hewitt. My mother's friend." That's when she started crying. Mould-heels: her mother's partner in midwifery. I remembered her telling me in that warm, lofty chamber in my mother's house, long ago in a different life.

"What do you mean?"

"It's my fault."

"What's your fault?"

"Now, now," said our acquaintance, uncomfortable.

"Will you leave us for a moment?" I demanded.

"*Leave* you? I cannot do that."

I fumbled at my skirts and took out my purse. "Here." I held out a penny and he fell on it like a starving dog. "You can leave us locked in, just come back when I call. Don't go far," I said.

He staggered up the steps, breathing raggedly, shutting the gate behind him and locking it again. His figure blocked the light momentarily, and only when he moved away could I see Alice again.

"Come up," I said, retreating up the staircase. "You need air and light."

She followed me and we sat on the top step with our backs against the gate. I tried not to breathe in the stench coming off her: stale sweat and vomit and something else that I knew at once to be fear. I'd never smelled it before on a human, but I knew it right away. She had stopped crying but the tears carved clean paths down her mucky face.

"Tell me about Katherine," I said gently.

"She is accused, too, of the same thing. It's my fault — she's done nothing."

"Alice, you have to tell me everything. Why are you accused of murdering John Foulds's daughter? He was the man at the Hand and Shuttle, wasn't he, when I came?"

329

She nodded and licked her lips, though her tongue was dry so her mouth made a sticking noise. "I loved him," she said in a very faint voice. "And I loved Ann. I loved them both. Me and John were . . . together. He used to come to the Queen's Arms, that's how I met him, a couple of years ago. He had a daughter — his wife had died. He was funny, and kind. At first. I thought we would get married. Ann wasn't two years old when we met. I used to look after her when he went to work, if I wasn't working. She was like a little angel, with fat cheeks and yellow hair that wouldn't lie flat no matter how much you combed it."

She was almost smiling now, her face lost in memories. Then it clouded over and she sniffed. "John said he wouldn't get married again, not after losing his wife. It was too painful, he said. So I stayed, and it was like we were married. I lived with him, and my dad as good as disowned me. He called me a whore. He said I'd never be a wife, that I was good for nothing but lying down for John after he'd been drinking. But I was happy, with John and with Ann. We were a little family."

She swallowed. "Then he started staying out longer, and later. Me and Ann were on our own a lot of the time. Most of the time.

John was either at work or at the alehouse, while I was pretending to be his little wife at home. I was lying to myself."

She shifted her feet and wrapped her arms around her knees. I looked again at the blood on the front of her dress, at her unwashed hair trailing from under her cap. I wished I could wash her and put her in a clean nightshift and tuck her in bed like a child.

"Even when folk started telling me he had other women, I didn't want to believe them. And life went on, and he got meaner, and cheaper, and me and Ann were living off my wage because he spent all his. And she started having these . . . I don't know what you call them. She would go stiff and her eyes would roll in her head, and her tongue was too big for her mouth. I thought she was playing up because her dad wasn't around. He didn't believe me when I told him. He thought I was making it up to get him to come home. I tried all the plants I could think of, all the herbs. I went to Katherine for help, but even she couldn't do anything. Ann was fine most of the time, it was just when this happened she was . . . it was like an evil spirit was choking her.

"One day I had to go to work and leave Ann at home on her own. John was nowhere to be found. He was supposed to come back. I was close to losing my job." Tears began leaking again from Alice's eyes. Her face was carved with sorrow. "I still loved him. I always loved him, even when he wouldn't come home. If we hadn't had Ann, things might have been different. I might have left. Anyway, I went to work and asked Katherine to keep an eye on her. The next thing, she came running in saying, 'Alice, Alice, come quick, you have to come now.' And we ran to John's and she . . ." Alice buried her face in her knees. "I shouldn't have left her."

I put my arm around her, feeling her thin shoulders. As I grew, she shrunk. My heart felt like it was breaking. It was a different break to when I found Judith. That time there was anger; this time there was only pain.

"There was nothing you could have done," I whispered, pressing my cheek to hers. Our tears mixed together and ran down to our lips. I tasted salt: mine and hers. We stayed like that as she shuddered beneath my arm, then after a while she grew still.

"I think that's why I wanted to help you so much," she said softly. "I thought maybe if I could keep your child alive, it would go some way to . . ." She stopped, struggling to explain. "I'd failed to save one child, so I thought if I could give life to another . . ."

I nodded sadly. "If the child is a girl, I will call her Alice Ann."

She did not smile, but something lit up behind her eyes. "I thought you wanted two boys."

"I do." I looked down at our skirts — shiny maize taffeta against filthy brown wool, and I held her hand. "That has not changed."

"It's awful in there," she whispered with her dry mouth. "It's like hell. You can't see a thing, and it makes you feel like the room's turning. There's a woman dying. Demdike. She'll die before the trial. There's no food."

I closed my eyes and thought of the food I'd had that morning all to myself. I hadn't even thought . . .

"I'll get you out of here," I said. "Alice, I promise. I will get you out."

Salty tears slid down her cheeks. "I can see what all this has cost you," she whispered. "I can't have you sacrifice any more."

"To hell with what it costs me." While I said it, I felt the baby move, and was aware at once that while all three of us were here and alive now — Alice, the baby and I — feeling the stone steps beneath us, and breathing in the dank air beneath the castle, one day very soon we might not, and there was no way of telling who would make it. The three of us were bound together in some dreadful destiny, and it was clearer now than ever that to survive, we needed one another just as equally, and just as desperately. The future for both of us was as dark as the hole at the bottom of the staircase — with Alice in there, I might not survive the birth, nor my baby its chance at life. But I was no use to her wherever I might be; except, no, I *had* to be. While she was in there and I was out here I could help; I knew I had to be able to in some way, however small.

"I will save you," I said again, gripping her fingers in mine.

She squeezed, once, and let go, and looked sadly at me, and her lively golden eyes were empty. "I am not a dog you can save from a bear pit," she said.

"I *will* save you from death, like you promised to save me. You will live."

"And Katherine," she whispered.

"And Katherine. She is in there with you now?"

Alice nodded. At that moment a great wail came from behind the locked door at the bottom, making both of us jump. Then fists were banging on the door and the wails turned to screams. Alice and I leaped to our feet as the gaoler from earlier hurried over and fumbled with the lock.

"You've set them off, have you?"

"What's all this?" said another voice. More men were approaching like bats from the shadows in the castle walls.

The gate clanged open and an iron grip held my arm. Alice and I were wrenched apart and suddenly I was outside the gate and she was being marched back down the staircase. "Alice!" I cried. "I'll come back. I'll come back!"

As a fierce bulk of a man escorted me back to the gatehouse, the shrieking escaped as the door to the dungeon clanged open. "She's dead! She's dead! She's dead!" The words came out like crows from a forest, echoing around the walls with nowhere to land.

Before beginning the long journey back I stopped at an inn in the town, where I ordered three roast chickens, twenty meat pies and two gallons each of ale and milk to send to the dungeon. I had four boys carry the food and roll the barrels up the hill to the castle, and made sure that the same wheezing gaoler from earlier carried them down those steep stairs and came back with empty arms. I left him with another penny to shine his palm and gave one each to the miserable guards, too. I told them I would be back, and they smiled at me like they knew better.

CHAPTER EIGHTEEN

The next morning there was a crowd of servants at the front steps when I came down to breakfast. Arrived back from Ripon, Richard's bare head was at the front of the crowd, so I pushed my way through. He was still wearing his cloak. But there was no one at the door, nor a horse in front of the house. Then I realized everyone was looking down. I stepped back in horror.

Richard's falcon had been slashed to pieces. Lying in a pool of her own blood, she was left as an offering on the top step, her wings folded piously as an angel's, her eyes glassy and unseeing. The servants were hovering like a pack of flies on rotten meat, so I sent them away, and could not help but put my hand on Richard's arm. His face was a mask of grief and anger, and I knew that one would soon surrender to the other, so I closed the door and led him back into the house.

"Do you know who did this?" I asked in the dark hush of the entrance.

"No, but when I find out I will kill them," he said quietly, though his voice shook with conviction.

I allowed him to collect himself, remembering suddenly the slash of fur, the glistening red I'd seen in the woods all those weeks ago.

"One of our tenants? Have you argued with anyone of late?"

He shook his head. Then he wrenched open the door, and knelt to gather up his precious bird. I watched his narrow shoulders slope in sadness, his hair stirring in the wet wind, and felt a powerful surge of love. But also something else: a despondency — a shame, previously unknown to me — that he could feel something so strongly for a creature, and not a human woman. I felt like leaving him on the threshold and going to where my breakfast was waiting in the dining room, but then an idea arrived. I asked a servant to bring a bathing sheet, then knelt and began to wrap the carcass up. The sight of it did not stir me — I had seen plenty of death. But something did cause me to hesitate: a few very fine, orange hairs were caught in its wounds. I folded the sheet and bound it carefully around the bird, aware all at once of my own fate hanging like a rain-filled sky.

We crossed the lawn and the heavens opened. I stood with my husband in the downpour as he buried the bird by the stables in a sheltered spot by the river. I felt the rain run down my neck, soaking my jacket, and I felt my child kick inside me. When we got back into the house, and Richard sent for some aqua vitae and pulled off his drenched jacket, I took his face in my hands. His hair was plastered to his head, and his eyelashes were wet. His gray eyes burned. "Richard," I said. "I need your help."

I spent a long time getting dressed, and for the finishing touch added my black velvet choker with the plump pearl hanging ripe as a peach from it that Roger had bought for me one Christmas. My cheeks were fatter than the last time I saw him. I pinched them and dabbed rose oil behind my ears, at my wrists and at the dip in my throat. When I heard him arrive downstairs, I stared into the looking glass for another minute or two, tweaking my collar, patting my hair and trying to breathe normally. I was pleased to see my hands weren't shaking, and said a silent prayer.

I heard Roger's voice before I saw him, telling Richard some tale or other. They were in the dining room, and I paused in the doorway to take a deep breath before gliding in. He looked the same as ever — shiny boots, wide sleeves, glittering rings. It might have been any day in our friendship, but the memory of the last time I saw him returned. Something told me to be very careful.

"Mistress Shuttleworth," he said genially with a graceful bow of his head.

I went to him and kissed him, trying very hard to do it as I might have done months ago. So much had happened since the supper at Read Hall, but one would never know it from his easy grin, his beaming cheeks. "You are looking very well," he said evenly.

"Thank you. Will you have some wine?"

"I will always have some wine, if there is wine to be had."

I went to the draw-leaf table to pour it and looked at the panels above the fireplace. Empty, gleaming wood filled the space around Richard's initials.

"The Tower lies empty," Roger was saying. "I told him I imagine it will be difficult to find a tenant afterward."

"I could ask the bailiff," Richard suggested.

"Tower?" I asked, going back to serve the wine.

"Malkin Tower," was Roger's reply.

I tried to appear lightly curious. "What is that?"

"The home of the Devices, near Colne. It's a very strange place to look at. You hear *tower* and think it to be grand, but it's like a spike coming out of the earth. It's tall and round and made of stone, with one room at the bottom, and they climb rotten ladders to sleep around the walls. But they won't have use of it for much longer — it's been empty a month or more. Since Constable Hargrieves found the teeth and clay dolls under the ground there, I shall be surprised if anyone goes in there again."

Silence fell as the food was brought in: a joint of roast beef, with fallow pasties and cheese. Roger eyed it hungrily. "Fleetwood," he said, helping himself to sauce. "A friend of mine saw you in Lancaster the other day. What were you doing there?"

I kept my eyes on the food, cutting the beef into strips. "I was visiting a clothier there," I said.

"All the way in Lancaster? Must be some fine material."

I smiled and licked my thumb. All he needed do was ask the guards or the keeper

341

Thomas Covell and they would tell him I had been there. "I stopped by the castle, too," I said thickly. "I thought I might visit my midwife."

I glanced at Richard. I'd told him of my whereabouts in case Roger did first, and was glad of it now, though he was not at all happy I'd ridden some eighty miles in a single day. I'd reminded him of Alice's advice: that if I had always ridden, then riding was as dangerous as walking, so that was one balm at least.

Roger speared his meat with his knife and did not look up. He knew, then. "And why ever did you do that?" His voice was low and dangerous.

I pushed my plate away and reached in my pocket for my handkerchief to dab my eyes. "I have been feeling very unwell," I said in a small voice. "I am worried for my health and the health of my child — I wanted to ask her advice."

"And there is not one other midwife within forty miles that could assist you?"

"Alice has been a very good midwife — the best I've had." I stopped dabbing and looked meekly at him. "I have never reached this far in childbed before, and I believe that is down to Alice. My lying-in will begin soon. Roger," I went on, dab dab dabbing.

"If you could just consider allowing Alice to live in custody here at Gawthorpe, for my own sake and for that of my child. Without her, I am afraid . . . Richard?" I pleaded, unable to go on because now I did feel tears come to my eyes.

I prayed he would say what I asked him to, and there was a pause in which Richard licked his lips. "Fleetwood was very ill," he said quietly. "You saw her. She could barely eat a morsel. Her hair fell out in clumps. Somehow she is better than ever now. Alice would of course face the assizes next month but we would keep her here under lock and key. She would not escape."

"And you could guarantee that how?"

"The same way you could guarantee it with Jennet Device, who I believe is still at Read," I said.

I have eyes in the forest, Roger had said all those months ago. "Jennet Device is not on trial for murder," he said calmly. He picked up his knife again. "You would invite a child murderer and a witch under your roof?"

"She is not . . ." I whispered, but Richard gave me a look, and I went silent.

"It is impossible," Roger announced.

I hated him then, for everything, but just then for toying with us, like a cat will place a powerful paw on a mouse's tail before letting go and catching it again. Roger enjoyed letting people wheedle, and persuade, and beg, letting them think they were in with a chance, when his decision was already made.

"I think the pair of you fail to grasp the seriousness of the allegations against the Pendle witches, as they are colloquially known. Witchcraft is punishable by death, but their crimes are altogether more serious — they have not only practiced witchcraft, but their actions have caused the deaths and madness of many people. They are a danger to society. How would it look to the king, to ask for their pardon until the trial? No, it will not do." He dabbed at his beard, where beads of sauce clung to the silver hairs.

"Which brings me to my next point," he went on, this time speaking directly to me. "There is no use visiting the castle again, because you will not be let in." My mouth fell open. "Visitors excite the prisoners, and what with your . . . condition . . ." He gestured vaguely at me, as though being a woman was a condition, which I suppose it was. "It whips them into a frenzy. Shortly after you barged your way into the Well Tower and had that door opened, a woman died."

344

"You are not suggesting —"

"I am not suggesting anything. I am telling you," Roger interrupted. His eyes were fierce, every line of his body taut with malice. "Do not go to the castle again. If you do, you will not be let out."

My knife clattered against my plate. I realized I had forgotten to breathe, that my mouth was opening and closing like a fish on a riverbank. I turned to Richard, who was pushing strips of fat miserably around his plate. He would not challenge Roger; I knew it. And I needed him on my side. Trying to disguise the fact that I was shaking violently, I sat back in my chair and let my hands fall to my lap. "Do you mean I would be a prisoner?"

"That is exactly what I mean. Be under no pretense, your advantage of birth is the only thing that stands in your favor. Had you not this house and husband, you think you would be permitted to tear around the country unchecked, making your inquiries? You are no threat to the course of justice, as much as you design to be. But if you think you are free from the grip of the manacles, you are quite mistaken."

At this, Richard interrupted. "Roger, be reasonable."

My blood had turned cold, but Roger was

not yet finished.

"One of the accused is Miles Nutter's mother. She, too, is a rich woman, a fine woman of standing, with educated sons. The problem is she curses her neighbors and they fall down dead."

I wish she would curse you, I thought, but my mouth remained shut.

Roger leaned in slightly to deliver his fatal blow. "In fact, Jennet told me you reminded her of Mistress Nutter. She can always be persuaded to think a little harder of who was there at Malkin Tower on Good Friday."

His pale gaze rested on me, and I think that was the first time I realized with a crushing certainty who I was pitting myself against. This was not Roger, my father figure, who dined and hunted and played cards with us; this was the former sheriff, the magistrate, the justice of the peace.

"That's enough!" Richard cried, stabbing his knife into the table.

We all jumped, and Roger sat back. I had not seen Richard this angry since the necklace went missing.

"I'll hear no more of it." He pulled the knife from the wood and began eating again.

"I am leaving this afternoon for Jennet Preston's trial at York," Roger began, setting his knife on his empty plate. "The same

346

judges are hearing the case who will be at Lancaster in August — James Altham, who is very experienced, and discreet, and Sir Edward Bromley. Do you know him, Richard?" Richard gave a tight shake of his head, his jaw set with fury. Roger did not seem to notice. "He is the nephew of the former Lord Chancellor who oversaw the execution of Mary, Queen of Scots. He is also the man who acquitted Jennet Preston at the Lent assizes." He shook his head and took a noisy sip from his glass.

I remembered how Thomas Lister seethed and shook next to me at dinner at the mention of Jennet Preston, how he had succeeded in committing her to trial twice in the space of a few months. One of the judges had found her not guilty a few months before: he could do it again.

"How many weeks until the trial at Lancaster?" I asked Roger.

"Three or four. I expect both of you will want seats in the gallery? I am expecting it to be busier than the Rose on play night."

When the two men went out to look at Richard's new gun, I stood for a long time at the window, thinking. Demdike was dead. Jennet Preston would be tried for murder by witchcraft tomorrow. While Alice was alive, and there was time before the trial, I

347

could still save her life and my own, as worthless as they were to anyone but us.

The next morning I set out to find Malkin Tower. My mother's voice rang in my ears as I rode out in my traveling cloak, my skin pricked with sweat even though it was cool for July. *Fleetwood, you are making yourself ridiculous. Fleetwood, you are making a mockery of your family.*

I thought back to those gentle, light-filled days at her house — a place I would never have imagined myself comfortable. The reason I found them comfortable was Alice. If I had sat night after night embroidering or reading Bible passages with my mother's sour face the only company, I might have been driven mad. No, how could I think that? What would drive anyone mad was night after night in a dank black cell, surrounded by other sweating, weeping, vomiting bodies, with no water or food or place to relieve yourself.

The reason Alice was in prison was Elizabeth Device, who wanted to save her child so desperately she had shackled herself to everyone around her. Perhaps she thought there was safety in numbers. She might never have expected her other daughter would turn the key in the lock. I wanted to

348

see where she came from, this astonishingly ugly woman with her spirit dog and bastard child. She had already lost her mother, and now the rest of her family was at stake — apart from the child Jennet. What life had this child, that made her deliver her kin to Roger Nowell? Roger had said Malkin Tower was a miserable place, but it was the only home she knew, with the only people. The lure of a bed of feathers and meat pies at Read Hall would surely not, could surely not be enough.

But you hated your home, a voice persisted. *And your mother.* I smoothed it over with my own assurance: I would never have reported on my mother. But then, I was not sure what it would take for a child to do so. Neglect? Cruelty? They were my old bedfellows, like Prudence and Justice now.

I did not know where to find the Tower, nor whom to ask, so I set out on horseback toward Colne. I left Puck at home and would regret it later when the wind whistled on the moors and Joseph Gray's wind-battered hovel came back to haunt me.

They burn witches, don't they?

With my cloak covering my head and stomach I might have been anyone, or no one, but nobody paid me much attention on the quiet road there. Three or four carts passed me piled with vegetables and bolts of cloth, but I kept my eyes down, remembering how I'd been seen in Lancaster. *I have eyes in the forest, you know.*

I knew that if I stayed on that road eventually it would lead to Halifax, and Abraham and John Law. To think a simple peddler who was asked for some pins started all this. To think what might have happened if he had given them. But even if he handed them over to Alizon Device, Alice would still have lived with her grief, would have gone on working at the Queen's Arms, cooking what little they could buy for her miserable father under the hole in the roof. And where would I be? I may have been dead; I may not. I may have never found out about Judith. But wherever I was, I would not be on the road to search for a stone tower sticking like a spike out of the moor.

Gray and green, gray and green, as far as the eye could see; now and again passing the odd home made of crumbling stone or crudely slapped together out of mud. Long, low farmhouses stretched along the hills like cats, but nothing looked like a tower.

I decided to ask the next person I saw: a man traveling on an exhausted-looking mule the opposite way to me. "Excuse me, do you know where I can find Malkin Tower?" I asked.

He shrank back in alarm like I had told him I was a witch, and without saying a word shuffled away on his dusty beast, glancing back over his shoulder once.

I sighed and came to a stop. Just when I was deciding what to do, two figures appeared on the road: a woman, dressed plainly, tugging her daughter along. "Excuse me," I tried again. "I am looking for Malkin Tower."

The woman stopped and her daughter, drowsy with the heavy summer air, almost walked into her. "What do you want with Malkin Tower?" she asked. Her dark eyes glittered suspiciously.

"I heard of the Devices and have a bet with my sister — she doesn't think they are real, or their house. I have a penny on finding it."

"It is real, all right, and so are they. Tell your sister she should believe what she hears, folk aren't likely to repeat falsehoods around here. They've been an odd family for years, and now we know why. My mother used to buy remedies from Demdike but I was having none of it. I leave the Lord to do his good work, I don't mess with the Devil." She was set on a path now and would not come off it. She licked her lips. Her daughter stared silently at my cloak, my face. "Where are you from?"

"Burnley."

"You've come a way to settle a bet." She nodded in the direction behind her. "Leave the road half a mile up and join the path up to the top of the moor. You'll find it up there. I don't like it myself. I don't like to look at it. There's something not right about it. Like I say, my mother used to go up there when we were ailing, she took me a few times. I wouldn't take my own there if the Lord told me to himself."

I thanked her and went the way she said, leaving the road for a narrow path between two dry walls. A dog barked in the distance, and I thought of the one I'd seen in the forest with Elizabeth and Alice. Had it been a familiar spirit or a family pet? To think Elizabeth Device had been so close to my house, with all its entrances and windows . . .

I shivered and leaned backward as the land rose up slightly with wide fields on either side. The brow of the hill came closer but there was no sign of the Tower. And then I was at the top and looking down the other side, and there it was: a dull, gray, tallish building like a short table leg; in the style of the old towers like the one built at Gawthorpe hundreds of years before. But the Devices were not a noble family or even yeomen — they were poor as church mice, so how they came to live in a tower was part of the mystery.

Great chunks of it had fallen off and were scattered around the bottom, and I went to what seemed to be the entrance: a large, thick door in the bottom. Arrow slits in the walls would be the only source of light, and probably a hole in the roof for the smoke to get out.

I climbed off the horse and walked once around the Tower. An odd little garden had been attempted and abandoned, squared off in bits of dry wall. I did not think I wanted to go in, but I needed to see where Jennet Device had come from to determine where she might want to go.

I went to the door and tried the ring pull. It jolted open easily — there was no lock. Inside was dark, and I thought again of the gaol cell the family now lived in, how much their home was like one. I left the door as wide open as it would go to let more light in and stepped inside.

There was a powerful smell, but what it was I was not sure. Damp, certainly, and decay, but something animal: like wet fur that had been left to dry. It did not take long to look at everything. A cooking pot bigger than Joseph Gray's sat in the center of the dirt floor. A straw mattress lay nearby, but there were no hangings to keep the draft out of the spaces between the stones. I watched a wood louse crawl lethargically over the greasy linen that covered the mattress. Plates and cups lay forgotten on the ground. A wooden ladder led up to a rotten-looking platform, where there must have been more straw beds. On my right, a table was pushed against the wall, which curved round in a circle. Some bits of things were on it and I went to it, and immediately recoiled. Here were the remains of Elizabeth's clay doll in an unshapely mound, stuck in places with pins. And in the lumps and crumbs of clay, they were apparent: teeth. I went to pick one up and held it in front of me, a creeping sensation flooding my scalp and going down my neck.

An almighty crash made my heart almost stop. The door had slammed behind me. I dropped the tooth and ran to it, fumbling in the gloom for the handle, and finding it, and pulling at it, panic rising to a high, clear note that sang in my head. The wind was on the other side, clamoring to be let in, but I pushed against it and was out on the

354

moor again, panting and frightened. What was I thinking, touching their devilish instruments? The creeping feeling came over me again, and I had the curious sensation of being watched.

My horse neighed and backed away, raising its legs in protest. I turned and saw the outline of a thin, ragged dog standing on the top of the hill, twenty or thirty feet away. It was still as a statue, watching me as I watched it. I moved first, swinging myself up onto the horse, using one of the fallen stones from the Tower, and by the time I collected the reins the dog was gone.

I was alone on the hillside, but I felt far from it, and I could not look back at Malkin Tower as I retraced the horse's tracks back to the road, though I felt it looking at me: the arrow slits were not unlike the thin strip of black in a cat's green eyes.

Now I had seen what she had left, how grand Jennet Device must feel staying in Roger and Katherine's house, with their thick curtains and Turkey carpets and ink quills and servants. How she must have told him what he wanted to hear to let her stay, thinking long and hard beneath her counterpane about the tales she could draw out, long and shining like a spider's web. Part of me did not blame the child, especially if she

355

thought she might be kept like that forever, a cuckoo in the Nowells' nest. As soon as the assizes were over, no doubt Roger would pawn her off to a farm in need of labor, or a house not unlike ours for a brewing or laundry maid. And how would she live the rest of her life: Would she believe herself elevated by fortunate circumstance, or be racked with guilt until the end of her days?

By the time I reached where the path met the road, it was only midmorning, and the sun was high but dim in the watery sky. I looked left to go farther to Colne, and right to go back to Gawthorpe. A moment later my mind was made up, and I clicked my mouth and squeezed with my feet to walk on.

CHAPTER NINETEEN

"You!" said Peter. I stood once again before the counter on the straw-covered floor of the Queen's Arms. "We never have ladies at all in here, now it's twice in one week." A few drinkers were straggled around the tables, porters finished their shifts or messengers breaking for the day, but they didn't take much notice and went back to their solitary tankards.

"I am looking for an address," I said. "You wrote a letter in March or April this year to a man named Abraham Law, a cloth dyer from Halifax."

Peter eyed me warily, his rotund middle denting where it butted against the counter. "I might have. What's it to you?"

I drew myself up to my full and insubstantial height. "I need to speak with him."

"What for?"

"I have a large quantity of cloth on order from Manchester and I would like a quote to have it dyed. Alice mentioned Master Law, so I thought I might try him."

Peter exhaled. "Well, the Lord knows you gentry folk have needs the likes of us mere mortals can't fathom," he said. "I'll go and find it, give me a minute."

I clasped my hands together and waited. Presently he was back with a single sheet of correspondence, which I all but snatched from his hand to read the address. "Many thanks, Mr . . . ?" I said.

"Ward," he offered.

"Mr. Ward. I shall write to him at some point."

Five minutes later, with *the sign of the raven, Haley Hill* repeating in my mind, I was on my way to Halifax, having left Peter Ward with a palm of silver. I thought about all the coins I had pressed into hands recently and wondered how I would explain my traveling all over the county to James. Then I remembered he would probably never question me on anything again — even looking at me sent the tips of his ears red after I'd found the paper trail that started in his study and ended at Richard's other life. I would take a much closer interest in management once all this was over — if I was around to. Soon there would be extra linen, towels, milk, caps and miniature gowns, not one set but two. It interested me to realize that thinking this didn't send me into a blind rage: it was a fact, and not even an important one at this moment in time.

I had to go fast, and by the time I reached the town I felt as though I had been put in a pillowcase and shaken within an inch of my life, and the baby inside me squirmed and kicked. Briefly I wondered if this constant journeying was doing it harm. But while it was moving, it was living, so I pushed the thought from my mind, dismounted, and paid the nearest boy to mind my horse and fetch it something to drink.

The timber house at the sign of the raven was crammed in by others on both sides and hung over the street on its highest floors, so you had to lean back to see it. Children ran barefoot up and down in the mud, and people walked with purpose in and out of shops and houses. It reminded me of the buildings on London Bridge, with everybody living in each other's pockets.

I knocked on the door, my knuckles making a pattern that sounded more confident than I felt. It opened into a dark hallway and a young girl appeared on the other side. She looked at me in surprise. I was wearing my traveling cloak and everything was covered, from my hat to my hem. "I am looking for Abraham Law," I said. "Is he at home?"

"He is at work, miss," she said. "I'm his daughter. Me mum's home if you want to see her?"

"Oh. I . . . Yes, I better had, then."

She stepped backward so I could enter, and I followed her into a warren-like low corridor with rooms leading off the left-hand side. "Wait here, I'll fetch me mum," she told me, so I stood, listening to the sounds of a busy household and the households on either side bumping and shouting and crying.

A slender woman approached from the end of the corridor, wearing a corn-colored gown and an apron that needed darning. Several strands of fair hair straggled from beneath her cap into a kind face, and she was wiping her hands on a rag. "Can I help?" she asked.

In that moment, seeing her distracted politeness, I was suddenly startled by the sheer weight of my own task, but also the indulgence of it. Here were people whose lives went on because they had to — she would have no idea who I was, or why I was here, and the effort of explaining myself suddenly seemed exhausting because I wasn't sure where even to start. But she must have seen this, for she asked me to come in and have some beer, so wordlessly I followed her into a wide room that was still dark despite the bright day, with old paneled walls that sucked the daylight from the room. Heaps of things were piled on every available space, and three or four children and a dog occupied the floor space, moving constantly so I had to step cautiously. There was a man in a chair facing the window looking out: I could see the top of his balding head.

I unfastened my cloak and held it, unsure of where to set it down. The air in the little room was stifling. The woman had stepped out and came back presently with a cup of beer for me. I drank it gratefully.

"I am Liz," she said. "You were looking for my husband?"

"Yes," I managed. The beer was light and good. "My name is Fleetwood Shuttleworth. Forgive me for trespassing like this . . . I hardly know where to start."

"Please, sit down." She indicated a chair on one side of the empty hearth and I waded through the mess of children's limbs and dog's to sit down. She took the other.

"I suppose I wanted to speak to Abraham about something that happened a few months ago in Colne."

Liz Law's face instantly took on a different expression, one of tiredness and even pain.

"With your father-in-law? What happened to him set off a series of events that . . . I'm not sure if in this county you're aware of what is happening in Lancaster?"

She shook her head, and one of the children wailed for her attention. She spoke to him kindly but firmly and turned back to me. Of course Liz Law knew nothing: she was up to her eyes in running her household.

"What's happened is . . . My midwife is a woman called Alice Gray." I swallowed and saw her eyes flick almost imperceptibly to my stomach, then back again. "She has been caught up in accusations of witchcraft, as have many others. About twelve, at the last count."

Liz was staring blankly at me. A small child was using her skirt to pull itself up, and began banging on her knee with a chubby fist. Was there no nurse, or maid to take them off her hands for a single moment?

"Alice Gray worked at the Queen's Arms, which is where your father-in-law was taken after he was . . . after he met Alizon Device.

Alice found him on the woolpack road and cared for him there, but the Device family began threatening her to change her story. Now they have dragged her into these horrid accusations, and there will be a trial in a few weeks at Lancaster."

Liz was still listening but I could sense she was distracted. She removed the child from her skirts and tried to put its hands by its sides, to no avail, and the child began to cry.

"Sorry, I know you are very busy. I wondered first of all how your father-in-law is, and second, if I could ask him some questions about what happened that day in Colne?"

She sat up straight and picked the child up onto her lap. "You can ask him yourself, but you won't get much sense from him. Dad?" She went over to the man I'd noticed before, positioned in the light from the window.

I followed her, and my mouth fell open. John Law was shrunken like an old apple, crumpled to one side in his chair. One side of his face looked as though it had melted, with the eye closed, and the other roved wildly over me and Liz, as though he was frightened. I had the impression of a much larger, stronger man who had lost a lot of weight quickly; his skin sagged, and I could have grabbed fistfuls of fabric from his clothes.

"Hello, John," I said, failing to hide my shock.

He moved about, but the side closest to me stayed limp and heavy. "Whaaant," he said loudly.

I looked at Liz.

"We understand him but no other folk do," she said. "Dad, this lady is here to see you. Do you know her?"

"Nnnnnnn," he cried.

"No, he doesn't," I said. My voice shook and I cleared my throat. "John, my name is Fleetwood Shuttleworth. I am a friend of Alice's, the woman who took you to the Queen's Arms after you were . . . after you were attacked."

He gave some lamentable cry, and I had no idea if he understood.

"Alice Gray?" I tried, but he squirmed and his eye moved away to look out the window again.

"He's been like this ever since," said Liz. The infant in her arms was tugging bits of her hair from under her cap.

"I thought . . . ." I swallowed. "I thought he could speak."

Liz shook her head. "He could at first, but

he's got worse as time's gone on. Some days he makes more sense than others but . . . today isn't a good day. I can leave you with him, so you can try to talk to him — he might say something. I have things to get on with. Could you just hold him for a moment while I clear this cloth?"

She handed the small boy, smocked and sticky, to me and began lifting piles of cloth from every surface and taking them from the room. It was the first time I had ever held a child. He dangled like a sack of flour from my rigid arms, staring at me with astonishment, and I at him.

In no time at all Liz Law was taking him back. My hands fell to my sides, they left the room and I looked around. With most of the cloth moved, the room was clean — the table was polished and free of crumbs, and the children's faces weren't dirty like the others I'd seen in the street. I realized that the Law household was one of modest respectability, and the addition of Abraham's father was stretching them beyond their means. They might have left him in a bed all day, but he had been placed before a sunny window overlooking a yard, where women did laundry and more children and dogs ran about. I pulled my chair up to John and sat beside him.

"Plenty to see, isn't there?" I said. He made a noise of agreement. "John, I do not mean to upset you or cause you further grief, but I was trying to find out what happened that day on the woolpack road in Colne, when you met Alizon Device."

"Hmmmza-tch. Seeurst me nnnnn kamme."

I watched him speak from one side of his mouth, trying to understand, but it was hopeless. His blue eye was fixed on me, willing me to comprehend. When I didn't, he dropped his gaze sadly and seemed to hunch even further. I covered his nerveless hand with mine. He looked at my rings, the gold and rubies and emeralds fastened around my fingers.

"John, do you know Alice Gray? Nod if you do."

His chin went down into his neck, then up again.

"Do you think she is a witch?"

His face went off in the opposite direction, then back toward me and again.

"Would you be prepared to say that at the assizes? Are you going to the trial?"

His head did not move; his eye roved wildly.

"Have you been invited to speak at the trial?"

He nodded, or what I understood to be a nod. If only he'd regained his speech, he could speak freely for the others' innocence.

"Do you think Alizon Device is a witch?"

He nodded, then shook his head. He looked greatly pained, and his searching blue eye filled with tears that spilled onto his face. His right hand moved as though to wipe them, but only got so far as his chest. I took a handkerchief from my pocket and did it for him. Poor John Law was a living puppet; he would be carried in as proof of what had happened, then carried out again, unable to use his own voice. Alizon Device could have walked away and none of this might have happened had she not turned up day after day at the Queen's Arms and admitted her own guilt. No wonder her family wanted to change the story: it was *her* story. This man had none.

I sat a while longer with John and we watched women bending over tubs and brushing sweat from their foreheads. The sun was high, and their work was hot. They were not afraid of their skin browning; they had no choice. On a day like today I would be riding by the river under the cover of trees or even sitting by the window like an ornament, no more useful or purposeful than John Law.

An almighty crash sounded from another room, and Liz Law began scolding someone. "Jennie!" I heard her shout, and one of the women in the yard looked toward the house, holding her hand over her eyes. It was the young girl who had answered the door, but really she was not much younger than me. I watched her walk back into the house, the smell of lye coming with her. I thought of her life here, with infants to play with and a mother whose lap she could rest her head on at night while her father read them a passage from the Bible.

There was banging at the door to the street, and shortly afterward Jennie came through to tell me the boy I'd paid to mind my horse had to be getting home. I rose stiffly and thanked John Law, and went to thank Liz, who was feeding a child with a spoon in the hallway, crouched on the floor. "I'm sorry to have troubled you," I said, having to step around her.

"Not at all," she said. "I hope you aren't too disappointed. John wishes he could talk, I know he does. We all do."

"He said he would be at the trial in a few weeks' time?"

She looked up distractedly. "What trial?"

"The assizes at Lancaster, where the witches are on trial."

"Oh, yes, someone did write about that. I will have to speak to Abraham and see if he can take him."

"Good day to you, Liz."

I stepped out of the dark house into the bright street, where at least there was a breeze. Sweat ringed my armpits and sat above my lip. I was no closer to anything; I felt as though I was walking around the center of it all in ever-wider circles, gaining nothing. And with little Jennet sitting high in her tower at Read Hall spinning stories, she was tying the family's nooses one by one. But she was a *child.*

I could not see a way out of it for Alice. John Law did not think she was a witch but could not say it; her own father was indifferent to her fate, and her landlord cared only about his business. Who else was to speak for her, then? I thought hard all the way home, but I felt like I was staring at a wall.

By the time I arrived back in the stable yard at Gawthorpe, I felt as exhausted as if I'd been carrying a sack of bricks. But I had an idea burning in my mind like a tiny ember. I just needed to give it enough space to catch alight.

CHAPTER TWENTY

Richard was away again when I got home, gone to Preston, which I assumed meant Barton, as it was the nearest town. He left no note, and I wondered if he was angry with me, then I remembered that I had every right to still be angry with him, but anger was difficult to summon. At least while he was away I did not have to be discreet about my wild ways, as he called them. Before all this, he indulged and even admired my lone wanderings, my propensity to leave the house tidy and arrive back muddy and wet with pink cheeks and bright eyes. Could he not see that those pursuits were girlish, and now they had purpose? But perhaps he saw more than I thought. I went to the study and took ink, a quill and paper to my chamber.

The next morning, the sky was a bright blue and there were no clouds. I took the two letters from my desk, written the night before, and tucked them into my skirt ready for the long journey ahead. Overnight my fingers had swollen, and there was a funny feeling in my chest, as though inside it was being pulled taut like a sheet. I ignored the persistent thought that these were symptoms of the sun setting on my earthly life, that the next one was drawing ever closer. Perhaps death was right behind me, stepping with me, moving in my shadow, and at any moment it would gather me in its cloak. I glanced behind me, as though I might see it. Then I gathered my nerve, glanced at Prudence and Justice, and went downstairs.

Katherine Nowell answered the door, her eyes wide with concern. "Fleetwood? Back so soon? Do come in."

I leaned on the doorframe with one hand; with the other I cradled my stomach. "Katherine, please . . . I need help. My child . . . I am in pain. I need my midwife."

"You are alone? Where is Richard? Fleetwood, you are full-bellied, you should not be riding now, surely." There was fear in her voice, and she helped me into the house. I gave another groan. "Where is the pain?"

"It started yesterday, I tried to ignore it but . . . it's not time yet, Katherine, it's too early."

"How bad does it hurt? Does it come in shocks?"

"No, it's constant."

I let her guide me to the great hall, where she had been embroidering a cushion. There were pins and thimbles and lengths of thread strewn over the draw-leaf table, and I thought of sparse Malkin Tower, and how all Alizon Device wanted was some pins. Katherine helped me into a chair.

"Should I call the physick? A doctor?"

"No. I need my midwife, Katherine. Ever since Alice was put in gaol I have got worse. I felt fine until she was in there. Roger said he would try to get her out, but I need her now with me at Gawthorpe. I asked him if she could stay with us until the trial — I will not let her go anywhere, you have my word and Richard's. Please, ask Roger."

This I said through labored breaths, and Katherine handed me a cup of ale brought by a discreet servant. Compared to the life and chaos of the Law house, here it was as quiet as Gawthorpe. Roger's father stared down at me from his portrait.

"Roger is away — I forget where. Oh, Fleetwood, I am so worried. Tell me, what can I do?"

"I need Alice," I said weakly. "I need to get her out of gaol. Only she can cure me.

She knows the herbs, and she knows the right tinctures."

"Perhaps the apothecary could help in the meantime? I will have our man ride out for him."

"No. I need Alice. Only she can help me. Only Alice. There is no time to write to Roger, or to the castle — I must go myself so she can help me."

"No, you should go home — but not until you have rested here. I will make up a room for you and I will tell Roger when he gets home that Alice should be released for your health. I think he is at York, actually . . . never mind, he will be home soon, today or tomorrow."

I thought of being shut up in one of Roger's chambers and thought it no better than the gaol at Lancaster: he might lock me in and throw away the key.

"Katherine, do you think you can persuade him to let her out?" I asked feebly.

Her eyes were wide with compassion, her lined face grave. She cast around helplessly for some words of comfort. "I had an excellent midwife from Liverpool, but this was many years ago, I would not know how to reach her . . ."

"No, it has to be Alice."

She wrung her hands together. "Fleetwood, I . . . She is a prisoner of His Majesty, I don't see how . . ."

"Just until the trial," I said hurriedly. "I am worried my life is in danger." For the first time there was fear in my voice, because what I was saying was true.

"But the woman is on trial for witchcraft. The penalty for that is death. She will not be allowed to roam free before the trial. She will disappear!"

I knew suddenly that we were being watched, and not by one of the painted faces around the hall. I looked toward the doorway and saw a pair of wide pale eyes staring back. Jennet Device did not look away, and her gaze was full of judgment beyond her years. I knew it was ridiculous to be frightened by a child, but there was something very strange about her. After all, she had stolen my necklace, and how without being noticed? I would not have wanted her staying in my house, gliding soundlessly over the flooring, appearing in doorways like a ghost.

"Katherine, might you have your man check on my horse? I abandoned him quite at the door in my haste to reach you. I hope he has not wandered off."

Katherine leaped up, hurrying from the room in her effort to help. With her gone,

Jennet slipped into the room and went over to the fireplace, kneeling in front of one of the stiff-backed oak chairs. She appeared to be carrying some scraps of cloth, and began setting them out on the seat, one next to the other.

Unable to disguise my curiosity, I stood and went to stand beside her. "What are those, Jennet?"

I noticed they were knotted in such a way they resembled human bodies — a large knot at the top for a head, with more knots and lengths between to represent arms and legs. I had seen these poppets before in church, in the fists of infants to hush them from crying or growing irritable. I felt certain Jennet was not a child who grew up with toys.

"Who gave you those?" I asked. "Was it Roger?"

"I made 'em," she rasped in her scratchy little voice.

"And you've stuffed them, too, how clever. What with?"

"Mutton's wool."

I felt certain she had only brought them in here to show them to me, like a cat bringing a mouse to its master. I looked at her thin, shapeless dress; unhappiness and neglect in every line of her. Because of this child, my friend and midwife was rotting in a place that light never reached, and would almost certainly meet her death at the rope. Because of this child, so many others were in there with her. I wanted to take her bony shoulders and shake her so hard her teeth rattled and her eyes rolled. I wanted to scream at her to take back every word, every lie she had told through her sharp little teeth. I could not look at her; I went back to the chair and sat facing away, staring instead at the genial face of Roger's father, Alexander.

Jennet was whispering something, and the sound of it made the hairs on the back of my neck bristle.

"What are you saying?" I demanded, so sharply she turned in surprise and regarded me with those wide, contemptuous eyes.

"A prayer to get drink," she replied, the picture of innocence.

"What do you mean by that?"

"Crucifixus hoc signum vitam Eternam. Amen."

I stared at her, piecing the vocabulary together. My Latin was poor because I had no attention for reading. Something about a cross, and eternal life? I wondered where she had learned it, because the words were pure popery. Had she said them in front of

Roger? And if so, were the Devices in gaol only because they were Catholic? It made no sense — half the families in Pendle were. Roger knew that, and as long as they presented themselves at church each week and kept their eyes to the ground he gave them no trouble.

Jennet came toward me and took the empty pewter cup at my elbow, and held it to the imagined lips of her poppets so they could drink.

"Where did you learn that, Jennet?"

"My grandmother," she lisped.

"You say that and she brings you a drink?"

"No," she said flatly. "Drink is brought."

"In what sense?"

"In a very strange manner."

I watched her tend to her flock. Everything she said was strange. Had I been this precocious as a child? Almost certainly not. So perhaps a different approach was needed. As Richard said with his birds, loyalty was earned not demanded. I would not bring up the necklace, then. And Roger's threat lodged in my mind: that Jennet might be encouraged to remember others present at her home. The idea was too grave to consider. I sighed.

"Jennet?" I glanced at the doorway. "I think you may know my friend. Alice Gray?"

She stayed hunched over her poppets. Her lank hair spilled down her back from beneath her cap. She did not reply, and neatened her cloth figures, brushing imaginary dust off them.

"Do you know her, Jennet?"

She lifted her shoulders: an acquiesce.

"You do know her?" I leaned forward. "Do you think you might have got it wrong about her being at your house that day, at Malkin Tower?"

"James stole a sheep for us to eat," she said, pointing at one of her toys. They leaned drunkenly on one another. She pointed at another. "Mother told him to."

I licked my lips. "Do you remember Alice being at your house? Is she a friend of your mother's, or had you not seen her before?"

At that moment I heard feet on the flags, and Katherine appeared bearing a tray. "More ale — are you recovered, Fleetwood?"

I sat back, disappointed, and eyed the child in front of me. Jennet was smiling, and when I realized what about, a chill saturated me from head to toe.

"Drink is brought," she said happily, and turned back to her little creations.

"Jennet, will you leave us?" Katherine asked in a strained voice.

The child gave her a look, and swept up her toys in an armful, sending the pewter cup I'd drunk from clattering to the floor. She did not pick it up, and glided silently from the room. Now it was Katherine's turn to sigh, and I noticed properly the lines around her mouth, the dull exhaustion in her eyes.

"How much longer will she stay with you?" I asked gently.

Katherine shook her head. "Roger cannot tell."

"Surely it is his decision?"

"While she is here she is . . . useful to him. So I suppose when she stops being useful."

Her bluntness took me aback.

Katherine sat back and sighed, reaching for her cup and drinking deeply. When she had finished she wiped her mouth and said, "I cannot tell you how glad I will be when the assizes leave and all this will be over."

"But, Katherine, how can you wish haste on the sacrifice of innocent lives?"

"Innocent?" Katherine was bewildered. "Fleetwood, you nor I can make judgment on that."

"Do we not have eyes and ears like our husbands, and the men who will condemn them?"

"You speak as though you know the out-

379

come already."

"But I do, everyone does! In history, when have witches ever been treated with lenity? Katherine, we must do something!"

Katherine gave a pleasant little laugh that made me want to slap her.

"Fleetwood, your head is full of fancies. You speak as if we are in a play, all with a part to act. You and I have no role in the king's justice. We support our husbands."

"We cannot stand by and let this happen!" I cried. "We must do something!"

"Fleetwood, please," Katherine coaxed. "Sit, you will exert yourself and cause harm to yourself and your child. Sit down. May I speak frankly with you?" It was unexpected, and all I could do was nod. "Richard loves you very much. He is very fond of you. The pair of you are lucky to be companions in marriage, not like most of our kind."

Briefly I wondered if she knew about Judith, or if Roger would have kept her in the dark about that, too, like he did all his women.

"You must concentrate on raising a family, and being a wife. People . . . talk around here, you see, Fleetwood. And I know we are out of the way here as gentry folk. We are far from large cities, we have a certain privacy in this corner of the land, but that

does not mean we can behave without pro-
priety."

I shifted in my seat, the silence of the hall
ringing in my ears. I waited for Katherine
to wet her lips before going on. "You are
very young, and very earnest, and dear. You
are mistress of the finest house around. This
child will make your life so full, and rich,
and happy. You must take care to involve
yourself in the right things, like the family
and the home, and not be so upset by things
that you have no agency over."

I felt as though she had crushed me like a
carriage wheel. The words died in my
throat, were lost in my sinking heart. "I
want to help my friend," was all I could say
without choking. "Or she will die. And I
will die with her."

The realization was lapping at my edges
again — the knowledge that without Alice, I
may as well have a rope tied, too. She had
promised to save me, and I had promised to
save her, and the chances of those things
happening were now so small they had
vanished from significance. I realized I was
thinking in days now. When I tried to
picture what my child might look like, and
me holding it in my arms, I could not.
Neither could I picture my life in five, ten,
twenty years' time. The date of the summer

assizes loomed, and my life as I knew it was contained in these short weeks.

"There is nothing I can do, Fleetwood." Katherine's voice was gentle. "Roger will not release her. She is on trial for murder by witchcraft — a crime punishable by death."

"Roger has it wrong. She has been cheated, by almost everyone in her life. I cannot let her down like the others. You must come with me to the castle, and plead for her release. You are Roger's wife, you must have some authority." I heard myself, and knew it was hopeless, and my shoulders sank in abject misery.

"You are distressed. You need to rest. Let me take you to one of our chambers."

"No, thank you. I must go."

"You cannot ride home — you are unwell."

"I will go slowly."

Katherine smiled. "You are more like a man than a woman. I insist on having our man ride alongside you."

I reached into my skirts for the letters I'd written in the early light. "I have a favor to ask of you, Katherine."

"Oh, Fleetwood . . . what have I just said —"

"Please. I ask nothing of you but this."

She was listening, and I gathered my nerve, and pressed the papers into her hands. The sealing wax was like bloodstains. "When is Roger next going to Lancaster?"

"In a day or two, perhaps. Are these for him?"

"No, and he cannot see them. I want you to go with him, the next time he goes. Say you wish for a change of scenery, and want to visit the shops — I don't know. But go, and when you are there, you must find a way to visit the castle, alone. They know who I am — Roger will have warned them, which is why I can't do it. You must hand these to the coroner Thomas Covell's clerk at the castle. Don't give them to anyone else — put them into his hands, and tell him to pass them *with urgency* to their intended. If the clerk asks questions, use Richard's name, and say they are from him."

Katherine raised her eyebrows. "I don't understand."

"Please, Katherine. I would not ask if it was not a matter of life or death."

"And there is nothing deceitful in this? Nothing that slanders my husband's name? Why can he not know about it?"

"He just can't. If you do not wish to have my blood on your hands when I die in childbed, then you will do this for me."

We stared at one another, and there was a flicker of something like defiance in Katherine, but not toward me — I could see her tasting it, examining how it sat on her.

"I will do it," she said, nodding.

I could have kissed her, and almost did, but settled for taking her hands in mine and squeezing them. She tucked the letters into her skirts.

"A thousand times thank you," I said.

"Roger will be back from York tomorrow I think, unless the execution is planned for then."

"Execution?"

"You have not heard? They found the woman Jennet Preston guilty of the murder of Thomas Lister's father. She hangs today."

Over the next days, I occupied my old role as the ghost of Gawthorpe, waiting at various windows for Richard. When I saw him approaching from the stables, I watched for a moment his easy swagger, the lightness of him after his trip to Preston, and I thought how untouchable he was, how easily he glided through life. The law would not touch him with a yardstick. Then I went to let him in.

He seemed surprised to see me opening the door, then read something in my face, because he stopped. "What is it?"

"Come inside."

His face fell. "You have lost the baby?"

"No, nothing like that."

Relief swept through him, clearing his face, and he mounted the steps, removing his gloves while I helped with his cloak. I led him through the house to the parlor and closed the door. Puck was dozing lazily beneath the window, and forced himself up to greet Richard, wiping his hands with his large tongue.

"Do you remember the other day when Roger came to dinner and told us about the Lords Justices at the assizes — Altham and Bromley?"

"Yes," was his weary reply.

"I have invited them to dine at Gawthorpe."

There was a pause, in which Puck wandered back to his warm spot. The baby adjusted its position in my belly, trying to get comfortable, and I rested a hand on it.

"You invited them to dine here. At this house." I nodded. Richard stared. "For what purpose?"

"For the purpose of illuminating the plight of the Pendle witches."

Richard did not blink. His voice was calm. "You are making things very difficult for yourself, Fleetwood. For both of us."

"This is not about me, or us. This is about Alice and how she did *not* murder a child."

"That is for the jury to decide, not you, or Roger."

"Roger has already decided!" I cried. "He has already decided!"

"Lower your voice," Richard roared.

He began pacing, his fury a clear, high note in the room. Pockets of red bloomed on my cheeks and I felt white-hot rage sizzle in my head. My ears rang, and I felt for my chair, sitting back down slowly. Puck whined and whimpered next to me, trying to reach my hands. I rested a trembling palm on his head and covered my face with the other.

"When are they coming?" Richard asked.

"When they pass through Lancaster next week."

"And Roger knows about this?"

"No."

He gripped the back of the chair and shook his head. "You are making a mockery of the Shuttleworth name. For far too long I have let you run around like an infant, and now this."

"*I* make a mockery of our family? *You* are the one with two families!"

"Damn you to hell, Fleetwood, I thought we were finished with that. Plenty of men have mistresses, it is not uncommon."

"We are common, then, are we? It is not the sort of thing that can be finished. I am trying to help an innocent woman — what is so wrong with that?"

Richard began pacing through the dust motes illuminated in a shaft of light, stepping into the beam then out again; lightness then darkness. "Why must you constantly undermine your own husband? Do you know how you make me look? And over a lowborn local girl you barely know — is she worthy of your attention? You have known her mere months. Why must you make such a spectacle of yourself, of us, for a woman who gave you some herbs?"

"If you do not understand this now, then you never will — *Alice is innocent.* And nobody believes it but me! Nobody wants to help! I *need* you, Richard. Who will you choose — your wife or your friend?"

"He was your friend, too! He was your friend!"

"I cannot be friends with that man after what he has done, and you shouldn't either."

"How can you say that? Roger is the closest thing to a father I have, and you. He has looked out for us. He has helped us through so much. He thinks I have what it takes to be sheriff. He sees me in Parliament one day. He *believes* in me, Fleetwood, like no one else ever has."

"You should see the gaol he has them in, then you would not think so highly of him. It is a corner from hell — dark and damp and they are locked in there with no light, standing and sleeping in vomit and waste and there are rats and Lord only knows what else. One of them died in there . . . Where is your heart? Do have a hole in your chest where it was? Where is the man I married?"

Richard was standing out of the shaft of light so I could not properly see him. What he said next made my blood run cold.

"Your lying-in starts now. I don't want to see you out of your chamber. You will stay in the house until the child arrives. It is mindless and foolish of you to go here, there and everywhere, putting yourself in harm's way. You are not thinking of our child, you are thinking only of yourself."

"What is so wrong with wanting to save her life?" I sniffed, wiping my eyes. "You were more grieved for your bird than the fate of an innocent woman. And you would prefer me dead anyway, would you not? Your life would be easier without me here, your friendship with Roger intact. You can marry Judith and forget I ever existed."

388

Puck whimpered and I stroked him absently. Richard's face was full of a private sort of agony. Before he could reply, I left the room, shutting the door behind me so he would not hear me cry.

CHAPTER TWENTY-ONE

The day of the dinner arrived, and the house hummed with purpose, but I did not. I'd followed Richard's wishes and stayed in bed, but I might as well have been running from a tiger because my heart raced as if I was, even when I was lying down. The thin sheet of pain was still wrapped around my chest, fine but tight, and my neck pulsed.

I had a new nightmare. In it, I was in the witches' dungeon. Even when I opened my eyes it was blacker than black, darker even than when my eyes were shut. There was the sound of dripping water, and someone was sobbing softly in the corner. I did not move, because the floor was wet, covered with what felt like straw and other things of unknowable textures. Just as I thought I would die from fright, close to me, very nearby, there was the sound of something eating. Not a person; something bigger, like a dog or some other creature. Teeth ripped easily through flesh, and the chewing was the worst thing, like it was in no rush at all, as though it was savoring every mouthful. That sound sent my stomach churning, my skin crawling, and I woke up drenched with sweat and fear, and my heart battering my rib cage.

I had no reply from the Lords Bromley and Altham, though I was not expecting one. But in my confinement I had not been able to ask Katherine whether or not she had carried out her task. By the time the morning arrived, my nerves were jangling like a bunch of keys. I sat in my chamber and imagined what was happening two and three floors below: the kitchen servants would be plucking, chopping and peeling; James would be selecting wines from the cellar; glasses and cutlery would be polished, knives sharpened . . . If they didn't come, it would be a splendid feast for two.

There was no sign of Richard: he was not speaking to me. I climbed out of bed and went to the looking glass, deciding to tackle my hair that hadn't been combed in a week. My arms ached, and I felt as though I hadn't slept in days, when really it was all I'd done. I cleaned my teeth and went to my dressing room, where I no longer took enjoyment. My notebook gathered dust in the corner.

Once I'd dressed in pale gold taffeta, the idea of going downstairs after so many days in my chamber felt strange. I had grown used to the size of it, like Alice and Joseph in their one-roomed cottage.

Just before midday, there was a knock at my door. Richard put his head in, his face tight. "Are you coming down?" he said.

I stood up. "Are they downstairs?"

"No, but the mistress who invited them should be."

The great hall was laid out for a feast, glinting with silver and glass and fresh linen napkins. Bowls of fruit brimmed with strawberries, plums, apples, pears and peaches. A very low fire crackled to take the slight chill out of the large room, and the sky blazed blue at every window. Richard and I stood in unhappy silence looking at it all, and then James appeared in the far-right doorway. "Master, your first guest has arrived."

Roger stepped into the great hall. Richard stepped forward to greet him. "Hello, Fleetwood," Roger said after shaking Richard's hand. His expression was mild. "Are you much recovered?"

I swallowed. "A great deal improved, thank you."

"You have Katherine to thank for that."

He smiled placidly.

My heart banged as loud as a musket going off. Richard moved to fetch him a glass of wine, ignoring me.

"The Lords Justices are not arrived?" Roger asked.

"Not yet. What time did you tell them dinner would be served, Fleetwood?"

"Noon, I think."

"It is unfortunate today is a fish day," Roger said to Richard. "That was a fine fallow you killed on Thursday."

"That was thirsty work. I think I shall wait for the weather to break before going out for that long again. The heat made the horses grow stupid."

"Your skill surpasses stupid horses. You would hunt well on a mule."

Richard laughed and clinked his glass with Roger's. He had not handed me one, so I moved toward Jacob, our red-cheeked, bright-eyed young server, who had noticed Richard's slight toward me and had flushed in embarrassment. I took a glass.

We made an odd triangle as the two men stood close to one another and I away from them, breathing deeply to calm myself, when James appeared again through the low doorway.

"Sir Edward Bromley and Sir James Altham." He gave a little bow and retreated, and as though appearing on either side of a stage, both doorways into the great hall were filled.

On the left, in the order James had announced them, Edward Bromley stood poised, a thumb hooked behind the velvet sash that cut through his middle. His doublet was very finely embroidered, with slashes through his sleeves, and his fan collar was tied beneath his chin with a green ribbon. He wore a wide black hat, and beneath it his eyes twinkled merrily. A mustache framed rosy cheeks, plump as apples that shone at either end of his smiling mouth. He was past middle age — at least forty — but handsome with it.

Standing ten feet from him in the other doorway was James Altham. Perhaps ten years older than Bromley, he was taller and slimmer, enhanced by a voluminous sleeveless gown thrown over one shoulder. His jacket was a pretty cream silk, cut close to his body with wide cuffs. His breeches were black velvet with gold stitching to match his jacket, and ribbons were tied around each of his slender knees. He was hatless, and had gray hair and serious dark eyes in a lined face.

As though hearing some silent cue, they

both stepped forward. Richard went to Sir Edward first so I hurried to the older Sir James at the same time, as was proper with guests of equal rank.

"Sir, thank you for coming to Gawthorpe," I said. "I trust you had a pleasant journey?"

"Mistress Shuttleworth, thank you for inviting us. It was very generous of you to entertain us while we are in the north."

His dark eyes fixed on mine as he kissed my hand, and I noticed their intensity.

The steward's voice interrupted, surprising me. "Master Thomas Potts," he announced.

I looked toward the door, my hand still caught in Sir James's, and saw a tall, slim young man standing in the entrance.

"Mistress Shuttleworth, I hope you do not mind my taking the liberty of inviting our constant companion during our tour. Master Potts is the clerk of the assizes."

The young man directed an elegant bow in my direction.

"Of course, welcome, Master Potts," I said.

The clerk moved inside and looked around the room, studying the coats of arms on the wall and the minstrels' gallery at the ceiling. He might have been younger than Richard, perhaps twenty-one or -two.

"Gentlemen." It was Roger's turn to greet our acquaintances, and he slid smoothly over to shake their hands. "It has been an age since we were last in each other's company. When was it . . . Tuesday?"

They all laughed heartily and the three arrivals were handed wine.

"Master Potts, you are traveling with the assizes?" I asked the youth.

"Yes," he replied in a gentle voice. Was there a hint of Scot about him? "We have just left York, and begin the Westmorland assizes the day after tomorrow."

"Ah, my mother lives in Westmorland," I said, regretting it instantly because she was the last person I wanted to talk about.

He nodded politely.

"Tell me." I lowered my voice, but the other men had moved toward the table and were talking loudly. "If you were at York, then you must have been present at the trial of Jennet Preston."

"Indeed," he said pleasantly, as if we were talking about a shipping merchant we had in common, not a woman hanged. "Are you an acquaintance of Master Lister of Westby?"

"Yes . . ." I trailed off, expecting something else would come to me, but it did not.

"This is a beautiful house."

"Thank you."

"How do you like living in the north?"

"I have never lived anywhere else." We walked toward the table, where a sixth setting had been discreetly made. "Is this your first tour of the assizes?"

"Yes, and very interesting it has been, too. I must say I find the people in the north very . . . *different*. Everything is different — the food, the humor, the towns. I am craving London already."

He smiled with sharp teeth like little pins. I smiled and took my seat, farther back than everyone else because of the size of my stomach. Roger was introduced to the young clerk.

"Pleasure to make your acquaintance," said Master Potts, repositioning his glass of wine.

Roger's eyes flicked toward mine, then away.

The first course was brought: salmon poached in beer, with pickled herrings. One glass of wine had helped me overcome the shock of Roger's arrival, and I turned to the two Lords Justices.

"How does your tour fare so far?"

"Very well, Mistress," said the genial Sir Edward. "We are over halfway through, with

Kendal next and Lancaster after that, as you know."

I colored slightly, hoping desperately that he would not mention in front of Roger the request I'd made in my letter, but he stopped there.

"So far we have completed Durham, Newcastle and York, and Carlisle is after Lancaster. And then we are on the long road home to the south."

"Tell me," I said. "You must have seen all sorts of fascinating arraignments in your work. For how long have you been justices on the northern circuit?"

"Two years," replied Sir Edward.

"And I just under ten," said Sir James.

"And this is my first time on the circuit," announced their clerk.

The men's eyes fell to their food and we began to eat. I could feel Roger's intense presence from across the table.

"I recently heard the news . . ." I tried to keep my voice steady. "That you found a woman guilty of witchcraft at York?"

"Indeed," said the older justice. "That was an interesting one, because the woman was also at the Lent assizes accused of the same thing."

"Again by Thomas Lister," I said.

The table fell silent. A piece of herring

trembled before Sir James's lips, having failed to reach its destination. "Quite right," he said. "You must take quite the interest in the laws of the realm."

"But this time she was found guilty."

"The woman was found to be guilty of the felony of murder by witchcraft of Thomas Lister Senior, yes." James Altham's voice was quiet, almost soft, as though cushioned. No doubt he saved its full impact for the courts.

I nodded and dislodged a salmon bone from the back of my mouth, trying not to gag.

"Sir Edward, however, did pardon her at Lent, so her life was graciously extended by some months." He spoke to his colleague. "I wonder if you had an idea then of how very *disparaging* her supporters were, and that was how you reached your verdict."

Sir Edward's eyes twinkled. "I knew nothing of the sort. They're a loud bunch, the Prestons," he explained to the rest of the table. "Poor Altham here has been vilified at every town from York to Gisburn. And that's quite a few."

I tried to imagine people crowding the streets in Padiham and Colne to protest against the arrest of the Pendle witches, and could not imagine so much as a single raised fist.

"And have you tried a person for witchcraft before this year?" I asked.

The pair looked at one another, considering for a moment.

"Never. In fact," said Sir Edward, "this is the largest group of people to be tried for witchcraft in this county."

"Ever?"

He nodded. I could not help but glance at Roger, who had been waiting for his turn to speak. "They have successfully hidden themselves all over the country, until now. It's like catching mice — when you find one, you know there's a whole nest. The king has long suspected Lancaster to be the hiding place of delinquents and sorcerers, so I am only happy to help root out the evil before it spreads and infects the rest of his kingdom."

"Would that imply you think evil is like a plague, Master Nowell?" asked Sir Edward.

"In certain neighborhoods. Look at the Devices and Redfearnes — they live not a hundred yards away from each other. Whether one household began with witchcraft and the other took it up to protect themselves, or something else, it's no coincidence. But old Demdike has been practicing for, oh, decades."

I realized I was staring at him and lowered my eyes.

Thomas Potts spoke. "Why do you think the old woman has avoided detection until now, if that is the case? Has no one accused her before this?"

"Not to my knowledge."

Our plates were removed and the second course of oyster pies was brought. I had three more courses to persuade the Lords Justices to . . . what, exactly?

"Where are you staying tonight?" asked Richard.

"A modest inn not far from here."

"Oh, but I insist you stay here."

"We will not intrude. We leave very early in the morning."

"Although a feather mattress would be quite welcome after so much straw," said Thomas, leaning in as if conspiring. The men laughed. I cleared my throat.

"I suppose you were relieved to cross the border and escape the Jennet Preston supporters," I said. I could feel Richard's eyes on me, but did not look.

"Quite, yes."

"And you have met no such protest on behalf of the so-called Pendle witches?"

"We have only just crossed into Lancaster," said Sir Edward, spilling open his pie.

"We are not so familiar with the cases yet, with Westmorland to come first. How many women are accused?"

"A dozen or so. But regrettably one passed away," said Roger, without a hint of regret. "However, I am investigating another case of a woman at Padiham."

"*Another* one?" I failed to control my voice.

"A woman named Margaret Pearson. My colleague Mr. Bannister is taking evidence tomorrow from her servant, who swears that she has seen Mrs. Pearson's familiar spirit."

"What is it?"

"A toad."

There was a pause, in which I'm sure a noise like suppressed laughter escaped from Thomas Potts. Roger ignored it.

"Mrs. Booth the servant says she was carding wool at her employer Pearson's house and asked her for some milk. They added wood to the fire to warm the milk pan, and when Mrs. Booth removed it, a toad — or a spirit disguised as a toad — came out of the fire. Margaret removed the creature with a pair of tongs and carried it outside."

"I am curious to know," I began mildly, "if you have yet seen any of these familiar spirits yourself, Roger."

There was an awkward silence, in which Roger chewed thoughtfully. "The Devil only appears to those who crave his company," he said eventually.

"Did you not say," I went on before I could stop myself, "that a familiar spirit is the surest sign of a witch? In which case, if a witch does *not* have a familiar spirit, they are likely to be innocent?"

Roger regarded me through heavy-lidded eyes and took a sip of his wine. "Or they keep it well hidden."

"Gentlemen," I addressed the Lords Justices. "*I* have a very large dog, who accompanies me everywhere. Should *I* not be accused of witchcraft?"

The table went silent, and my gaze landed on Roger, who regarded me coolly. "It sounds almost as though you are inviting accusation, Mistress. I would be very cautious, if I were you. You have your husband's reputation to consider. His name, the Lords Justices have told me, has already been heard of at Whitehall for the right reasons, so let there not be a wrong one."

The Lords Justices exchanged an uncomfortable glance.

"Is Padiham in the forest of Pendle, too?" Sir Edward asked politely.

"The boundary is that river there." Richard indicated with his knife. His tone was generous, but his mood unreadable. "So you are safe in this house."

"You cannot swear to that," Roger said. He was looking directly at me. "Seeing as one of the accused has been a guest here, and may well have left her evil stain on it."

Several powerful, intelligent gazes turned on me at once, and my voice died in my throat.

Roger's massive presence commanded the table, and the men peeled their eyes from me to look in disbelief at him. "One of the accused is a woman called Alice Gray, and she was Fleetwood's *midwife.*" He said the word with the same incredulity as if she'd claimed she was a mermaid.

Sir James pulled a puzzled face. "How very unusual."

"Quite." Roger did not move his eyes from my face.

In that moment, I hated not only him but Richard for inviting him, when he knew my mission. Things would have been entirely different with them both out of the way. I could have pleaded Alice's case and perhaps made some difference. But here we were, all together like one unhappy family. At that moment, the main course was brought out: a huge pike curled gracefully on a platter the size of a carriage wheel.

Richard's eyes met mine, and there was danger in his look, but also something that looked like guilt. Perhaps he realized now why I had invited them to dinner, and how he had made it impossible.

"Gentlemen, before we enjoy our next course, may I speak with my husband's permission?" I glanced again at Richard, who gave a quick, solemn nod. Roger cleared his throat, but I went on. "The woman who has been a guest here was my midwife, and friend, and her name is Alice Gray. She is on trial at the Lancaster assizes, accused of murder by witchcraft."

An attempt at a protest came from Roger, but I continued. My voice was high, and nervous, and I prayed it wouldn't falter. "Alice was working for me for some months, and she is an exceptional midwife. She is highly skilled, and learned her skill from her late mother, Jill."

I swallowed and looked at each of them directly, and they were all staring back at me, rapt, as though they had never heard a woman make a speech, as though I was a performer and they'd paid a penny.

"Alice is very generous, and obedient, and kind," I went on. I knew I was standing on the edge of a cliff with one foot dangling over; one mistake and I would slip. "A long time ago she was . . . She . . ."

I faltered, then I felt the most curious thing: waves of encouragement were radiating from somewhere close by, like heat from a fire. I breathed in, and felt warm, and comforted, so carried on. "A long time ago she found herself in a terrible situation no woman should be unlucky enough to experience. She has few family and friends — her only friend is sitting in the dungeon at Lancaster. I hope that . . ."

I blinked as tears came to my eyes. My throat became thick with emotion. "I hope that you will not punish her for the tragedy she endured, because she has already suffered immeasurably —"

Roger cut me off, shooting up in his chair. "I think we have heard quite enough. This is not a courtroom and the woman's plea will be heard where and when it is appropriate." His face was a dark red-purple with years of wine and getting his own way, his eyes little beads of malevolence.

I nodded and turned again to the Lords Justices. "I invited these men to my home, and I'm sure they do not consider it impertinent of me to talk fondly of my midwife, who they will soon meet in different circumstances. Are you offended, gentlemen?"

406

They shook their heads, bewildered but polite. Silence covered the table like a dust-sheet, and the only noise was the rain falling softly against the windows.

"Gentlemen, when we are finished eating I will show you around the house, if you would like to see it," Richard said.

Everyone was glad of the change in atmosphere, and the mood lifted as Richard cut fish for everyone and told a brief history of his uncles. Only Roger and I sat like dark clouds, wondering which of us would burst first.

CHAPTER TWENTY-TWO

One dreary, rainy afternoon a few days later, I was lying in my silent confinement when Richard knocked on the chamber door. He told me Lord Montague's players were in the area and would perform at the house that evening. Usually this would thrill both of us, but things were different now.

"Why in heavens would James agree for them to come at a time like this?" I asked, moving to sit upright.

Richard sighed. "I asked him to invite them months ago. They only announced their arrival this morning."

He left immediately and, wearily, I forced myself out of bed to get dressed.

I should have been surprised to see Roger sitting in the great hall, his hands knitted together resting on his large belly. But when I walked in, with Puck at my hand, my eyes were drawn not to Katherine, pale and drawn-looking on his left; instead they fell on the dark-haired woman sitting on his right. Her eyes were cast down into her lap, but her white collar lifted her features and pulled them from some distant corner of my mind. Behind the table, she had attempted to conceal beneath folds of brocade and taffeta her huge stomach. My head swam.

"Mistress," Roger said pleasantly. "May I introduce Judith, the daughter of my great friend Jeremiah Thorpe of Bradford — not to be confused with the Thorpes of Skipton, but perhaps a distant relative?"

There was a stunned silence, broken moments later by footsteps in the passage. Richard appeared in the other doorway. It took less than a second for him to take in the scene before him, and the color drained from his face.

What little resolve I had, the kernel of hope stuck deep inside me that had got me this far, vanished, like some tiny object being pulled into a great, powerful river. I knew it the moment it went, and I knew, too, that it was gone for good.

"Roger," Richard managed to say. But he was not angry; he was as breathless and surprised as if his friend had stabbed him.

Then several things happened at once. Puck began barking, unsettled by the awful feeling in the room; James arrived in the doorway to announce the Lord's players, who could be heard assembling in the hall; Richard regained his color all at once and turned an unsightly beetroot purple — I had never seen him so angry — and Judith looked up. When I watched her, all the noise in the room and in my head quietened. Her heart-shaped face was the color of cream, and her plump cheeks were the delicate warm orange of roses. Her liquid dark eyes gazed fearfully at Richard, but there was also guilt there, and admiration, and respect, and I could not deny it: love.

The chaos of the room came back and I put my hand to Puck's head, which silenced him instantly. He whimpered once and stood still. James trembled in the doorway, his mouth a perfect hole of surprise.

Richard strode over to where Roger was sitting at the table, a thorn between two trembling roses. "Roger, what do you mean by this?" he roared. "What on *earth* possessed you to do this?"

Katherine looked tearful, and had lost more weight since the last time I saw her. With a distant pang of guilt, briefly I wondered what it had cost her to defy Roger for me. Judith looked terrified, her lovely features arranged in an expression of anguish.

"Answer me now before I get that sword down and run it right through you, damn you, Roger, answer me!"

Roger's eyes traveled uneasily to the monstrous weapon that glittered above the fireplace. "As you know, Richard, Judith is a friend of the family, and I invited her to stay at Read Hall for a spell as she is sometimes short of company. So when Lord Montague's men announced their arrival in Pendle and inquired as to whether I would enjoy a private performance at Read, I found out they were also performing at Gawthorpe, so naturally I saw the opportunity to bring our families together for the . . . occasion." He spread his hands wide to encompass everyone in the room.

If I felt my resolve be swept into a river, then Roger was the river. I did not know where his evil stopped: it could not be stopped. It was so forceful and smooth, gathering everything up as it went along and swallowing it.

"Master?" James tried timidly to thaw the frozen scene before him. The only person who was at ease was Roger, drumming his ringed fingers. Behind him, where the low voices of the players buzzed a minute

411

before, there was a hush as they awaited instruction.

Very slowly and stiffly, Richard turned to face me. His face was a mask of grief. It probably mirrored mine. "Fleetwood, will you join us?" he asked, his voice thick with emotion.

I blinked through tears at Judith, the woman with whom I shared a husband and now a home. She kept her gaze on her hands, which were folded in her lap. I sniffed and nodded, taking a seat next to Richard.

While wine and sacke was brought, six or seven men trooped into the gallery and took a bow. "Good evening, ladies and gentlemen." A young, handsome one in the middle spoke. He had a wide mouth and a clear, gentle voice. "Master and Mistress Shuttleworth, thank you for inviting us into your splendid home. Tonight's play is a national favorite from one of the greatest living playwrights, and it is certainly one of *our* favorites to perform. A tragedy of ambition, a maze of morals and with a touch of magick, cast your imaginations to deepest, darkest Scotland — which should be relatively easy in these climes." He paused in anticipation of a titter of appreciation, so no doubt the collection of stony faces a few

412

yards below unsettled him. "Ladies and gentlemen, William Shakespeare's *Macbeth*!"

With a flounce of his cloak, the assembled men left the gallery save for three, who had pulled their cloaks up over their heads and sat hunched in a tight circle. I was vaguely aware of all this, but my mind was occupied by a dull kind of numbness. I had seen the play before.

"Round about the cauldron go;
In the poison'd entrails throw.
Toad, that under cold stone.
Days and nights has thirty-one . . .
Double, double toil and trouble; fire burn,
    and cauldron bubble."

While the players chanted, from the corner of my eye I was aware of Judith, sitting still and upright, her face turned up toward the players but perhaps looking about at the room: at the china vases in the cabinets, the polished sconces on the walls, the portraits, all ordinary things, but no doubt of great interest to her eyes. She would be drinking in every detail of his house to savor and think of later, to imagine him wandering about the rooms where before he would have wandered about in her imagination.

413

Unless, of course, she had been here before.

Rain lashed at the windows; the players could barely be heard and were raising their voices, sounding slightly hysterical.

"Scale of dragon, tooth of wolf,
Witches' mummy, maw and gulf.
Of the ravin'd salt-sea shark,
Root of hemlock digg'd i' the dark."

The rain lashed, and Judith's presence was loud as a bell. I could feel her casting glances at me, but I kept my face on the gallery. How lifeless we must all look, how dull and bored. The clock ticked loudly. I thought of the stairs down to the dungeon, and the door closed on the darkness. Tick, tick, tick.

Root of hemlock, digg'd i' the dark.

A servant taken ill. A rag poppet on a bed, tied with black hair to a child. A bowl of blood, vanished. A falcon ripped to death. A nightdress in the dark, floating palely, coming ever closer.

"Stop!" I shouted. "Please, stop."

Richard leaped up in alarm and clapped his hands. "Gentlemen. My apologies, but my wife has been taken ill."

I was vaguely aware of confusion, and apologies, and the gathering up of things

414

and more faces appearing in the gallery, and the clink of coins. I sat staring at my hands that were ice-cold and dead-looking. Soon I might actually be dead, and Alice, too, but this room and these people would remain, and the year 1612 would become a distant memory, a long time ago. Wine would be poured for Richard and his new wife, and Roger and Katherine would play with their pink-cheeked child. I could feel the other child's presence in the room, feet away from me, waiting to be born, waiting to claim its place, and Judith mine.

Even in life I had been the little ghost, and now I was consigned to death. I held my stomach, and imagined disappearing. It would come soon, no doubt, but it would not be gentle, like the light leaving the sky. It would be painful, and terrifying, and lonely, with no cool hand on my head, no amber eyes willing me calm. There would be a trial, and Alice would die, then I would die, both of us killed in an outbreak of misfortune. I closed my eyes, and thought of my child, and how much I wanted us both to live. My earthly life was coming to an end, and the end was nigh.

CHAPTER TWENTY-THREE

It was the day before the assizes opened, and almost every man and woman in the county and those surrounding it had come to see the fates of the Pendle witches unfold. The streets of Lancaster were thronged with horses and carts and people and dogs and cows and chickens and children and all kinds of obstacles that led our coachman to curse audibly and repeatedly behind Richard and me as he navigated the cart carrying our luggage and a travel-weary Puck. Sat tall on my horse, I kept my eyes down as we crossed the cobbles to join the throng moving up the hill, feeling my skin prick with stares. I wanted to disappear, but with the size of my stomach I was as conspicuous as if I'd grown a beard. The narrow streets were a mass of brown clothes, white caps, black hats and unwashed skin. I watched a little boy of one or two stumble into the road in front of my horse and be wrenched back by his mother before the horse's plate-sized hooves claimed him. She caught my eye, and I think she was surprised at how indifferent I was, how unmotherly.

Richard and I traveled all the way in a numb sort of silence with Puck occasionally padding at our sides or trundling behind us, whining occasionally with discomfort. It was a welcome relief when the noise and distraction of Lancaster arrived. By mid-afternoon we were pulling in to the yard of the Red Lion, a modest inn shielded by trees, tucked away down a narrow road leading to the river. I barely noticed the room we were shown to on the third floor, but it was clean and well furnished, with carpets on the cupboards and a handsome four-poster bed. I glanced around the room for the truckle bed for Alice, before realizing there was none, and there would not be one again. When my trunk was set down with a thud I jumped, and the porter looked at me with curiosity. The baby bucked and rolled inside me, invigorated by the long and bumpy journey. I was so big my skirts hung inches away from my legs, and so far from the floor I might have grown upward, as well.

Bread and milk was brought for the dog, which he ate gratefully before setting on the

417

Turkey carpet in front of the fireplace. I could not settle so easily: I was cold and shivering, and lay on the bed, drawing my knees up to meet my stomach.

Richard stood at the window, his hands clasped behind his back. Since the dreadful dinner a week before, I had barely spoken. I had barely eaten or slept. I drifted up and down the long gallery, my legs planted wide on the polished wood to balance my massive stomach. Or I sat at various windows, facing out, and the baby moved for both of us. I could tell Richard was still anxious I would lose it, and I felt like telling him there was no need to be so worried about things that were out of our control, when there was so much that we could have done, and had not. The appeals we should have made; the help we should have offered. I dared not think it was too late, but part of me knew it was: for me, for her, for everything.

"How do you think it will go?" Richard spoke.

I stared at the wall. "They cannot be found guilty," I replied. "Their only witnesses are each other. They are like children telling tales."

"People are hanged for a lot less. Do you really think they know the Devil?"

I thought of Malkin Tower poking up from

the moorside like a finger from a grave. How the wind had howled there; how it would drive you mad. I thought of Alice's home, open to the sky; the damp streaming down the walls; the child she knew as a daughter buried in the thick wet soil. What was there for them in this life? In the shadows cast by their fire at night, perhaps they did see things they wanted to see. "If the Devil is poverty, and loneliness, and hunger, then yes, I think they know the Devil."

Richard went to the castle to find out when the witches' trial would start. For the rest of the day I lay fully dressed on the bed, staring out the window at the trees, with Puck lying next to me, thumping his tail happily at being allowed on the counterpane. Even with the glass separating me from the street, I was aware of a strange quality to the air — it seemed to be oozing down the slope from the town toward the river, and I realized it was excitement. The trees shivered with it and it bounced off the walls and flags of the yard like rain. More carriages were arriving at the inn, and the yard was full of people with brightly expectant faces talking to one another. Women carrying babes cradled them patiently; men stood astride the cobbles with a sense of purpose. I knew that if I could listen I would hear a hundred different opinions, all of them certain. Neighbors denouncing neighbors, which was how the dungeon was filled. It was the most reliable trait of humanity. Rumor spread faster than disease, and was just as destructive.

A maid brought a tray of food and set it on the cupboard, bowing clumsily, flinching when she saw the dog. I didn't look at the tray, let alone touch it. I felt for the paper in my pocket I had put there the night before — my statement defending Alice's innocence that I hoped to read aloud before the judges. A more eloquent version of my speech to the Lords Justices, I had written it at least five times, the paper blotting with ink and tears and tearing under my shaking hand. If they would not let me speak, I would try to have Richard stand for me. He did not know this yet, because I could not face him refusing me this one kindness, though I would never ask anything of him again. I did not know if they would let me read it at the assizes, did not know of any time when a woman had been allowed to stand up and speak when she was not in the dock. The idea of doing it sent my legs to melting, but then I thought of Alice's face, blinking in the light after being kept in the dark. She had to be there, yet I had a choice. Roger had said no witnesses would be brought, but the Lords could surely not ignore the polite request of a member of the gentry, when they had dined at his house? I would leave it until the last moment to ask Richard, because I was not convinced myself that it would be enough, and until I was, I could not persuade him with conviction.

As more people arrived at the inn, the passages filled up with voices and the sound of boots on stone. I listened vacantly over Puck's snores as women chatted and scolded their children, men bellowed, trunks scraped and dogs barked.

I was holding the paper so tightly I thought it might tear, thinking of how not so long ago I'd held a different letter — one that gave death, while this one gave life. A noise in the passage: much closer. A man's voice drawing near; a door opening and closing.

Suddenly I was wide-awake. I pushed myself up on my elbows, bringing my head in line with the top of my stomach. The child must have been sleeping, for once. I went to the window and looked at the sky; I did not have a watch. Where was Richard? It would soon be dark, and from below came the sound of the kitchen getting the supper things ready. Barrels rolled in the yard and the traffic in the streets had eased. I had what felt like a hair's breadth of time to make a decision: it had to be now. I did not need more than that.

I woke Puck from where he lay next to me and beckoned him to the floor, where he landed ungracefully on a pile of orange hairs by the door and began sniffing. He had not lain there; this room must not have been cleaned properly. Enough of that — it did not matter. I went to one of the trunks, thanking Prudence for blessing me with her gift earlier, and pulled out the long, wrapped package I had inexplicably buried among several nightshifts. I went to the cupboard and scrawled a note for Richard. Then I cast a swift look around the room, making sure I had got what I needed, and left for the stables with my dog at my heel and the package slim and discreetly at my side.

CHAPTER TWENTY-FOUR

John Foulds's house was down a dank little alley in Colne. By the time I arrived it was almost midnight, and I was breathless from navigating the horse along the black paths. But the moon was on my side: full and bright, it had shone all the way from Lancaster, lighting the way for our ghostly procession. And I had Puck with me, so I felt safe, and I held his head with one hand and knocked on John Foulds's front door with the other.

The street was silent and there were no lights in the windows. I'd knocked on four doors where I saw the yellow glow of rushlight from the house, and the fourth occupant — a woman, her face creased with tiredness — told me in surprise that John Foulds lived one row behind the market street, three doors from the right. Luckily the moon was full and watery over the village, and the alehouses were long closed, so

I could see, but would not be seen.

I knocked again, and Puck gave a low growl from deep inside his throat. I looked around, and could see no figure at either end, but did have the sense of being watched. It was too dark to see into the shadows pushing up against the houses. I shivered and set my eyes on the wooden door in front of me, knocking more impatiently this time. Then, suddenly, all the hairs on my neck stood up, and I knew there was someone in the alley. Puck immediately began barking, straining from my grip and directing his aggression to our right, and in the gloom I saw something low and spindly slink around the last house. An animal, then. I banged furiously on the door, and a man's voice shouted from behind it, and then I was looking into the face of John Foulds.

Tousled dark brown hair hung down on both sides of his face, and he was dressed for bed, wearing a loose cotton smock, untied at the neck. He was as handsome as I'd remembered, but there was something in his eyes that was not — a coldness, perhaps — that impacted on his features in a way that no end of clothing or pomade or jewelry could disguise.

Whatever it was died when he saw what I

held to his stomach: Richard's musket, which I'd carried with one aching arm beneath my cloak. And then he saw the dog, and there was fright there, and even resignation, as though he had been expecting this very thing to happen to him: a four-foot-eleven pregnant woman arriving on his threshold with a gun.

He angled himself so that he was standing in between the door and the wall, and I could not see into the small house. I pushed the barrel of the musket into his chest, and was thankful for how heavy it was, because I was shaking so badly. "Will you let me in?" I said.

"Are we to fight a duel?" he said dryly, his lip curled.

Puck growled, and he eyed the massive dog anxiously, then gave me a look and opened the door wider. I went in, Puck padding behind me.

The tiny house had one room downstairs and one up, accessed by a steep set of narrow stairs against the back wall. John Foulds held the only rushlight in the room, and from the glow it cast out I could see a few shapeless objects: a couple of chairs by the fireplace, a low cupboard covered with a cloth and pots and pans. John went to light another rush, and the fatty fumes were choking, but I watched his every move, looking for a flash of silver in case he had a knife, because I had no idea how to use Richard's gun.

"Who are you?" he asked, holding the torch up to my face.

"You don't know me," I said. "But we have a mutual friend."

He made a noise like forced laughter. "I wouldn't call him a friend."

"Who?"

"Roger Nowell. Is that not who you are here for?"

"No." I stared at his flickering face, half-hidden in shadow. He scratched his neck and glanced about nervously. If he moved an inch I would move quicker. "Did he give you money?"

"What if he did?"

I let the musket's barrel fall, heard the mechanisms clink inside. The weight of it was exhausting. Just as I'd reached Colne, it had started to rain very lightly, and now it was coming down harder, thudding into the dirt in the street. John Foulds's eyes glittered in the candlelight.

"Why is Alice Gray on trial for murdering your daughter?"

"She's a witch," he said simply.

His neck was warm and brown in the

rushlight, the top of his chest smooth.

"She loved you," I said, trying to stop my voice from shaking. "And she loved Ann."

"Who are you?"

"It doesn't matter."

"Who is your husband?"

"It doesn't matter. But you will give me something tonight. I will not leave here without a written testimony from you that says Alice Gray did not murder your daughter."

He looked at me as if I was crazed. Then he started to laugh. I smelled something else then, masked under the dripping grease of the rushlights. Ale. Fermentation. Decay. John Foulds was still a drunk.

"If Alice is hanged, it will not bring your daughter back. Why would you see an innocent woman killed?"

"Innocent? She's a bitch," he spat. "Anyway, I can't write."

My heart sank. I'd brought paper and ink and a quill and tucked it in the pack of the horse I'd ridden like a madwoman for the last few miles. The horse was tied outside and would now be soaked, if it hadn't been stolen already. The musket was so heavy it was making my arms hurt. I could not turn my back on him.

John Foulds had checkmated me.

427

The stairs creaked, making me jump, and someone began walking down them. A long white smock descended from the ceiling, then the rest of a plump body, and a plain-faced woman in a cap appeared, her mouth a little round O as she took in the scene before her. Her eyes widened when she saw Puck; he might have been a wolf in the dim light, and certainly looked monstrous in the little room.

"John?" she said.

"Go back to bed."

"Who is this?"

"Now," he barked.

The woman turned with difficulty on the dark, narrow staircase, holding the wall with one hand, and before her head disappeared I said, "Wait." She froze. "Bring me paper and ink, and a quill."

She looked quickly at John, and nodded, but did not move.

"Now," I said, and she disappeared, creaking up the stairs. "You are literate, then," I said to John. "Your wife?"

He regarded me with vicious hatred. "No."

"How much money did Roger give you?"

"None of your business."

"It is the business of the king's peace. How much?"

He moved his jaw; his eyelids lowered.

"What is of more use to you — money or ale? I have a brewery. If you do what I want, you will have a hogshead sent every month." His eyes widened. He was listening. "I presume that's what you spend your money on. Unless you prefer brandy? Wine? What will it be?"

"How will I know you will keep your word?"

I loosened my grip on Puck's collar and he lurched forward, snapping his mighty jaws. John Foulds leaped back and gave a cowardly whimper. What did Alice see in this weak, selfish man?

The woman padded back down the stairs and handed me the things I'd asked for, never moving her eyes from the dog. As soon as I took them she ran back upstairs.

"They say dogs can smell fear," I told him. "I would try to mask it, if I were you. But I know how hard it is when you're terrified. I am scared, John. I am scared that my friend will be hanged for a crime she did not commit. And not only her — *her* friend might be hanged, too, for trying to save your daughter's life."

I looked round at the unhappy room, with its stench of fat and ale and the chill that came from the bare walls, and shivered. It was no place for a child. Maybe it was cheerful once, when his wife was alive and they had their new baby wrapped in fresh linen, with the front door open to the street so the neighbors could come in and tell them how blessed they were.

"And what if I don't," he sniffed. "You'll shoot me?"

"Yes. Unless you would prefer to be worried by the dog?" His dark eyes went from one to the other. I handed him the paper and quill, and nodded. He sighed and carried it to the low cupboard, bending over to flatten it out in the pool of light.

"What do I write?"

"The truth."

I stood shivering and waited as he scratched down his words in an untidy, barely legible scrawl. I listened to the horse exhaling outside, and the floorings creaking above, and the rain on the street. My chest was tight with fear, and relief, and I thought of the long way I had to go in the morning. I would ride back to Gawthorpe tonight and sleep for a few hours, then leave for Lancaster before dawn.

John Foulds handed me his testimony, and I read it through quickly. "Add a line about Katherine Hewitt," I said. "She is arraigned for the same thing."

He rolled his eyes. "I am not writing a

whole book."

"You will do what it takes. Add a line."

He flounced back to the cupboard and scratched a fierce black scrawl at the bottom of the paper. "There," he said. "Good enough?"

"I don't know," I said, taking it from him and folding it into my pocket. "You had better hope so."

"Meaning?"

"If it isn't, I may pay you another visit, and don't expect me to be in a bargaining mood. The assizes start in the morning, should you wish to face what you have done like a man. Good night." I turned to leave, but it was only a couple of steps to the door. The rain teemed down outside.

"If that bitch hangs, I'll still get my ale, won't I?"

I stopped in the doorway, and without turning round, released my hand from Puck's collar. All John Foulds would have seen was a streak of copper and a flash of teeth as the dog threw himself at him and sank his mouth into his arm. He cried out in high-pitched terror, then cursed, rolling about and gripping his elbow. Blood bloomed dark on the dirty white linen. I called Puck softly, and he came back to me. I turned to face the weak, trembling, cowardly man whom Alice once loved.

"Yes, you will still get the ale," I said. "Because if my dog doesn't kill you, that will. And the slower the better."

An hour later, I realized I was lost. I meant to head west along the river to Gawthorpe, but the rain was coming down so hard and was so loud I couldn't hear the water, let alone see in the darkness, or even think. There were only trees, and mud, and clouds flitting across the moon, making it impossible.

I was soaked. The horse was soaked and plodding ahead miserably, stopping now and again in protest. Puck trudged on next to us, exhausted as I was, his drenched coat dark brown. My stomach felt heavier than ever, and my heart was racing despite the slow pace. I turned left and right and left again, hoping to find the wide roads that ran between villages. All I could think of was the two pages in my skirts: my testimony and John Foulds's. If they were wet, they were ruined. Something was lodged in my stomach, and I thought it might be despair, but I would not submit to it. I would not cry; I would find my way home, even if it took all night. I would go to Lancaster tomorrow and stand up in court and hear my own voice ring through the hall, pronouncing Alice's innocence, and everyone would listen, and her chains would clatter to the floor, and she would be free.

I was slumped forward over my stomach, riding at a snail's pace through the woods, with tall black tree trunks gliding past me surrounding me on all sides, and the rain seeping down my neck, and my dog whining at my side, and the horse's hooves thudding into the mud, and then The Nightmare began.

The horse stopped suddenly, as though startled, and that's when I heard the grunting. It was low, but distinguishable even over the rain. Cold fear drenched me from the head down, and I felt dizzy with it. I closed my eyes and opened them in case I had fallen asleep and was dreaming, but that sound: I knew it, had heard it many times throughout my life, but always in my sleep. Now I was awake, and alone in the woods. Puck barked, and there was a low squeal, and another chomping, grunting noise, and I knew it was closer, but I could see nothing on the ground. I kicked the horse and shouted for it to go, but it staggered about in terror, and then I felt it land against something, and it neighed, and reared — and I began to slip down.

I screamed and it bucked again, and I jerked sideways. The soaked musket that had been in my lap clattered to the ground, and I gave a cry, gripping desperately to the reins but finding only the horse's mane and damp neck. It reared once more, and I kicked my feet out of the stirrups lest I get dragged for miles, but then I was falling backward into the blackness. The world tipped upside down, and the rain fell on my face, and my feet were over my head, and there was a moment — a clear, pure moment of rapid fall, where my mind was empty, and I was flying, no, falling — and then I hit the ground, landing on my side, my stomach smashing into the mud.

I lay with one cheek to the ground, and somewhere close by Puck was barking furiously, and the sound of hooves grew quieter as the horse galloped farther away, and the rain continued to fall. I could not move, but I could hear, was listening for the grunts I knew would come. And then I heard them. There was more than one, a boar coming from somewhere behind me, and one in front, and Puck was nearby, thrashing and barking and growling and snapping, and there was an explosion of squeals, and I had no idea how many of them there were, or if Puck would survive their ivory tusks, like little daggers shooting from their faces.

I closed my eyes because I knew they would reach me — they always did — but it was what happened after that I did not know. And while Puck wrestled with one or two or three, I felt a curious nudge on my leg, then heard the sound of grunting, greedy with hot breath and blood-soaked teeth. I was wet, with rain or blood or my own piss, and my legs were damp under my skirts, and that's when the pain started.

Perhaps a tusk pierced my stomach, because it was instant and fierce, a great crashing blow, and my heart pounded in my chest, and I could not move. But then, just as quickly I was empty, my body ringing with its shocking absence. And then it came again, and something was nuzzling my neck, my face, something hairy and then soft — was it Puck? Something else? And I closed my eyes and began to cry, my tears mixing with the rain, and then the pain came again, harder, driving right into my body, into my spine, and I could not move, with agony or terror I did not know, but I was blind with it.

I was dreaming, I had to be — I had been knocked out, or I was sleeping. I was at home, at Gawthorpe, in my bed, and the window was full of stars — no, I was lying on the forest floor, in the rain, miles from home, miles from anywhere, and I was alone, and about to die.

Her earthly life will end.

I was too frightened to cry, but this was a different kind of fright to how I felt in my nightmare. There was knowledge now, and understanding, but still terrible fear, and I could not decide what was worse: the fear or the understanding that this was it.

My dog. Where was he? I had saved him from a life of violence and misery, and I loved him. I opened my eyes to look for him, and there was a streak of copper, bright as a flame before my eyes, and I closed them again. I knew he was near, fighting for me, that great beast I had carried around and petted and kissed and told secrets to, who could kill a bull but wouldn't hurt a fly.

My baby, who I would never meet, and who would never meet me, but we knew each other, and that was enough. Agony seared me again like a branding iron, creasing me in half, and I hoped my child did not feel it, and was not afraid.

Her earthly life will end.

The sounds seemed to fade away, but I was pinned to the ground, still pinned to this life under great rolling waves of agony. I might have been under a carriage wheel going back and forth, back and forth.

The rain was soft, like Richard kissing my shoulder.

The papers in my pocket would be soaked.

Alice. I had to save Alice.

I opened my eyes, but it was as black as if they were shut. I closed them against the pain, and waited for the darkness to come.

"Mistress?"

Birds were singing. The sound of them was so cheerful. Arms lifted me. Another stab of pain coursed through me, like I was lowering myself into a scalding bath.

"My God, look at her."

"Is she dead?"

They sounded afraid, and I had no wish to open my eyes and look at whom they were talking about.

"Is she bleeding?"

I was being lifted up, but I was heavy, my dress soaked with rain. More pain, too much to make a sound, and cold — so cold.

"She's shivering."

"Quick, be quick, man!"

Then I was moving, with a steady rhythm like a baby being rocked in a cradle, and I could see green leaves and dark branches waving above me, and hear the wind sliding through the woods. I liked the woods, and felt safe there, and I must have fallen asleep because suddenly I was being carried upstairs, laid across a powerful chest like an offering. Strong arms held me, and we moved upward, and I wondered if this was God taking me to heaven. Then I was in my chamber, being lowered into bed, and the counterpane was pulled back, and all the drapes opened, and people were standing around the bed, but I did not have time to look who they were because another crease of pain was starting, and it brought me back to life, because although I was awake, I felt as though I was dreaming. And that's when I realized where I was, and what was happening to me.

The baby was being born.

I screamed, and tried to sit up, and at some point my gown and jacket and farthingale had been removed and I was lying in my smock, which was stained red from my waist to my ankles. "No," I murmured. "No, no, no. Richard! Alice, where is Richard?"

"We are fetching Richard," said a small voice next to me, and I saw one of the boy apprentices from the farm standing inexplicably by my bed.

"The boars," I told him. "I need Alice. Send for Alice."

He wrung his cap in his hands, frightened

out of his wits.

"George, go back outside and wait for the midwife," said another voice, and it was James the steward's, who was standing at the foot of my bed. His face was gray.

"Midwife?" I asked, aware that another roll of pain would soon knock me sideways. "Is Alice not coming? Only she can help me. Where is she?"

And then I remembered. I had left Lancaster to visit John Foulds, and have his statement, because the trial was today. Alice was standing trial, several miles away, and I was here, bleeding, and that only meant one thing. My earthly life was ending, and so was hers. A great roaring wail came from somewhere in my stomach and escaped from my mouth. "Alice! I must get to Lancaster — the trial is today. Am I too late?"

"The master is on his way, Mistress, he is almost here, and a doctor, too, and a midwife." James's dark eyes were shining with terror.

"Where is my gown? Fetch my gown."

Someone — not James — brought it to me from where it must have lain crumpled on the floor, wet with soil and blood and rain.

"The pocket, open the pocket." I could

not do it myself; I was braced against the pain, propped on my elbows, trying not to look at the blood coating my smock and the sheets, trying not to cry. But I was so terrified, and no one knew what to do, least of all me, and if I was going to die on this bed I at least wanted to hold my husband's hand while doing it, because I loved him, and I forgave him everything, and hoped he did me. Bits of paper were being drawn out of the ruined gown, and I snatched them out of the woman's hand — a kitchen servant — and cried out with relief, for they were dry, protected by the lining.

And then I was being trampled, again and again, by this great wheel of agony, and then it went away, and someone came and told me to sleep, and bathed my head with a cloth, but it was not Alice, and it was not the same.

"Alice is innocent. I saw John Foulds," I muttered, and this voice said "shh, I know, I know," and then perhaps I did sleep, because the next thing I was awake, filled again with panic that the trial was happening several miles away and I was not there, and could not move.

And then Richard was in the room, filling it with his compelling power and authority, as if the king himself had walked into my

440

chamber.

He fell on me, taking my hands, and his face was wet. "My little ghost, what have you done?"

I was vaguely aware there was another woman with him, a stout, wide sort of presence with pink skin, and I thought in horror that it was Miss Fawnbrake. But Richard told me it was a midwife from Clitheroe, and she would . . . But I was not listening, because now he was here, something strange was happening, as though I was sinking into sleep. But I had something to give him — I felt around on the bed for the papers, and thrust them into his hands.

"Richard, you have to go now, you have to read these at the assizes." My mouth was very dry, and my voice faint.

"What is this?"

"Richard, *please,* listen to me. These statements could set Alice free." Another bolt of pain seared me like an iron white from the furnace. "You have to go and insist they be read, or read them yourself. It's my statement, and John Foulds's." My head was spinning, my vision blurring. *Her earthly life will come to an end.*

"Of course not, Fleetwood, I am staying here, with you."

"You have to do this!" I all but screamed.

441

"Get her out, Richard. Get her out! Only she can save me, and only I her!"

"Enough!"

His voice was like the voice of God, swimming around in some great cavernous darkness, because I was drifting away from him, from my chamber, from everything. I thought I knew the pain, but it turned out I'd only had the best of it, and the worst was to come.

I was being stabbed with knives. I was being washed with flames. Chains covered me, and kept me down, though I tried to lift myself, and couldn't. My limbs: full of water. My body: cut in half, sliced from the scalp. Every inch of me screamed, except for my mouth, because when I opened it nothing came out. Water — I needed water in my mouth. Water to extinguish the flames that licked along my spine. I was on fire. I was dying, I was dead, and must be in hell. I could feel water streaming out between my legs, because they were wet — I needed it on my skin, in my mouth. Darkness came again, mercifully wrapping me in its thick black cloak.

"Fleetwood."

"Fleetwood."

"Fleetwood."

There was love in the voice, and grief, and

it was shaking with both of those things. A woman's voice, or was it a man's? Was it God's? The pain — I *was* pain, it was not separate from me, was not something happening to me. Darkness came again, and I was grateful.

A blackbird sitting on the bedpost. The sheets white, and clean, and tidy. Blue sky framed in the window. The bird cocked its head, expectant. *Samuel,* I thought. His feathers gleamed, but were streaked in parts. He shook out his wings, and a black cloud appeared, like smoke. Soot. He had flown down the chimney, and wanted me to let him out. "All right," I sighed.

A streak of fur against my arm. I knew it was a fox before I opened my eyes. It was standing on the floor by my bed, staring at me with wide amber eyes. It looked as though it was desperate to tell me something, and I laughed, and said "What is it?"

And then the strangest thing happened: the fox opened its mouth and spoke, and it was female, and what it said was: *"Honi soit qui mal y pense."* Shame on him who thinks evil of it.

The darkness went on for so long, I could not remember what light looked like. But then there was candlelight, dotting my vision like pearls on a black velvet dress. A cool hand on my head brought me out of the darkness. It was the hand of light, but the hand of darkness tugged at my feet, at my arms. *No, I want to stay in the light.* I tried to brush it away, concentrating on the small, cool hand — or was it a cloth? — on my head that was anchoring me to the room in the wild, dark sea that raged on inside me.

"Push," a voice said. "You have to push."

A white cap. A twist of golden hair tumbling from it. It was the girl from the forest with the bag of rabbits. What was her name?

A wave of pain crashed into me, and to end it I had to strain against it, to push it away and out of my body.

"Push!"

Something spilled, and there was a gush like a barrel of fish knocked over. The wave was coming again, building slowly, then crashing, and I strained harder, harder, harder, until I thought I might burst.

"When it comes again, push!"

Oh, did it have to come again? Yes, it was coming now, and I was ready for it this time, braced against it like I was about to do battle with some ancient deity, and knew that I would lose, but would do my best anyway. There was a horrible cry, an agonized groan, and I wished whoever it was would stop, but then I realized *my* mouth was open and *my* lungs were emptying, and it felt good, like I was wringing myself out, because it was louder than the pain.

And as my cry died, another one started up. But this one was much softer, and in short little bursts rather than one great long note. The crashing waves had stopped, and were coming now in little lapping motions, like bathwater against the tub. That strange noise again, almost like a lamb, or a kitten. Suddenly I felt more tired than I'd ever been in my life. I wanted to sleep, and although my limbs were heavy as lead, my heart drummed on furiously, going *bang bang bang.*

But there were people in the room, and they were being loud, even though I wanted to sleep. I heard the word *blood* over and over, and they sounded panicked. Had they never seen blood before?

Sleep — I needed sleep.

"Fleetwood, stay with me. Fleetwood, stay here."

Where else was I going? I was too tired to move. The darkness that had been tugging me earlier had now wrapped my hand in his, ready to take me with him. Ah, that's where they meant. Don't go with him. *I can't go,* I said. *I have to stay.* Another tug, more

445

insistent this time, and with it I knew it would be quiet there, and peaceful, and safe. I was already lying down — it would be so easy to surrender to warm, thick darkness.

"Fleetwood, drink this."

Just wait a moment, I need to have a drink. A drink would be good. With difficulty, for he was strong, I removed myself from his silky grip, and felt a cup at my lips, and something warm and sweet in my mouth. Then the liquid was replaced with something hard and earthy, and I was told to chew.

As I came to my senses, the room was mercifully quiet. A single bird sang outside the window, framing the light gray sky, and the fire burned merrily, filling the room with the scent of woodsmoke. A woman was bent over the fire with her back to me, stirring a pot, and the sharp tang of herbs scented my chamber. Pain echoed around my body still, and every part of me wanted to sleep. I watched her, and saw the creamy curve of her neck, and the mischievous way her hair refused to go neatly in her cap. She stood and went to look at something at the foot of the bed, and made a gentle noise.

"Alice," I whispered, and I don't know she heard me, but she looked up, and I saw

446

she was crying. She moved toward me, and knelt beside my bed. I went to sit up, but she put a firm hand on my arm. We looked at one another for a long time, and I wanted to ask her things, but the effort of speaking would not be worth the answers, because for now they did not matter.

"Willow bark," she said, and I realized the bitter wood was still in my mouth, and it was perhaps helping, for my mind felt clearer and my heart no longer galloped. I wanted to wipe her cheeks, because tears were falling down them freely, collecting on her jaw and running down her neck. "You should sleep." She moved to stand up, her skirts rustling.

Obeying like a child, I closed my eyes. There was another rustle, and the comforting scent of lavender, and I felt on my forehead her lips, very softly, and her breath on my cheek.

When I reached again for the darkness, it was not there.

■ ■ ■ ■

PART FOUR

■ ■ ■ ■

"Kind friends know and keep."
KAY-SHUTTLEWORTH FAMILY MOTTO

CHAPTER TWENTY-FIVE

Richard Lawrence Shuttleworth was born just before dawn on the twentieth day of August 1612, the same day that ten witches were hanged on the hill overlooking Lancaster.

Alice Gray was not one of them.

It was only because Puck had run from that deep pocket of forest to Gawthorpe, which was actually only a mile away, that all three of us — Alice, my son and I — survived. His barks at the cellar door roused the servants, who woke James, who woke some of the apprentices, and my dog led a torchlit procession through the trees back to where I lay in the mud, arriving as daylight broke on the first day of the witch trials. One of the men — the best rider on the fastest horse — raced forty miles to the Red Lion at Lancaster to fetch Richard, who was worked into a frenzy not knowing where I was, and having asked at every door in Lancaster if anyone had seen a small woman with a large stomach and a huge dog. All I'd left was a note saying I'd be back before the trial started. He had even gone to the home of Thomas Covell the castle keeper, but the words died in his mouth as he realized Roger might be sitting in the parlor with an ear to the door, so he stammered an apology, and left.

When his man from Gawthorpe arrived before breakfast, he said he heard the hooves on the cobbled yard beneath the window and knew it to be a message about me. He wasted no time, and rode home without stopping, sailing like an arrow in the wind. He told me how the skies were peach and blue, and reminded him of my dresses, and how he made a deal with himself that if I lived, he would have me a gown made in each of the beautiful colors he saw that morning. He said he made all sorts of bargains with himself — if I lived, he would refurbish my mother's house from cellar to gables, with fresh plaster and paint and rugs and more books than she could read in a lifetime. If I lived, I would never sleep alone in our bed again, if that's what I wanted.

The servants had fetched the cook's midwife sister from her bed in Clitheroe.

When Richard arrived, breathless and shining with perspiration, she'd told him in plain terms that she did not hold out much hope for me, and that the Lord seemed ready to take my child and me into the next life. And Richard was white with rage, and dismissed her, and bid the servants find another one. As she left with her nose in the air, she passed him the papers from my skirts that he'd dropped on the floor by the bed, trampled by so many feet going in and out.

And that was when Richard decided the only person who could save me was sitting in chains in the castle. So without changing riding habits or even stopping to eat, he rode all the way back to Lancaster, knowing he might never see me alive again.

He left his horse at the gate, both of them almost expired, and burst — if a thirsty, exhausted man can burst — into the castle, and demanded that the Lords Justices allow him to read two testimonies relating to the trial of Alice Gray, which had already begun.

He was barely aware of the ripple of astonishment from the gallery, or Roger's thunderous expression from his seat by the judges, or the grand, high ceilings and rows of gleaming benches, or the jury, or if any of them were familiar to him and owed him money. All he knew was the paper in his hand, and his heart hammering in his chest, and Alice's wretched face where she stood with the other prisoners, and the chains around her wrists and ankles.

Lord Bromley granted his request, and Roger almost exploded with anger, rising up to protest, but the law prevailed, and Richard faced Alice at the bar and read my words, though his hand was shaking and his voice trembled. And after that he read the words of John Foulds, though he struggled even more with them, because his writing was so poor.

And the jury went out, and Richard had to wait in the gallery, soaking wet and tired from riding almost eighty miles in less than a day, and when they came back in he searched their faces, every last one of them, and when a few of the gentlemen looked him in the eye — for by now he was certain he had played cards with a couple of them — he did not know what that meant, and thought he would die with the agony of waiting.

When the foreman said the words *not guilty* he watched Alice drop like a stone a few yards away, and a great gasp went up from the crowd, and he had to shake his head to take in what he had heard, and he turned to the jury and whispered *thank you.*

"And then what happened? Tell me again."

"And then I fainted."

I laughed and clapped my hands together. I was sitting up in bed, in a clean white nightgown, beneath fresh bedding — the previous had to be burned, along with the mattress. Little Richard was in my arms, and although he was small because so was I, he was perfect in my eyes. He had threads of black hair, fine as silk, and rosebud lips, and cheeks round as apples. His eyes were dark like mine.

The first time I fed him, when I had time enough to look over every lovely bit of him at length, I noticed something on his arm, and was about to call the nurse when I realized what it was. In the crook of his tiny elbow was a brown birthmark, no bigger than his little fingernail, in the shape of a crescent moon. It matched the scar I had in the same place, where Alice drew blood from me. I checked the next morning to see if it was there, and it was, as much a part of him as his fingers and toes, and I folded his neat little sleeve down again and smiled to myself.

"And then?" I sipped my warm milk, spicy with healing herbs.

"Well, then we had to wait for the rest of

the verdicts," Richard said. Half-heartedly, he jangled the rattle he had bought all those months ago. It was not all happy news.

Richard had been unable to read John Foulds's final sentence, scrawled in a drunk's shaky hand in that pitiful candle-light, absolving Katherine Hewitt of any blame. The poor woman, a friend to Alice and her mother, had been found guilty, and hanged. Richard told me how after he had spoken for Alice, Katherine's arraignment came next, and Roger was determined on seeing his own needs served. He bullied the jury, he shook his fists, and spittle fell from his lips as he drove the point home again, again, again how that woman, alias Mould-heels, who had delivered so many babies and made so many women mothers, killed a child for no reason other than the Devil told her to.

It was too much for Alice, and Richard said she dropped onto the floor of the hall like a stone. After her chains were removed, she left the castle without looking back and wept all the way to Gawthorpe, clinging to Richard so tightly she ripped his jacket. She was free, but her freedom had come at a terrible price.

Nine people from Pendle hanged that day, including Elizabeth Device, her daughter

Alizon and her son James, leaving Jennet alone in this life. Six more went with them. All were present at Malkin Tower. Alice was the only one of the group to be set free.

One woman was found guilty and given four days in the stocks and a year in gaol as punishment. Her name was Margaret Pearson, whose servant had seen a toad climb out of the fire. She was not present at Malkin Tower, so Roger was only half-interested in her fate, and was not prepared to go to great efforts to see her swing.

Richard told me that in Bromley's parting words to Alice, he urged her to forsake the Devil. That would have been easy, because as soon as she left the room, she was free of him.

"Someone is here to see you," Richard said to me a few days later. "Shall I send them up?"

"Who is it?" Hope bloomed in my chest.

Richard smiled. "You shall have to wait and see."

Fatherhood suited him; he was besotted with his son. Somewhere he might have another one, or a daughter, but I pushed the thought from my mind.

"I will come down," I said. "I haven't been downstairs yet and am forgetting what it

457

looks like. Richard?" I said before I lost my nerve and he left the room. He paused in the doorway, one hand resting on the door-knob. "I'm sorry, but I shall have to buy you a new gun." He looked puzzled. "I took yours the night I . . . the night I came back here. I lost it in the forest."

"You took my musket?" He seemed more astonished than annoyed.

"Yes. I didn't intend on using it — I didn't know how. It doesn't matter. It got soaked, besides, so I ruined it anyway."

He smiled. "You surprise me every day, Mistress Shuttleworth."

"Would you sit with me a moment? There's something I want to ask you."

The mattress sank under his weight, and the baby mewled in my arms, flailing his little fists in his sleep before settling again. I handed him to his father and went to my cupboard in the corner of the room, mov-ing carefully.

I pulled out the doctor's letter, which was torn and flimsy as an old rag by now. I held it in my fist and looked out the window at Pendle Hill. Then I handed it to Richard. "Why did you not tell me about this?"

He frowned and took it with the hand not holding the baby. I watched his eyes move over it, then understanding cleared his face, and he frowned. "Where did you get this?"

"James gave it to me months ago."

"You were not meant to see this."

"Do you not think I would wish to know that my own life —"

"You were not meant to see this because it is not about you."

I fell silent. "What do you mean?"

Richard sighed. "This letter is about Judith."

"Judith?"

He patted the bed next to him and I went to sit. Months of turmoil were ringing in my head, and it took all my effort to listen.

"You were not visited by this doctor — he is from Preston. I had him visit Judith at Barton when she lost . . . she lost the first child."

I closed my eyes to let his words sink in. "But it says *your wife.*"

Richard bent his head, and said very quietly, "I had to tell him she was."

Black ink from the ledger swam to the front of my mind: *Mr. William Anderton to bring marriage license from York.*

"Why did you have a marriage license brought?"

"That was for James's niece. She married last month. There is nothing now you do not know, I promise you."

I sat quietly, letting his words sink in. "Why do you go to her?" I whispered.

He seemed to consider his answer for some time, and covered my hand with his. His rings glittered, and his voice was almost a whisper. "I saw how you were when the babies died. I saw how ill it made you. I was afraid of hurting you again."

Even then, after all I had been through, I could not hate him.

"And now I could not be happier that we have a son." Holding the baby in one arm, he took from the bed the rattle shaped like a sword, and smiled down at him. I watched them sadly, and happily, and wretchedly. It was too much to take in.

"Did you say someone was here?"

"Yes, in the dining chamber." He left a kiss on the baby's head and went so I could dress.

I stood and twisted my hair into a cap. It had stopped falling out, and was strong and thick as a rope. I put a sleeveless gown over the top of my smock, and picked the baby up again to show him the rest of his house. I paused briefly on the stairs beneath my portrait and remembered how Alice said I reminded her of someone, and realized she must have meant Ann. My son might never know the woman who saved our lives, but perhaps it was better that way.

Alice had gone when I was asleep, and the blood washed away and the baby wrapped, slipping out of my chamber without anyone noticing. Richard said it was a full day and night after our son was born, and the house was busy with people coming up and down the stairs bringing bowls of hot water and fresh linen, so nobody noticed. She was there, and then she was gone. She had not said goodbye, though she had kissed me with a mother's tenderness I'd never known.

A tiny, glinting part of me hoped it would be her sitting in the parlor. I wanted to cherish the thought for longer, so I made my way very slowly down the stairs, rocking and murmuring to the baby. The servants were enamored with the new addition to the household, and could not stop beaming at me. They assembled in a little group in the entrance hall to smile and watch me carry him down the last of the stairs, and I smiled back.

The parlor was empty.

"Mistress?" one of the kitchen girls said at my back. "She is in the dining chamber. She is hungry from her journey so asked for food."

My mother rose from her seat the moment I entered, with her face serene and arms

461

outstretched like the Virgin mother. "My grandson," she cooed, and came to take him.

I hesitated, then passed him over.

Richard beamed wider than he ever had showing off a new gun or a suit of armor — this was a different pride altogether.

"Richard, would you leave us for a short while? I want to spend some time with my daughter."

"Of course." He bowed and stepped out.

My mother's eyes raked over my skin, my hair, my body. "You look well, Fleetwood. Your pregnancy was not a kind one."

"No."

"You are recovered?"

"I think so. I lost a lot of blood, so Cook has me eating meat almost every hour. This is my first time downstairs."

She smiled and put her face to little Richard's. He blinked slowly and flailed his tiny fists, and she put her finger inside his palm.

"A little boy," she said happily.

But there was something she was hiding; I knew it in her voice. "What is it?" I asked, and she turned to me, and smiled bravely.

"Richard is a father twice over."

"Why are you telling me this?"

The feather in her hat trembled. "Because I wanted you to hear it from me, and not some newsmonger in the village, or in someone else's dining chamber." She sighed. "I know you might never forgive me for keeping what I did a secret, but I thought it was the right thing to do, and knowing would only bring you unhappiness. Who would want that for their child, if they could help it?"

She looked down at the baby, and I noticed the lines around her eyes and mouth as she spoke. "When your father died, I was . . . adrift. I was alone with an infant daughter, and . . ."

"You could not wait to be rid of me," I said dully. "You married me off straightaway."

She shook her head. "That was a decision your father and I made together. We needed a man to take responsibility for us, and your father was ill. What would have happened to us? When Master Molyneux came to your father with an offer, he had little choice but to take it."

"I did not know Father arranged it."

We sat in silence for a minute or two, looking at the fine black hair on Richard's head, and his pink ears like little seashells. Already I missed his weight in my arms, which hung uselessly in my lap.

"I was so unhappy in that house," I said.

"I spent every day of my childhood worrying that the next day you would send me away to him."

"I would not have done that."

"You threatened it when I misbehaved."

"For that I am sorry. I would never have done it. It's difficult, raising a child without a father. You will say anything for a moment's peace."

"You know he . . . When he came for the first time, he . . ." My voice shook. "You left the room."

My mother looked away. Her eyes were darker than ever, and her mouth turned down at the corners, though her hand went on reflexively patting the baby, and she was rocking very gently. I had never seen her with an infant before. "That is why I had the marriage annulled."

I stared at her. "You knew?"

"When I came back, I could tell what had happened. He looked guilty as sin, and your little face . . ." For the first time in my life, I watched my mother's eyes fill with tears. "I felt responsible," she said. "I didn't know what to do, how to get out of it without your father to tell me. I knew I could never, ever hand you over to that man." Her voice trembled with emotion.

"I thought it was annulled because Richard was a better match."

My mother sniffed, and smiled weakly. "And wasn't he?"

Slowly, I sat back in the chair. Sunlight streamed in through the windows — it was a beautiful late-summer day. "I am glad Richard put his woman in there because now I never have to go back."

"I hated it, too," said my mother, surprising me. "I never settled there. I hoped that when you married you would put me somewhere else, and you did."

Richard did. I had nothing to do with it, had no interest in my mother's desires when I married.

"Well, now it has a new mistress. Judith Thorpe of Barton. She is welcome to it."

My mother leaned in. "I took all the best silver before I left."

We smiled at one another. I was about to ask if she'd had a son, or a daughter, then decided I did not want to know.

The servants began bringing in dinner, and Richard came back in. We sat down to a joint of roast beef and a huge wood pigeon dripping in sauce. My appetite was unrecognizable from five months ago — I could have eaten the whole pigeon myself.

"I saw on my way through Padiham a woman in the stocks with a bag over her head that had 'witch' on it," my mother said as we ate.

"Margaret Pearson," said Richard. Since attending the trials he'd taken a keen interest in the events of that summer. He even had a theory about our old friend Master Lister: that Jennet Preston was his father's mistress, and with his mother still living and frail, he wanted her out of sight and out of mind. Either that, or she knew something about him, and he would rather have her dead than have it known.

As for Roger, our paths would certainly cross again, but the magistrate had disgraced himself slightly on his voyage for power. He had shown himself as a man who traded lives for a comfortable retirement; souls for new furnishings afforded by the king, all for the sake of adding a final few glory days to a golden career in justice. Among the gentry of the north, such ruthless ambition was considered rather desperate, and many dining chambers had closed to him.

"She will do four market days in the stocks and then go to gaol, where she will probably die, because she will not be able to pay her bail once her sentence ends," Richard was saying.

"Why was she not hanged?" my mother asked.

Richard shrugged. "A shred of sense prevailed? I don't know."

My mother shuddered. "I heard there were thousands in Lancaster on hanging day."

"Nothing excites the living more than death," I said.

"What happened to that girl Jill? Or was it Alice? Was she not arrested?"

Richard and I shared a glance. "She was found not guilty."

"Well, that's remarkable, is it not? I certainly thought they'd find them all guilty if they found one. Weren't they conspiring to kill Master Lister?"

"Who knows?" I said. "There were no witnesses, apart from a child. Besides, Alice was innocent."

"How do you know?"

My hand went to the scar at my elbow and traced it over my sleeve. "All she wanted to do was help people," I said.

"Where is she now?"

"I wish I knew."

"She didn't tell you?"

I shook my head.

"Has she family?"

I thought of Joseph Gray, drinking himself

467

to death in his house made from mud. "No."

At that moment the baby began crying from his cradle in front of the fireplace. The nurse was eating with the servants, and my breasts were full and threatening to spill, so I got up and went to lift him from the oak cradle my mother had given me all those years ago. I stood up slowly and came face-to-face with the set of engraved panels on the mantelpiece.

I blinked, and looked all along them, then stared again. I could not believe what I was seeing. Next to Richard's initials, in the space that had been left blank since the house was built, was the letter *A*.

I would recognize it anywhere, had seen it scrawled dozens of times in the shaky hand of someone learning to write. But there it was, whole, and clear. I stood frozen in astonishment, and then I began to laugh, and tears came to my eyes.

"Fleetwood? Why are you laughing?"

I spun around, lifting Richard up above my head and dancing with happiness as my husband and mother looked at one another in baffled amusement. "She is well!" I cried. "She is well."

Alice Gray was the only friend I ever had. I saved her life. And she saved mine.

CHAPTER TWENTY-SIX

Five years later

Richard was dressed to hunt. He put his head in the great hall, where I was sitting mending Nicholas's silk stocking. With two sons, I had grown much better at embroidery because of the rate at which they poked holes in things, or skidded on the floor and tore their cloaks, or ripped their collars climbing through branches. At one elbow was the mending, and at the other was an ever-growing list of things I wanted James to fetch from London. Whenever something came to me I would take up the quill and scribble it down. I had just remembered I needed ambergris for my perfumes, when the boys, who were clashing wooden swords together in an attempt at a duel, dropped their swords to the floor with a clatter.

"Father, will you duel with me? Nicholas fights like a baby," said Richard, thrusting his brother's toy at his father. He took after me, with coal-black hair and serious dark eyes.

"He *is* a baby," I said, smiling at Nicholas, who was as different from his older brother as I was from Richard. He had his father's warm gold hair and gray eyes, with rosy apple cheeks.

"I will when I'm back, so don't splinter them before then." Richard pressed a sword into each of his sons' arms and wandered over to me. He looked distracted.

"What's the matter?" I said, briefly looking up from my sewing.

"The king is touring the north."

I stared at him. "When?"

"Next month."

"And does he plan to stay here? He is not welcome."

"Thankfully not, although to refuse him would be treason. I'm glad the tour is not next year when I am sheriff, because he almost certainly would. But he does plan to lodge at Barton."

"At *Barton*? Why?"

"Your guess is as good as mine. He is staying at Hoghton Tower before that, and Barton is halfway between there and Lancaster."

"But it's empty."

"The king does not concern himself with

inconveniences."

I put down Nicholas's stocking. "We would have to furnish it, and hire servants . . . It will bankrupt us. The king travels with a party of a hundred or more."

"It's the king," Richard said simply. "I am no more happy about it than you."

"That house," I muttered. "It's like a curse."

Richard ignored my remark. I knew he kept Judith and their son somewhere in Yorkshire now, but I had no interest in where. As long as she was out of sight, and I had my boys and my home, I could quite easily ignore the whole thing. Richard nodded at my list on the table.

"You know what ambergris is, don't you? Whale vomit."

"Richard!" I batted him away and he darted out of my reach, straight into the sticky grasp of his sons, who pawed at his legs and begged him to play.

"Enough! I am going hunting and if you do not let go of me this instant I am using both of you as bait." He picked Nicholas up by the ankles and tipped him upside down. Nicholas shrieked and squealed, helpless with laughter, and his brother pretended to jab him with the sword, crying "Die! Die!"

Puck, who was used to their noise but

declined to participate in his old age, watched lazily from the carpet. Sometimes they forced him to take part in their japes, but today he was spared.

"Why are boys so loud and badly behaved?" I asked. "Why could I not have had two lovely daughters to sit and sew with me?"

Nicholas collapsed to the floor, breathless and giggling.

"Father, take me hunting with you!" Richard demanded, pulling at Richard's cloak.

"Not until you are older."

"What do we say to Father when he goes on a hunt?"

"Don't kill the foxes!" they both cried, each trying to be the loudest.

I smiled, and Richard sighed in a playful way.

"Even though they kill the hares and rabbits, and make it much harder work for my birds, I think your mother would turn the musket to *me* if I came home with a fox pelt."

I nodded sternly, and smiled, but I was troubled by the news he brought. He left the hall and the boys went back to their games. I went to the window and looked at Pendle Hill.

■ ■ ■ ■

I set out at first light, leaving Richard and his light snores. The bag I'd packed and hidden under the bed the night before, and I swept it up silently and went to dress, arriving at the stables before dawn. The morning was clear and fine, with a bright sun and a slight chill. One of the apprentices appeared in a doorway at the sound of hooves on the stable yard, and was startled to see me.

"I am going to spend the day with Mistress Towneley," I told him as he blinked sleepily, reminding me of my boys. "Please tell the master to expect me back by evening."

The road out of Padiham was deserted, and I made a good start. By the time I arrived a few hours later, my thighs were aching, my corset digging into my stomach, and I was drenched with sweat. I hadn't ridden this far in years, and felt it in every muscle. When I got down, I leaned against the horse for a moment, its coat hot and gleaming under the midday sun. I tied it to a tree out of sight, and trudged the last few hundred yards with the string of the bag digging into my wet palm.

I fumbled in it for the key, and unlocked the door. The last time I was here it had been nighttime, with shadows dancing everywhere, but now its mystery was gone. It was just an old, dusty, empty house. The final few survivors of furniture stood listless, and I went to the old cabinet in the hall that had been my father's, running my hands over its grooves and edges. But I could not take it, or anything else, so I patted it as though it was a pet, and moved on.

I looked in every room and opened every cupboard. No doubt the servants would have been through every room after Judith left, taking candle stubs and needles and broken vases forgotten in cupboards and every scrap of food. I wanted to avoid the parlor, where I'd been taken away from my dolls to meet my first husband, but I went in and appraised it swiftly. There was the fireplace in front of which he had sat, but with no furniture it was just an empty room. I saved my chamber for last. There was just one bed frame in there — mine — my mother's was moved to a different room. I thought of her sleeping near me every night: I had thought it torture, but now knew it to be something quite different.

I went to the window and looked at the waving trees, and the farmland stretching flat behind them. It was a beautiful summer's day, with barely any wind. I made sure all the doors were open before I went back downstairs to the great hall, where I had met Judith five years before. It was as though the ghost of her was here, watching me as I went to the large windows overlooking the front of the grounds. The curtains were still there, thick with dust, no doubt too high and heavy for whoever cleared the house to get down. There was no chair to rest on, no table to set down my things. I knelt on the cold stone floor beneath the window, and the sunlight streamed in and bathed my face, and I lifted it up to feel the warmth, closing my eyes.

Then I set to work. I took the little silver tinderbox from my velvet bag and opened it, and bunched the charred cloth in the bottom to air it. I was pleased to see my hands were steady. I took out the flint and the steel and began striking them together. In the empty room, the clinks rang as loudly as they did in a blacksmith's workshop. After half a minute of effort, a spark caught the scraps in the tinderbox, and I leaned in to blow it gently into a flame. Fearful of it going out, I held a splinter to it, and when it had caught put it to the bottom of the curtain. Flames bloomed immediately on the dry, dusty fabric, and I cheered silently as fire licked the bottom of the scarlet threads, rising like damp. There were no mattresses, no firewood in the house — I had counted on this working, and it was. I sat and watched it for a minute, and by the time I stood up the curtain was half covered in flames. I thought of the time my skirts had caught in Joseph Gray's house, and I stepped backward and gathered up my things, shutting the front door behind me and locking it.

The king could not stay in a house that had burned down to the ground.

I stood on the front lawn for a long time, watching the front room swell with flickering light that was hard to see in sunlight, but would be magnificent at night. The wainscoted walls caught easily, and when the windows were black with smoke and I felt sure the fire was big and angry enough to attack the rest of Barton, I turned to go home.

Someone had been watching me. I jumped, startled, as a movement caught my eye at the edge of the trees. A stunning red fox fixed me with its wide amber eyes and placed a hesitant paw onto the grass. We stared at one another, and time stood still. The fire raged on behind me, and my breath caught in my throat. Then I blinked, and it was gone.

AUTHOR'S NOTE

Fleetwood and Richard Shuttleworth, Alice Gray, Roger Nowell, the Device family and many other characters in the novel were real people, but *The Familiars* is a work of fiction. Fleetwood Shuttleworth (born 1595) was mistress at Gawthorpe during the witch trials, and had her first child in 1612, but there is nothing in history to connect her with Alice. However, her husband, Richard, was present at the assizes — at which Alice Gray and the other ten Pendle witches stood trial in August 1612 — possibly because it generated so much interest at the time. Very little is known about Alice Gray other than from Thomas Potts's account of the trial, *The Wonderfull Discoverie of Witches in the Countie of Lancaster.* For some unknown reason, Alice's transcript is not recorded in Potts's book. Why she was the only one of the Pendle witches to be acquitted remains a mystery.

ACKNOWLEDGMENTS

If it takes a village to raise a child, it certainly takes a hamlet to raise a book. To start with, thank you, Juliet — friend first, agent second — for making my dream come true and holding my hand through all of it. In no particular order, the following people deserve my utmost gratitude: Katie Brown, Francesca Russell, Felicity Jethwa, Becky Short, Felicity White, Kate Hilsen, Claire Frost, Catriona Innes, Cyan Turan, Ed Wood, Lauren Hadden, Beth Underdown, Rosie Short and John Short. Thank you for your sharp eyes, bright ideas and enthusiasm. There aren't the words to tell my editor, Sophie Orme, and all at Bonnier Zaffre how thrilled I am that *The Familiars* found its home with you. I knew you were The One as soon as I met you, and you've made the whole process a joy. I am grateful to Rachel Pollitt at Gawthorpe Hall for answering my questions and Robert Poole for modernizing Thomas Potts's account of the trials. Last but not least, thank you to my parents, Eileen and Stuart, and brother, Sam, for your endless support and love, and Andy for being my number one cheerleader in life. You're always there when I need you, and I always will.

ABOUT THE AUTHOR

Stacey Halls grew up in Rossendale, Lancashire, and has always been fascinated by the Pendle witches. She lives in London and has worked as a journalist for *Stylist, Psychologies* and *Fabulous. The Familiars* is her first novel.

The employees of Thorndike Press hope you have enjoyed this Large Print book. All our Thorndike, Wheeler, and Kennebec Large Print titles are designed for easy reading, and all our books are made to last. Other Thorndike Press Large Print books are available at your library, through selected bookstores, or directly from us.

For information about titles, please call:
(800) 223-1244

or visit our website at:
gale.com/thorndike

To share your comments, please write:
Publisher
Thorndike Press
10 Water St., Suite 310
Waterville, ME 04901